MY AMERICAN EDEN

Mary Dyer, Martyr for Freedom

A Novel by

Elizabeth S. Brinton

BURD STREET PRESS
SHIPPENSBURG, PENNSYLVANIA

This Burd Street Press publication
was printed by
Beidel Printing House, Inc.
63 West Burd Street
Shippensburg, PA 17257-0708 USA

The acid-free paper used in this book meets the guidelines for permanence and durability of the Committee on Production Guidelines for Book Longevity of the Council on Library Resources.

For a complete list of available publications
please write
Burd Street Press
Division of White Mane Publishing Company, Inc.
P.O. Box 708
Shippensburg, PA 17257-0708 USA

Library of Congress Cataloging-in-Publication Data

Brinton, Elizabeth S., 1953-
    My American Eden : Mary Dyer, martyr for freedom : a novel / by Elizabeth S. Brinton.
        p. cm.
    ISBN 1-57249-348-8 (alk. paper)
    1. Dyer, Mary, d. 1660--Fiction. 2. Massachusetts--History--Colonial period, ca. 1600-1775--Fiction. 3. Rhode Island--History--Colonial period, ca. 1600-1775--Fiction. 4. Executions and executioners--Fiction. 5. Civil disobedience--Fiction. 6. Christian martyrs--Fiction. 7. Women immigrants---Fiction. 8. Quakers--Fiction. I. Title.

PS3602.R5319M9 2003
813'.6--dc22

                                                                    2003060790

PRINTED IN THE UNITED STATES OF AMERICA

To the man written in my heart, my huckleberry friend, husband, father, healer, Howard Nicholas Brinton, with thanks for loving the pilgrim soul in me and for walking me into the light.

CONTENTS

 PROLOGUE

We landed with no thoughts of religious freedom in mind. We sailed to Boston because my mistress read one of Governor Winthrop's pamphlets, circulating through London in 1635. Hearing of a place where the people were knit together as one, she set her sights on going. Mary convinced her husband to plunk down the required fifty pounds necessary to buy a share in the Massachusetts Bay Company. They planned to leave England behind for good. She longed for a friendly village, a place to build a home where citizens would be judged by their good deeds, not by who their father was, or wasn't. She grabbed hold of that vision and clung to it even till the end. What if you crossed an ocean to join a close band of people escaping persecution, only to have them turn around and kill you because of your Christian beliefs? Twenty-five years after we set foot in Boston, Mary Dyer chose her fate. The first woman executed on American soil because of religion, by her death, she set a standard. Without freedom, she declared, her life was not worth living.

To the sound of two hundred men pounding drums, the marshal escorted her to the Hanging Tree, twice. She climbed the ladder twice. She had her face and feet bound twice. The noose went over her head twice. The first time resulted in an eleventh-hour reprieve from the governor; the second broke her sweet neck.

I put the shroud in her hand that she carried with her into Boston, vowing to look their bloody laws in the face. We knew they would rip the clothes off her after they cut her down. We understood all too well that she would be lying dead on the ground, stripped bare for all the Puritans to see. Reverend Wilson, her first pastor, the man who promised to transport all the passengers on board the *Arabella* to glory, covered her face with his own handkerchief. Repent, they said, but she refused, even unto death. They called out to her to repent even as she had her foot on the first rung of the ladder. One man said, "Do you want an elder to pray for you?"

Mary answered, "Bring me a babe, then a child, then a young man, then a strong man, before you bring me an elder in Christ Jesus."

Quietly, soberly, and dressed in sad colors, the people stood in a clump under a gray sky. On this first day of June, in 1660, the people of Boston struggled to breathe the close air. A storm had been pending all week. Some feared it would spoil the hanging, but they were not disappointed. They got to see the executioner push her off the platform. They bore witness to her collapse. After the fall, all drumming, all noise, all talk ceased. A gust of wind blew across the Common, catching Mary's skirt, puffing it full with a snap. Her dress billowed as a sail does when suddenly grabbed by the wind. Someone said, "She hangs there like a flag." The chorus repeated these words until another voice boomed, "She hangs there like a flag for others to take example from."

But I must go all the way back to the beginning, if I'm to do this story justice. We'll stay by the fire where it's warm until the storm blows over. It suits me to tell this tale on the eve of Thanksgiving. I'm ninety years old now with thirty-six grandchildren sitting at my feet. I can tell you all a thing or two. When I'm done, you'll know all about Mary Dyer, and why she is called the Rebel Saint.

CHAPTER ONE
Boston

Arriving in the late summer of 1635, we found a town reeking of new lumber. Right off the boat, I struggled to gain purchase. As we took our first uncertain steps up from the wharf toward the nearest pub, we passed two men sitting locked in the stocks. Onlookers pelted them with a collection of foul-smelling vegetables. Each man wore a sign pointing out his crime. One said "Drunk." The other said "Lazy." I felt as if I had been hit in the face with a kind of rotten truth. I asked a man holding a shrunken cabbage head, in the process of taking aim, if the fellows in the stocks had broken any laws. He nodded and swung.

A steady, warm wind blew in from the harbor, whipping my hair around my face. Still a bit dizzy from being at sea, I got myself into a wide stance and asked, "Will we be subjected to a quota of work then and a ration of ale?" Mary threw back her head as she laughed. Mr. Dyer took me by the elbow suggesting we head into the pub. I clammed up and obediently followed. Inside, I took a great pull on the leather flask handed to me full of the most delicious water I had ever tasted in my life.

"Are you for works or grace?" asked the man behind the bar.

Mr. Dyer hesitated, not knowing what to say.

"Straight off the boat, are you? Well, you'll be taking a stand soon enough."

"Which side do you favor?" asked Mary.

I could feel a mass of discomfort emanating from Mr. Dyer.

"Grace," he said. "You go to church on Sunday, hear what Pastor Wilson has to say and then on Monday morning, you go down to see Mistress Hutchinson, the midwife. She lives right across the street from the Winthrops. You'll find half the town there. She can preach rings around any man. In the beginning, only the women went there, but she

1

soon got every important fellow we have in this town hanging on her every word. Here, let me pour you all a drop of ale to welcome you to Boston. Bottoms up to Mistress Hutchinson," he bellowed. We sat stunned as we saw the whole crowd raise their flasks and cry, "Bottoms up to Mistress Hutchinson!"

A great, gorgeous smile crossed the face of my mistress. In my mind's eye, I can see Mary as she was then. Her body swollen with life, and every bit of her keen to give this New World a go. Mr. Dyer looked a bit green at the gills and got us upstairs to our rooms as quickly as he could.

I had no idea what the barkeep was on about. As I helped Mary unpack, I immediately pestered her with questions. What did he mean, I asked, when he wanted to know if we were for works or grace? She said he spoke of two schools of thought having to do with heaven and hell. Old testament, New testament stuff, she said. Works meant following a clear set of steps to salvation. That sounded reasonable enough to me. Then I remembered something, which made me wonder if these Puritans would ever be able to pull it off. God gave us free will, I reminded her. "Do they want us to give it back?" I asked. She thought my idea funny and later repeated it to Mr. Dyer. It seemed to me that we were going to have our hands full in this place, making sense of the whole business. I knew, being Irish, that the clergy would never succeed in legislating the sin out of everyone, least of all me.

Bright and early we were up and out in the streets exploring. As it was then, the spirit of the place flowed as the water running under Beacon Hill: sweet, cool, and pure. The abundance of the New World left us thunderstruck. I could not get over the size of the trees, the smell of the balsam firs, the sky black and loud from the sheer multitude of birds overhead. White pines climbed up straight, thirty or forty feet high, before they threw any branches, so the woods were open enough to walk, or ride through. I guess I had been fixated on an idea of a New World, so it surprised entirely to be walking through old forests. We crossed rivers where the alewives swam upstream to spawn. The water near boiled from the numbers of them. Lobsters, cod, and oysters; the sea teemed so with life, you could almost accuse God of overdoing it. Paradise, as far as the eye could see, oh I believed it. I had only one goal then; I wanted to care for my new family, and to see to it that we all prospered. In seven years, I'd be on my own. My duties with the Dyers would be over and I would be free. If I played my cards right, I could bring my brothers and sisters over, the whole Cary brood, one by one.

William Dyer, being older than his wife and a man who worshipped the ground she walked on, wasted no time securing a lot on the corner of Summer Street and Corn Hill Road. As an established merchant in the cloth trade, he looked ahead to the opportunities they would have. Because of this investment, they became church members right away.

We found the town fairly well established in 1635. Five years had passed since the landing of the Arabella, so we were five years into the great experiment when we got there. The houses stood surprisingly close together, as initially they had been built all huddled around one common pasture. Some homes listed like drunken sailors, crooked and useless at keeping out the cold. Many men didn't have a clue how to build; they never had to learn in England. Lucky for us, Mr. Dyer had a knack, and our house went up straight and true. How I thrilled over our planked floors. The wooden chimney though, all we could manage due to the shortage of bricks, gave me no end of fear. Mary's baby, a son she named Samuel, came as soon as we had a roof over our heads. Our lives revolved around keeping body and soul together.

The church they called a meetinghouse began as a crude mud structure with a twig roof, nothing more than a sieve to hold in the dampness, if you ask me. We had to spend the entire day there on Sunday suffering through sermons five hours in length. I sat fingering my rosary under my apron, the only gift my mother had to give me; the one she put in my hand as she said goodbye forever, and the one thing that got me through everything. With too many of us at home, I had to leave Ireland and go out in the world to make my way as an indentured servant. I had to go it alone, hanging on to the one true faith. In the meantime, I had to face the fires of hell by darkening the door of this Puritan stronghold. Craggy Protestant pastors warned us up, down and sideways that a second Eve would be our downfall. Demons, called out by name, Beelzebub, Leviathan, and Old Gooseberry, lay in wait to slither under our door, attacking us women through our weaker wills. They had taken a notion to declare Boston as a second try at the Garden of Eden. We were a collective of Adams and Eves, you see, trying to get it right this time. One slip-up, and we'd all be evicted. I thought I detected some comments from the pulpit directed at Mary. Caps, done completely in needlework with gold and silver thread, had no place amongst the righteous. Long, bony fingers would point at her, declaring, with utter certainty, that mankind would never be granted another chance. Expect no goodness; anticipate no mercy, they said. This American experiment represented the final hope of mankind. Asking God for mercy once had been extravagant; twice was definitely out of the question. How I longed to hear just one Mass.

On Mondays, the women received absolution and comfort in the home of Anne Hutchinson. She gathered us all in, took us under her wing, befriended Mary instantly and as promised, did indeed preach rings around everyone else. I remember the smell of cedar smoke and the ever-present band of children clinging to her skirts. Her warm hands always held a whiff of walnut oil. She wore an air of newborn babies. She delivered so many of them, the heavenly scent and spirit of them hung around her in a celestial cloud.

Perhaps we could have lived there forever, a happy little band, cautioned indefinitely as to our upcoming fall from grace. Surely the first years went well enough. The past is a different country though, my darlings.

In the autumn of 1637, fate intervened with the birth of that second baby born to Mary in Boston. After that, everything changed for me. I stood helpless in the face of her pain. I could do nothing to make things right. It altered the course for Anne, because afterwards they did everything they could think of to reduce her influence. Mary's standing became the most stained, because from that day forward, whispers followed her everywhere she went, declaring her the mother of a monster. That was the cross she carried as long as I knew her. How do you help a friend carry a millstone that heavy?

CHAPTER TWO
The Maligned Birth

On a bright morning in early October, Mary and I launched into a full day of soap making. Because of the heat, we had put off the task for as long as possible. With a chilling wind blowing in from the north, Mary announced that the day had come. Color eased across the leaves. The neighboring changes spurred Mary on to a burst of energy. Twenty-four pounds of grease and six bushels of ashes were boiled outside. Our great pot rested on a circle of bricks. The soft soap would be used to tackle the month's washing. Spreading clean linen across lavender bushes to dry represented our only fleeting glimpse of domestic triumph. Yet it did not come without a price. I feared the smell of boiling grease would put Mary right off her food for days.

Even though I offered to do the job single-handedly, Mary adamantly refused to let me do it without her supervision. "Soap can be tricky," she said.

"I've always had good luck with it," I insisted. "So did my mother. She taught me the trick of using the potato to test the lye. Mine always bears it up."

"No doubt, Irene. I need to help you so we can get at that wash. We have to get this done before the weather turns."

By the time of the noon meal, the soap appeared to be on its way. As we sat down to our stew, the smell of the grease lingered on with Mary; she couldn't eat a bite. Suddenly, her head dropped down to the table.

"What is it?" I asked.

"Cramp. It must be the cider."

"Take some rest then, mistress. I'll finish up."

"I hate to be lazy."

"How could any woman living in Boston be accused of that?"

"I think I will go to my bed. Just for a bit."

"Aye, ma'am. I'll set the soap."

To my eyes Mary looked as if she suddenly did not care about the soap, about the wash, about her house, her family, or even herself. I don't think she cared about a thing except crawling up on her bed. I heard her yank the curtains shut. They were heavy curtains, thickly embroidered with wool, suffocating on a hot day, but I knew she would sleep soundly today. A stiff breeze continued to pick up, developing in its wake the first bite of the season. What a blessing, I thought. To be done with the heat of summer. Soon we'd have bitter cold, but for now it was nice to be on the brink.

As Mary drifted off to sleep, I kept up a fast pace. I decided that as soon as I got the soap finished, I'd have a talk with Anne. Nothing was going well. Mary, for all her saying the child would pick up, had not gotten any bigger. The baby still did not move past a little quiver. I'd already seen her through one birth, so I knew these were quite unlike the vigorous kicks Samuel used to throw at this stage, bending her double. We stopped asking what was going on inside her. My efforts to get her to eat fell on deaf ears. We all knew it wasn't going well, but we lived in a conspiracy of silence, hoping against hope that the baby would pick up in the last two months. I prayed for Mary every day. I prayed I hadn't cursed this house. What if my sin brought some terrible fate down on all of us?

Checking the small wooden tub into which the lye leached through the outlet, I placed an egg gingerly on top. The lye was not strong enough. I added more ash, and kept stirring. In a while, I tried another egg. Then I gave the potato a go. It rested nicely on top. Victory. I ran straight in to tell Mary. As I peered through the curtains, I could see that my mistress was asleep. I thought she might be hungry when she woke up. I could make Appoon, baked from corn meal, for supper, I thought, if I could get the soap done soon enough. Mary hadn't cared for the midday stew. She wouldn't eat oysters. Maybe a lobster would do the trick. Chowder, Appoon, and squash. That would take her mind off the grease, I decided.

When I finished up in the yard, I gathered a few squash from the garden for dinner. All was quiet inside. I couldn't remember when it had been so quiet in this house with Samuel off playing with the Hutchinson children and Mary asleep. Bustling around the kitchen, I got the Appoon in the oven. With that cooking, I listened by the door of Mary's room. Still quiet. I guessed it would be best for me to slip quickly down to the docks and see about the lobster. I figured I'd be back before Mary woke up. Surely, if my mistress were to be wakened for a simple question, she would be irritated, because anything about food made her cross these days.

I climbed the hill from the wharf, lugging a great fat lobster. Inside, I pitched it into a pot of boiling water hanging from the lug pole. Jabbing the seven-foot-long logs stoked the fire, setting it to crackling. There was still no noise from Mary's room, only the desperate sounds of the poor creature in the pot. Then it dawned on me that perhaps Mary could have woken up and gone to fetch Samuel. So I went in and opened the curtains surrounding the bed.

"What is it?" I found her up on her hands and knees with her head jammed into the pillows. The bed had become a total jumble with the heavy covers pushed back. The sheet, ripped to shreds. I lifted the bolster from Mary's head and found the sheet in her mouth, clenched between her teeth. Her face carried all the anguish of a trapped animal. "Pain?" Mary dropped the sheet. A wretched wail cut me like a knife. "I'll get Anne," I blurted. "I'll be back as soon as I can."

I had only to go as far as the end of her street, when I ran into little Bridgett Hutchinson. "Run, dear. Get your mother. Quick as you can. Tell her to come to the Dyers right away. Do you understand?"

The child nodded.

"Run now, run like the wind," I screamed as I took off to get back to Mary. "I'm going to put the water on," I announced.

When Anne came rushing in she said, "Is it—"

I did not even let her finish. "Travail." I told her. " I'm certain, two months early."

"How long has it been going on?"

"I can't say for certain. I've been checking on her. She was so quiet. She slept after our meal. I went down to pick up a lobster. She didn't eat anythin' at noon."

"How long were you gone?"

"Longer than I planned. When I got back, the curtains were drawn. She could be three hours in already."

"Come with me."

In the room, Anne started by saying, "Let's try to get her more comfortable. We'll start with this bed. We'll get you cleaned up, Mary."

As I took the shredded sheets out to the wash pile, I thought how unlike my mistress it was to have done such a thing. The flax, spun by her own hand, the cloth fashioned, and all the sides hemmed, and she'd even taken the trouble to add a bit of embroidery. It was not like her to destroy any of her work. She took such pride in it. Two months early. This child could not live. Mary must have thought of this as soon as she'd gone into labor.

Back in the house Anne took me aside in the kitchen. "Irene, do you know Goody Hawkins?"

"The witch?" I asked.

"She is not a witch."

"Folks call her that."

"She is better known as a midwife. I'm going to need her to assist me. The baby is in the wrong position."

"Is it the travail for sure then?"

"Yes."

"Too early. She isn't big enough."

"We will do what we can. Right now we have to see to the delivery. I need Goodie's help. You must fetch her."

"I will, ma'am."

"Ask one of my boys to find Mr. Dyer."

"Aye. I'm on my way."

"Good. I'll see you shortly."

With that, Anne went straight back to Mary, finding her sunk down into the pillows. I heard them talk as I took off my apron and put on my cap.

"How is our Mary?" asked Anne with such tenderness it brought tears to my eyes.

Mary cried bitterly, "Everything is going wrong,"

"We have to do the best we can. Don't think ahead. Don't think beyond the next pain. Right now we have to concentrate on getting this baby out. That's all."

"It's too early. It hasn't moved. It hasn't been right. I couldn't eat. William accused me of being willful."

"What do men know? They know nothing."

"Stay with me?"

"Yes. I'm right here. Come what may, Mary, I'll be with you."

I left then, but to my relief, found Mr. Dyer at the gate. I got him filled in and then added, "The pain is very bad. This is going to be a difficult birth. Anne has asked for Goody Hawkins to help her, sir."

"Isn't she the one who burns spiders and ants?"

"She falls into superstitious ways from time to time, I guess, but Anne says she is helpful and we are going to need it. The baby is breech."

"I see. We have to do what is necessary."

I returned with the extra midwife at my side. Had I known I was ushering in a traitor, I would have stuck out my foot to trip her, right there on the doorstep, rather than bring her into our home. Anne told me to go ahead with the lobster stew. It looked like we were in for a long night. The labor crept on and on, picking up a momentum like ocean swells on an angry sea. William sat in the kitchen with his head in his hands. Mary struggled along to the pushing stage, but there she hit a wall. Deep into the night, she fought a desperate battle.

Eventually, we began to get somewhere. Anne managed to get a hold of the baby's body. Mary pushed. Anne tugged gently. Nothing. When the pain took a momentary breather, Anne asked Goody and me to follow her outside.

By the fireplace, we saw William leap to his feet.

"No. Sit back down. We are going out to the yard to get some air," said Anne.

"Can I get you anything, mistress? Irene cooked."

"No thank you."

In the yard, Anne said to Goody, "The problem is the head. I fear it is stuck. The womb is tightening up again. Did you bring any belladonna?"

"Yes. Do you think the baby dead then?"

"Dead and stuck. We'll have to give her enough belladonna to put her in a deep sleep. A big whacking dose of it. Not enough to kill her, mind you. Do you know how to do this?"

"I do."

"Are you sure?"

"Absolutely. I had one like this in St. Ives," said Goody, whose tone struck me as morbidly conversational. "It has to be done. The gates of the womb shut like a noose around the baby's neck. They'll both die if we don't get it out. The mother has to be so deeply asleep that she feels nothing. Then you push her legs way, way up. You get your hands in, and try to ease the head. We must not tear the baby apart though. When that happens, you have to get a surgeon to cut it up. The mother almost always dies."

"Aye. We can't tear the womb either," said Anne. " She'll bleed out if that happens. We must proceed slowly and hope the belladonna relaxes her enough to let me ease the baby out."

I followed them back in, silently beseeching the Holy Mother to spare her.

Back in the house William asked, "'Will it be much longer?"

"No way of telling," I said.

In Mary's room we propped her up and held her as she drank the bitter herb. "What is it?" she asked.

"Something for the pain," Anne told her.

"But you said there wasn't anything."

"We're getting near the end. The baby is stuck, Mary. The womb has clamped down around the head. You've done all the work you can. If I don't give you this, I can't do anything. This will make you go to sleep."

"It's dead then."

Anne said, "It would seem so."

"Don't tell William," begged Mary. She grabbed the goblet, downing the liquid, looking like she hoped it would kill her too.

I crouched down in the corner and hugged my knees to my chest. I used to sit like that through the births of my sisters and brothers, all twenty of them. Inwardly, nothing went through my mind, but one Hail Mary rushed into the next. In the pocket of my apron, I fished around for the rosary. Goody and Anne said few words as we watched Mary slip out of consciousness. Anne kept a vigil on her pulse. When she gave us the go-ahead, Goody and I took a hold of Mary's left leg.

"We've got to get the legs up and open as wide as we can. We have to push them all the way up to the shoulder. Understand? Let's give it a go," commanded Anne.

We proceeded.

"Lift up higher. Get the whole bottom off the bed a bit. The head is still in the womb. I'm going to have to get it up over the chin till I can get it to give way."

All three of us held our tongues, hoping Anne could work some kind of magic.

"The muscles are starting to slacken," she said. "Come on now. Give it up."

"On the count of three, Irene," said Goody.

With the legs back up, Anne went in again. "I think I can get it. Irene, hold both legs. Lean against them. Put your whole weight over her. Goody, grab the baby. Give it a gentle pull with increasing strength. Put your other hand on her belly and push down. Gently now, mind."

Jesus, Jesus, I said to myself as I followed orders. Both midwives were quiet, until I heard Anne say, "There! It is coming out."

Lifting my head, I got the first look at what lay in Goodie's hands. "Where's the head? What happened to the head?" I cried.

"There's a face. Sort of," said Goody, "But no skull. The feet are twisted too. What a mess."

Blessed Anne did not even flinch. "Cut the cord, then wrap it up. Irene. You hold it, or put it aside. We still have the mother to tend. We need to get some mugwort into her somehow. We have to deliver the afterbirth."

"Should I get more hot water?"

"Yes, but say nothing to Mr. Dyer just yet. We have to take care of Mary."

"Aye."

Into the kitchen I sped. William jumped up again. I shook my head and fetched the water without saying a word.

Back in the room, I told them I would mix up the mugwort. "I know how," I said. I pried her mouth open and put drops on her tongue. She did not stir and we concluded we were not going to be able to get any more of it into her.

Anne raised no objection. She and Goody kneaded Mary's belly as calmly as if they were making bread.

"I hope we don't get a bleed," said Goody, with her hard little mouth in an even, straight line. "Given everything else that's happened here, we'll be lucky if she doesn't bleed out on us. Irene, get a bucket and put it down here just in case. It'll come out in torrents if we're in for it."

Anne stayed mute until the afterbirth was expelled. Due to her skill, Mary was spared. Saints be praised.

Anne helped herself to a drink of water. I made her sit. "Dear God," she said. "What do we do now? We have to act quickly. We have to figure out what to do. I say we bury the child before the sun comes up."

My mouth dropped open in pure shock.

"Do not think of your religion now, Irene, think of your mistress. They will say this is God's judgment. It will be called a manifestation of evil, her own evil. God has spoken, we will hear. It will be portrayed as Satan's child. Do you want to hear her called Satan's whore?"

"Shall I send for Mr. Dyer now?" I asked.

"Yes," Anne answered.

"I'll wash the baby. Then I'll get him."

"Are you sure?" asked Goody, turning up her nose.

I unwrapped the poor wee creature, washed her and dressed her in a beautiful little frock full of delicate little tucks and English smocking, made by Mary's loving hand. Then I swaddled her in bleached linen, choking back tears as I bound her tiny face.

Anne remained in the rocking chair, in the corner of the room, holding our bundle of sorrow as William rushed in.

Anne whispered, "It didn't go as we had hoped, sir."

"Mary?"

"She fainted from the pain. She was delivered of the child while she slept."

"Is it stillborn?"

"Yes. Mercifully. A girl. I think you should take one look at her, sir. Mary will ask you about her. The baby is deformed. We need to bury it quickly. If word of this gets out, it will be very bad for your wife."

"Let me see," he said.

Anne slowly removed the wee shroud. William stood frozen. Anne studied him and then declared: "I think we should bury her tonight."

"What of the church?"

"I could ask John Cotton."

"Can you trust him?"

"I have no choice."

"Go then," he told her. "Irene can go with you. Give the baby to me."

Out in the night, we scurried along quickly. The leaves on the trees made rustling noises, unfamiliar after the softness of summer. I could hardly keep up with Mistress Hutchinson. The Cotton household lay in complete darkness as we tiptoed in. Anne called to the reverend outside of his room. He emerged in his nightdress and cap, carrying a candle, looking most irritated. She explained the situation.

I could see him thinking about what to do, weighing the risks. Studying our faces he said, "Wait outside. I'll be right there."

Beacon Hill loomed beside us in the darkness, as we hurried down Court Street, to School Street and then along Corn Hill Road to the Dyer house.

Upon our arrival, William thanked him for coming. Then he said, "This cannot be God's judgment on my poor wife." For the first time in my service to the Dyers, I witnessed his tears. "I could never believe He would do this to her. She has not sinned. She is a good woman, a beautiful soul, the greatest blessing in my life. I know God because of her. I see God in her eyes."

"I have agreed to help bury the babe tonight, sir," said the reverend.

"In the churchyard?"

"Yes, I will baptize it."

"I am indebted to you, sir."

"We must hurry."

Slipping stealthily through the streets like thieves in the night, we managed to reach the cemetery without being spotted by the night watchman. John Cotton dug the earth while Anne kept watch, prepared to distract a passerby if need be. Goody stood there like the useless witch that she was. I held my sweet burden while Goody glared at me for kissing the poor darling. I could have been exchanging endearments with a dead pheasant, judging by the disdain on her face. I should have gotten an oath from her that night. I should have threatened to boil her in oil, or to drag her to the Hanging Tree myself, but my mind was all taken up with prayer over the poor wee soul going into the ground.

With the deed done, an exhausted Anne headed back to the Dyer house. It would only be an hour before Boston rose to greet another busy day.

"People will awaken oblivious to all that happened," I stated.

"Let's make sure it stays that way," said Anne.

Why didn't I cut Goody's tongue right out of her fat head that morning? That's what I ask myself now.

CHAPTER THREE
The Drawing

"Dead?" asked Mary when she opened her eyes.

William took hold of her hand. "Yes. I am sorry, my love."

"Boy or girl?"

"Girl."

"Oh, the poor little thing. I knew it. I didn't want to know it, but I knew it. She didn't move. I couldn't eat."

"It wasn't your fault."

"Where is she? Can I hold her?"

"We had to bury her, my dear."

"What?" Her eyes were wide with fear. "Why did you bury her? How could you do such a thing?"

Tears rolled down William's face and mine as well. "I'm sorry. She didn't turn out right."

"What are you talking about? Where is Anne? You get out of here, William!"

"I'll send for her," he said while getting up slowly.

"I'm sorry, mistress. Truly I am," I said with my apron over my face.

When Anne arrived, she took William's place beside the bed.

"What was William saying? What was wrong? Why did you bury my little girl before I could even see her?"

"There was no skull."

"What do you mean?"

"It sloped straight down to nothing. There was no brain."

"Deformed?"

"I heard of one like that in England. I'm sure it's very rare, but something went wrong, that's all. We buried her because of what people would say, if word got 'round. We can't help these things, and there is no explaining them away."

"It's my own blackness," announced Mary. Her face settled into a dull stare, which I knew from experience, I would be seeing for months to come. "I produced a demon child, a monster."

"No. I won't have that, Mary. It was a stillborn birth. That's all. You can have other children. You are young. You can try again. Next time will be better. Now. Can we try to get you up? I need to see how you're doing."

"Why didn't you let me die?"

"You'll get past this. It will be very hard, I know, but you'll get past it one day. I will help you all I can. I promise. Let's get you up."

Anne motioned to me and we got Mary up with her arms around our necks.

"Did you see her?" Mary asked me.

"Aye. A wee girl, God bless her."

"Irene washed her and dressed her in the little gown you prepared," said Anne.

"Was she a monster?"

"No. No, no. She was a precious wee lamb, just missing something, that's all."

A gut-wrenching moan came out of Mary. William heard her lament and ran back in.

Back in the bed, she immediately drifted off. "Leave us, please, sir," requested Anne.

"It's not her fault. It's mine," I whispered.

"How could the fault be yours?"

"I brought sin into this house. That baby was cursed because of my sin."

Anne shook her head. "Maybe this thing came down through William's family. Who knows? Don't blame yourself, child, and don't let Mary blame herself. This is not a punishment. Our God is merciful."

"There was a child born in our village once that had no bones in it at all. It was like dough."

"And did that family think they were cursed?"

"Aye."

"What did the priest say?"

"He said they conceived the child during lent. They swore that they didn't. He asked them what sin God was punishing them for, in front of everyone. It was terrible."

"What happened to them after that?"

"He took to drink. She slipped away—lost her wits."

"I will not have anyone say things like that to Mary. I won't. This is not anyone's fault. Something went wrong. We can't explain it, period."

"She's comin' round."

"Get her some water. How are you, dear?"

"Anne, Anne. You must be very tired," whispered Mary.

"Me? Goodness gracious, do not think of me. How are you?"

"Irene, walk her home. You can send William in. He can take care of me. Where is Samuel?"

"He's with my sister. Catherine said to tell you that we can keep him at our house today," offered Anne.

"No. I want him here. Will you get him, Irene?"

"Yes, ma'am."

"I'll come see you tomorrow. Well actually, it's morning now. Later on today, " said Anne as she squeezed Mary's hand.

"Pray for us?" Mary asked.

"Yes, my dear. Always."

I slept less than two hours before I was up and out in the yard with the wash. Word spread by this time and people were beginning to come by with pots of food. By staying in the yard, I managed to thank them for their offerings, but to keep visitors at bay. Mary slept all morning. Samuel kept up his steady stream of questions. William sat quietly by his wife's bed till noon. Shortly after the midday had passed when the sun was no longer overhead, I saw Mary step slowly out to the garden. She looked around at the trees. It was as if she had forgotten all about the transformation, the bright orange color, and it shocked her. It was almost obscene to my eyes too. Mother Nature, never known for her compassion, had perversely transformed our world into a hideous display of garish death.

"What are you doing?" I gasped, running to grab her arm.

"The wash. I have to get at the wash."

"I'm at it, ma'am. Look, I've got the linens drying already. I've begun to do your shifts. I'll get it done. You rest."

"Can't," she cried. "Had to get up."

"Why?"

"I want to see my baby. I think tonight I'll go the churchyard and dig it up."

"You can't do that!"

"Why not? She is my child. I want to see her. I can't go through the rest of my life hearing that my child was a monster."

"No one will say that. The only people who saw her were Anne, Goody, William, and myself. No one else. None of us will breathe a word."

"You saw her and I didn't."

"But you know why it was done."

"I can't accept it!"

"Why?"

"Because I want to see my baby! We would have buried her today anyway. What difference does it make? I want to see her."

"I'll help you," I offered.

"In the churchyard?"

"No. I mean I'll help you see."

"How?"

"I'll tell you everything as it happened. When I was a girl, my grandfather died in an accident. They were getting in the hay. He fell and a cart rolled over him right in front of me. My grandmother was back at the cottage. I was only seven at the time. I told her about it over and over for as long as she was living."

"All right," said Mary as she sank down on a little stool beside me. "Give me a bit of wash to do. I have to do something with my hands."

That night, William remained at his wife's bedside with his Bible in hand. Mary turned her face to the wall.

"Would you rather be alone?" he asked.

"No. You can read," she answered. "Don't ask me to talk."

"I'm sorry you didn't get to see our baby," he told her. "I did it to protect you. I couldn't bear the thought of you being hurt."

"I am hurt!" she screamed at such a volume I feared the neighbors would hear too.

"I know."

"I don't give a fig what people say about me. It won't change anything anyhow. The grief is mine no matter what people say. The grief is still mine."

Suddenly, his expression changed. "I'll draw you a picture," he said. "I can manage a fair rendition, I think. It will help you see." With that, he headed for the door.

Mary sat back on her pillows. She stopped crying, and stared dully ahead.

I saw him get a bit of blackened wood from the fire. He looked around for something. Samuel and I had torn off a big sheet of birch bark and stacked it behind a bin of potatoes in the pantry. I handed it to him.

I helped Mary into a clean shift and was brushing her hair when he entered the room gingerly. He had two sketches to show her. There was a profile and a frontal view.

Mary let the bark drop from her hands.

All of us in the Dyer house fell asleep that night to the sound of her weeping.

In the night, I woke with a start. I descended the ladder in time to see Mary standing fully dressed by the door.

"What are you doing? Why are you holding your shawl?" I asked.

"I am going to see my baby."

"You must come back to bed," said William as he surfaced, pulling up a pair of breeches. He got a hold of his wife by the arm, as it was the only way to stop her. She fought.

"Let me go, please."

"No. We cannot break the law. I insist. You will not disturb our daughter's grave."

"Leave me alone, William! Get out of here, Irene."

"Mary. I know you are upset."

"You know nothing!" she wailed. "You know nothing."

"I know you are not yourself."

He managed to get her into a chair. I came to her with a goblet.

"I asked you to leave us," she hissed.

"I heard you. I brought you some brandy."

"Why?"

"For the pain, ma'am. For the pain. I could think of nothing else, being Irish."

"No. There is nothing for this, nothing." Heading back to bed, she dropped her shawl on the ground.

Chapter Four
Disenfranchised

The following days were somber ones for us. Mary retreated to a territory of silence, sitting near the fire, reading the Bible. I carried on with my duties and shouldered Mary's as well. Samuel was farmed out often as Mary had some trouble with her nerves. The Hutchinson children took him under their wing. Recovery was so difficult for her with the problem of drying up the milk and all. Outside, the leaves began to fall. The new earth of the grave was soon covered in a blanket of burnished red. William thought she would never forgive him for burying the child. What else could he have done? If only she had been awake, that part may have been easier. She maintained that the opinions of the town should not have been a factor in the decision made without her consent. She said it should not have taken precedence over her needs as a mother. She stuck to her belief that the deed was done in shame and horror. I did not know if this was unfair to William or not, as she alone was going through the bulk of the suffering and I felt that if it helped her to be mad, then she could just go ahead and be mad.

Anne took a similar path. She advised William, in her usual kind and motherly fashion, to give her time. The subject drifted into a zone of silence, and there it would have remained if the scab had been left alone to heal instead of ripped off in such a painful way.

Mercifully, winter descended in one ghastly blow. To Mary, it was a welcome sight as the forlorn season mirrored the state of her soul. She resumed her solitary walks in the woods. William busied himself with the woodpile, tending it with great fuss and precision, as was his character.

In early November, the snow flew in earnest. The talk of the town turned to the upcoming meeting of the General Court. The four days prior to the session, we had a bout of snow, which fell solidly without any letup. The Charles River froze right over. It came as no surprise to the people of the commonwealth that the meeting moved to Newtowne. Getting there posed a great problem.

Mary voiced her will, stating she would not be deterred from attending. Events leading up to this meeting had divided Boston into two camps. All the clergy on this side of the Atlantic met that fall to grill Anne Hutchinson on her theology. Even though she told them that in the game of quoting the Scriptures she was up by two, they produced the edict that Anne Hutchinson had eighty-two blasphemous opinions. At issue was her Monday morning meeting. When it grew to encompass men, it was noticed across the street in the Winthrop home. Leading merchants, Boston's wealthiest citizen, a young man named Harry Vane whose father was on the privy council and had the ear of the king, the surgeon, the fence viewer and his wife— they were all there posing an ever growing threat. Mary vowed to show solidarity to Anne, as we all feared this meeting would take direct aim at her.

I did not want Mary out in that cold. William had run out of fight as far as she was concerned, so he was no help. Five short weeks after the maligned delivery, on November 12, 1637, she defied me altogether and wrapped herself in a series of heavy woolen garments, covering all in a thick cloak. We dropped Samuel at the Hutchinsons in the very able care of Catherine Marbury, Anne's sister.

Through the two miles from the house to the ferry, we slogged through deep snow crusted over on top. The heavy layers of Mary's skirts became stiff and dragged around her legs in sheets of ice. Mine did as well, which only made me more beside myself with worry for her. Our feet got soaked through, causing non-stop pain.

At the river, Tom Marshall told us we couldn't sail. When our faces fell, he assured us that he could pick his way through a path of broken ice and row us across. We sat bunched together in the scow, trying to keep each other warm. Arriving in Newtowne, we were presented with a new obstacle. The ladder, our only avenue to the dock, had become all caked over with ice. Falling could be deadly, but by the grace of God we made it.

Over the five-mile trudge through the woods, Winthrop's name was cursed more than once for moving this meeting from Boston. Inside the unheated meetinghouse, we collapsed in our seats like frozen blocks of wood. Some people exchanged clipped greetings. Mary sat in silence with her hands in her lap. On her head, she wore her beautiful needlepoint cap, its gold and silver threads drawing stares. Her dress, plain enough except for the color, drew all the attention in her direction. Experiments that summer in mixing pokeberry and alum produced a shocking shade of crimson. Since this dye was her own invention, she alone possessed the ability to create such a brilliant red.

Mary found a way around laws passed by the magistrates restricting finery, too. They forbid hatbands, needle cap belts, ruffs, gold or silver girdles and beaver hats. She pointed out that it was the purchase not the wearing that comprised the actual letter of the law, so she moved trim from old dresses onto new ones. Maintaining that her needlepoint cap had come with her from England, she refused to leave it off until she was ready. No law limited color.

The court came to order. Maybe it was the cold and the bitterness of the scene altogether that incited the magistrates to cruelty. We heard them banish Anne's brother-in-law, Reverend Wheelwright from Wollaston, as they objected to a sermon he preached on New Year's Day. He was given twenty-four hours to collect his things and disappear! We all sat there wondering how he could possibly survive. Roger Williams had undergone a similar fate the year before. Word filtered in that he was dressed in skins and living with natives, but still alive. A petition had been written by William Aspinall, signed and sent to the king by Anne's group on Wheelwright's behalf. Fashioned in order to prevent such action, we now saw that our efforts had been foiled.

Mr. Aspinall's name came up next. As the author of the petition, it was pronounced that he would be disenfranchised. At first I did not know what the word meant and thought he was reduced in status or something. It did not take long though, by seeing the looks on everyone's faces, to understand that it meant something worse. I quickly figured out that by spring, he too would be forced to quit the commonwealth; he would have to leave Boston altogether. We sat by helplessly as we saw our good friends receive the same fate, one after another. Convicted of the crime of being a strong supporter, we heard Mr. Coggeshall's name called out next. For a split second, I had the feeling that these men had been unfairly singled out as examples and that would be the end of it. There was a pause, but Governor Winthrop clearly looked as if he had a lot more ammunition in his pouch. Four other men were called before the court for meddling in public affairs "beyond their skill." Thomas

Marshall, William Dynely the barber, and then Richard Gridley the brickmaker met the same fate.

Where would this end? As if Winthrop read my mind he glared at us. William Dyer, "known as Mary Dyer's husband," was sentenced to disenfranchisement. We sat there as if slapped. Mary and William were both stone faced. I know my mouth hung open and my mind raced along wondering how on earth he could do such a thing. After all, we were their neighbors. How could he force them all to leave their homes, their farms, their friends, and all they had built? This man who had enthusiastically taken their money when they bought their share in the commonwealth, this man who had invited them all to join him in this mad venture. How could he live with himself? What about the children? How were we to explain this to little Samuel? How could he tell his fellow townsfolk that they would no longer be welcome here? He was the man who declared he would build a city on a hill that would be a beacon of light to shine to the rest of the world so they would take example. We were such a small number compared to the size and scope of the place. Shouldn't we all stick together? Dividing and splitting. Splitting and dividing, all over what had been voiced in the pulpit. I just could not make any sense of his thinking.

Anne did not appear until the court convened for the afternoon session. She heard the morning pronouncements just as she reached the meetinghouse. The magistrates, Thomas Dudley, Roger Harlekenden, Increase Nowell, Israel Stoughton, Richard Bellingham, John Humphrey, John Endicott, William Coddington, and William Colburn, sat facing the people. The ministers in their black garb with the stiff Geneva collars looked like a row of blackbirds. Behind his honor guard, Governor Winthrop swept in to take his place where he would act as both judge and jury.

"Mrs. Hutchinson," he began. "You are called here as one of those that have troubled the peace of the commonwealth and the churches here; you are known to be a woman that hath had a great share in the promoting and divulging opinions that are the causes of this trouble, and you have maintained a meeting and an assembly in your house that hath been condemned by the general assembly as a thing not tolerable nor comely in the sight of God nor fitting for your sex. Therefore, we have thought good to send for you to understand how things are, that if you be in an erroneous way we may reduce you." After pausing for a breath he continued, "I would entreat you to express whether you do not justify Mr. Wheelright's sermon and the petition."

"I am called here to answer before you, but I hear no things laid to my charge," Anne replied.

I squeezed Mary's arm and whispered that Anne would put up a fight.

"I have told you some already and more I can tell you," he answered with the irritation plain on his face.

"Name one, sir."

"Have I not named some already?"

"What have I said or done?"

"Why for your doings, this you did harbor those that are parties to this faction."

"That is a matter of conscience, sir."

"A pivotal law has been broken by you, Mrs. Hutchinson. Honor thy father and mother. You do endeavor to set forward this faction and so you do dishonor us. These twice weekly meetings do dishonor us."

"I conceive there lies a clear rule in Titus, that the elder women should instruct the younger. I must have a time wherein I can do it," she spoke.

I could see by this tactic that she was going to maintain her strategy of keeping the theological arguments in play, which was good, because I knew she would outscore them every time.

Winthrop looked energized by this challenge. He said, "Suppose a man should come and say, 'Mrs. Hutchinson, I hear that you are a woman that God hath given his grace unto and you have knowledge in the word of God. I pray, instruct me a little? Ought you not to instruct this man?"

"I think I may," she said. " Do you think it not lawful for me to teach men? Then why do you call me to teach the court?"

There was a bit of a stir on our side and we would have laughed if circumstances had been different.

Winthrop's face turned red. "We do not call you to teach the court but to lay open yourself! You have a plain rule against it. I permit not a woman to teach. You have seduced many simple souls," said Governor Winthrop. "Honest persons have become infected with your opinions which are known to be different from the word of God. You have caused such persons to neglect their families. Time has been lost. By venting strange opinions you have made a potent party. You have disparaged our ministers. Great damage has come to the commonwealth which we as Fathers of the commonwealth are not to suffer."

"I categorically deny those allegations," she stated.

"We are your judges, and not you ours. You show not in all this by what authority you take upon you to be a public instructor."

"Priscilla with her husband instructed Appolos. Phoebe was a deaconess in the early church. Deborah was a judge," she said.

"All the present troubles have arisen from those who attend your meetings. We see no rule of God in this. If you will not stop these meetings we will have to restrain you."

"It is just as lawful for me to do so as any of the ministers. Is there one standard for men and another for women? There are questions in the minds and hearts of the women who come to me, questions which would otherwise go unasked."

At this point, Anne had to lean forward and grab the rail. Having been forced to stand all this while had clearly taken its toll. As she was expecting her thirteenth living child, you would think they would have offered her some break. Seeing that she was growing ill, the tone of the interrogators changed. They came to their senses momentarily. Simon Bradstreet brought her a chair.

The clergy present were invited to join in the discussion. Theological debate galloped ahead, but Winthrop grew restless and impatient. Anne was too good at it. He feared things were going nowhere.

At last he said, "The court you see hath labored to bring you to acknowledge the error of your way so that you may be reduced. The time now grows late. We shall give you a little more time to consider of it, and therefore desire that you attend the court in the morning."

Mary and William left the meetinghouse in stunned silence. I trailed miserably along behind them. We traveled straight to the inn and were shown to our rooms. I set to work trying to warm Mary's feet and get her out of her damp clothes. William stared at the floor.

Mary spoke first. "I refuse to be defeated," she said.

Sparks flew from William's eyes. For a terrible second I thought he might lose control.

As usual, she faced him squarely. "They said we have until spring. Boston is not the only settlement on these shores. Roger Williams survived banishment and he did it all by himself. Maybe we can go somewhere with our sort of people and start a better colony. Perhaps we will become the example for the rest of the world to see. We will be the foundation of a new world of our own making. It will be one built on the principles of freedom."

I knew she was being ridiculously optimistic, but I did admire her spirit. I too, could not help but to share in her budding dream. William, being more practical, seemed to be only focused on the enormity of the challenge. His vision centered on how difficult it would be to protect his family. He knew full well that wherever we ended up, there would not even be so much as one fenced pasture, or a single roof over our heads. We would be at the mercy of this wild, untamed land.

I tried to stay with what we needed to do at that moment and said, "I have a dry shirt and breeches for you, sir, in my satchel. Why don't you let me go down and get you something to eat? You are frozen solid."

Mary joined forces with me. "We should go down by the fire," she said. "The innkeeper will have something to warm us up. The others will be there. We are not without friends in this predicament. We need to figure out a way to help Anne tomorrow."

"A hot brandy, Mr. Dyer, and some good conversation," I suggested.

William remained silent. Reluctantly, he accepted the offer, but he still sat there like a man who had been shot. Mary pulled him to his feet. It was only the thought of strong drink that got him down the stairs at all.

The Hutchinsons were staying with relatives and going over the testimony so they could prepare some defense for the next day. We found the rest of the disenfranchised set sitting at round tables pulled up close to the fire. They were all engaged in the task of figuring out how we had arrived at this pass.

"It's the Pequot War, " said John Coggeshall. "We refused to support it. Now we are being punished."

"We did the right thing. That war did not deserve our support. Why should we take up arms against innocent souls deemed by the clergy to be Satan's seed? What bollocks. If I have to be banished for this, so be it. At least we do not have to atone for the lives of the nine hundred men, women, and children burned as they slept," said Mr. Brenton.

"Religion isn't the issue. They may be trying to make it so, but we all know they were restricting trade to suit their own purposes. Boston needs bricks, tobacco, sugar, and horses from Barbados. Those are the real issues. We need to open up our own port somewhere and run it as we like," said Mr. Coddington.

"Shall we go up the Connecticut River then? We can navigate it as far as Canada," asked Mr. Aspinall.

"Yes, well, now because of the blasted war with the Pequots, no English traders can be safe from Indian reprisal. If we go up there, we'll have to look to Boston for protection. Plus, it has been sought by the Dutch and the French," added Mr. Coddington.

"Maybe we should go south then. Perhaps we'll find Roger Williams," suggested Mr. Brenton.

Dorothy Brenton, owner of the inane remark, said, "He made the women of Salem wear veils. How am I supposed to wear a veil made out of skin?"

All fell silent while they looked at her and tried to figure out an answer. Mary came to her rescue. "It doesn't matter so much where we go, I suppose, as long as wherever we end up, we form a town with a basis in English liberty."

"Then you could wear a beaver hat," said Dorothy.

"Precisely," she answered, smiling for the first time since they had gotten the news.

Some optimism was born that night for Mary's vision. She kept it up with anyone who would listen. A cornerstone of Mary's character was that she gained strength when her back was against a wall. I learned that from her. An inner core of solid iron seemed to rise up to fight the good fight. I always admired that quality. She had a great hand there that night at the inn in Newtowne in creating the world we live in today. She swayed and convinced the men. I think they would have followed her to the moon. They all pledged to stay together, come what may. All they could salvage out of the situation was that they were right, had been within their rights all along, and somehow justice would have to prevail.

The next morning, after a hearty breakfast and a brisk walk across the Newtowne green, the proceedings began again. Governor Winthrop started with a summary pronouncement of the hearing the day before.

Anne had spent the night reading Preacher Wilson's notes taken during her meeting with the ministers. Furious that she had been misquoted, she began by bringing this to light and saying, "I find things not to be as hath been alleged. Therefore, if the ministers accuse me, I desire it may be upon oath."

"Only the court can make a decision about requiring oaths, and furthermore this is not a case before a jury," he sneered. "Let those that are not satisfied in the court speak."

"We are not satisfied! We are not satisfied!" shouted the spectators. John Coggeshall jumped to his feet and urged that the ministers be put under oath.

John Endicott, rushing to the governor's aid, said, "You, Mr. Coggeshall, are guilty of further casting dirt upon the faces of the judges."

At this, Winthrop interjected in an attempt to sidestep the oath issue by saying, "Mrs. Hutchinson, you have walked by such a rule as cannot stand with the peace of any state. If these opinions of yours be allowed to rule in one thing they must be admitted a rule in all things, for they being above reason and scripture, they are not subject to control. I will however, allow you at this time, to call forth witnesses."

Reverend John Cotton came up and sat beside Anne. I thought this was a good sign and would bode well, but I was proven wrong. Winthrop asked him to state what he could remember about the December conference where the ministers had come up with the eighty-two blasphemous opinions charge.

"I did not think I should be called upon to bear witness in this cause and therefore did not labor to call to remember. If you put me in mind of anything I shall speak of it," he said.

That henchman of a man, Reverend Peters of Salem, jumped in with an attempt to get a confession regarding Anne's statement that all ministers except Mr. Cotton were preaching the covenant of works. I remembered her statement made in December, when she said they could preach no more than they knew. I thought they were going to trap her on this and that they had been waiting for this chance ever since she uttered those words.

Anne, at last given the chance to speak, went straight to the heart of the matter. "I will tell you of the time when the Lord did reveal himself to me," she started. "He was sitting on the throne of justice and all the world appearing before him. I understood that I must come to New England, yet I must not fear or be dismayed." Quoting from Isaiah, she fortified her position by adding, "The Lord spake thus to me with a strong hand, and instructed me that I should not walk in the way of the people."

Now I knew we were really in trouble. Unfamiliar as I was with all the Protestant teaching, I could not have matched wits with any of them, but my grandmother taught me a thing or two. She used to tell us the tales of the saints, and what Anne was saying was saint talk to my ears. So I shook in my boots, knowing how the men would respond.

"How do you know it was God that did reveal these things to you and not Satan?" demanded Winthrop, who was now leaning forward looking like one ready to go in for the kill.

Anne calmly replied, "How did Abraham know that it was the voice of God when he commanded him to sacrifice his son?"

Thomas Dudley piped in with the words, "By an immediate voice."

"So to me by immediate revelation. You have no power over my body; neither can you do me any harm. I fear none but the great Jehovah, who hath foretold me of these things, and I do verily believe that he will deliver me out of your hands. Therefore take heed how you proceed against me; for I know that for this you go about to do to me, God will ruin you and your posterity, and this whole state."

Now it was Winthrop's turn to look stunned. "Reverend Cotton, please deliver your judgment about Mistress Hutchinson and her revelations," he said.

Dudley stepped in. "I desire Mr. Cotton to tell us whether you do approve of Mrs. Hutchinson's revelations as she hath laid them down."

"This is a thing I cannot bear witness against."

"Do you believe her revelations are true?"

He sat in silence.

"Good sir, I do ask whether this revelation be of God or not."

"I should desire to know whether the sentence of the court will bring her to any calamity, and then I would know whether she expects to be delivered from that calamity by a miracle or a providence of God."

Anne answered, "By a providence of God, I say I expect to be delivered from some calamity that shall come to me."

At this, Winthrop made his move. "The case is altered and will not stand with us now. I see a marvelous providence of God to bring things to this pass and made her lay open herself. The ground of all these disturbances is to be by revelations."

John Endicott, the man who later sentenced Mary to death, twice, said, "I speak in reference to Mr. Cotton. Mrs. Hutchinson hath spoken of her revelations as you have heard. Do you witness for her or against her?"

"This is that I said, sir, and my answer is plain. If she looks for deliverance from the hand of God and the revelation be in word, that I cannot deny."

Endicott answered by saying, "You give me satisfaction."

Increase Nowell stated that Anne's revelations were a devilish delusion.

Dudley added, "I am fully persuaded that Mrs. Hutchinson is deluded by the devil, because the spirit of God speaks the truth in all his servants."

Winthrop found an escape hatch by insinuating that perhaps Reverend Cotton was not obligated to denounce her. So he said, "Mr. Cotton is not called to answer to anything but we are to deal with the party now standing before us."

Seeing that Winthrop was about to pronounce his final word, Mr. Coddington interrupted in a last gasp to save Anne. "Sir, her charge is her speech to the ministers. It is the rule of the court that no man may be a judge and accuser too. I do not for my own part see any equity in your proceedings. Here is no law of God that she hath broken, nor any law of the country that she broke and therefore deserves no censure."

That only served to set them all off again. Now they all jumped into the fray.

Roger Harlekenden broke in with, "If she had behaved as women are supposed to, this never would have happened."

Israel Stoughton added, "I say now this testimony doth convince me. I am fully satisfied. The words were pernicious and the frame of her spirit held forth the same."

"We all grow sick with fasting," whined the deputy governor.

Winthrop remained quiet until he decided that he too was hungry and should bring things to a vote. "The court hath already declared themselves satisfied considering the troublesomeness of her spirit and the danger of her course amongst us, which is not to be suffered," he stated. "Therefore, if it be the mind of the court that Mrs. Hutchinson for these things that appear before us is unfit for our society, and if it be the mind of the court that she shall be banished out of our liberties and imprisoned until she be sent away, let them hold up their hands."

Only Mr. Coddington and Mr. Colburn voted against the sentence. To our everlasting disappointment, we saw John Cotton raise his hand along with his fellow ministers.

A pleased Governor Winthrop carried on, "Mrs. Hutchinson, the sentence of the court you hear is that you are banished from our jurisdiction as a woman not fit for our society, and are to be imprisoned till the court shall send you away."

"I desire to know wherefore I am banished."

"Say no more," yelled Winthrop. "The court knows wherefore and is satisfied."

So that was it. From that moment on we were all forever unwelcome in the little town of Boston. It was not God the father who had spoken and told us we had to leave the Garden of Eden. It was the father of the commonwealth instead. Thinking he was acting on behalf of the almighty, he had no qualms about his decision, as the clergy had sanctified it. He went home well satisfied. We departed in a state of shock; barely able to grasp that it had come to this. And we still had the rest of the winter to endure.

CHAPTER FIVE
House Arrest

Two days later Anne had to leave us. She was to be sent out to Roxbury Neck, a cold lonely spit of land, to the home of a minister named Thomas Weld. To say that the tears flowed like a river is to do her an injustice. All women expecting babies were near hysteria. Goody Hawkins, whom I wouldn't trust to deliver my cat, held their fates in her fat, stupid hands. But it wasn't even the healing and the midwifery that were the biggest loss. It was her motherly confidence in all of us that we thought we would die without. No punishment meted out against Anne Hutchinson could ever be construed as anything but a crime against nature.

The morning they came for her we were all out in force. I stood beside Mary.

"I'd rather take my chances out there in the cold and have the children with me," said Anne. "Why must I be put under house arrest? What does he think he can accomplish by separating a mother from her children?"

"I will come to see you, Anne," vowed Mary.

"You won't be allowed. William will never let you risk yourself. I don't want you to risk yourself."

"I don't care," Mary answered. "I don't care what anyone says. I will come to see you, and I will tell you how your children are faring."

"What am I going to do with no one to talk to but that wretched man? Have you ever seen him? Tomas Weld? He looks just like a walnut, and I daresay a walnut would be better company. My sons are better men than any of those magistrates, or ministers. Better men by far. Why couldn't I be put under their custody, or my husband's? At least then I could see to my duties. Will you be all right, Mary?"

"Goodness, Anne, don't think about me!"

31

"I can't stop thinking about everyone. What will become of us all? Boston is not what it used to be."

"They're coming for you, Mother."

"No tears, children. No tears. They mustn't see us crying. They mustn't. There is no victory here. God asks much of the faithful. He asks much of us this year. We will endure. What cannot be changed must be endured. We are made of better stuff than this lot. We will show them a brave face."

"I will keep my promise, Anne," stated Mary. "God be with you."

After she was carted away, we trudged back home with the weight of the world on our shoulders. Coming around a corner, we nearly slammed smack dab into Reverend Wilson. He pardoned himself, and then his eyes raked up and down the length of Mary's dress. She wore a beautiful Lincoln green that day. It was another one of her triumphs at the dye tubs. He opened his mouth to speak. She raised her hand in a gesture that simply said, no. It stopped him in his tracks. We swept on past him.

A full week went by before Mary managed to get any word to Anne. Blinding snow and bitter cold keep her housebound for the first four days. When the sky cleared, she made an attempt. It was so cold the water in the wash basin in her bedroom was frozen solid. I walked along behind her. She kept telling me to go home all the way out Roxbury Neck. The minute we arrived, the minister spotted her from across the street.

"Mrs. Hutchinson is not to have any visitors, save the clergy," he announced.

"I have been sent by the midwife Hawkins," Mary lied. "She is in dire need of help. I am instructed to ask a question. We need the benefit of Anne's experience. The consequences could be quite terrible."

"That would be God's will," he replied, looking over Mary's shoulder.

"No, sir, I beg your pardon, but in this particular incidence, if the woman were to come to harm, the fault would lie with you. I know, sir, because I had a similar situation occur to me. Mistress Hutchinson saved me by her skill. The baby I speak of today is presenting in the breech position. Delivery is extremely difficult, but can be achieved with proper help. Perhaps you have seen this kind of thing happen with livestock?"

"I am not a farmer, madam."

"I do not expect you to fully understand what I am talking about. I had hoped though, that if you were to understand the particular problem with breech deliveries, you would then understand how badly we need Mrs. Hutchinson's advice. Without it, the mother will die. The child will die. These are two deaths we could avoid by your Christian charity. Surely the woman's husband will have cause for much complaint if his wife and child are permitted to perish, rather than be helped when help is available."

"Mistress Hutchinson is under house arrest. There is nothing to be done."

"She needn't be brought outside, or me inside, if that is the only obstacle. Could I not talk to her through a wall? No rules would be broken. You could stand with me. I will limit my conversation with her to this one particular situation. For the love of God, sir, can we not give this suffering woman and her child a chance to live?"

Thomas Weld sighed. His dark eyes studied Mary, who held forth with a resolute expression. Eyeball to eyeball they stood. Mary did not flinch. Finally, he said, "Very well. Go to the back door, and then turn left. Stand just past the woodpile. I will see that Mistress Hutchinson is there. I will stay with you until you have finished. I will tell you when to leave."

"Thank you," said Mary. We proceeded to the specified spot. "Can you hear me, Anne?"

There was no reply. After two more tries the answer came.

"What is the problem?" asked Anne. Her voice was very hoarse, which alarmed us.

"The baby is breech."

"Has she begun to push?"

"She hadn't when I left. We were wondering if we should continue with the mugwort?"

There was a pause. I understood the ruse and knew that Anne would as well, as mugwort only comes into play with the afterbirth.

"Tell Goody not to pull on the baby. The body must be allowed to expel the child of its own accord. It can be done. Tell the Goodwife Hawkins to be patient. Much patience is required. I have delivered twelve this way."

"Twelve who are all doing well. Twelve of whom you can be quite proud. At what hour should I tell her that she could expect to deliver the child?"

"If she started today then it is my guess that she won't be done till right before midnight."

"What can we do to alleviate her suffering? We are all concerned about her pain."

"That can be endured. Give her walnuts crushed to a pulp."

"That's enough," shouted Reverend Weld.

"Very good, sir," said Mary. "I will make haste to return."

That night, Mary stepped outside after Samuel had been put in bed. The wind howled and the snow flew around in torment. She could not risk it. William went out and shouted at her to get inside.

"What the devil were you doing out there?"

"I don't mind the cold as much as you do," she said as she poured herself a flask of water.

"There will be no more trips out Roxbury Neck."

I held my breath.

"I'm not quite sure what you mean."

"Yes, you do. I know you well enough to know what you are thinking. Sensible people are not leaving their houses, save to make a trip to the woodpile. There have been several cases of frostbite and one death already this winter. Do you want to lose the nose off your face? Anne will survive."

"I can tell you I am not going anywhere tonight. That's the extent of my promise."

"'Will you never cease?" he yelled.

"Cease what?"

"Cease from bringing trouble down on our heads? Have you no thought to what you have caused us already?"

"You wanted to accuse me ever since you heard the words 'husband of Mary Dyer.' Why don't you go ahead? Why don't you invite Governor Winthrop over to join you? Why don't you just say that this is all my fault?"

"What you wear, and how you behave in this settlement, is a reflection on me. Any mishap this winter will have us thrown out to the bloody wolves. You need to think of your son and stop flouting convention. I am not your accuser."

"But you wish you were," she said. With that, Mary grabbed a pillow and blanket from her bed and climbed the ladder to spend the night with me, up in the loft.

The next day the house was silent and tense. Samuel, out of sorts, had one fit of temper after another. It was too cold and windy to take him anywhere. He whined and complained all day, begging to be taken down to the Hutchinsons. Catherine welcomed any visitors, but in this cold they were a gloomy lot over there too. William whittled by the fire and kept watch on Mary. She wondered if his attitude toward her was ever going to soften.

By evening, the weather cleared. The sky seemed bright enough to give hope. William posed the biggest problem. Mary waited until she heard his deepest snoring, before she quietly dressed in his clothes, knowing they would draw less suspicion from the watch.

Out in the dark, she skipped along carrying her lantern. I followed behind without her knowledge. I didn't tell her because I knew she'd send me back. I couldn't let her go alone. If she were to fall, or come to any mishap, she could be dead by morning. The two miles along Orange Street fell behind us as we headed out the narrow neck. Every house stood still and silent as the grave, locked up and dark. The sober Weld home was as black as night when we reached it at last. Plunked down in a dismal spot that got continually blasted by the biting Atlantic wind, it was hardly an inviting sight. Mary snuck up to the place where she had conversed with Anne. She threw a chunk of ice against the wall. Then she tossed another. My heart pounded as I crouched in my perch behind a huge white pine. I lurked there unsuspected. Mary waited for a sound and was prepared to throw more ice when she heard Anne faintly call her name.

"Anne, thank God. How are you?"

"Fine. Is William with you?"

"No. I snuck away."

"Will you be all right then?"

"Yes, don't worry. I can always pretend to be a midwife again. How are you?"

"I don't know. I feel as if I'm slipping."

"How so?"

"This pregnancy. It doesn't feel right. It isn't like any of the others."

"Are you being kept out here?"

"Yes."

"This is no better than a shed! Do you have any heat at all?"

"These people have no right to call themselves Christians, I can tell you that. How are my children?"

"Fine."

"I have been told Reverend Wilson is trying to turn them against me."

"You know that will never happen, Anne. You mustn't fear such a fate. It would be impossible. They turn a deaf ear to whatever he says."

"Good, that's good. It's what I had hoped. How is my husband?"

"Well, he misses you."

"I miss him. Can you tell him that?"

"Yes. Do you have a Bible with you?"

"No, nothing. They are trying to break me, Mary. They have used every method. He even put his hands to my throat. He wanted to strangle me."

"Who?"

"The walnut. Say nothing of this. I fought him off. Actually, I could have snapped him in half as easily as cracking a piece of dry kindling across my knee. I had to exercise restraint, I don't mind telling you, because I would have enjoyed killing him. That's the devil at work, right there, getting me to contemplate murder."   •

"You are not alone there." Mary paced from one foot to the other, holding William's coat close to her neck.

"They want me to repent, you see. It will be a great victory for them, if I announce the error of my ways. All I have to do is admit that Satan got the better of me, but that would be a lie, wouldn't it, and I will not lie just to please them. What kind of example would that set for my children?"

"If there is repenting that is needed here, it is not with you, Anne."

"You should see how the women in this house are treated. He castigates them and humiliates them at every turn. He is convinced women have no intelligence, none, no more than a dog does."

She stopped talking then. Mary and I both knew she was crying. A tone in Anne's voice sounded so low it shocked us.

"Remember how Jesus was tested," said Mary.

"Yes," Anne replied in a quiet voice.

"Remember that God is always with you."

"Yes, God, not the devil."

"Hang the devil," hissed Mary. "There is more of God in your little finger than in all the Weld relations down to their wretched third cousins."

"Mary, it is good to hear your voice."

"It's only a few months, Anne," she continued. "You must be resolute. You must. Your children want the same mother they have always
known. They want you back unchanged."

"I know."

"We will leave in the spring. Word has been sent to Roger Williams.
Negotiations are being made with Chief Miantonomo. We will all head
south to Aquidneck. You only have to get through this winter. Nothing
like this will happen in our settlement."

"Yes."

"I'll come again as soon as the weather permits."

"Don't risk yourself for me."

"I would risk anything for you, Anne."

"You better get back before you get too cold, love."

I emerged from the shadows, unable to hold my tongue another
second. "God love you, Mistress Hutchinson!"

Mary jumped a foot, but accepted the inevitable.

"Pray to the Blessed Virgin," I added.

On the way home, we both concurred that Anne's state was worse
than we had expected. We had all grown so used to her intrepid spirit
that we found it hard to hear the sorrow in her voice.

Back in the front yard, we stopped talking and crept along slowly.
We entered her house like two mice. To our horror, we found Mr. Dyer
up and sitting by the fire. "Well? How is our friend?"

"I know you didn't want me to go William, but I'm glad I went," she
added, raising her chin.

"You didn't answer my question."

"She is not well. It will be a miracle if she doesn't freeze to death
out there. Her spirits are exceedingly low."

"Let me know the next time you plan to make the trip. I will escort
you."

"Why did you change your mind?"

"I didn't. I only know that my efforts to stop you are falling on deaf
ears."

"You are not happy with me."

"Really?"

"You blame me for everything. I could not help what happened with
the baby."

"Mary, surely you don't think that of me."

"You accused me of being willful!"

"I don't remember any such accusation."

"When I couldn't eat, you said I was just being willful."

"We need to put that behind us. We need to put everything behind us. We need to move on, or we won't get through these next few months without worse consequences than we are facing now. All we have to do is hang on till spring. Is it too much to ask that we comply with the laws until then?"

"Yes," she answered.

"What?"

"It is too much to ask of me. I will wear clothes of my own choosing, the way any other English lady does, and I will not leave my friend out there to suffer alone."

With that she headed off to bed.

CHAPTER SIX
A Pair of Lepers

We made it through the next few months making additional trips out to Roxbury Neck without being caught. Winter descended in all its cruelty. We had the hurdle of Christmas to deal with. Stripped bare of all feasting and fun, it turned into a time of ghastly homesickness and sadness, endured with utter cheerlessness by the Puritans. The onset of winter always brought on a feeling of terror. This year, in 1638, it doubled. The darkness, the frigid winds, plagued us; sleeping behind a wooden chimney, waking every time the fire started to go out, prevented a solid night's sleep. Our diet shrunk to a wretched succession of pumpkins and beans.

Through that winter we never stopped looking ahead to our eventual move. Mary suggested we make as many candles as possible, doubling our supply, so we could take as many with us as we could carry. Gathering our fellow partners in crime, the former attendees of Anne's women's meeting, we now set our sights on collective work parties, organized to see to our future needs. We had two huge kettles hanging on trammels from the lug pole in the fire place, hot as Irish love, filled with boiling water and melted tallow. Two long poles were strung across the room propped up by chairs. Candle rods hung from there. Wicks, made from roughly spun milkweed, were wrapped around the rods, ready to be dipped in the precious tallow and then hung back on the pole to dry. The shortage of tallow, the bane of the first settlers, was finally beginning to ease as the number of cattle increased. This would not be the case where we were headed, so we knew we were in a race against time. Deer suet, moose fat, and bear's grease had all been tried. Dorothy Brenton pointed out that no one had tried raccoon fat, and perhaps that might have a pleasant odor. When asked why, she reasoned that since their faces were so cute, the fat must be sweet. Mary wound beeswax from the hives kept at the farm. I saved every bit of fat from pots, or roasts, as well as what I could glean from the bayberry bush. As we worked, conversation only went in two directions. Concern for Anne, on the forefront of everyone's mind; we noted how long the congestion remained in her chest. Secondly, we tried to anticipate, in whatever way we could, what lay ahead.

Mary told me that we would not manage another crop of flax for quite sometime. She urged William to buy up as much as he could. We knew that many households had baskets of fibers waiting to be spun. Knowing how many steps were involved in turning the crop into thread, I knew she was very likely right. In the summer, the flax had to be pulled and spread through an iron wire comb to break off the seed bobs. Stalks tied in bates were stacked and then watered to rot the leaves. If we managed to get a crop that far, we would be stuck at the next step because after that, the strong men had to come in next to apply the ponderous flax brake. Through the violent pounding, the flax remained resilient, until it was twice broken. An open-tooth brake and then a close brake followed by pounding the strikes in a pestle-shaped beetle. How would we manage all that? How long would it take to get the tools? She decided we should spin our fingers to the bone that winter. If, in the future, we were able to get a few looms to our godforsaken outpost, we could then weave ourselves some cloth. Otherwise, our clothes would turn into rags and we'd be in skins before the year was out.

On March 15, 1638, Anne was called to the meetinghouse to be officially cast out of the church. This shameful affair was set for ten in the morning. Anne arrived late, and her tardiness was the first issue addressed.

How could this be an issue when she was a prisoner? It was a perfect example of how badly the tide had turned against her in recent months. Her son Edward and her son-in-law were the only males present to speak in her defense. The rest, including Mr. Dyer, had sailed down the coast in search of a new place to hang our hats. Edward and John both pleaded for leniency, but were immediately castigated by Reverend Cotton.

"I do admonish you both," he said, "to consider how ill an office you have performed to your mother this day. You have been instruments of hardening her heart and nourishing her in her unsound opinions. By your pleading for her, you have hindered the proceedings. Instead of loving and natural children, you have proved vipers to eat through the very bowels of your mother to her ruin." Then he turned to Anne. "You have been an instrument of doing some good among us. Let me warn you and admonish you to consider seriously how these unsound tenets of yours and the evil of your opinions do outweigh all the good of your doings. You cannot evade the argument that was pressed upon you that the filthy sin of the community of women, and all the promiscuous filthy coming together of men and women without distinction or relation of marriage will necessarily follow. I have not heard that you have been unfaithful to your husband in the marriage covenant, yet that will follow upon it. More dangerous evils and filthy uncleanness and other sins will follow than you imagine or conceive."

Anne, quite rightly objected, "I ask leave to answer this immediately." With permission granted she said, "I did not hold any of these things before my imprisonment."

Reverend Cotton continued. "You, madam, by your speech and behavior did open the door to Epicureanism and libertinism, and if this be so, then come, let us eat and drink for tomorrow we shall die, then let us fear neither hell nor the loss of heaven. Do not sully the hearts of young women with such unsound and dangerous principles."

This denunciation of her went on until eight in the evening! The stamina of these Protestants for staying in Church and putting up with effusive ministers was beyond me altogether. Forced to stand for the duration with no break for food or natural relief, an exhausted Anne was finally allowed to leave. This time she went into the custody of John and Elizabeth Cotton. For another week she was held under house arrest and subjected to constant argument. They forced her to give over and make a statement.

A triumphant John Cotton marched her back into the meetinghouse on March 22. Once again they brought her in front of a gathering of church members and clergy who were all on the edge of their pews waiting to witness her repent.

"I spoke rashly and unadvisedly," she admitted.

Mary, sitting in the front pew, looked down at the floor. Up in the upper deck where I was relegated to, I thought my heart had stopped beating.

"I do not allow the slighting of ministers," continued Anne, "nor of the Scriptures, nor anything that is set up by God." Anne lifted her face to the heavens. "It was never in my heart to slight any man, but only that man should be kept in his own place and not set in the room of God."

Audible fury rippled across the bench of ministers. One by one they rose to denounce her. Reverend Thomas Shepherd called her a heretic.

Zachariah Symes said, "She has not yet known sufficient humiliation."

Pastor John Wilson added, "You interpret other men's sayings and sermons after your own mind!"

Reverend Hugh Peters flared his nostrils and said, "I would recommend this to your consideration. You have stepped out of your place. You have rather been a husband than a wife, a preacher than a hearer, a magistrate than a subject, and so you have thought to carry all things in church and commonwealth as you would, and have not been humbled for this."

Reverend Wilson sought to fortify Peters' position by adding, "I took her as a dangerous instrument of the devil, raised up by Satan amongst us. Whereas there was much love and union and sweet agreement amongst us before she came, yet since, all union and love have been broken. The misgovernment of this woman's tongue has been a cause of great disorder. She says one thing today and another tomorrow. Therefore we would sin against God if we should not put away from us so evil a woman, guilty of such foul evils."

Reverend John Cotton, the man the Hutchinsons lovingly followed to the New World, declared, "God has let her fall into a manifest lie, and therefore as we received her amongst us, I think we are bound upon this ground to remove her from us."

The moment Pastor Wilson lusted after had at last arrived. His face, carved out of wood on a good day, now looked as ugly and mean as a hound of hell. He got himself all wound up for another garrulous diatribe. "Forasmuch as you, Mrs. Hutchinson, have highly transgressed and offended and forasmuch as you have in so many ways troubled the church with your errors and have drawn away many a poor soul and have upheld your revelations, in the name of the church, I do not only pronounce you worthy to be cast out, but I do cast you out and deliver you up to Satan that you may learn no more to blaspheme, to seduce and to lie. Therefore, I command you in the name of this church as a leper to withdraw yourself out of this congregation." He pointed his wretched, corpselike finger to the door.

My stomach, tied in knots as it was, nearly left me when I saw Mary rise from her bench. Dressed in dark wool, she would not sit in her seat and hear Anne Hutchinson called a leper; and she would not leave her friend to walk out of the meetinghouse alone. Anne grabbed hold of Mary's outstretched hand, and out they went together.

The building remained frighteningly quiet until they reached the door. Then Anne threw back her head and gave it to them. "The Lord judgeth not as man judgeth! Better to be cast out of the church than to deny Christ."

That was the last word, and the last input, Anne Hutchinson ever had with the First Congregational Church of Boston.

One person in the front pew asked, "Who is that woman who walks with Anne?"

Then I heard the words that I thought I would never hear. I had prayed I would never hear them and I would have cut off my right arm rather than hear them. Someone, I still don't know who, but some weasel in the group, said, "Mary Dyer. She's the woman who gave birth to a monster!"

"What? What is that you said?" asked Governor Winthrop.

"Goody Hawkins told me that Mary Dyer gave birth to a monster!"

Winthrop turned to the ministers and asked them if they knew anything of this event. Under Winthrop's gaze John Cotton crumbled. He confessed to the secret burial.

Then I heard another woman say, "It had a face without a head. There were two mouths and hooves instead of feet."

"No! You are all wrong," I shouted.

My cries fell on deaf ears. All the chins in the place were wagging like a school of cod feeding on a dead shark. The ministers and the clergy were all in conference. I heard them say the child would have to be exhumed.

I fell back in my pew, sitting there like a mute statue. I did not know what to do. My courage failed me. There was nothing I could think of to save the day. Tears sprang to my eyes. I knew that would make everything worse, but I could not stop them from flowing. My mind raced around, casting about for a savior. Mr. Dyer was still away. She had no protection. It would be up to me to take care of Mary. I took my leave and headed straight to the Hutchinsons. Without Anne to run to I could at least speak with her sister. Samuel needed to be collected anyway. I hoped Catherine would be able to offer me some comfort.

She told me she would be lending us Anne's son Francis to guard our door.

CHAPTER SEVEN
The Mother of a Monster

I found Mary in by the fire stirring a big pot of stew. A great smile greeted me as I gingerly shut the door behind me.

"Everything is going to be better now," she said. She had turned her face back to the fire and was not reading me. "The worst is over. They have no more ammunition. I feel very hopeful." She looked at me again. Her generous hair lay down about her shoulders as she had released it from her cap. In her soft dress with her dark waves framing her face, I stood there wishing for any divine intervention, even if it meant my own death, anything at all that would prevent me from having to watch her lovely expression change. When she heard no agreement come from me, she turned and regarded me curiously. "What is it? Where is Samuel? Did you not collect him? How strange you look. William? You have not heard news from the dock?"

My heart sank to the ground. "No, ma'am. I am sure Mr. Dyer is fine."

"What is it then?" she asked. "Come on. Out with it."

"Oh, mistress," I cried.

"What is the matter?"

"It's Goody! Jane Hawkins! May she burn in hell!"

Suddenly, the color drained from Mary's face. "Has she spoken?"

"Yes. Oh God. I'm sorry, ma'am. I am so sorry. They all know. The whole place."

"What are they saying? Are they calling my baby a monster?"

I nodded. "Goody is a liar! She is a witch! She said it had claws and hooves and two mouths. I shouted the truth but no one listened. Things had gone too far already. Reverend Cotton confessed in the church. Pastor Wilson says he's goin' to dig it up."

Mary fell. She slumped down to the floor. Her forehead went right to the ground. I rushed to her, but was no help. Mary's arms hugged her chest as if a great gash had opened and she struggled to stop the flow. I could do nothing but sit by her.

Catherine arrived with Francis and Samuel. "I'm sorry, Mary. I'm so sorry," she said as she rushed right over. "The men should be back any day now. We'll leave as quickly as possible. We'll get out of here and say goodbye to this place."

"Escape?" asked Mary, lifting her head.

"Yes. We can have the things shipped if they are packed. We can leave right away."

Mary could not say anything

"Francis will stay over. You should have some male protection."

"Thank you."

"Just think about getting out of here," said Catherine "God gave you more than your share of courage. Remember who you are. You know who you are."

A ghastly, bitter look shot across Mary's face. I wanted to change the subject, or figure out something better to say.

Catherine continued. "You have more courage than anyone I know, Mary. You are one of the strongest women I have ever met. We are in awe of you. Do not let this shake you. We stand with you. Put on the breastplate of righteousness."

Mary squared her shoulders, looked Catherine in the face, thanked her and then said, "I will pack."

Catherine left. Mary opened the big chest by the door. Her hands reached through the linen wrapping and extracted a beautiful, little ball gown. Many times before she described the day she had worn it. It was a scene she relived over and over. At the age of nine, she was presented at court. They had all approved of her, you see. The king smiled and nodded, clearly pleased with her. For Mary, it had been one of those pivotal moments that one never forgets, that the brain stores the way a good man keeps track of his tools; it is a useful memory to be brought out when one's sense of self needs a rescuer. Tears flowed as she clutched the silk garment and held it up to her face. I could see that in her mind she traveled all the way back to the day she had worn it to Whitehall. Stiff and straight, walking behind the Barrett girls; she had been so afraid they wouldn't take her, yet for once she received equal treatment.

"I don't know who I am," she stated, staring dully ahead. "This dress is my only clue."

I wasn't sure what she was getting at. "But you were a Barrett before you were married."

"That's what everyone thinks, but I don't know who my father was. No one knows the real truth about me, but William, and the man I wanted to marry."

Stupefied, I had no idea what issue to address first.

"You love Mr. Dyer. I know you do."

"Yes, I grew to love him."

"So, who was the other man?"

"He came from a prominent family. The Holders and the Barretts were very close. I thought I could trust him, so I told him. He went to France after that and I never saw him again. Now if he hears of this, he'll think he made the right decision."

Her face crumpled up again. I wanted to rush in and say that word would not travel as far as England, but I couldn't. I knew it would. It would spread everywhere and precede her everywhere she went. My mind jumped around, desperately searching for a way to help her. "What did he look like?" I asked.

"Like the devil himself maybe," she said. "Black hair, and bright blue eyes."

"Does Mr. Dyer know about him?"

"No," Mary answered. "And he never will."

"I won't say anything."

"I know," she said.

"What is his name?"

"Christopher. Christopher Holder. We were in love. Madly, passionately. We would have married if I had kept quiet about being an orphan. He did not want to take the risk, I guess. Maybe he feared something like this would happen. Maybe he was right. Anyway, he climbed up on his big black horse and I never saw him again."

"But you—I don't understand. I thought you were a Barrett."

"As does everyone. I was raised in that household, but as a ward. I have no idea where I came from, who I truly am. The dress was sent when I was presented at court. I was not told who sent it though."

She left then and walked out in the yard. I had a thousand other questions, but I knew the door had closed. I watched her go out the gate with Samuel. I tiptoed over to the chest and sat with the dress. It wasn't the first time I had done this either. I was learning the needle arts from her and I had never seen the like of this garment. I never have since either. She was nine years old then, when presented to the king. The dress was little, but encrusted in the finest embroidery you can imagine. I liked to picture her then. Proud, handsome, marked for court life, and not stuck in plain garments, dyed in sad colors, in a world that could have been on the moon for all its distance from home. So Mary had a broken heart, I thought. Well, it did make sense after all, this desire to come over. We often seek to put an ocean between our person and our misery. Escape will always be a theme in this distant land. What can we do but make the best of it though? I knew she told me her secrets so that I would understand what she faced. Those were the true serpents lying in wait. Buried burdens of the past were the old gooseberries Reverend Wilson was always whining about. He had it wrong though; they weren't sea creatures, or twisted demons; they were only our own regrets and shattered dreams. I came from a poor family in a little village in Ireland, but I was welcomed and loved. Not belonging was as foreign to me as anything I could ever fathom. I could only imagine what she suffered and I saw it as a deep cave existing inside her. I had to help her with that; I had to help her in her quest to fill up that dark hole. It was a good intention, as all roads to hell truly are.

We spent the bulk of the next two days sorting and packing. Mary did not leave the house. Nothing further was said of her mysterious past. I knew it was a subject I could only hope she would bring up again. It wasn't my place to mention it. Onlookers gathered, but were ignored, or sent on their way by Francis Hutchinson. God love him.

Then Mr. Dyer returned.

Believe it or not, the Boston Harbor was a welcome sight to the men who had been away on their adventure. William practically raced up School Street to tell Mary his exciting news. His first glimpse of Francis standing by the door told him something was amiss. When he saw Mary, tears sprang to her eyes and mine. The story came tumbling out between the sobs. The church trial, the words "leper" and "monster" hit like twin blows.

She said, "I'm sorry, William. I am so sorry I have brought so much shame to you."

"No, no, my Mary. My sweet Mary. These men have shamed themselves."

"But you tried to spare me. I wanted to see my baby, that's all. Now they are all going to see it. I can't bear the thought of them disturbing the little grave. Why can't they just leave it be?"

"I'm going to Governor Winthrop's."

"No. Don't. Please. That will only make it worse. Anyway, they've probably done it already. Can't we just get out of here? I thought we were going to leave as soon as you got back."

"I got us an island, Mary."

"An island?"

"Yes. We will have our own island."

"To live on alone?"

"For livestock. It is a little island off the shore of a big island named Aquidneck. As soon as I can sell this house and the farm, we can be off."

"How will we get there?"

"We'll have to wait another month to sail."

"No! I can't stay here that long. I'll die."

He brushed his hand along her hair, comforting her and thinking at the same time. Then his expression changed. "We can walk then. An Indian trail goes all the way down. Then we could have someone pick us up and take us across."

"What about Samuel?"

"We'll carry him when he gets tired. We can do it. The captain said it would take several trips to get us all there. If we walk we can all arrive at the same time."

"Where will we sleep? What will we eat?"

"Roger Williams showed us how the natives manage."

I had Samuel in my arms and I just about dropped him with this news. I thought I was a pretty hardy soul, but the notion of adopting native ways gave me pause to wonder if Mr. Dyer had taken leave of his senses.

"We're going to sleep in a hole in the ground?"

"Yes. We can find caves once we get there. I'm not saying it will be easy, but it will be better than staying here. No one will be called a leper for their beliefs."

"If we are not gone before May, we will have to appear before the General Court."

"They can keep their bloody court and their bloody church as well. We have already formed a new government. It is to be called the Bodie Politic. I will be clerk."

"But what about a charter? Surely we can't just go off and form our own government."

"The land has been negotiated for. The people of Plymouth are in accord. Eventually, when the time is right, we'll get a charter. It will work. I know it in my bones."

"So you don't think we should go back to England?"

"No. Have you been thinking of that?" he asked, perplexed.

"I won't be called the mother of a monster there."

"Mary. You'll be with friends on Aquidneck. It would be awfully hard for Samuel to go back to England. We want more children. We don't want to lose them all to disease any more now than I did when we first sailed. England is played out. This New World is where the future lies."

I thanked God for William Dyer. I had heard that the grave had been disturbed already and the hooves and claws verdict stood. Gossips were having a field day all through the town. I went to the spring every morning to spare her, but I heard it all. They were all going on about her crimson dresses and her cap and laces. She was branded as the devil's whore. I even lurked about in the Winthrops' kitchen, desperate to hear an admiring word. Save for the kind sentiments of Catherine Marbury, they had all turned on her and feared her as if she were a princess of darkness. I kept silent. It pained me terribly not to come to her defense at every turn, but I knew it would only make matters worse. Like Mr. Dyer, I did what I could to help turn our faces to the future. I thought he was right. Whatever lay ahead, we could face together. I had faith in him and in the other men as well. To be done with Boston was a relief. It taught me the greatest lesson in my life, and one I have never stopped instilling in all of you. Starting over is not the worst fate to fear. Trust in the Almighty, put yourself in his hands, look to the beasts of the field and the fishes in the sea and do what it takes to survive. If only we could have been done with Boston for good, all would have been well. But that was not meant to be. It was just not meant to be.

CHAPTER EIGHT
Cast Out

In single file our small band of Hutchinsonions set off trudging through the woods. Snow clung to the dark, wet hollows along the trail. Icy swollen streams, forded with great care, kept us all mindful of one another. It took a hard week's journey to get down to Mount Hope. Anne's condition gave us pause more than once as she struggled through the mud and water. Mary found the grueling trip to be a welcome relief. As I said before, she grew stronger when cornered. Every step she took, placed her one angry foot away from the people she had grown to despise. All the hardships: the dirt, the sleeping in hovels, the squatting on the ground, she relished with grim satisfaction. The farther she removed herself from civilization, the better it seemed to her because all she wanted was to be with a close group of friends who would not judge her or hate her. Can you imagine? To this day it tears me up to have to think of it. I can still see the looks on the faces of our former neighbors as they stood silently by to see us off. This small band of English settlers, engaged in a great experiment, sent us off from the city on the hill, with hard faces and stony hearts. We left them to carry on with their mission of setting an example for the rest of the world. We left them to do this without the help of their fellow members of the commonwealth who had the most to offer. I couldn't get over it. Their behavior was a total contrast to everything I ever knew of village life in Ireland.

The group marched along bravely, with one exception. Dorothy Brenton never stopped sniffling, or whimpering. Nothing anyone could say would convince her that she was not traveling headlong toward disaster. No one questioned her misery. We did our best to jolly her along, but we became resigned to putting up with her whining. Anne's face grew graver with every bend in the path, but bless her soul, she stayed right by Dorothy and got her singing. We got the best encouragement

from the children. The Hutchinsons never failed to keep our spirits up.
They were concerned for their mother, of course, but they were also full
of adventure. Oh, but I cannot think of those darling children, so many
of them now dead and gone, without crying.

When we reached Mount Hope we found ourselves stranded. We
waited on a beach off an inlet in a broad bay, which opened to the Atlantic, many miles to the south. We searched hopefully for any sign of our
savior who was to arrive in the form of Mr. Coddington on his pinnace.
When it finally rounded the point and came into view, we jumped for joy.
In little groups, we were ferried across to the northernmost tip of our
blessed Aquidneck Island, landing in a place called Pocasset. I kissed
the ground and cried. I could feel it down to my bones. I am an island
creature after all. And it was so beautiful!

Once there, we got right on the task of finding shelter. A few caves
in the side of a bank were selected by some, including the Brentons. Not
satisfied with that option, Mr. Dyer wanted to try his hand at building
temporary quarters, Indian fashion, by bending birch branches into a
mushroom-shaped dwelling. Mud and twigs slapped onto the sides became our first home here. Mary and I got to work right away weaving
twigs into thatch. When we crawled inside, the enormity of our fate
washed over us like a cold wave. I clutched my rosary and prayed myself to sleep. The night did not pass peacefully. The sound of howling
wolves, crying as if their guts were being ripped out, had us all sitting
up as if frozen.

Wee Samuel wailed in fright. His father picked him up and stroked
his hair.

"Eat me?" he asked.

"No, son. Do you think you are as tasty as a hog? Hmm?"

"We need to protect the livestock!" gasped Mary. "How can we shelter them, William?"

"I don't know!" he said.

The next morning, William found the men all caught up with the
same question. It was decided that an emissary would have to be sent
down to the southern tip of the island to find Roger Williams. We desperately needed him to help us. Without him, I seriously doubt we would
have fared as well as we did.

We were squatting down at the beach the next day, washing our
wooden plates, when a fleet of canoes rounded the point. Struck dumb,

we scanned the faces until we spotted one white man, dressed all in skins, leading this small armada. He landed on the shore with his two hundred Narragansetts! We had seen the odd natives wandering about Boston, but nothing like this. Everything was different now. For one thing, we were acutely aware of being on their turf now, at the mercy of their charity, and that reality did not sink in without a healthy dose of dread. The English transplants stood awkwardly by while the Indians got right to work, digging a pit in the sand. Then they all vanished into the forest. It was just as if the woods just swallowed them up. We did not have any way to communicate or figure out what they were doing at all.

"Where are they going?" I whispered to Mary.

"I imagine they are off to catch something they can cram down into that hole for bait."

Sure enough she was right. It did not take them very long to return with a young deer, felled by the sting of their arrows, which they stuffed into the pit. The deer screamed in protest. The natives whooped and brayed. Their plan worked and they succeeded in rounding up the wolves. Arrows flew and we took ghastly satisfaction in the death of every creature.

There amidst the blood, the howls, and the slaughter, Mary made a vow. She informed me that she would learn the ways of the Narragansetts—just as Roger Williams had. She pledged to learn how they hunted the food and cooked it, how they wove the baskets and made the mats. She would learn their language and eventually, she told me, she would even unlock the secrets of their God. I pretended I didn't even hear the last bit because all we needed at that point was more blasphemy, but I did ask her if she would teach me the language once she learned it. She nodded as if it was understood. I loved that about her. I was not indentured to her more than a week when she taught me how to read and write. She did not look down her nose at people; the opposite was true. She had a mission her whole life to bring everyone else up to her level and to befriend them every step of the way. That is the true mark of quality. Don't ever forget it. I shared her enthusiasm for all the challenges ahead. I hoped we would not be dressing in skins, but if we had to, I said I would get the hang of chewing fat and save her from that fate at least.

And so the next months became days of building, building, planning, planning, working and working. A crude mud and twig meetinghouse went up right away. John Clarke, a man I did not know too much about except as a doctor, became the preacher. A common fenced pasture, the next immediate need, was seen to right away. Then the allotment of land for six-acre parcels established everyone's place in the grand scheme of our little settlement. All summer the axes swung and trees were felled in a race against time. Mary embraced every aspect of the task. William, obsessed with building and survival, took notice of little else. Anne, likewise preoccupied with the survival of her brood, didn't pause to even take a breath.

So it was only me who noticed a new fierceness in Mary. I saw her turning savage, losing all care for her appearance, and somehow relishing the break with civilization. It was not uncommon to go wild, as they used to say in Ireland. Get evicted, lose your land, sleep on the ground; it only takes a week, or two, for civilization to fall away entirely. It worried me to see her changing. So one afternoon I decided to try to get on her about it and offered to comb her matted hair.

She turned and snapped, "Leave it be!"

"I'm only trying to help you, mistress," I said. "Do you think I don't notice what's happening?"

"You can go back if you wish," she answered.

"Did I say anything about going back? Don't let Winthrop and his lot get the better of you, mistress, that's all I'm saying. You don't have to fight them anymore."

"It is not your place to speak of such things, Irene."

"It is. I may be indentured, but that doesn't mean my heart is on a seven-year loan. I care. I care about wee Samuel. And Mr. Dyer. I care most about you, whether you like it or not. I care, and I don't like what I'm seeing."

"What do you see?"

"Fierceness. Bitterness. Loathing. It's no' like you."

"I can't help it," she said, suddenly sinking to sit down on the ground. "I know I look ugly. I feel ugly. I am ugly. What spewed out of me when I gave birth to that monster is what's inside. There is nothing I can do about it."

"Your little daughter was lovely. But for the one missing part she would have been as beautiful as her mother. I know what is inside of you and it is strong and true. Everyone sees it. The king saw it. So don't go telling me anything different because I will never believe you."

Her eyes filled up with tears, but she said nothing.

"I'm moving out," I announced. "I'm sleeping with the Brentons until the house is finished and we can have separate quarters."

"Who gave you permission?"

"Mr. Dyer did."

Mary made a move to storm off in the direction of her husband, but I stopped her. "You need another baby, Mary. He is the only one who can help you. I'll no' watch you slip away."

She glared at me then. She squeezed my arm. Squeezed it 'til it hurt, but I did not flinch because I knew it was the only way she could think of to tell me what was going on inside. I stood my ground.

A few days later, Mr. Dyer found us down by the shore sitting on a rocky outcropping. He noticed that something about Mary looked different, and wouldn't you know it, he had to struggle to figure out what it was.

"You look very beautiful tonight," he said. Then when he got closer he added, "You smell wonderful. What is it?"

"Raccoon fat," she answered.

He laughed. "No. What?"

"I let Irene take care of my hair. We had to use walnut oil to get the tangles out."

I had to give him some help as I could see he was still puzzled. "It's braided, sir."

"Oh yes."

"Clever of you to notice," she said, but her face looked sweet and she was not aiming to wound him with her words.

"I'm sorry. I've thought of nothing but the house in months. I came to tell you that Baulstrade has succeeded in making ale. It's crude, but not too bad. Would you like to come with me and get some?"

"Maybe we could cook a fish down here tonight. I wouldn't mind washing it down with ale. We could spread a blanket and look at the stars. Somehow, I have no desire to be with the crowd."

"It's just as well. Everyone is setting into that ale already, I can tell you. There isn't much privacy here, is there?"

"Irene says that I need another baby. She thinks if the next one comes out right, I'll get over what happened."

"And what do you think?"

"I think that baby was who I really am. The monster was me."

William suddenly threw his hat on the ground. "How dare you, Mary!"

"What?"

"She was our child! She was not a monster! She didn't turn out right, that's all. Nothing black, nothing evil, nothing bad. She was a lamb of God. To take all this on yourself is selfish."

"Selfish?"

"It is not up to us to question these matters. It is something over which we have no control. We simply have to accept it."

"If that is true, then why did the good people of Boston look at it as a judgment upon me?"

"Ignorance, that's why."

"Is Governor Winthrop ignorant?"

"No, but he took advantage of the situation for his own political gain. It happened at a fortuitous time for him, don't forget."

"I don't want to have another baby," she announced.

"Why not?"

She sat with her head down.

"I understand," he said quietly. Then he added, "It's not like you to be ruled by fear."

Her head shot up then. I was silently cheering for him. He found the right words. She turned her gaze out to sea.

That evening we took the newly made ale, a blanket, some cooked fish, and a crude hunk of coarsely ground corn bread down to the shore. William brought along the Bible.

"Listen to this," he said.

St. John 1
In the beginning was the Word and the Word was
with God, and the word was God.
The same was in the beginning with God.
All things were made by him; and without him was
not anything made that was made.
In him was life: and the life was the light of men.
And the light shineth in the darkness; and the darkness
comprehendeth it not.

"Without him was not anything made that was made," Mary repeated. She thought for a bit, pondering things. Then she said, "Then why did God make a deformed baby in my womb? If God made the baby, then God wanted me to have this trial, this pain; God wanted to punish me just as they all say. How are those words supposed to comfort me?"

"No punishment was sent to you. No pain was sent to you. God is present everywhere. We can find him everywhere in the good, and in the bad; in the happiness, and in the sorrow."

"Anne told me once that she found Him in her mother's agony."

"Exactly. It is as she said. Nothing is separate from God. The feeling of separateness is the source of the pain. Feeling singled out is causing your distress and you needn't suffer this discomfort. I can hardly bear to see it."

"Me neither," I added.

Mary stared at the water. After a time she spoke. "This ale is good. I might just drink my fill of it tonight. Read me some more, William. I do find comfort in the sound of your voice. Why don't you read from The Song of Solomon? You know the chapter I mean."

He smiled at her with great tenderness in his eyes.

I told them I would take Samuel and put him to bed. As we strolled away, I could hear William's voice.

"Very well. I shall read from Chapter six."

How beautiful are thy feet with shoes, O prince's daughter!
The joints of thy thighs are like jewels, the work of the hands of a
    cunning workman.
Thy navel is like a round goblet, which wanteth not liquor; thy
    belly is like a heap of wheat set about with lilies.
Thy two breasts are like two young roes that are twins.
Thy neck is as a tower of ivory; thine eyes like fishpools in Heshbon
    by the gate of Bathrabbim; thy nose is as the tower of Lebanon
    which looketh toward Damascus.
Thine head upon thee is like Carmel, and the hair of thine head
    like purple; the King is held in the galleries.
How fair and how pleasant art thou, O love, for delights.
Thy stature is like to a palm tree, and thy breasts to a cluster of
    grapes.
I said I will go up to the palm tree, I will take hold of thy boughs
    therof; now also thy breast shall be as clusters of the vine, and
    the smell of thy nose like apples;
And the roof of thy mouth like the best wine for my beloved, that
    goeth down sweetly, causing the lips of those that are asleep
    to speak.

Come my beloved, let us go forth into the field; let us lodge in the villages.

Let us get up early to the vineyards; let us see the vine flourish, whether the tender grape appear and the pomegranates bud forth: there I will give thee my loves.

The mandrakes give a smell and at our gates are all manner of pleasant fruits, new and old, which I have laid up for thee, O my beloved.

CHAPTER NINE
Not a Baby

About a week later, we women went off in search of wild blueberries. Everyone was chatting away happily, delighted to be engaged in such a simple endeavor. The mood was broken very swiftly, however, by a sudden gasp erupting from Anne. Mary, looking up, saw that Anne's skirt lay wet, soaked through down the front. We made a chair with our hands, and carried her all the way back to the village. William Hutchinson ran off to get Dr. Clarke, totally ignoring his wife's protests. It was the first time any of us had ever seen him go against her.

Anne grabbed Mary's hand. "I don't want that man to tend me," she stated.

"Why not? He is a physician."

"I know this child is not right. We must do what we did for you back in Boston. Irene can help you. She knows what to do. I don't want them to use this against me. If you deliver the child, no one will know but us. It will be between us."

"I understand, but I don't think your husband will let me take such a risk. I am not an experienced midwife."

"But I am. I will tell you exactly what to do."

"Then I shall do my best to persuade him."

"Good."

John Clarke, waylaid in his mission by Mary, found her planted in front of the doorway to Anne's room. As she explained both Anne's will and the logic involved, the doctor appeared pained and did not disguise his irritation. He turned to Mr. Hutchinson for an answer. To our dismay, he held fast in his position, refusing to take the chance of leaving his wife to our care. He insisted that the doctor remain.

Mary stepped forward. "Might I assist you then, sir?"

He studied her rather coolly and then agreed.

Mary brought me with her. I prayed not to be sent away. He said nothing, so I slipped into a corner of the room behind the fireplace on the main floor of their small, makeshift cabin. I knew we'd be in for trouble because Anne had been resigned and silent for months. I asked her once if she felt any movement and she wouldn't answer me at all. I took that for a no. I had no means by which to write my priest in Ireland for help.

We slid into the afternoon and evening. Anne put up with the pain. She endured her travail quietly, but I did not like her color. Her face wore the mask of stony determination. She said nothing to Dr. Clarke. He grew impatient with her. Mary and I glared at him. We gathered in closer when she got to the pushing stage. Just when I thought we were never going to have a delivery, and I had resigned myself to hugging my knees to my chest and rocking in the corner, something started to happen. I jumped up, but was not able to do a thing. What gushed out and ended up in the doctor's hands, was not a baby. I don't know what it was exactly, or what to call it, but it was not a baby. I guess you could say it was a large clot or something—a shapeless clump of flesh and growths.

"Let me see it," thundered Anne.

When John Clark shook his head, to say no, Mary snatched the bundle right from his arms.

"Mistress Dyer! Have you forgotten yourself?" He looked absolutely stunned.

"I have forgotten nothing, sir," she said.

He stormed out in a huff, showing no sympathy, no kindness, no understanding at all. He barely disguised his revulsion, and I went back to wishing Mr. Hutchinson had let Mary and me tend her.

"I'm so sorry, Anne," whispered Mary, handing the bundle to Anne.

"Here, let me wash it, mistress. Mary, you must deliver the afterbirth. I'll help you."

"This will be used against me," said Anne. "Just swaddle it in linen when you are done Irene. We'll have William in, and then we'll have to see to the burial."

"We will ask everyone to respect your privacy," said Mary.

"This will get back to Governor Winthrop. He has already been snooping. Every time a pinnace lands here, inquiries have been made. They're still at it. Winthrop wrote letters to every governor up and down the coast describing what happened to you."

"He did?"

"Surely you knew that?"

"No, I heard nothing of this."

"Your husband tried to shield you, I suspect. I wouldn't have mentioned it had I known. Sorry."

"What difference does it make? No letters needed to be sent. Word travels of its own volition. I bear an uncommon renown. I'm the mother of a monster. I'm that woman who took the devil to her bed."

"Now I am too," cried Anne.

I thought I was going to go plum crazy hearing this. So I spoke up. "I am the only witness to both births," I announced. "Mary's baby was a poor wee soul who had no chance at life. This is not a child at all. People may not listen to me now, while I am nothing but a poor indentured servant, but as I live and breathe, I will set the record straight. I won't be a servant forever. I simply refuse to hear of people speaking ill of either of you. I hope and pray to the blessed Virgin, keeper of all women's sorrows, that I won't have to say anything at all as far as this day is concerned. I would not have wished this on you for all the world, Mistress Hutchinson. If Dr. Clarke can be trusted, this need go no further than this room. If that old man in skirts, Winthrop, wants to go poking his nose into your business, then nothing need be said but that it is a stillborn."

Anne squeezed Mary's hand and turned her face to the wall.

Weeks went by. With bated breath we scanned the shoreline daily for any sign of ships. Samuel first spotted the pinnace rounding the point. A letter for Anne from her cousin Francis Marbury, who had chosen to remain in Boston, arrived. After running to fetch her, to our disappointment, the letter got tucked up in her apron and taken home to read.

I kept the door open all afternoon. A lovely salty breeze cooled the main floor of our small home, but did not bring Anne in with it. We did not hear a thing until the next day.

A stream ran down the hill behind our tiny village we called Pocasset. A waterfall further up the hill gave off enough sound to transport us to another time and place, far away from our troubles and woes, heavenly, in all its purposes. Women gathered water in the soft pool there every morning. As we had done in Boston, we chatted, washed the little girls and enjoyed the privacy of the fragrant woods. A hush fell over us as we heard the familiar sounds of the Hutchinson girls coming up the path. Seeing them clustered around their mother gave us the first clue. The sight of Anne's face banished all hope. We wished we could run to her and envelop her in our arms, but out of respect, we kept quiet.

After sitting down on a spongy patch of moss, she began by announcing the verdict. "Thirty inhuman monsters."

Stunned into silence, we sat dumfounded, waiting for her to continue.

"Governor Winthrop made inquiries, as we suspected he would. Dr. Clarke responded. Apparently, he wrote that he beheld, first unwashed and then washed with warm water, several lumps, some greatly confused, and if you consider each one of them, they were altogether without form. Of these several lumps there were about twenty-six, or twenty-seven, distinct and not joined together. It was from those words, 'distinct and not joined together,' that my great friend, the esteemed Reverend Weld, my constant companion last winter, ascertained that I gave birth to monsters in the plural. He is quoted as saying all over Boston and up and down the coast, probably as far as Halifax, that it was thirty in all. Note how the number jumped from twenty-six. I'm surprised that it didn't jump to eighty-two so as to coincide with my eighty-two blasphemous opinions. He said that some were smaller, others bigger, some of one shape, some of another, few of any perfect shape, and none at all of any human shape."

The air took on a tinge of frightening quiet, disturbed only by the sound of falling water. Then a hint of wind came through. I had forgotten to breathe. Tears spilled down cheeks, Anne's girls' faces crumpled and I felt the hair on the back of my neck stand up.

"This can happen to women going through the change," I cried. "Surely it will be noted, by the women at least, that this is a common enough occurrence."

"Since when do we count?" asked Dorothy.

"What did your husband say?" asked Mary.

"Well, he is very upset and sorry. He went over the assurance Dr. Clarke had given him, at the time of the delivery, that my privacy would be respected. To his everlasting regret, he believed John Clarke to be a man of his word. I am not speaking to my husband at present, so I have little else to report."

"Did your cousin say how it was going over in Boston?"

"Yes. She did not fail to report that the few friends I have remaining in the town, and my son, of course, are leaping to my defense. But we all know it is of no use. 'The sin of misshapen opinions led to misshapen births.' This is the cry from the pulpit, bearing, of course, Reverend Wilson's stamp."

"Well, at least you are among friends here," said Marie Coddington.

"Am I?" asked Anne.

None of us knew what to do with that question. We all understood her feelings of betrayal. We also knew that she was as low as any of us had ever seen her. Each of us cast about for words of comfort. Mary reached over and squeezed her friend's hand. A deep sob erupted from Anne. Her daughters crept up and encircled her. Hands rubbed her back. Worried concern etched on every face, which within moments, gave way to collective tears. There we sat, by the pool, by the sweet, cool water, and wept together. Eventually, a little boy came up the path, sent by the men who were all wondering what we were up to. Full of weary resignation, we rose to resume our duties.

With our faces washed, we set down the path, each of us bearing the yoke of our buckets. Heavy clouds rolled over the settlement. It occurred to me that we still had the whole winter ahead of us. It wasn't long before we were all working our collective garden again, at our characteristic feverish pitch.

Due to the scarcity of fencing, and the plentiful deer population, our production had been simplified to one group effort. Tending it, knowing that we could starve if our one stab failed, lent extra vigor to every move we made.

Anne scraped the earth ferociously, hour after hour. By the set of her jaw we could easily guess what was going on in her mind, even though she hacked away in silence. By late afternoon though, she stopped to speak. "I can't see myself sitting in John Clarke's congregation. I'm not willing to take my children to him for instruction either."

Our whole operation came to an immediate halt. Mary and I both leaned on our hoes, which were desperately makeshift implements, fashioned only from clamshells wrapped around sticks.

Then Anne posed a rhetorical question. "Why do we have to have John Clarke as our pastor?"

"Well, I suppose he is the only one among us who is qualified," said Dorothy.

"Why do we need this artificial qualification? Who says that a man should be the one to teach—a man with a certificate. Christ had no official certificates."

"Would you like to be the preacher then?" asked Mary.

"Yes, actually, I would."

I thought that we were in a bit of a flight of fancy here. If it would cheer Anne up at all to think on this topic, I would have been all for it, of course. What happened next is something for the history books, for we went through a sea of change, right then and there.

Mary piped in with, "Well, let me be the first to join your congregation."

Dorothy plopped down right in the dirt and sat there with her mouth open. When Anne and Mary's faces both lit up, I knew it was as if we had been out on Mr. Coddington's pinnace and he had thrown the tiller all the way over and shouted "prepare to come about."

"We could meet in my home, same as before," Anne continued. "Only this time I will not wait till the service is over."

"You mean you are going to set up a separate church?" I asked.

"Well, how much is our current situation a real church? We arrived here, we built it, and we started attending. I'm simply going to offer an alternative. Since it is written into our Bodie Politic that I can't be run out of here for my beliefs, I will carry on in my own way, in my own time."

"I will attend your church, Anne. I swear it. I don't care what William says. I will join forces with you," announced Mary.

The rest of us fell to silence. I knew the other women would not dare utter a word until they had discussed this with their husbands.

Back home for supper, I felt a growing knot developing in my stomach. We prepared the meal in uncharacteristic silence. Mary did not ask for my opinion; so for once, I kept my thoughts to myself. When Mr. Dyer came in, I gauged his mood. He dropped into his chair, removed his hat and wiped his brow.

Mary wasted no time in delivering her declaration. The blow was not softened, the way was not prepared, no wheedling, no pleading—she simply told him flat out what she intended to do.

Naturally, he responded forcefully. "No. I forbid it," he said. "Anne cannot do this."

"Why not? She has every right to feel betrayed. Dr. Clarke should have known better, William. I cannot listen to a single one of his sermons. He will not be my pastor either."

"I understand your feelings, and Anne's. That does not change the fundamental fact that she will have to be dissuaded from this course."

"Good luck," she answered.

"Look. You need to listen to me here. If Anne does not wish to attend, then fine, she can stay home by herself and keep her children with her. That is the limit of what she can do. To try to have a separate church, with my wife in attendance, is an entirely different matter."

"Are you saying she can't do this because she is a woman?"

"Yes!"

"But why? Who is to say we have to have an ordained minister? Where is it written that a woman cannot preach?"

"Don't do this, Mary. Don't even think about it. Everything we have built here will fail if this whole business starts up again. The clergy of Boston will have a field day. Every fool in England will want to land here thinking they can become whatever it is they imagine themselves to be."

"Isn't that what we want?"

"No, it is not. We want to form a good solid town; we want to grow and prosper until we eventually get our own charter. Surely, you know this. I should not have to spell it out. I'm shocked that you would even contemplate a plan so detrimental to our common mission. I'm surprised at you."

"You can go listen to John Clarke if you want to, William, but I will not be joining you," she told him.

"Are you saying that you would send Samuel and me off to church alone?"

"Yes. I would prefer it if Samuel came with me. If you insist on taking him, I will not stand in your way. Since you do not know what it is like to be a woman, you have no understanding. Dr. Clarke betrayed the dearest friend I have in the world. I simply will not go and listen to his ideas about Christianity."

"Winthrop pressed him for that information."

"He could have pressed me with stones and I would not have divulged a word."

"No doubt," he answered.

Mr. Dyer grabbed his hat and stalked out of the house, taking huge strides, but saying nothing.

He came back later, entering slowly, carefully shutting the door behind him. Mary, at her place spinning, gave him a brief glance before turning her eyes back to the wheel. I sat nearby sewing, with my eyes going from mistress to master.

Mr. Dyer crouched down beside her stool and spoke in a gentle tone. "What if Dr. Clarke were to give Anne a public apology, from the pulpit, and ask for her forgiveness."

"Don't ask me what she will do. Ask her."

"If she could forgive him, would you?"

"No."

"No?"

Mary's eyes flashed with anger. "Do you have any idea what he has done? There is no place in the whole wide world to which she can escape. Everywhere she goes, people will stare at her and wonder how many times she received the devil in her bed."

"How do you know what people are thinking?"

"How dare you ask me that question, William?"

"All right, I grant, it is a difficult cross to bear, but I have heard it said that God never gives us a burden we can not carry. It serves no purpose to blame people for their ignorant superstition."

"John Clarke fanned the flame of superstition by divulging that information."

"He thought it his duty to tell the truth," said William. "Winthrop was determined to find out. How would you have answered the letters?"

"I would have said that Anne was delivered of a stillborn child. I would not have seen any further cause to elaborate."

"And if asked for the specifics?"

"I would have replied that Anne had been delivered of a stillborn child who currently resides in God's merciful heaven."

"Well, I suppose Clarke could have responded that way, but he didn't consider such a reply truthful."

"There was nothing else that could have been said. It was not a baby, but you don't try and explain that. Any midwife would have described either Anne's misfortune or my child as stillborn! Born and has mercifully died, is the only explanation. If pressed, he could have defended Anne's privacy. That is what I would have done. What business is it of Governor Winthrop's to go poking his nose into these matters? Is every issue born on this side of the Atlantic his affair?"

"No, and I agree with you. John Clarke, however, thought he had no choice. Yes, he should have asked. Yes, he could have decided differently, but he is a physician, don't forget, and quite used to relaying the facts in plain English. Is there no room in your Christian heart to forgive him?"

"He has not asked for forgiveness."

"But if he were to, could you forgive him?"

"No," she said.

He stood up and shook his head. "It is not like you to be hard hearted."

"Well, maybe my heart grows harder every day."

"But why?"

"Maybe it comes from working eight hours in a field. Maybe it comes from sleeping on the ground. Maybe it comes from wearing dirty, worn-out clothes. Maybe it is because my garments are all in shreds. Clout upon clout hardens hearts."

He held up his hand. "You have said enough."

"I will not change my mind. On Sunday, I shall be with my friend."

"On Sunday, Samuel and I will take our places in church."

"So be it then," she stated.

"Nothing good will come of this," he added.

"Yes, I expected you to say that."

"Mary. I have no wish to quarrel. I don't agree with what Clarke did. I would not have handled the inquiries the same way. But I think he deserves our allegiance."

"Fine. I understand your position. You may tell him for me that he has, forever, lost mine."

I crept away to the back door in search of breathing room. At the shore, I sat and tried to look down the road. All I could conclude of the matter was that the Protestants were all gearing up for another division in their church. I began to wonder if that was all they ever did, split and divide, argue and break apart. I suddenly longed for home with such a passion that I wept bitter tears of utter despair.

CHAPTER TEN
On the Move Again

Roger Williams came by to tell us that the Narragansetts foresaw a tough season ahead. Winter winds swept off the ocean early, biting us hard. Candles, hoarded and rationed, sputtered to nothing. Without the tallow to make more, we burned pitch and fat in great, gloppy messes. Plentiful game and no shortage of fish, our Godsend that year, kept starvation from us, but we had to go months without flour. The cold enveloped all, permeating our very bones. Ragged skirts whipped our legs. Some days the chamber pots had to stay full; we couldn't even get out to empty them.

Mr. Dyer fussed over the fire, day in and day out. Poised like a cat, he waited for the right minute to add another log. Once again, we had to live with a wooden chimney. The woodpile had to be rearranged and resorted according to the varying sizes and degrees of the timber. He reminded me of a miser continually counting his money. He and I had words because I needed a hot fire for cooking, and it was like pulling teeth to get him to build it up.

Sometimes at night, I would look up at the moon and think that if human beings ever tried to start a colony there, I would know exactly what they were in for. As a few craft had sailed in over the summer, we could receive news, however disconcerting, and also the odd bit of belongings that were ferried to us in dribs and drabs. But as winter covered us up with snow, it also cut us off from everything. We feared what we did not know. Yes, we felt marooned. It only served to increase the tension in various households.

On Sundays, Mary and I traipsed over to the Hutchinsons for what I called in my mind, a makeshift church. Since I could not write to my priest, I pretended that one Protestant gathering was the same as another. It made us a congregation of three, not counting the children. We

68

had hopes that it would grow. As I said earlier, Anne could preach rings around any man. Sometimes, on those Sunday mornings, the heat of the fire would create steam rising from our wet clothes. It would sit over us as a celestial cloud. How can I describe the feeling we shared in her cozy cottage? It was as close as I ever came to home, to feeling at home, to being back in my own church, in our parish in Derry.

Mr. Dyer never stopped objecting, but he did witness the sweet smile on Mary's face when she returned for cold supper on Sunday. He stopped saying anything after awhile. We knew he did not like it, but he loved his wife, worshipped the ground she walked on, and her well-being meant more to him than anything.

Not until March did we see a ship or hear any news. The wind still pierced our worn-out dresses and cloaks. My heart shot to my throat when I heard we had a letter from Harry Vane. My face betrayed me as usual. Flaming red it went, like I'd painted myself for battle the way the natives do. Mary concealed a smile at the sight of me. Back in our Boston days, back to the first day I saw his long curls and scarlet vest, I went plain nuts over the man. Even though Mary continually pointed out that Harry Vane's father was the most powerful man in England next to the king, I still worshipped him and was daft enough to entertain foolish notions that he had feelings for me. Telling me that class divisions were going to be different in the New World, I was as deceived as any other servant girl has been since the dawn of time. My mistress helped me through it by telling me that with Englishmen, all class divisions disappear when they lie down, but the minute they are back up on their feet, they are stronger than ever. After Harry Vane defeated Winthrop and became governor, he never looked at me twice. We would never have had all our troubles, if he had remained in power. Once Winthrop was reelected and got his seat back, Harry went back home, taking my foolish, girlish heart with him. Boston sent him off with a great volley of shot. I wanted to shoot myself.

Word from England began with the chilling missive that the king's forces met defeat at the hands of a well-disciplined Scottish army some twenty thousand strong! The Scots wanted their own church and they were willing to fight in order to get it. The secret thrill of solidarity I felt, I kept well hidden, believe you me, but I did feel it, I must confess. Everyone else was dumbfounded.

Mr. Dyer went on and on that night over what a mistake the king had made in dissolving Parliament. It must be remembered that democracy had been in place in one form or another for three hundred years, so who was he to think he could do without it? King Charles seemed to totally forget that without a governing body, he had no way of raising funds for war. Hence the defeat at the hands of the Scots, which really stuck in the English craw, I don't mind telling you. Those who should have been in Parliament gathered themselves together under the banner of the Earl of Stratford. They sought to form some kind of government whether the king was for it or not. Harry Vane wrote that this Parliament would open up a conflict with the king—the likes of which had never before been seen in England. As it turned out, that became one of the great understatements of the century.

Coddington, Dyer, Hutchinson, and Clarke all send back letters imploring Harry Vane to keep them informed. Otherwise, the Old World could come to an end, and we wouldn't even know. I prayed for dear Ireland too, because I knew that every time England gets in any kind of pickle, they take it out on us.

As soon as we could emerge from our various hovels, we spread our wings. Mr. Coddington sailed to Boston, in May, to see to business matters. John Clarke and Mr. Dyer went off exploring to the south end of the island. Mary and I took on the challenge of planting a kitchen garden.

Shortly after the men left, Anne rushed over to our house, right before the noon meal.

"We're going to do it," she announced rather breathlessly.

"Do what?" asked Mary.

"We're going to put my husband in as judge."

"Your William? How can you do that? What are you talking about?"

"We're electing him. A few of the magistrates will be replaced too."

"How?"

"By election."

"How can you have an election?"

"We're going to call one. Didn't Coddington put himself in as judge more or less? We're not under a royal charter here. This is our own government. The people want a change."

"What people? Half the men are gone, including Mr. Coddington. What is wrong with the Bodie Politic as it is?"

"I thought you'd be excited. This is our chance for real influence."

"Whose chance?"

"Ours. Yours and mine."

"I never said I wanted to run anything. I am not unhappy with William Coddington. He has done no harm. To take over like this while he's away, isn't right."

"The time has come to take a stand. I thought you'd be with me, Mary."

"I cannot sanction this move."

"Right. And the fact that you don't support my husband as judge—what does that mean?"

"I'm sure he would make a fine judge, in due course. That is my only point. Is my husband still clerk or has he been removed too?"

"No, he hasn't been removed."

"This is a matter for the men to hash out," said Mary. "It is none of my affair."

"Why? Why should the men run everything? Why should you be running to your husband to get his opinion? He tells you how to worship. Isn't that enough?"

"You may not speak against my husband in this house," Mary answered with her eyes flashing a look that could cut any man, woman, or child in half.

Anne turned. She paused with her hand on the door, but must have thought the better of saying anything further, as she left without looking back.

Mary and I stood rooted to the spot until we looked at each other and tried to figure out what had just happened.

"I agree with you, mistress," I said. "It's no' right."

"Which part?"

"Replacing Mr. Coddington, for starters. I don't think Mistress Hutchinson is herself these days."

"I told her last week that I was thinking of splitting my Sundays, one with her and one with William. It is nothing against her, of course. I have my husband and son to consider. If I go to hear Dr. Clarke, my husband will be happier, but she will be mad, so where does that leave me? I hate it when William is unhappy. There is no middle ground here. What should I do?"

"I have no advice when it comes to this Protestant splintering. I think you were right to stand up for your husband though. Religion is one thing, but politics is quite another. Never the twain shall meet. This cabal will be brought up short when Mr. Coddington returns, mark my words. Perhaps Mr. Dyer suspected she was after more than just her own church. How can this be a fair election when so many are away? The miscarriage took the wind out of Mistress Hutchinson. She's just tryin' to get it back."

When Mr. Dyer returned with John Clarke they both went immediately to the Hutchinsons' house. Convinced that he could talk some sense into his friend, he found his efforts falling on deaf ears. Quietly and sullenly, he crossed his own threshold, hours later. "He wouldn't budge even when I told him he'd behaved no better than a thief. How did this happen?" he asked, as he jabbed the fire with his poker.

"Don't look at me," replied Mary. "I had no hand in this. For once you can't blame me."

"I had no wish to blame you. I merely asked you a question."

"Irene, could you pour us some ale, please? William, sit down. I haven't even heard about your trip. How did it go?"

"I think we should move," he stated.

We both nearly dropped in our tracks. I poured the ale. Mary pulled up a chair and dropped as if shot.

Mr. Dyer, seeing the looks on our faces, sped along. "We found a remarkable harbor to the south—a perfect natural harbor. It's so deep a ship could sail right in and tie up. There are fields of rich grassland all around."

"But how?"

"They were cleared long ago by Indians. When they left or were killed off by disease, the natural grasses took over. The land is ideal for grazing. Now that this has happened, it might be time to pull up stakes."

"Surely you jest," said Mary.

"We could end up with the main port on this island. We could get bigger tracts of land and maybe even another island. Do you realize how many years it will take us to make pasture land here? I'll be pulling out stumps for the rest of my life."

"Have you given no thought to your family at all?"

He glared at her, plainly insulted.

She continued, "We spent the winter trapped in here like animals. We slept in a wigwam last spring. Those are not experiences I care to repeat."

"We didn't have time to really explore before. There is no reason not to begin again. We might even sell this house."

"To whom?"

"More fools coming over to be with Anne."

"Don't speak of her that way. I can't live apart from her."

"You may have to."

"William, please stop saying such things. I cannot bear it."

"If Coddington wants to try out this harbor, I'd want to go with him. I have no wish to remain with this lot if he goes."

"But what if I do?"

"You would be out of luck, I guess. Once we get there, you'll see the difference. The wisdom of the move will be very clear."

"Is that what you want? You want someone who just goes along with whatever you say? Well, fine, I'll go to your bloody new port then. Take me away from the best friend I ever had, and the only hope of finding spiritual guidance—just take me away like you did when you took me from England."

"Mary," he pleaded. "I see no reason to become unhinged."

"Unhinged? We have no hinges but leather!" With that she slammed the door and marched out of the house.

When Mr. Coddington returned, all speculation ended. He, along with the Dyers, Aspinalls, Coggeshalls, Brentons, and Eastons decided to swarm to the new port in the south. The deeds of land, the only official records of who owned what in Pocasset, would be smuggled out, safely tucked up under William Dyer's shirt.

When we climbed the path to get our water those last few mornings in Pocasset, we would fall into silence. Certainly, the setting lent itself to such reverence, but we clammed up for other reasons. Nothing was said of the split. No one wanted to broach the subject, so it landed in the realm of the unmentionable, until the last day. As we had been so much in the habit of taking all our cues from Mistress Hutchinson, we waited until she was ready to speak. On this morning, we heard her singing as she headed up the path. Her clear voice, rippling through the trees, caused most of us to tear up. I dared to think, by her good cheer, that she had come 'round at last and would join us after all.

Mary must have read my mind, or had similar thoughts as she began by saying, "It's good to hear your voice this morning, Anne."

She laughed at the sight of our hopeful faces. "Did you think I'd changed my mind?"

"Have you?" blurted Dorothy. "Please say you have."

"My dears, we are all island dwellers, after all. We are creatures of an island race. We'll be together, after a fashion, just the way we always have." She knelt down and dipped her cup, filling it with cool, refreshing water.

Glum, mute expressions registered on every face. Mary tried again. "The door is always open. If you change your mind a week from now, you can still join us, no questions asked."

"I know. That sentiment runs both ways. Don't think for one minute that I don't hope and pray you will be as chickens coming home to roost. If not, then we'll all prosper, each in our own way. I've had word from Plymouth that there will be people joining us here. We'll form two towns on this island, two American Edens. One shall be guided by Dr. Clarke; the other will be led by me. I just want you ladies to remember that we all have duties to our husbands, but our first duty is to God."

The peace and goodwill of the setting came to a screeching halt. We heard, to our shock and dismay, something sounding like a war whoop coming from Mary. She stood up with her fists clenched, her teeth bared, and her face in a furious grimace. For a second, we did not know what she would do next. "Do not, " she yelled, "question my faith. Not in my husband, not in my choices and least of all, in you." She hurled her buckets in the water with such force she had to wade out to get them. With her wet skirt weighing her down, she took off down the path at a near run.

"I must have hit a nerve," said Mistress Hutchinson.

"I have to go," I said. "I'm frightened, Ma'am," I told her with my eyes filling up with tears. "I'll have no use for any sodding paradise if it doesn't include you."

"Don't be afraid, my dear. Your mistress needs you to be strong. I will see you before long." She reached out and stroked my cheek. Then she squeezed my hand. I took up my buckets with the weight of my heavy heart doubling the load. If I had known then that I would never set eyes on her again, if I knew what terrible fate lay in store for her, I would have put a halter around her neck and dragged her to safety. Instead, I comforted myself with the idiotic notion that she wouldn't remain behind in Pocasset for long. I thought she would get lonely and change her mind. She would miss us all too much, I reasoned. But we were the ones who were going to miss her. I still grieve for her to this day. I never again saw the like of her, not in old England, or new.

Jammed on Coddington's pinnace, his loyal followers and their live-stock set sail for the south. Most families took a male servant; they chose their best builder and farm hand; the Dyers took me. When they questioned Mr. Dyer about his choice, he stated that any man in his shoes would have done the same thing. We indentured souls were assured that when our time was up, we would be granted small parcels to farm.

Dorothy Brenton did not whimper as much as she did when we left Boston, but her face now had a bitter cast. Mary stared sullenly out to sea, saying nothing to anyone. No further words passed between her and Anne upon parting. The Hutchinsons were down in the harbor, of course, and Samuel wailed his head off over the separation, but the two brave spirits said nothing further. The men shook Mr. Hutchinson's hand, but that was all pretty clipped and restrained too. I could only try to fathom this new reality. The forests were so dark and thick, so vast, so endless; it seemed utterly unbelievable that we were dividing again. I could not understand any part of it. Governor Winthrop used to say he wanted us to be knit as one, yet we just couldn't seem to keep two stitches together on the needle!

Mr. Dyer, on the other hand, embraced the sea breezes and pointed out all the sights to everyone. He had Samuel up on his shoulders half the time, giving me fits.

Into the fantastic harbor of Newport we sailed. What a sight greeted us. Not since setting foot in New England had we seen open pasture land. One small and rudimentary, fenced pasture had been all we could manage in Pocasset. Even in that crude corral, the tail end of stumps remained. To see these great open fields before us, there for the taking, set us all to pointing and exclaiming. Mary's arm hooked through William's. Doubt and fury had given way to delight that was almost childlike in character.

On shore, the children whooped and brayed like savages. I ran down the beach with my hand in Samuel's. Soon Mary joined us. We swung him to and fro laughing. The bluffs, the wide-open vistas, a dear little island just off shore, lent a higher tone to our voices than had been heard in some time. Every sound we made seemed to have gone up a whole octave since leaving Pocasset. It was a sweet spot, but it never thrilled us like Newport did. No weary travelers ever shed their cares so quickly as we did when we lost our winter woes in one great moment there on the beach. So open, so wide, so high were the bluffs and so beautiful the vistas, that we barely could keep our feet on the ground. Flanked by the forest primeval, huge trees stood guard as centurions to the depths behind them.

The men's eyes raked the shoreline looking for choice pieces of land. As judge, William Coddington had the job of allotting the parcels. He decreed that the sizes of the pieces should be given by rank, reasoning that resources and means would have to be put to full use in order to make the land produce. Mr. Dyer surveyed the landscape with Nicholas Easton and John Clarke. John Coggeshall, William Brenton, William Coddington, and Nicholas Easton snagged all the large points and promontories. The Dyers chose this spot we're on right now—south of Coddington's point, opposite Coaster Island. When Mary told me they would deed some of it to me when my time came, I fell and kissed the ground. Anyone with a drop of Irish blood in their veins will know the true scope of my rapture.

There I was dancing in a jig, hair down and wild, skirts torn and ragged, when I felt his eyes on me. Your grandfather Sean O'Neil stood with his feet firmly planted, liking what he saw. I had been introduced to Mr. Coddington's new man on the boat, but we hadn't exchanged two words. Later, he told me he'd made up his mind then and there to make me his wife. Newly indentured, he knew it would take seven years, but he would not be deterred.

While all this was going on, Mary saw me taking notice of him. Since I was the only female servant to make this move, I thought I was the only port in the storm. Over the years, I always accused him of taking me out of plain desperation. He came by and asked me which piece of land I would take if I had my choice. That's how it started. It began with us dreaming about the future.

Later, as the Dyers huddled over a campfire trying to warm some beans and salt pork, Mary asked me if a romance was in the cards.

"I do believe I have my pick," I answered.

"Well?" asked Mary.

"He has great curls and long eyelashes," I told her. "He's full of ambition, not for glory, mind you, just for land, and a family."

"What do you know of his background?"

"Good stock. Simple. No one on the privy council to the king."

"Now, mind me, Irene," she whispered fiercely. "You must not tell him about Harry Vane."

"I'm no fool," I answered. "I wouldn't be the first woman to resort to a bit of pig's blood on the wedding night."

"You can marry before your time is up if you like. I would have no objection. We would want you to continue to work for us, of course. In fact, if William agrees, we could even plan for it when we build. Sean can help. I'll see what William says."

"Hold your horses," I said. "He's no' goin' to get me that easily."

That evening as we crouched close to the ground busily weaving a twig shelter, the buzz of mosquitoes had us swatting and, under our breath, cursing. A nearby swamp had become home to these infernal creatures and our arrival created a banquet for them. The children, unused to such a swarm, cried in frustration. The night proved miserable, our initial ecstasy short-lived, and by morning we were all in a terrible temper.

"This place is no good, William," Mary announced. "We cannot stay here."

William, whose eyes were all but swollen shut, said, "What?"

"I say we all get back on the boat and find a place where we won't be eaten alive. I cannot live here."

"No. Out of the question—not with this harbor."

"Look at the swamp. If you can see at all. Is it any wonder we're having our blood sucked dry?"

"Maybe the natives have a salve or something."

"Raccoon fat? Bear grease? Is that what you would like to smell on your wife?"

"Look. We'll solve this problem."

Help arrived the next day. Mr. Brenton, standing on the shore discussing the bugs, saw a group of canoes come around the point. After waving them ashore, he made several gestures imitating nasty bites and stings. The Indians, once they understood the nature of the problem, did, in fact, have a solution. With our help, they set fire to the brush. Then by digging a series of trenches, the marsh drained. We filled it with sand, giving thanks yet again for natives coming to our rescue, right from the start. We were ready to build. Just in time too, as it became evident to me that Mary was expecting again. She kept the news to herself.

All summer the sound of swinging axes and the scent of freshly cut timber marked every waking minute. I took the chance to get a good look at Sean O'Neil as he helped Mr. Coddington. I must say, now it was my turn to like what I saw. I found any excuse at all to go to Coddington's Point and linger awhile if I could.

The livestock went out to the islands, which couldn't have formed a better natural barrier for keeping the animals put and the predators out. This also freed us from clustering around a common pasture, and as the settlement rose up, we were able to spread our wings.

Mary happened to ask William, on a summer evening, what he planned to do with the extra pork, as it occurred to her that they were going to have more than they could use. His answer surprised me.

"It can be shipped as far as Barbados," he stated.

"Salted, boxed, and shipped then?"

"Yes. We plan to export as much as we can."

"Then why should a farmer spend so much time doing all these different tasks? We can grow beans, squash, pumpkins, and corn all together in their little hills. Keep our own dairy. Shouldn't we only grow enough barley to feed the beasts in the winter and concentrate the rest of our efforts on raising animals for export?"

"Three steps ahead of me at all times. You are a driven creature. You're right. It won't be long before we see transoceanic trade."

I had to stop my cooking for a minute and sit down on my stool, just so I could indulge in imagining this far ahead. Export. That word brought a grand ring to my ears. After using everything we had, just to stave off starvation, living like near savages, we were heading into uncharted waters with this new plan.

"Should we consider tobacco then? Isn't tobacco profitable?" asked Mary.

"Yes, but I don't think it will fare as well here as it does to the south. Coddington is going to give it a try. I say let him. Pork and mutton are our best bets for now. Bushels of corn will travel well. It will be a rarity in England. As more and more people arrive up and down this coast, they are going to want livestock to get started. We could supply Connecticut and Massachusetts. We could even ship horses to Barbados. We will prosper. Mark my words. Did you know that Governor Winthrop wrote Mr. Coddington asking to graze livestock on a suitable island in these parts?"

"Are you certain?"

"Yes. He disagrees with everything we do, but he does not want us, for one second, to get ahead of him. They're still badgering Anne."

"When did you hear that?"

"He said that a contingent had come to Pocasset with the intention of 'reducing' her. They have also been asking William Hutchinson why he seems to do nothing but obey his wife. He told them she was the dearest friend he had in the world, and that he had more call to obey her than the clergy of Boston. Anne apparently added, 'Don't call them clergy, call them the whores that they are.'"

"She called them whores?"

"She did," he said, picking up his knife and a stick for whittling.

"She's sticking her neck out awfully far."

"With so much room in this New World, maybe it's best for little groups to set up their own settlements and carry on their affairs, in their own fashion. It seems preferable to trying to unite everyone under one banner."

"Then all settlements in the Americas will consist of odd little patches, run by the tyranny of public opinion and petty judgments meted out on one person after another."

As the house was under construction, we were crowded into a little shed while this conversation took place. The frame of the new house, up and standing, loomed nearby in the twilight. Straight and sound, ordered and simple, it stood. I recall wondering why the rest of the picture never seemed to be so true. Full of ambition, I could not settle down that night, as the prospects ahead seemed so bright. Maybe I envisioned then all that I am blessed with now. A family able to flourish and stay together, not forced to be sent out in the world alone. Riches, mine for the taking, up for grabs to those willing to work for it. This place has always struck me as a perfect spot to build a home, to raise a family and to see them all thrive. My goals never changed. I set my sights on a bright future. I guess it was just as well that I didn't know then of the troubles lying ahead.

CHAPTER ELEVEN
New Life

By the end of the summer, the Dyer house, standing snug and strong, set a standard for all newcomers to follow. Thick pine planks, set down in straight lines, changed life around the hearth for the better. With the high-backed bench now in front of the fire, life returned to what passed for normal. As the Dyers were able to build a bigger house this time, the kitchen and pantry made up the ground floor. Upstairs, we had a parlor with a desk for William, a loom for Mary, and chairs and benches for visitors. Another floor held four bedrooms.

One evening, as Mary worked at her loom, she said, "I want to raise sheep."

"Sheep? Wouldn't children be more appropriate?"

"We will have as many children as we are blessed with. I don't want to spend the bulk of my life raising them though."

"If you don't, who will?"

"Irene."

"What if she decides to marry the lucky Mr. O'Neil?"

"Please, sir," I begged. "Do not tease me."

"That wouldn't mean she couldn't continue working." She turned to William then and repeated, "I want to raise sheep."

"Whatever for?"

"Profit. I have given this a great deal of thought."

"Don't you have enough to do? You are working your fingers to the bone as it is. And you are asking a lot of Irene."

"She can take on extra help."

"How? Help is scarce."

"By next spring we'll have new arrivals. With all this grazing land around here, I sense that we can raise a great number of sheep. I want to devote myself to this endeavor."

He jabbed at the coals in the fire. Without looking at her he said, "I thought it was your intention to devote yourself to your family. Why are you suddenly getting all muddled about your duty? It has always been perfectly clear."

"No. Nothing about our life here is perfectly clear. When we settled in Boston we were living in a town with farmland nearby. You had to be off tending the cattle and doing a hundred other things, including the group work projects. Then we moved to Pocasset under great duress and did whatever it took to keep from starving. Luck and brains will turn this venture into a thriving port. Once our wares are shipped from here, captains will seek us out, word will spread, and Newport will grow. It will be possible, at some point in the not too distant future, to drive the livestock to Boston and other New England towns."

"All right then. I will raise the flock."

"No. You can do the same thing with the hogs. You have the rest of the livestock: the oxen, the horses, the cattle, the goats, and the chickens. One man can't do everything, you see; that's why my idea makes such perfect sense. If you take care of the crops, the building, and your duties as clerk, I can concentrate exclusively on the sheep. Irene can tend the children."

"Sheep crop the grass low to the ground. One or two seasons and the pastures will be bare. Grass has to be replanted. You have not thought all of this through."

"Some of us here have more meadow land than they can use. I have discussed this with Mr. Coddington. He kindly offered me the use of his pastures, should I have the need."

"You talked to him without consulting me?"

"We talked in a general way. It came up one day when I was visiting. He, unlike you, seemed to have faith in my idea."

William walked out on us then, having heard enough.

I kept at my sewing, looking at the baby dress on my lap rather than at Mary, because I was not sure she was being entirely truthful. Yes, she did have a very sound scheme in her head with the sheep. Her desire to head up to the hills, walking with the wind in her hair, did not have a basis entirely in commercial aspirations. Another need lay at the heart of this scheme. No one save me ever knew what it was. Mr. Dyer would have been hard pressed to understand her motives, even if she'd tried to explain it. Looking back, I can say now that she would have done well to try.

Roger Williams paddled into the harbor often that summer with his usual flanking canoes full of natives. We had taken Samuel down to Easton's beach one gorgeous morning. All of us crowded around trying to catch up on the news from other little outposts on Aquidneck. Mary angled to get close to Roger Williams. A young brave, bare-chested and strong, stood beside Mr. Williams. Planted there, legs apart, as straight and silent as a great oak, his eyes never left Mary's. The natives were not subject to English manners, and we had grown accustomed to their habit of staring, even though it often made us uncomfortable. That did not seem to be the case then, however.

I don't want to insinuate that a romance, or anything of that nature, began to bloom, because I'm pretty sure that wasn't the case. In light of her condition, it would seem highly unlikely. We were all used to the amount of attention she attracted. There was something about Mary that drew men to her, and I'm not even sure it was necessarily for the usual reasons. Maybe they trusted her intelligence, or maybe they sensed her courage and sought her counsel for that reason. I cannot rightly say. To be sure, it was a thread that ran through the whole of her life. Mr. Coddington said once that she could converse as well as any man, and on any subject. To tell you the truth, I believe it was because she was so brave; her sheer fighting guts brought out the best in everyone in her midst. Whatever the reason, something instantaneous happened on the beach that day, something that altered the course of her destiny.

Looking at the young man, she turned to Roger Williams, posing a question, "Could you ask him where he looks to find the Great Spirit whenever he feels lost or alone?"

Roger Williams raised his eyebrows and, for a minute, I thought he'd silence her. Before he had the chance, the native raised his hand. The son of a chief, he knew enough English to understand her. Solemnly placing his hand on his chest then lifting his arm up to the sky, he pointed out across the glassy water. For a split second, I wondered if he pointed to England, which would have been about the last place I'd ever look. Mary searched his face, desperately trying to figure out what he meant. Then this fellow knelt down and ran his hand over the earth. He pointed to the immense forests ringing the shore. With his arm sweeping over the horizon, he bore his eyes into hers and then brought his hand back to his chest. He said a few words in his native tongue, which translated to Mother Earth and Father Sky.

"From the land?" Mary asked.

"In the land," said the Indian. "In the sky. In you." He reached out and gently placed his hand on Mary's belly.

Her condition had not yet begun to show. I glared at him for being too familiar. She didn't flinch at all. "From nature?" she asked. His eyes met hers again, this time registering even more approval. Rooted to the spot, a peculiar look crossed her face, like she drifted away from everything. Her eyes dropped to his feet, to his worn moccasins.

Williams became uncomfortable with this whole exchange, and brusquely changed the subject. They all got back in their canoes, with the chief's son in the stern. Mary's eyes stayed with him, and his with her as he dipped the blade of the paddle in the water and, with a swoosh, backed away.

On the long walk home, she told me the meeting had stamped something irrevocable on her mind. "Nothing that was made was not made by God," she quoted, "yet all the rituals of worship take place indoors," she said. "Why not lie on the ground and breathe in the Holy Spirit through every drop of dew, on every blade of grass?"

"You'll never get the English to prostrate themselves for any reason," I announced. "Can you picture any of the ladies here, not to mention Boston, in that posture? I'd keep this to myself if I were you."

She took up the notion to abandon her hearth for the great outdoors from that day forward. She fancied herself a shepherdess. She imagined she could grope her way to glory; that the forces of nature would rise up through her feet and transform her into a holy creature. I had trouble picturing the point of it all, especially in light of the fact that we had this new wood floor, which thrilled me every time I crossed the threshold. What understanding did I ever have of these Protestant yearnings? I was fully aware that her condition could have been a factor and I guess we all indulged her for that reason.

I should have paid more attention though. It wasn't long before she slipped away to meet the Indian in private.

In the early March of 1640, William swept into the house full of high spirits.

"Great news," he announced.

"What? Have the ewes arrived?" asked Mary.

"William Hutchinson sailed into the harbor this morning."

"Is Anne with him?"

"No, but Mr. Coddington has asked me to gather the General Court together. There will be a reconciliation."

"Why didn't Anne come?"

"You'll have to ask her husband that question yourself. I invited him for supper. Irene, what do we have? Do we have any beef?"

"We have plenty of ham in the smokehouse. Will that do?"

"Good. Yes. Let's make an occasion of it."

"Why don't you get a bottle of port, then, William? He loves port. I think I can get a roast beef from the Coddingtons. You did ask them as well, I hope."

"Yes, absolutely. I rounded up the Eastons, the Brentons and the Coggeshalls as well. It will be like old times. The two settlements are going to be joined. We must do whatever it takes to see this through. Do you realize, Mary, that if we manage to iron out our differences, you'll be able to visit Anne often?"

We set the table with a gleaming white cloth and all our household and larder had to offer. By the time the guests arrived, they were greeted by the delicious smells of a great roast turning on the spit. We found William Hutchinson in fine spirits.

Pocasset, it was determined, would now be known as Portsmouth. Mary asked immediately if they had considered moving to Newport. Mr. Hutchinson told her, full of pride, that Anne had too many followers to consider leaving. Moving would leave the place deserted, he stated. His jolly conversation carried on, but I noticed Mary looking down at her plate. Dorothy Brenton ventured to ask who their pastor was. The whole table fell silent. Anne, he said, held the fort for now, without objection. When asked whether the clergy of Boston were still trying to "reduce" her, he nodded and added that with spring coming they should expect a contingent to arrive any day now.

"Is it true then that she referred to them as fallen women?" asked Marie Coggeshall.

"Strumpets," he bellowed. "She calls them strumpets. But that's why this move of bringing the two groups together is so important. Boston is still lusting after us, you see, trying to get us and all we have built under their jurisdiction. We won't be out of the woods until we get our own charter."

"All in due course," announced Mr. Coddington.

"What does it take?" asked Dorothy.

"Money, power, influence—that's all."

"The crown will not want to see the Dutch try to take over. Once we establish a substantial base, they'll want it protected," offered Mr. Dyer.

"But couldn't that be accomplished by having us under the Massachusetts Bay Company Charter?"

"Our laws regarding freedom will be fully recorded and established by then and will be totally incompatible with Boston's. If we have built enough influence and contacts, they will have to grant a separate charter," said Mr. Easton.

"So how have you set up the government between Pocasset and Newport?" asked Mary.

"The chief magistrate will no longer be judge, but governor. Instead of the magistrate, there will be assistants. The governors and the assistants will hold the jurisdiction of justices of the peace."

"Just asses to you," joked William Hutchinson. Then he turned to Mary and remarked, "Portsmouth demands that no one be allowed to hold office for more than a year without being reelected."

"Have you established rules for the elections?" came Mary's next question.

William frowned and cut into his meat. Mr. Hutchinson answered with no discomfort at all. "We will follow election rules to the letter. I give you my personal guarantee."

At this, Mr. Coggeshall bellowed, "Hear, hear," and they all raised their goblets.

The next day, Mary invited Mr. Hutchinson to walk with her up to their pasture so she could show him her flock. I was on my way to take a pudding to Sean, so I walked with them.

Mary was the first to speak. "I miss Anne very much. I hope she will come and visit us soon."

"It was a shame that you two didn't part on better terms. My wife can be a wee bit stubborn, you know."

"She loves you so fiercely," answered Mary. "She would not take a stand against you. I guess I felt upset that she didn't understand my position. It was not personal. I just didn't think it was right to replace Mr. Coddington as judge when he and my William were not present."

"I know. Anne felt strongly about the division of land. She thought that we should take drastic steps so that the land be divided up evenly."

"I beg your pardon?" asked Mary, stopping in her tracks. "What are you talking about?"

"Well, surely you understood that the election, or the coup, depending on your point of view, took place over land issues."

"I knew of no such thing. I recall asking what Mr. Coddington had done to warrant such action. She did not say a word."

"Let me see. If I remember correctly, she assumed your concurrence in the matter."

"I didn't think of the issue one way or another."

"When you arrived in Newport and Mr. Coddington gave each of you these great promontories and pastures, did you question the fairness of it then?"

"No, because it was explained to me that those with capital would be able to handle more livestock. It was reasoned that those without should start slowly, say, with a small farm they could manage themselves, and if they were to grow in fortune as the years went by, then they could purchase more. I had no idea this whole thing was over land."

"Roger Williams is mired up to his neck with the same problem. Some want even divisions, but now the people who have been there longer, argue that since they had to bear the burden of getting the settlement established and had to pay for common fencing, they should not have to be put on equal footing with new arrivals who bore no note of this burden. Every ship that sails over brings more of England's fair sons and daughters chomping at the bit for land. We must do what we can to see that we don't trample over one another in our zeal."

"Surely Anne does not think that of me."

"I daresay she is in the dark as to where your heart is these days."

"My affection and admiration for her has never wavered. I had to support my husband, just as she had to support you. Actually, when I think of all that's happened I could kill my husband," said Mary.

"Why is that now? What has he done?"

"He told me nothing of this. I had a feeling that I did not know what was going on in Pocasset. I was caught up with my own troubles."

"As was my dear wife. Well, it's a simple misunderstanding. Let bygones be bygones, eh? I think the whole thing worked out for the best, actually. If we hadn't had this strife to begin with, Newport may never have been established, or it would have been established with Portsmouth being abandoned, and it is a dear little place, you know. It will all work out, my dear, you'll see."

Pregnancy prevented Mary from traveling to Portsmouth that summer. Her longing for her old friend increased as she neared her time.

While very conscious of her diet and health in the early months, she preferred not to discuss her condition at all. I kept a watchful eye, but did not talk about it either—not until she wanted to. I did sew baby smocks in the privacy of my loft. I wrote to my priest asking that both he and my mother and sisters pray for a safe delivery. The household remained in a conspiracy of silence.

Fall came suddenly, surprising us with a burst of color. Off the ocean, a strong easterly wind swept in, bringing with it rain, and Mary's travail. Taking Samuel over to the Coddingtons, at her request, I had hold of his hand. In spite of his endless protests, I kept a firm grip; the winds were that strong. I had not known her time was upon us when I left the house. Since it was my custom to do her bidding, I thought she needed some peace. After her awful time of it in Boston, the poor thing just wanted to be alone. She would not have Dr. Clarke tend her, even if it were a matter of life and death. I knew she longed for Anne because she had voiced that concern to me many times. There was nothing she could do about it though. Can you believe she mixed up the mugwort and brought a bowl of water into her room? She was determined to bear her child in utter privacy, keeping the onset of it a secret, even from me. Like the Narragansett women wander off in a field, troubling no one, she decided to bear her child all by herself.

Mercifully, it arrived quickly—much more quickly than the last time. Later she told me that after her water broke, the baby came out in three big pushes. I am sure she must have looked, bracing herself for the worst, but to her sheer amazement, what lay on the bed was a perfectly formed, beautiful, little girl. Mary grasped the baby with one hand and wiped the little face with her other, clearing the nose and mouth. At this, the baby cried and Mary erupted with a shout of pure joy.

By this time, I had just come in the door. Hearing her shout, brought me flying to her room, as I thought her time had arrived. At the sight of Mary holding the baby I cried, "Jesus, Mary and Joseph! What have you done?"

"Look! Look! It's a girl! A beautiful girl. Will you get something to cut the cord and some twine, please? Isn't she wonderful?"

"I was nearby. Why did you not send for me?"

"Everything is right there," said Mary, pointing to a table by the bed.

I took one look at the twine, the bowl of water, the swaddling linen, and the mugwort and said, "Are you daft? You planned to have her alone, didn't you? Why on earth?"

"I didn't think she would live. I thought, well, I thought I had to do it myself so that I could see her—oh I know I was a goose, but it's all right now. It's a miracle, isn't it? Where is William?"

"I'll go and get him, once I've seen to you. Let me take the wee girl now and get her washed up. Oh, she's beautiful. She is the prettiest baby I have ever seen. She's going to have your hair and brow. Look at the color of her! A lovely pink."

"I've never been so happy in my entire life. Where is Samuel? Is he outside? Can I call him?"

"I'll get him. I'll find William as well. We'll get the baby settled and cleaned up and then you can show her off to all the world."

"Is this how all women feel when they have girls? I didn't imagine that having a daughter would make me feel this way. She is the best part of myself."

William flew in the door, tossing his hat on the floor. Seeing the greatest smile he had ever seen on Mary's face, put him right in tears. He pulled up a stool and took his place beside his wife. Then he gingerly took up the precious bundle. He pressed the newborn babe to his wet face.

Mary threw an arm around him. When she felt him shaking she said, "What is it?"

"I am overcome," he whispered. "Can we call her Mary after the bravest, strongest woman I have ever known? Can we name her after you?"

"If you like."

I proudly produced the baby dresses and set about getting both mother and child settled. Pleased as punch myself, I gave thanks for the baby's safe passage. I thought we had turned a corner then, crossed over a great obstacle and as far as I could see, we were heading into the fullness of our lives, with everything bright and rosy ahead.

CHAPTER TWELVE
Marriage

For the rest of that year the Dyer household became possessed by one consuming passion, which was caring for little Mary. Winter was not nearly as bad as it had been in Pocasset. We were able to get big ships to land on their way north from Barbados. With them came supplies like candles and sugar. No purchases of any kind were forbidden by our Bodie Politic, so Mr. Dyer, to his everlasting credit, bought some beautiful bolts of fabric. What a joy it was to load up on gold and silver thread! Mary wanted to turn her training and my skills loose on the world. A little shop was set up in the town. We planned to band together with the other friends in order to sell our wares.

With me working on the sewing and Mary out in the field as soon as she could manage, it looked like another servant would be needed to help out in the house. I got the brilliant idea of asking the Dyers to bring over my sister Moira. Knowing it may take a long time, not to mention the cost, I held my breath waiting for their answer. To my great relief, they seemed to be willing to give it a try.

By summer, Mary and Mr. Dyer announced that they would allow me to marry. I insisted on waiting until my indenture was finished, so I could take my rightful place in my own home. Sean would be allowed to live with me, but carry on working for the Coddingtons. This was a very Aquidneck kind of arrangement, the likes of which would never have been seen in Boston. But that is how it was here from the beginning. Dividing lines were crossed over, due to the good people in our midst.

My only fear came over the service itself. In the weeks leading up to the great event, I cried my eyes out daily. Not having my mother and father, and the village folk, was bad enough. Those sorrows paled in comparison to the thought that I'd have to be married by that dried up cornstalk of a man, Dr. Clarke. I said I'd rather go over to Portsmouth and be married by Anne, but Sean wouldn't hear of it.

I prepared myself as best I could. The dress, lovely beyond my wildest dreams, fashioned by Mary, went over my head in a great cloud, yet I still had so much sadness hanging over me. I stared out the open door, telling myself to buck up, when I caught sight of Mr. Dyer heading up the road. Behind him, I saw the familiar robe of a Jesuit priest. Giving me the greatest gift I ever could have asked for, Mr. Dyer brought the priest to marry us, all the way over from Maryland! I broke down entirely, but with tears of joy and relief this time. My nose stayed bright red through the whole ceremony, but your blessed grandfather married me in spite of it.

A new chapter in my life began. We built a little house in back of the Dyers, so I could care for the children. Samuel, a strong lad now, continued to grow like a weed. I took to marriage like a duck to water.

The great excitement of our life then revolved around the arrival and departure of ships. Sails spotted from the bluffs sent all the children running around calling from house to house. Women and men alike dropped what they were doing to run down to the harbor.

The last ship to sail into Newport in 1641 brought a long letter from Harry Vane. His first announcement was that of his marriage. A well born woman named Frances Wray, daughter of Sir Christopher Wray, had become his bride. The rest of his letter involved a curious tale that led directly to the utter ruin of both England and Ireland.

Shortly after Harry's wedding, he received word from his father's steward that he must come to London to settle some legal affairs. The steward informed him that he would be permitted into the treasure room, in order to iron out some of the details of the marriage settlement. Sir Harry Vane, the elder, I gather, had remained in the north and was unable to see to these matters personally. Harry searched for the proper documents. In so doing, he happened upon a red cabinet, covered with velvet. He wrote that while in the grip of an impulse to open the forbidden cabinet, he felt somehow in harmony with God's will and because of this, whatever action he took while in this state, would keep him free from harm. I thought this had to be the most daft Protestant reasoning I'd heard yet, but I guess it didn't surprise me. Well, Harry, thinking he was under divine protection, put aside doubts, judgment, common sense, and loyalty to his father in favor of asking the steward for the keys.

When he opened the box, he found notes describing advice, given to the king, in the Privy Council, by the Earl of Strafford. He read these words: "You have an army with which you may reduce this kingdom."

After reading this, Harry Vane determined the words to be treasonous and that the information must be made public. So he sent word to Prime Minister Pym. Then, sick with fear over the enormity of making such an accusation, not to mention causing great harm to his father, he fell ill with a fever. He thrashed about until the next day when he got the prime minister to read the document. Like two thieves, they tiptoed into the treasure room again. Prime Minister Pym declared that the information was God's way of preserving church and state. So the famous Long Parliament came into being. On the morning of November 11, 1640, the doors of St. Stephen's Chapel were closed and locked; the keys were placed on the table; no strangers were permitted to enter; no member was permitted to leave, until the articles of Strafford's impeachment were delivered to the House of Lords. In late November, Strafford was arrested and sent to the Tower of London.

There was a trial. King Charles, determined to stay by his man, forbid any action. As is so often the case, a good search through the law books usually provides some back alley. An ancient rule stating that Parliament alone could try a man for treason became the method of dealing with the Earl of Strafford.

King Charles, ever bent on getting his own way, tried to take control of both the tower and the prisoner. The governor, Sir William Balfour, closed the gates. The mob, some of whom were armed, continued to cry for justice. Eventually, with no other choice but to put pen to paper, and sign the death warrant of his dearest adviser, King Charles capitulated. Two hundred thousand people, probably the biggest crowd ever seen in London, flocked to Tower Hill to witness the execution.

Mr. Dyer put the letter down at this point. We had several people over for the reading, but they grew quiet. "These events took place months ago. My God. This is all unbelievable. The king is in serious trouble."

Mr. Coddington spoke first. "Members of the House of Commons locking themselves in a church, the gates to the Tower closed, the angry mob, the people demanding justice, two hundred thousand people in the streets calling for blood. Royal prerogative has broken down completely. The part that Harry Vane played in all of this will not be forgotten. No sir. He took a great risk to do such a thing. We must send words of support right away. Frankly, I am surprised. I didn't think he had it in him."

"He did take on the Boston clergy and Governor Winthrop," said Dorothy Brenton.

Her husband gave her a withering glance. "A gesture awfully pale in comparison to incurring both the wrath of his father and the king. Do you realize that they could both have been ruined by Harry's move?"

"It wasn't clear to me what Strafford meant by his comment of 'they had an army that could reduce the Kingdom,'" said Dorothy.

My blood boiled over. I had heard all about the Earl of Strafford's army, as letters from Ireland were full of him. I knew Irish souls would curse his name for a thousand years. "It was the army he trained and brought over to Ireland to slaughter us like sheep. He was talking about using it against his own people. You have an army with which to reduce this kingdom. Don't you see? Reduce. Reduce. Isn't that the favorite word of the Boston clergy? He was insinuating that he had an army that would make short work of the Puritan uprising. He was boasting that he could do to the English what he did to the Irish, only this time he was talking about turning on his own people! Twenty hangings are too good for that wolverine. Why did the king listen? Why would he remain loyal to a traitor? If he could even think of using an army against his own people than you can count your blessings you're on this side of the ocean. That king of yours is a despot. England is going to splinter into a thousand pieces and Ireland is going to bleed."

Silence fell on the whole gathering. Seven years had been too long a time for me to keep my mouth shut, I guess. Newly free, and mistress of my own house, I thought I was now able to voice my opinions, but that night, I learned to remember that I was still living amongst the English and mustn't speak against the king, no matter how much I might want to. As was her constant pattern, Mary came to my defense.

"Irene is right, William. She knows. She's read me letters about the Irish rebellion that came of Strafford's invasion. If he planned to bring that army into England to 'reduce' the kingdom, then it is as Harry said. He did the right thing. It shows he has backbone. It makes me want to go back."

"To England?" asked William incredulously.

"Yes."

"But why?"

"I don't know. I feel a sense of duty."

"Your duty is to your family and that pasture full of sheep."

"Don't you want to go back to England when you hear of these events? Don't you want to do your part? The king keeps forgetting that he is not an absolute ruler. People like Harry are right to remind him of that fact."

"You want to get in the thick of all this, and I want to be as far away as possible."

"It will be months before we hear anything more. Something will have to be done to counteract this action."

I took my leave and stepped out to a warm summer evening. The wind faded to a whisper of a breeze leaving the sea flat and calm. The ripe aroma of the harbor worked on me like a tonic. Children ran up and down the beach. A few canoes traveled between the islands and the mainland. I met up with Sean and we walked hand in hand, down the beach, past the wharf, beyond the little town springing up with ever increasing vigor, and up the long path leading to Brentons Point. I felt glad to be in Newport. We had peace in our world. What happened back home was so far away now. I knew it did not seem so to the others. I wondered if it would always be like this down the years. Would we wonder what these events had to do with us and with our little settlements on the other side of the world? Would we lose a sense of who we were and where we came from in favor of fashioning our new home here?

England would have less and less of a hold over us in time, I suspected. Laws would be passed and we would be held to them, but our influence in the making of them would dwindle. I could tell that is what the English feared most. And what of this Puritan tide they all feared so much? Scotland had fought and won the right to keep their own church. What if parliament started making rules along the lines of what we had gone through in Boston? Then we would be back to the wretched dress code again, which went squarely against my own ambitions. That night on my walk, after discussing this with Sean, as odd as it sounds to my ears even now, I thought that if I were to take sides, which I hoped I would never have to, I don't think I would throw my lot in with the Puritans. Not after what I'd seen of them so far—and that was only the beginning.

CHAPTER THIRTEEN
Murder

Word landed one afternoon in the fall of 1642 of William Hutchinson's sudden death. A large contingent of Newport citizens climbed onto Mr. Coddington's pinnace and sailed over to pay their last respects. Mary, pregnant once again, was unable to travel. All she had time to do was to scribble a hasty note and implore Anne to come and visit.

When William returned from the memorial service, he said, "Anne has a strange notion."

Mary stopped scrubbing the table and looked up. "What now?"

"She wants to leave Portsmouth and start over with the Dutch."

"Where?"

"A place called Pelham Bay. She is going to take the youngest children with her."

"How can she do such a thing by herself?"

"She said she had some followers going with her."

"Did she say the word 'followers'?"

"Yes."

Mary shook her head. "That's the way it is with her. I believe she still wants me to be a proselyte."

"I have never heard her speak a word against you, Mary."

"I know she wouldn't say it out loud, but deep down inside, she is hurt that I'm not one of her flock. She expected it of me. Did you ask her to come and visit?"

"Yes, but she said she wouldn't have time as she is so busy with packing."

"Why the rush?"

"Those Boston clergy have never stopped pestering her. She fears them."

"Anne has never feared anyone."

"That's not true, Mary. She had a very hard time when she was sent out to Roxbury Neck. After her misfortune, she never fully regained her strength. She fears them now more than ever. They still want to reduce her. So much so that she is willing to run off and live with the Dutch. She thinks it is the only place they won't pursue her."

"How many are going with her?"

"That remains to be seen. I believe there are at least seven. Apparently, they will be joining some other English settlers. She said they plan to settle between a river and a trail."

"This doesn't feel right. Surely she would choose Newport over living with the Dutch. We can stand up to those Boston blackbirds, as Irene calls them. She should come here with us. As soon as I have this baby and can travel, I'll go over and see if I can't talk her into coming here."

"Maybe you'll have better luck than the rest of us did. None of us like the thoughts of her going off by herself. Perhaps she'll listen to you."

A few weeks later, we were hit with more news. William came up from the harbor with a wild look in his eye. "A ship came in to port today. Two thousand armed sailors went right up the Thames. The king had to flee with the queen to Hampton Court."

"Here. Sit. I'll serve you. You must start at the beginning," said Mary.

"Vane proposed a commission to manage religion in England. It got out of hand. A vicious mob entered churches, breaking rails, and smashing altars. It was an utter humiliation for the king—one which his French wife did not fail to point out. In response, he was advised to impeach five members of the House of Commons and some of the Lords."

"Was Harry Vane one of them?"

"No. Why, I don't know. Perhaps he is still protected by his father. The king went down to the House of Commons, accompanied by four hundred of his cavaliers. However, a lady from the queen's bedchamber managed to leak the news, and the members in question slipped into a boat and escaped on the Thames."

"What did the king do when he realized they weren't there?"

"He said, 'I see the birds have flown.'"

"Then what happened?"

"He withdrew. The mob was on him and then the barges escorted him out of London."

"Good God. Do you mean to tell me that he can only return to London if the Parliament and the mob let him?"

"Yes."

"Has our world come to an end then?"

"I don't know. I don't know what is going to happen."

It took us a while to digest this news. It looked to me like the English monarchy was done for. Everybody went into a tailspin. With London now off limits to the crown, I grew certain there would be civil war. The rest of them didn't think it possible. They all started to worry about their financial holdings though.

Winter arrived with the usual clobber. We were cut off from the old country till spring, so we had no choice but to huddle up by the fire and pray for a peaceful outcome.

Mary's third child, a boy named William, came to us in late June. He burst on the scene with a ferocious temper and an equivalent appetite. Mr. Dyer joked that his mother had finally met her match. Nothing stood between wee William and what he wanted from the world. His demands, coupled with caring for the new lambs, kept Mary working from dawn till dark. Hoping to travel to Portsmouth sometime that summer, she learned to her dismay that Anne had already set off for Long Island.

One morning in August, Mary, up on the hill with her flock, suddenly stopped. A queer sensation gripped her heart and her hand shot immediately up to her neck. Deciding to bring the sheep down to their fenced pasture, she herded them in, fed them, and settled them as she would for the night. Then she came down to her house to check on the children.

"Mistress, I'm glad you are here," I said.

"What is it? Are the children all right?"

"Yes. I've been hovering over them like a mother hen. Young Mary is in a temper. I had this awful feeling, though. I haven't been able to shake it. I'm afraid."

"Are you feeling well?"

"Yes," I said, rubbing my swollen belly. "I called my Sean in awhile ago. Why are you back so early?"

"I thought I should check on the children. Something strange came over me. I can't explain what. Maybe something happened in England. I have this sense of dread. It's odd that you feel the same way, isn't it? Maybe a storm is coming?"

"There isn't a cloud in the sky. I guess someone walked over our graves."

"I beg your pardon?"

"It's just an expression. I have not lost my wits. Anne Hutchinson told me that when you get a queer feeling, it means someone has walked on a grave."

"Oh. Well, I've pastured the sheep. I guess I might as well stay home for the afternoon. Would you like to go back to your house?"

"As soon as I get this stew done. I wish Mistress Hutchinson stopped here on her way out. I miss her. I wish she could deliver my baby."

"I'll help you, Irene."

"I know, but I was there in Boston with her that night we tended you. I watched her in action. You would have died without her. I'm sorry. I know you don't like to speak of that night anymore. I didn't tell you everything."

"What didn't you tell me?"

"I didn't tell you what she did to get the baby out."

"I thought it just came out by itself when I fell asleep."

"No. That's what everyone said."

"Tell me now."

"She and Goody Hawkins gave you poison."

"Poison?"

"Aye. It's too true. Belladona. They gave you almost enough to kill you."

"Why?"

"The baby was completely stuck. It was dead already, you see. The gates of the womb clamped down on the tiny neck and shut tight. Do you know what a surgeon would have done? He would have cut you up, cut up the child, and pulled it out in chunks. Anne put you as close to death as a person can get. She risked committing murder. Goody and I had to pull your legs up around your ears. Anne worked and worked. She literally pulled the womb over the jaw and eased that baby out. Without her, you and the baby both would have died. She did all that without damaging you. It has always amazed me that you have been able to go on having children after that night."

"Did William know? About the belladonna?"

"No. That's just it, you see. She took matters into her own hands. Then she went out in the dark of night and buried that poor babe herself. How many friends would have done that?"

"I must see her. William has to take me to Long Island after the shearing."

The next day thick heavy clouds rolled over us. The air, so close, made breathing difficult. We went about our chores until Dorothy Brenton came flying in the gate, and shrieked out the whole terrible story, sparing me nothing. The shock alone could have driven me right into my time. I sank down to the floor in a collapse. Her head plopped onto the table and her wailing grew near Irish in its quality. That's how Mary found us.

"What is it?" she cried.

We stared, unable to say anything. William ran in flushed, hot, and out of breath.

"Have you heard?" he gasped.

"What?" shouted Mary. "Will someone please tell me? Are the children all right? Where are they?"

"They are at the Coddingtons'," I said.

"Why? William, what is the matter?"

He sat. His head dropped to his hands. "Anne Hutchinson was killed yesterday morning."

"No!"

"Anne, and all her children. They were attacked by Indians and slaughtered."

Mary gaped at him shaking her head. "No," she moaned. "Why?"

"No one knows why. There had been some trouble between the Hudson River Indians and the Dutch. That's all we know."

"Was anyone else killed?"

"No."

"Why all the children? Zuriel, Susanna, Catherine, Mary, Francis?"

"All of them that were with her, yes."

"So where did her great faith get her then?" cried Mary. "Where? She said God would protect her."

"Don't ask yourself these questions, Mary."

"Why not?"

"Because there are no answers."

"Do our children know?"

"Yes. I told them."

"Why are they at the Coddingtons?"

"At first we weren't sure what was going on. We didn't know if a full-scale uprising was under way. It seems to be a local incident, though."

"She shouldn't have gone there," whined Dorothy. "Why did she go off by herself?"

"She wasn't alone. There were English families there," answered William.

"Then why did she settle in a place that was obviously in dispute? That is not like her. Didn't you say it was between a river and an Indian trail? Maybe they weren't supposed to settle there."

"No. The land was bought or negotiated for—whatever. Why torture yourself with these questions?"

"If Anne had prospered, then all her prophecies would have come true. I have suspected all along that the Boston clergy could not afford to let her succeed. She felt it—that's why she left. Don't forget who is always charged with witchcraft. Widows. Older women. Now they will say that she was wrong; they will say that she was obviously not protected, not favored by God. They will say this is a judgment. Mark my words, William. This is exactly what we are going to hear from the Boston clergy."

"We cannot prevent them from uttering cruel words. They can say what they like. Nothing will alter our high opinion."

"And nothing will bring her back," wailed Dorothy.

"I cannot accept this!" cried Mary.

Dorothy suddenly lifted her head from the table. "Why? Are you trying to cover up your own guilt?"

"How very kind of you to ask that question, Dorothy. Strumpet is too good a word for those men. They should be called lying, murdering sons of whores! They should be put to death!"

"Mary," said William softly. "The children will be coming home soon. Samuel adored Francis and Zuriel. This is going to be hard for him. We need to come together as a family now and offer the kind of strength and solace that we would expect from Anne. That is what she would have us do."

Mary sobbed. "I can't stand it, William. I can't—those darling children. I helped Susanna with her first sampler. Dear God! Francis stood by my door, that time."

"I know. I know. We'll go over to Portsmouth as soon as we can. There will be a service."

Mary came to me then and crouched down where I remained slumped by the wall. "I knew it. I knew it," I whispered, as I rocked back and forth. "Sweet Jesus, Mary and Joseph, I felt it in my neck."

"So did I."

"We'll never know another woman like her. Never. She treated me like an equal. She never, for one minute, treated me like someone's servant."

"Would you like some ale, Dorothy?" asked William.

"No. I don't want anything. I only want to turn back the clock. I begged her not to go. I even asked her to come and build a house on our land. I knew she would be vulnerable. She was afraid. She didn't say anything, but I knew she was afraid. Anne never had any trouble with Indians. Why would they do this her? The murdering savages. How can we live in a land full of such depraved people? I wish we could get rid of every last one of them. Don't look at me, Mary. I know you think they are saints or something. I think they are animals."

"We don't know the details, Dorothy," stated William, who by this time was trying to hang on to his patience.

"I wish I could go there," said Mary. "To Pelham Bay. I want to see that they are buried properly. I want to put flowers on their graves. I want to talk to her followers."

Dorothy, still spoiling for a fight, came back with another shot. "You didn't make much of an effort before."

By this time I was pretty close to letting her have it.

"I was wrong!" cried Mary.

"Look," William stated. "We have to calm down here."

"I'm going back to the pasture."

"Mary!"

"I need to be alone. I'm sorry."

I watched her run up the hill. She did not look back. Up in the field, she fell on her knees and grabbed one of her ewes. Burying her face in the sheep, she looked like she was trying to hide herself in the creature. I could see her there clutching the animal, trying to burrow into the thick wool.

Who had been struck first? I wondered. Probably Anne. She would have been defending her children. Or Francis. Anne left alone, with no friend to stand beside her, no friend to help her protect her children, no friend to help her shoulder the burden of motherhood, no ally in her hour of greatest need, no fellow soldier to fight off the attackers. If Anne had seen her children murdered, how could she be at peace now? A woman who never feared death, who always talked about it as something she looked forward to— another great adventure. How could she be at peace with her children slain? Yet, they would be together, I thought, and Anne always had a pack of children at her feet. A mother, first, foremost, and always.

Mary remained with her flock until it grew dark. In the black of night, she returned to her hearth—tired, numb, and dirty. She couldn't forgive herself, she told me.

The next morning William rose early and built up a small fire. The smell of smoke woke me up and I slipped across the yard and into their kitchen. William had his Bible. Mary wore a shawl over her nightdress. She slumped into a chair near the fire.

"Word has come from Portsmouth," said William, who had been sitting by the fire reading the Bible. "There will be a service, but it will be at the home of Catherine and Richard Scott in Providence. Anne's sister was closer to her than anyone else and she insists it take place in Providence. She has room for Anne's older children. It makes sense to have it there."

"I wonder if Catherine sees this the same way I do."

"What are you saying, Mary? Are you saying that the Boston magistrates hired those Indians to kill her?"

"Is that so preposterous?"

"You must keep these opinions to yourself. We have absolutely no proof, no way of substantiating your claims. These are serious allegations. If word gets back that you have been going around saying this, it will be your neck next. Yours and mine and our children's, as well."

"I know I have no proof! I can, however, bear witness, and bear witness I shall."

Somberly and quietly, I carried on with my duties that morning. What kept rolling across my mind was the picture of Anne's hands: helping hands, healing hands, caring hands. Hands that never passed by a child without sweeping across the hair, hands that never failed to go to a shoulder or arm of someone in distress, hands that cradled each new life as it came into the world. Hands high above her head when cast out of the church, hands that must have reached to her loved ones in the last moments of her life. How could hands that had touched so many, helped so many, healed so many, be folded and laid to rest? How could we have missed the chance to touch those hands in parting?

A lake of tears flooded the home of Catherine Scott. Catherine took the lead, just like her sister, in spreading words of love and comfort. Anne's four surviving children, with their husbands and wives, were in attendance.

We lingered on another day and as evening descended, we all headed off to the tavern. Mary had a chance to talk with Edward Hutchinson. William hovered close by. Edward surprised us all by making his suspicions known. "They will declare a complete victory for their side," he stated. "We have to be prepared."

Feeling like she was getting somewhere, Mary seemed to hang on his words. "What will you do?"

"I will do what I always do," he replied. "I will say nothing."

"Even if your mother is attacked personally?"

"No one will say anything to my face, Mistress Dyer. That is how Boston operates these days—behind a polite veil. There is always a semblance of decorum. Plots and schemes are hatched behind closed doors."

"Can you live with that?"

"Yes. I can, strange as it may seem. I made that decision years ago when I decided to remain behind. Mother and Father supported me, to their credit. Mother told me that I am of a unique generation, one of those born in England, but raised in the New World. She said that I should keep the character of the initial group alive."

"I always wanted to be more like her."

"Didn't we all?"

"What did she do to keep her spirits up? I know she prayed. What else did she do?"

Edward smiled. "She sang."

"I remember her on the trail from Boston," added William Dyer. "I believe she sang the whole way to Aquidneck."

"He's right," chimed Dorothy Brenton. "I cried and she sang. Eventually, she got me to join in. Why don't we do that now? Maybe we should sing! We could sing some of her favorite songs. Please, please, let's."

Rain fell outside the narrow windows. Inside the tavern, a mist of vapor rose from the clothes of the mourners, just as it had in those meetings in Anne's house. Bridgett Hutchinson got the group singing. I felt Anne's presence in the sad smiles filling the crowded pub. I became gripped with the feeling that the memory of this moment had been locked in time. It would last forever.

"The essence of Anne had to do with friendship," Mary told me later when were back home in Newport. "'Greater love hath no man than this, that a man lay down his life for a friend.'"

With a weary, sad expression on her face, she told me that night what troubled her most. As I listened to her speak, I did not try to separate her from these feelings of guilt, because I could see that there wasn't any use at all. I knew that she revealed something that would be in her heart till the day she died, at the hand of the executioner. Her loyalties had been torn and once ripped, she could not mend the fabric. One side went to William, the other to Anne. The rift opened up a great gash inside her that she could not figure out how to close. If chance presented another disciple, another person like Anne, Mary vowed to me that night as we sat side by side on the high-back bench in front of the fire, sipping water, that she would never make that same mistake twice.

As for Boston, well, their time would come. "They may have won the battle, Irene, but I swear that as long as I live, they will not win the war. The how, the why, the wherefore, I may not be able to solve now, but one day, I swear, I will. So help me God. I will find a way. The true story of Anne Hutchinson will be told, and whatever part I must play in the telling, I swear, I will play it."

No amount of trouble coming down on our heads will ever bring her back. Those were the words I wanted to say. I was too tired to say them though. I was just too worn out. What I kept saying, over and over, was that I wished Anne had just come with us to Newport and lived to a ripe old age. As it turned out, I was the only one to manage that feat.

CHAPTER FOURTEEN
Civil War

My baby did not live. Mary placed a stillborn son in my arms, not long after Anne's death. I could hardly bear my sorrow. Sean assured me that there would be more children, that this was only one misfortune. As tears slipped down my cheeks, I did not have the nerve to tell him that I feared I was cursed.

In 1644, Mary's fourth child, Maher, came next. His full name, Mahershallaber, is the longest name to be found in the Bible. I took hold of him in my arms and would not let him go. He is the one who healed my grief. Mary headed back to the fields. Her ewes delivered at the unheard of rate of two a year. This yielded her twenty pounds from each ewe. As she prospered, so did Newport. We began exporting and competing with Boston. Roger Williams sailed to England with the hope of securing a charter.

News from the other side of the Atlantic dribbled in with the arrival of each ship. Letters were shared, read aloud, and events were discussed at great length. As I predicted, England split in twain. The task of declaring allegiance was not any easier in the New World. In Newport, they asked themselves this one question: which side did God favor? Should the king govern as a God by his will, and the nation be governed by force like beasts? Or, should the people be governed by their own laws, and live under a government derived from their own consent?

Most of Newport leaned toward the latter, but we were all fully aware of the unsuspected form of tyranny that lay in wait on that path. The snake of public opinion, theocratic measures, imposed from the pulpit by newly ordained despots, could be worse than what they sought to replace. We were in a unique position to see those dangers after our experiences in Boston. We also knew that England had not, as yet, been through this kind of experience. Puritans in Parliament, as well as the rising class of merchants and tenant farmers, wanted a hand in shaping events of the future. I wondered how much New England, the New World in general, was a factor in all this commotion, because everything was opening up. Too, England would not have the same luxury we enjoyed in Newport, that of pulling up stakes and starting over again, forming policies to suit our like-minded natures. In the old country, they would be hashing all this out in families and in villages where they had lived together, united, for centuries. We knew those leaning to the Puritan, or Roundhead side, as they were beginning to be called, knew nothing of these dangers. We understood that events had put us on an unalterable course, which would not be settled without first witnessing, and from a great distance, a sea of blood spilt on the old sod.

The king, his cavaliers, and his royalist supporters preferred keeping the status quo. Those who have solid positions will always favor hanging on to what they have rather than risking all in changing times. Geographically, the north and the west fell in with the king's side. They stuck to what they liked to refer to as their ancient duty. Catholic nobles, hoping for a return to the one true faith, threw in everything they had with the king's cause. The Marquis of Newcastle is said to have given a million pounds. The nobility became royalists, with only a small faction supporting Prime Minister Pym's Parliamentary cause.

The middle section of the country favored the Puritans. Sir Harry Vane described in a letter his new great friend and ally, Oliver Cromwell. I didn't know much of the man at this point, so I did not yet spit whenever I heard the mention of his name. Ireland was not yet saying, "May the curse of Cromwell fall on you," but in time they did. That curse will be hurled a thousand years from now, for no one individual ever caused us more grief. As for me, it was a name I grew to hate more than any other name in the wide world.

News of the first battle came to Newport months later, but hearing about it so long after it had taken place, did not take the bite out of the sting. Five thousand English lay dead on the field. We learned the queen sold the crown jewels in Holland to raise money. The University of Oxford melted its plate.

Wave after wave of fear, anguish, and guilt washed over our little port as people ran from house to house shouting the horrible news that England had fallen into civil war.

Mary told me she felt as if a great beast had a hold of her round her middle and wouldn't let go. Shaken one way and then the other is how she put it. "How did this happen? How did it happen? Will England ever be one country again? Can we heal this rift, or will we keep dividing into smaller and smaller parts? What must it have been like for the king to see all those soldiers lined up against him? How can we ever get back to our simple faith in king and country? Perhaps we should go back."

"How can you, for one minute, even consider such a thing?" William asked.

"I feel a great need to be there, to do something—even if it is to stand with a crowd in London."

"The king's forces could have marched on London. The fighting could have taken place on the very skirts of London. No one in England has any great understanding of what's happening. Both sides say they are fighting for the same thing. It will not be over quickly. We can only look to our duties here, our children, our farm, and try to keep a steady head. England may lose the monarchy."

"Surely events will not go that far."

"I hope and pray they don't, but do not speak of returning. We've had enough upsetting news for one day."

Mary took her place at her wheel. As she spun, she told me she pictured women, all over England, spinning and weaving cloth for the soldiers.

"Aye. It is an ancient task. Through the ages the men start fighting and the women get to work: winding sheets, bandages, warm stockings, and coats. No time to dye the cloth, no refinements added; it will be dyed red soon enough. All the women are bound up in the same duty, yet the men are tearing each other apart. Isn't that just the way of it? The fabric of the country is being torn in two, and all the cloth in the world will not stop the blood from flowing. Mothers will be losing sons. Fathers are fighting sons."

Tears spilled down her cheeks. I decided to say nothing further because I was too gloomy with my own troubles.

"Why couldn't they have reached some agreement with the king? Why has it come to this?" she asked again. "Peace reigned for seventy years. Now entire towns are torn in half. Village life is the warp and weft of England. How can we get it back? In all my times of darkness, through the nights we rocked sick babies, the days of endless snow, the first night in Pocasset when we heard wolves howl all night long— through all those episodes, where we felt like little creatures marooned on a distant shore, it has been thoughts of England, thoughts of our English mettle, that have seen me through. My husband's firm ways, Anne squarely facing her accusers; I have been sustained, Irene, by our resolute ways."

"To be sure, mistress. But no war, civil or otherwise, could ever take the Irish out of me. It runs clear through. If I ever have children, it will be in them too, even though they will not even know it."

"We are a civilized country," she added. "Don't misunderstand me. I know very little about Ireland. In the most desperate of circumstances, it is always our civility that can be counted on; it is what we depend on. Now it is being ripped to shreds. Harry Vane betrayed his own father," she added. "That's when it all began."

When ten more skeins were done, she went off to bed. I took a look at the bright stars before I wrapped my arms around my husband. I asked myself how many women had been torn from how many men. And what of dear Ireland? What of my brothers? My nine darling brothers. God bless them.

The winter dragged on and on. As the bright grasses of spring sprang up, both young and old scanned the horizon for any sign of a ship. At first sight of the distant sails, we ran down to get news. Letters came from family and friends. Snippets and bulletins were read aloud right on the spot. That night, most of Newport gathered at the tavern to compare notes. William Coddington read aloud his letter from Sir Harry Vane. We heard of the death of Prime Minister Pym. Then came the story of the battle of Marston Moor. The Scots army, hired by parliament, joined forces with the Puritan armies and faced the king with twenty thousand foot soldiers, and seven thousand on horse. The Royalists numbered eleven thousand on foot and seven thousand on horse. At six o'clock in the evening, Cromwell attacked, taking them by surprise. As they thought the battle would take place the next day, they were caught unawares. When all was said and done Cromwell stated that "God made them as stubble to our swords. Then we took their regiments of foot with our cavalry, and overthrew all that we encountered." With no quarter given, four thousand men fell.

On the walk home, we discussed these events with William. Mary walked quickly with a troubled look on her face. "People cheered in the pub tonight, William. I don't understand. How could they all abandon their duty to the king so easily? I know he is unpopular, but he is still the king. He was outnumbered at Marston Moor. He would have known at first sight that more of his subjects had taken arms against him, then stood behind in defense. England cannot throw away the monarchy. It would be disastrous. And why are people insinuating that they should even think of such a thing?" asked Mary.

"Would you side with the Royalists then if forced to send your sons into battle?"

"No. Neither side should be fighting at all. Does no one feel as I do?"

"Yes, but there are lots of citizens of Newport who were driven out of England for being Puritans in the first place. Perhaps they look to Cromwell as a champion for their cause."

"Is Cromwell such a man? I could see feeling that way about Mr. Pym, but Cromwell is something quite different; he strikes me as a ruthless man. The king's side is losing."

I had to admit that it looked that way to me too.

As spring grew into summer, the Dyer household taken up with work kept our noses to the grindstone.

A bright July morning brought us down to the docks, as we all had a hand in arranging a shipment of breeding stock to Boston. Mary spotted the captain who brought us news from England. She asked him how the repairs on his ship were faring. When he told her that he planned to set sail by the end of the week, I saw a frightened look on her face.

"I can't stand stayin' here and not knowing what's going on. I have a son fighting," he said.

"Which side?"

"For the king," he answered coldly. "What other side is there? I may join in myself. He needs every man he can get."

"We need you to come back, Captain Trevice. Don't leave us in the dark here."

"After Marston Moor, who knows what I'll be goin' back to?"

"So you have no qualms about fighting on the side of noblemen and the aristocracy?"

"Bollocks. Pardon me, mistress, but does it strike you as right that a hired army of Scots should march into England and tell us all to be Presbyterians?"

"No."

"Nor I. They can make a lot of talk in London, but in my humble opinion, it is a sin to raise an army to fight our king on English soil. By the time I get back, it could be finished."

"The war?"

"The monarchy. We could be seeing the last of the Stuarts."

The color dropped from Mary's face. The captain urged her to sit on a barrel.

Once home, she put on a pair of sturdy walking boots and slipped away. She was gone for the rest of the day, and I was asked many times where she went. I only said that she had always garnered strength from long, solitary walks.

I hoped I was telling the truth, but I did not know for sure.

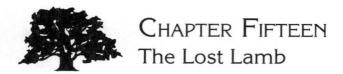

CHAPTER FIFTEEN
The Lost Lamb

Late in the fall, Mary burst into our cottage one night calling for me. "Irene. I need you. Come. Maher is really sick," she cried.

As Mr. Dyer and Sean were both away fishing, we couldn't send them out to get help. I knew it would be up to us as I grabbed my shawl and followed her out the door.

We found the wee lad burning up with fever. "Have you sponged him?"

"Yes. I can't cool him."

"How long has he been like this?"

"Only hours, but he's getting worse. What shall we do?"

"We have to get the fever down," I told her. "This water is not cold enough. How can we get it colder?"

"I don't know. I've been thinking the same thing. Maybe we should take him down to the ocean."

"He'll catch his death!"

"Irene, listen to me. We have to take this chance. We have no choice. If we don't get this fever down, we will not be able to do anything. Let me take him."

"No," I screamed. I grabbed the child and held him close.

"He's my son, Irene. Give him to me. Come with me. Grab a lantern."

Mary peeled him out of my arms, even though I was still clinging. We sped along in the dark, down the path to the sea. When we got there, I tested the waters by sticking my hand in the ocean. She's going to kill him, I told myself, and I can't stop her. Mary put her hand over his little nose and mouth and plunged him right under. He gasped, giving her a look of horror. His little eyes went straight to mine, as he wailed for help. I prayed to the Holy Virgin who I've always felt is so dependable in these kinds of circumstances. The baby took another breath and howled.

At the second he exhaled, she covered his mouth again, and dipped him into the sea. Driven to distraction, I hopped from one foot to the next. Pulling him out, Mary wrapped him in her shawl and ran like the wind back up the hill. My feet didn't even touch the ground. I got him dried and then we sponged him again. Then I fell to my knees with my rosary and remained there for hours. Near dawn I must have crumpled over and fallen asleep.

I felt a hand on my shoulder and Mary whispered, "The fever has broken."

"Sweet Jesus, mistress, you saved him."

"Watch him closely. I'll go down and get Dr. Clarke."

"He wouldn't have done what you did. How did you know what to do?"

"I didn't. I thought of asking Anne. The answer came to me then."

"She was with us. I know it."

"Yes, she was."

Tears jumped to our eyes. "I miss her, Irene. I miss her so much."

"Aye."

Mary sighed and wiped her face on her apron. "I'll leave now."

Two weeks later, when Maher was fully recovered and Mary was up in the pasture, I ran up the hill, like the devil himself was after me. No cap on my head, hair wild and streaming down my back, I could not get to her fast enough.

"What is it? Stop. Catch your breath," said Mary.

"Susanna!" I blubbered. "Little Susanna Hutchinson. She's alive. She's been found."

"Where?"

"Mistress Brenton got a letter from Catherine Scott. Susanna was off picking blueberries when it happened. Her blessed mother sent her into the woods with her little pail. She was found in an Indian village. She doesn't speak a word of English."

"Oh dear Lord. Thank God. Is she living with Catherine?"

"Aye, but Bridgett wants her sorely. She'll go to her."

"Come," said Mary. "Help me get some things together to send her. She'll need clothes. The poor child."

"She has no memory."

"It's a blessing."

"It's a miracle. Saints be praised."

As we started down the hill, Mary suddenly fell quiet.

"What are you thinking?" I asked.

"I was thinking of how powerfully Anne lives on. Her light has not been dimmed. I have the sense that her spirit lingers."

"That's right, mistress. Of course you cannot ask anyone Irish such a question. She's with me all the time."

"You're certain?"

"Aye."

"How do you know you're not imagining these things?"

"What's the difference?"

At this, Mary laughed, linked her arm through mine and the two of us ran down the hill together like little girls.

In November, the last ship of 1645 sailed into Newport. The great advantage of the Newport house was the second floor sitting room. After supper, Mr. Dyer would sit at his desk going over his papers. We would spin and sew. Children whittled, or worked on samplers. One floor away from the fire, the cooking, and the endless household chores made this room a great luxury in my eyes. When a letter arrived from England, usually from our faithful correspondent, Sir Harry Vane, we would gather and digest the news.

In a matter of fact tone, Mr. Dyer read Harry's description of the battle of Naseby. He wrote of the royal foot soldiers surrounded by a flank of Roundhead reserves led by Cromwell. He described the king's order to charge, but an aide, recognizing the desperate futility of the command, got hold of the king's bridle and forced him to retreat. Cromwell put one hundred Irish women, present at the battle, to the sword, supposedly on moral grounds. Vane confidently stated that the end seemed to be clearly in sight.

"What does that mean? What will come of this?" asked Mary as she rose and started pacing back and forth, wringing her hands.

William, looking up from his letter, saw her expression and said, "Calm down, my dear. You must think of your child."

Pregnant, Mary sat rubbing her swollen belly. To my relief she asked, "What moral grounds did Cromwell have to kill all those Irish women?"

"Prejudice, I should think."

"I do not like that man."

I knew this would irritate him, and it did.

"Mary, we know next to nothing."

"I don't like him." she repeated. "Did he say anything about the princes? Where are they in all of this? Rumors have been flying about them."

"Hang on. I haven't got to the end yet. Here. He said they are still abroad under the tutelage of the Earl of Clarendon—" He stopped dead and looked up.

"What is it?"

"And William Seymour."

"The name your aunt Mary whispered to me when she was dying?"

"It means nothing. She was not herself."

"How do you know it means nothing? Why did that look cross your face when you saw his name?"

"There was no look."

"Yes there was, William. Why are you being evasive? Do you know something?"

"There is no need for any further discussion."

"Why did she whisper his name to me? You know I have always thought William Seymour could be my father. Why else would she have done that? You belittle me when I speak of it, but I don't see why else she would have whispered his name. Is William Seymour my real father?"

"Your ancestry is unknown."

"If you know something and are not telling me, I will never forgive you, William."

He looked at me and then at her. I knew it was my cue to leave, but I could not make myself go. Was there a mystery father that William Dyer knew about? What kind of cruelty would allow anyone to keep this knowledge from her? Her uncertain ancestry gave her no end of anguish. She once told me that the Narragansetts worshiped their ancestors, so where did that leave her? Not knowing had always been a trial. If Mr. Dyer did know anything, why on earth would he keep it from her? And what of this aunt? William's aunt, who was a close friend of the Barretts, arranged their marriage. All I knew of her was that she had introduced them and, for all intents and purposes, handed Mary over to Mr. Dyer's care.

"Those are harsh words," he said.

"I mean it. A husband should not keep secrets from his wife. If you know something you must tell me."

"A husband cannot keep secrets from his wife. It is not possible. This subject is closed and I will hear no further discussion. Irene, if you would be so kind as to see to the children, I think we'll just call it a day."

The next morning, Mary and I slipped down the shore to the Coddingtons. As we entered their gate, we heard the muffled sound of horses hooves on bare earth. Mr. Coddington rode his big gray stallion at a sitting trot and then a walk. After he dismounted and we greeted one another, he said, "Will you walk with me while I cool my horse down?"

Sidling up beside him and without any lead-in, she blurted, "Do you know anything about William Seymour?"

"Why do you ask?"

"I heard that he was in exile with the Prince of Wales. I am curious as to what kind of man he is."

"I have not met him personally. He's had a colorful past though, what with that business with Lady Arabella."

"What business?"

"They were married in secret. King James put them both in the Tower."

"Why?"

"Arabella was the granddaughter of Henry VII, and niece of Mary Queen of Scots. A great favorite in her court, Arabella was charming and educated along with the king. He did not care for intelligent women; he never arranged a marriage for her, so she married Seymour in secret. He has royal blood too, through the House of Suffolk. A child of that union would have a double claim to the throne. So, in order to prevent the threat of a challenge to his supremacy, the king slapped them both in the Tower. He could not take the risk of any of her issue having a stronger claim than his own. Lady Arabella died a few years later. There were rumors of a baby, a girl. It could be possible too because they made good one escape. She dressed as a man and got as far as France. Seymour was to travel in a separate boat and meet her there, but his brother reported him, and they were both captured. Some say they left their baby in France. King James spent his whole life looking for that child, but nothing ever turned up."

"What happened to William Seymour?"

"I guess after Lady Arabella's death he was free to go. If that daughter lived, she has never been heard of since."

On the walk back home, Mary's mind began to race. "Could it be possible? Do you think I could be their daughter?"

I thought long and hard as to what to answer. I was silent for so long she repeated the question. No one knew her secret but me. Mr. Dyer, being mute on the subject, would never discuss this with me, so the task of either affirming or denying the sense of this fantasy, lay squarely on my shoulders. I knew the stand Mr. Dyer would have taken. He would have done everything in his power to dissuade her and most likely would have referred to it as a foolish notion. I could have taken the same approach, but some gut feeling steered me off that course. Gazing out to sea for help, I decided to stop walking so I could devote my mind fully to the task. Harry Vane's assertion that he had been in the presence of the divine when he asked for the keys to the red casket somehow popped into my mind. Curiously, I felt the same cool hand of fate on my shoulder. Her face searched mine imploringly, and I guess, in the end, it was my love for her that carried the day. "It would explain why you turn heads wherever you go," I declared. "To learn that you have royal blood would come as no surprise to me, mistress. I thought you might have been a queen, the first day I saw you."

This sent her away to the races, as I knew it would. In my heart of hearts, I thought it would be good for her to think of herself this way. I grew to learn why Mr. Dyer had taken the measures he had; his motive was to protect her. I should have had the same intention, but I was never as learned, nor as wise as he.

"See, it does make some sense to me because why else would William's aunt have whispered his name? This is incredible. Could he be my father? Was Lady Arabella my mother? Do you realize, Irene, that I actually could be the king's first cousin! No. It's too much. No one will ever believe me. Where is the proof? William must never hear of our conversation today. It is between you and me and no one else. Do you swear?"

"I swear."

"You know how angry he gets if I even talk about it at all," she continued, with her mind galloping on. "That is another thing—why does he get so cross whenever the subject comes up? I thought he was ashamed of my uncertain origins and does not like any reminders. There is not a living soul who will consider me anything less than mad if I ever speak of this. But what if I could meet him? What if I got the chance to ask William Seymour to his face? What if I were to ask him how I ended up at the Barretts? How did I become their ward? It's so maddening not to know. Enduring playing second fiddle to the Barrett girls was bad enough, but that pales in comparison with living my whole life not knowing. I've lived in this conspiracy of silence long enough. If there is a ghost of a chance of finding out, I should take it."

"How?" I asked her as my blood ran cold. "William Seymour is in exile with the princes and you are in the New World."

"I have to find a way to get to England," she stated. "I bet I have enough to pay for passage if I sell off my flock."

Now I really started to panic. I knew better than to try to talk her out of it, as that would only make matters worse. So I tried to be practical. The war would prevent it, I told myself. William would not let her go for any reason. There was the baby to consider, but then I remembered she had made the passage before, carrying Samuel. I told myself that it was only a plan after all, one which could not possibly become a reality. She wouldn't sell her whole flock; it was too important to her. She had developed a reputation as a right good breeder. She wouldn't give that all up for this daft notion. Maybe she just needed the idea of having a secret plan. It would be a distraction, that's all, a lifeboat in a stormy sea. So I said nothing to dissuade her and only nodded.

On the way home, we stopped at the pasture and I watched her counting and calculating. The determination in her face scared me. I found myself wondering if she could have Stuart blood. I tried to remember all I knew about the Scots Queen. Then it came to me. The tapestries. I had heard that through all the years Queen Elizabeth kept Mary Queen of Scots imprisoned, the prisoner worked magic with her needle. We had even heard of those tapestries in Ireland. It comes in the blood, my grandmother told me, the skills with the needle. Mary could spin, sew, embroider, and knit rings around any other woman I had ever met. Her designs were masterful. I used to tease her by saying angels sat on her shoulder while she worked.

I didn't have any answers yet, but I did think there might be something there. To be sure, I knew we'd crossed over a threshold. It was as if a door had swung open and then closed and locked behind us. To return to the place we had been before Harry Vane mentioned the name "William Seymour" became about as possible as it would have been for me to return to Ireland.

CHAPTER SIXTEEN
The End of the English Monarchy

By the spring of 1649, Mary, now the mother of five children, had yet another on the way. Samuel, at fifteen, had grown strong and bull-headed. Mary, ten, was quiet and prim. William, nine, barely civilized; eight-year-old Maher had a love of bugs and building. Then there was wee Henry, a fat and charming toddler.

Mary's children took up the lion's share of my heart as I was still without. Three sorrows followed the stillbirth.

When Captain Trevice sailed into the harbor in April, a throng of eager faces greeted his ship. It was a clear morning, with a cool breeze brushing at our hair and caps. The sight of his solemn expression and his slow, careful manner coming down the plank brought a hush over us all.

"It is my sad duty to be the bearer of bad news. King Charles is dead."

The crowd stood stock still and silent until one cried out, "How?"

"Executed. Beheaded. At Westminster, with the army standing guard."

"Under what law? What charge?" rang out many anguished voices.

"Cromwell's army is the law now."

"What of the rest of the family?"

"They are still alive, for what it's worth to them. No doubt you'll read all about it in your mail."

Mary and William quickly headed home. We all gathered around the hearth.

"Do you have a letter, father? Did someone write and tell us what happened?" asked Samuel.

"Did they murder the queen?" added young Mary.

"I'm looking at what I have here," he said to Mary. "I've been sent several pamphlets. One seems to be an account of the execution. Shall I read it?"

I had my eye on Mary. She poked at the fire with one hand over her belly. The children pulled up their stools. Maher liked to sit right in the hearth at the corner.

Mary stood, rubbing the small of her back. "I don't think I can bear to hear it, William. But then I must, mustn't I?"

He began softly by saying, "They started off on December 23, 1648, by appointing a committee to discover how to proceed against the king in a legal fashion. When they learned that he could not be tried under the law of any court in existence, they had to pass an ordinance to create a new court."

"What did they call it?"

"The High Court of Justice," he answered.

"Doesn't all justice begin with the sovereign?"

"Yes it does, but they found a way around that too. They created a new base from which they attempted to establish justice. Let me see. I'll read this part. 'On January 4, 1649, the House of Commons passed a resolution. The people under God are the source of all power and the House of Commons, chosen by and representing the people, holds the supreme power by delegation. Their acts need no concurrence from a king, or a House of Peers'. This," he added, looking up, "was the authority which constituted a court of one hundred and thirty-five commissioners. They were the judge and the jury."

"There is no House of Lords? So they are now saying that the House of Commons is the supreme ruler of England? That is not how our government works. That is not how our laws work. In one fell swoop they have changed everything—centuries of history. Was there no opposition to this? No argument?"

"Yes. Apparently many refused to serve. Algernon Sydney is quoted as saying, 'First the king can be tried by no court; secondly no man can be tried by this court.' Then Cromwell replied, 'I tell you we will cut off his head with the crown upon it.'"

"I told you! Didn't I tell you? They tried him in an illegal court!"

"On January 20, the trial began with only sixty-eight of the judges present."

"And what about our friend Sir Harry? Was he part of this sorry lot?"

"No, he was quoted as saying he opposed putting the king on trial because of 'tenderness of blood.'"

"How did they stage this travesty?"

"In Westminster Hall they put up a whole row of seats for the judges, and had the king face them on a red velvet chair. The galleries were packed."

"Why didn't the people riot? How could they stand there and let this happen?"

"Apparently, the military presence stood by in full force— both inside the hall, and all through the streets. They even covered the river in barges."

"Dear Lord," cried Mary. "This is awful. Military dictatorship. Imagine how the king must have felt."

"It says here that he carried himself very well."

"Tell me, please."

"He wore black with a jeweled George around his neck on a blue ribbon."

"What charge did they read to him?"

"It's lengthy and goes into all his 'crimes'. He was tried as a 'tyrant, traitor, murderer, and a public and implacable enemy of the commonwealth of England.'"

"What?"

"Your reaction is very similar to his, my dear. He laughed out loud. Then he was asked to answer the charge. A masked woman cried out from the gallery, 'It is a lie, not half, nor a quarter of the people of England. Oliver Cromwell is a traitor.'"

"Do they think they can govern in the name of the people when great numbers have openly opposed this government to the point of meeting them in the battlefield? How did the king respond?"

"He asked by what authority he was being tried. He was told that the authority lay with the people who had elected him."

"Elected?"

"Yes. Your response was exactly the same as his. He added that this was a 'strange point and new' as he had always assumed he had inherited this position."

"The trial was a farce then," said Samuel.

"It would seem to have those elements, son. Yes, " continued William. "He would not enter any plea, so they were forced to adjourn. The troops escorted him out crying 'justice, justice.' The civilians started shouting, 'God Save the King.' Then our friend from Salem, Reverend Hugh Peters, went out into the square, raised his arms above his head and cried, 'This is the most glorious beginning of the work.'"

"Hugh Peters? He was actually in favor of this?" Mary asked incredulously.

"The Puritan clergy have been for this since the beginning, Mary. Think of the heights to which they will rise if the Anglican Church is abolished," he added.

"If Hugh Peters thinks he can go in there with this army behind him and impose that cold, rigid Puritanism on the English people, he has another thing coming."

"He preached the next day to the judges."

"Does it say what text?"

"Yes. 'To bind their kings in chains and their nobles in fetters of iron.'"

"He has the king's blood on his hands! It's unbelievable. One of the men who denounced Anne Hutchinson has had a hand in murdering the King of England!"

William went on. "Monday, January 22, the King was brought back to the court and again they told him he must plead either guilty or not guilty. Shall I read you his response?"

Mary nodded.

"'It is not my case alone; it is the freedom and liberty of the people of England; and pretend what you will, I stand more for their liberties; for, if power without law may make laws, may alter the fundamental laws of the kingdom, I do not know what subject he is in England that can be sure of his life or anything that he calls his own.'"

"He's right," Mary stated. "Children, you must understand that he is right. Parliament believing that it speaks for the people could be more tyrannical than the greatest tyrant who ever sat on the throne. He does his duty as monarch to remind everyone of that salient fact. If this new faction, which began by imposing war, and then murdering the king, proceeds now to dictating religion and, from there, God only knows what, liberty as we have known it will come to an end."

"The king was brought in for sentencing," said William. "He asked to speak before the Lords and the Commons in the Painted Chamber. This was refused."

"What would he have said?"

"There is only speculation now. Some say he may have offered to abdicate in favor of his son."

"Would he risk this sham of a court setting up young Prince Charles and then murdering him?"

"We won't know that now," sighed William.

"No. Oh God. Go on."

"Perhaps you don't want to hear it," said William, looking at her anguished face with concern.

"Every English subject must hear," she stated with a coldness that startled him. "Our children must know their history."

William paused. In a hushed tone, he said, "The deed took place on January 30. It is reported that the night before, Thomas Herbert, the king's most faithful retainer, dreamt that Archbishop Laud came to the door and bowed so low to the king that he fell."

"Did the king hear of the dream?"

"Yes. He called it 'remarkable.' Then he rose, asked for a warm shirt, and warm underclothing as he did not want to be seen shivering. 'I fear not death,' he said. 'Death is not terrible to me. I bless my God I am prepared.' He received Bishop Juxon and then they came for him." Seeing the tears spring to Mary's eyes, William asked. "Are you sure you want me to continue? You must think of the child, my dearest."

Mary bent over in her chair rocking. "I have to hear it," she whispered. "Where did they do it? At the Tower?"

"No. They built a platform outside of the Banqueting House."

"Why there?"

"They needed a place big enough to hold all the soldiers. It is also surrounded by army headquarters; a battery of guns were moved into place."

"Did he say anything?"

"Yes. He said, 'An unjust sentence that I suffered to take effect is punished now by an unjust sentence on me.'"

"He blamed himself for the death of the Earl of Strafford?"

"To the degree that Strafford said the same thing at the time of his death. Both men reminded their executioners of the law of the land."

"Was that it? That was all he said?"

"No. The king added that he had forgiven 'all the world; especially he had forgiven his enemies.' He said that what he most wanted was peace for his people. He also wished for their liberty and freedom, which he stated, could only be found in a government of laws. He felt that if he had submitted to the power of the sword, he would not have come to the scaffold. Then he said, 'and therefore I tell you (and I pray to God it not be laid to your charge) that I am a Martyr of the people.' Then he added that he would die a Christian, according to the Church of England as he had found it left to him by his father. When he finished speaking, he tucked his hair up in a white cap, lay his head down, stretched out his arms and then gave the signal for the executioner to strike."

"Then what happened? Did the people react?"

"The executioner peeled off the cap, grabbed the king's head by his gray hair and held it up to the crowd. He said, 'Behold the head of a traitor.' The soldiers were dead silent. A sobbing sound like a low moan ran through the crowd. It was described as the most awful sound imaginable."

"So they remembered then that they were English," she whispered.

"At that moment, yes. I do not think that the specter of that pronounced military presence sat well with the people either," added William.

"We must do what we can to turn this tide. I am sorry. There is no question of which side I am on, and as long as I live, I'll be damned, William, if I am to be quiet from here on in." She rose to her feet and started pacing, "By God. I do not feel proud to be English today." Then she stopped, bowed her head, and sobbed. "He smiled at me. When I was presented at court. He smiled," she choked, "as if he knew me."

The children gathered round her skirts. William rubbed her back for a time. "I will never accept this. Never!"

"Has this ever happened before?" asked Samuel.

"Battles have been fought over the succession, but the victor always claimed the throne. What just happened is a military coup and that is different," explained Mr. Dyer. "The throne is empty now. No king or queen wears the crown. This is unprecedented."

"How will it affect us then, over here?" asked young Will.

"Good question, son. Laws will change. Who knows how justice will be meted out? We will carry on as before, until further notice, that is."

"Should we say our prayers, Mother?" asked little Mary.

"Is the war over then?" asked young William. "Are there still Cavaliers? Should I fight?"

"Prayer is what is required most now," said Mary.

I left them in favor of discussing this turn of events with my husband. Naturally, we were very concerned about how this would affect Ireland.

Over the next few days in Newport, people went around as if stunned. Their feeling of helplessness had never been worse. News spread from house to house as stories were compared. The Brentons had a report of a rumor floating around London in regard to the executioner himself. Since it was reasoned that no normal subject worth his salt would slay his own king, they speculated that a fanatic Puritan, perhaps Hugh Peters of Salem, wielded the fateful ax.

Mary threw herself into work. As the summer progressed, she presided over her largest and most prolific flock of sheep yet. Telling William one day that she had set into motion plans to sell off the whole lot of them save a few for domestic use, made me stop in my tracks.

He asked, "Whatever for?"

I held my breath because I was thinking about what she said earlier about getting to England.

"I don't want to carry on this responsibility after the baby is born. I will have six children to care for, God willing. The older ones need more of my attention with their schooling. They must learn history and Latin."

"How can you sell so many sheep at once?"

"I have been working on it all summer. It will be possible."

"It will mean a reduction in our income."

"I know."

"Well, it seems as though you have your mind made up. Actually, it is not a bad time for us to have a bit of working capital. Who knows what taxes may now be imposed on us."

"Surely we will resist any taxation from this band of scallywags."

"How? Are you talking about armed sedition?"

"No. I don't know. William Coddington plans to sail to England next year. Don't you think he can secure the charter?"

"There are no guarantees. Fewer now than ever before."

In late fall, after the harvest, Mary sold all her sheep. Two weeks later, safely delivered of a son, she told me as I placed him in her arms that she would name him Charles. The night before his birth she dreamt that she had lifted the coffin of the slain king and found a live baby boy lying on his stomach.

As winter drew near, Mary stayed close to the fire, tending her baby and teaching her children. Perhaps the weight of all those years of history, or conceivably the weariness brought on by the difficulties of motherhood dragged her down; for whatever reason, a state of melancholy hung over her like a winter fog. Some days she did nothing more than sit and stare into the fire.

One day when I could not stand to see her hang her head like this for another second, I said, "I am writing to Catherine Scott."

"Why?" asked Mary.

"Anne Hutchinson had remedies for women like you."

"And what is that supposed to mean?"

"Women in the midst of sinking into a bog. I'm going to write Catherine and ask her what we can do."

"Don't mention me by name."

"Why not? It is a common enough occurrence, especially after birth; there is no shame."

"I know. I'd rather you didn't, that's all."

"Fine. I'll say it's me who is under the table then."

"Its not as bad as all that."

"It is. You don't see yourself."

"I get like this in winter. Everyone does."

"Maybe it's the selling of the flock that's got you stuck in a tub of butter."

"Irene!"

"It's just an expression. It's what my mother used to say."

"You don't feel the same way about the war because you're Irish."

"Don't think we don't have our own problems! Cromwell's brought his men over to slaughter us like sheep, all in the name of God!"

Seeing the color rise to my face, Mary said, "I know, I'm sorry. I didn't mean it that way. Write to Catherine. I'll be interested to hear from her."

In a few weeks' time Catherine's letter arrived. She recommended rest, solitude, St. John's Wort, pennyroyal, hops, and valerian root. While her letter was full of news and local gossip, what intrigued Mary most was Catherine's description of a man of whom she had learned through her cousin back in Alford. She described a person who could be seen walking from Leicester to Suffolk, disrupting market days and storming into churches, asking the congregation if they wished to hear from hireling priests only. Dressed in leather breeches and wearing long, shaggy hair he had been beaten, jailed, and fined for his trouble. Yet according to Catherine's cousin, he had not only gathered quite a following, he had formed a new sect called Children of the Light. Catherine wrote that her cousin praised him as a man who spoke in the manner of Anne.

By spring, the first ship to arrive brought me my sister Moira. She would be indentured to the Dyers, but would live with Sean and me. The sight of her drove me wild with joy. As prepared as I had managed to get myself, the reality surprised me. Never doubt the saying that blood is thicker than water. God forbid any of you will ever be separated from all your kin, like your old granny here was, but if you ever find yourselves in such a bleak predicament, you will know what the sight of her did to me.

William took his pouch of mail to his desk and read it with great concern. Seeing the look on his face, Mary begged him to let her know what happened.

"It seems Mr. Coddington has had the charter granted to Roger Williams annulled in favor of a new one."

"That's good, isn't it? Isn't that what we wanted?"

"He has had himself appointed as governor for life."

"What? Is there some mistake?"

"No, this letter is from him."

"Anne," said Mary, burying her face in her hands. "She was right about him."

"Evidently so."

"What will happen now?"

"We will have to set a whole move in motion to get another charter. This is a disaster. I have other bad news as well. The firm handling both our estates is closing. I have received a letter informing me that the account has been turned over to someone else. It is a name about which I know nothing."

"How can they do that?" she asked.

"I imagine they have left London due to the current political climate. Now that the House of Lords has been abolished, what laws are in place to protect our holdings? Some have taken everything out of England," he added.

"Shouldn't we do the same?"

"How? How can we do that from here?"

"One of us must go over and get what we can. Otherwise, we will be robbed blind. We could lose everything with absolutely no recourse."

"I can't go over there now. It would be impossible," griped William.

"Then send me," she said.

"You're joking."

"I certainly am not. Look, I have given birth to six living children. If anything were to happen to me now—well my work is done." She watched him shake his head vigorously. "No. Listen, William. Hear me out. If I were to meet up with an accident, you could marry again, have more children and continue providing for all of them. If something happened to you, we would all be left nearly destitute. Since the funds in question are largely from my estate, I can handle the transfer. It makes the most sense."

"What about the children?" asked William.

"I am thinking about the children. If we lose this money they will be tied to the land for generations. I cannot sit here and let someone steal their inheritance. We must act quickly. I can go over this summer and be back before winter."

"What will you do by yourself in London?"

"I will contact Harry Vane. With his protection, I can succeed in getting our money out."

"What will you do with it then? Carry it around in your purse?"

"Do you have so little faith in me—so little trust?"

"No doubt Sir Harry may be of some assistance, but I don't think this is worth the trouble, or the risk."

"Our children deserve to be educated and to take their place in the world. My mind is made up. Oppose me if you will, but I am determined to do this."

"Why must you be so stubborn? Why must you leap to every notion that pops into your head without thinking of the consequences?"

"What have I done in all the years you have known me that would give you cause to believe I could not be trusted with this mission?"

Thinking he was playing his trump card, he announced, "I will not pay for your passage. I cannot risk you undertaking such a journey."

"Then I will pay for the passage."

"You cannot pay for anything without my say."

"Yes, I can. Have you forgotten about the proceeds from my flock?"

"Your flock? You think of it as yours?"

"I do."

With that he grabbed his hat and lurched for the door.

I stood there like a mute sheep not knowing what to do. Then she surprised me altogether by asking me if I'd come with her.

"I can't leave the children. I can't leave my husband," I protested.

"Moira is wonderful with the children. We won't be gone that long. We'll be back in September. I thought you might like to go to Ireland and see your family."

"Do you mean it?"

"Of course I mean it. This may be your only chance. William might soften if he knows you are coming."

The following day Mary marched straight down to the harbor to speak to the captain. She booked our passage with September 30 listed as the estimated date of return.

Sean was dead set against the idea. I told him that if I went home and sought absolution from my priest, the curse on me might be lifted. I told him it might be the only chance I'd ever have to see my mother again. The army was marching on Ireland and I knew my brothers would fight. I begged him to give me this one chance. He knew he would never get home again. He could have been mean and made sure that I didn't either, but he decided to spare me that pain if he could. I saw his eyes fill up with tears at the thought of the Emerald Isle, and in that fit of nostalgia, he gave in.

As the date of her departure drew near, William barged into the house one night with Dr. Clarke, the Brentons, the Eastons, and the Coggeshalls. The group seemed to be united in its purpose. Mary had to be reminded of her duties as a mother and as a wife.

"I must confess I am touched by your concern and care," she said. "But I am puzzled by why you all feel that this journey is such a perilous undertaking. I know it is unusual for women to travel without their husbands, but it is not impossible. You all seem to be implying that I must have taken leave of my senses. I am merely traveling, a good distance I admit, but traveling, nevertheless, to see to a matter that concerns me and my children. How can a mother sit back and watch her children being robbed? Am I not best suited to defend their rights? I cannot stay here knowing that a band of thieves will help themselves to what I intend to pass on to my children. I could not live with myself if I let it slip away to nothing. Fortunes change hands in times like these. We all know that. I am not one to throw up my hands and let it happen."

"But is it worth risking your life for?" asked Dorothy.

"Yes," Mary answered. "I would give my life for my children, gladly. I would give my life in an instant if it would benefit them."

"And if your ship were to go down? How would that benefit them?" asked Dr. Clarke.

Mary glared at him. "Then they will know that their mother died with their best interests in mind."

A few days later, friends, children, and most of Newport lined the bluffs to wave the ship off as we set sail for England. Mary and I stood on the deck and shouted our goodbyes. My heart raced with fear and joy at the same time. William had given her a stiff nod that morning on his way out the door. As the ship pulled out, he trudged along behind their ox and plow.

Resolve turned to dread as we lost sight of shore. We slept that night in fits and starts. The sound of young Will's voice came to Mary in a dream and she woke with her heart pounding. Had she been at home, she would have climbed the narrow staircase to the children's rooms upstairs and checked on them. Now she could do nothing. We wouldn't know if one of them fell ill or became hurt, she said. We would not be able to answer their questions, or sort out their difficulties. We would not be able to comfort them. Every wall of water the ship climbed over and every trough it slid down, put more distance between the children and us. Nothing in our bodies felt right. Our equilibrium was off. Flesh fell away from our bones. I kept telling her that the children were safe in my sister Moira's care. I told her how we raised the little ones together back at home, that she had all the skill in the world and a loving heart as well. But I knew how she felt because it was just the same for me.

Then it ended. Plymouth. We were on solid ground but an entire ocean, a whole world, lay between us and our families.

CHAPTER SEVENTEEN
Reduced by a Third

In the spring of 1652, when we arrived in London, soldiers stood in clumps like clusters of flies on dead meat. Rigid, black-clad, somber-looking men and women filled the streets. Poverty, rags, stumps instead of limbs, and everyone scratching and clawing to keep body and soul together—that's what it looked like to me. I had not remembered England with such an angry look. The military presence did not sit well with Mary either. As they had turned her world upside down, she longed to play some part in ridding England of this plague. I decided that it was a good thing she brought me along.

Mary contacted Sir Harry Vane immediately. A man arrived at our inn the next day, all turned out in a fine uniform. The sight of him shocked me. Do you have any idea how long it had been since we had seen a footman? The note he delivered bid us change our accommodation immediately, in favor of residing with the Vanes. The carriage stood in wait until we gathered our things.

The handsome Charing Cross town house, not imposing from the street, but unfolding on and on inside, seemed like a palace to our modest New England standards. I walked around the most splendid house I ever set foot in with my jaw hanging open. Henry's wife, Lady Frances, a beauty by anyone's standards, greeted us. Her calm manner and kind face put us at our ease right away. Mary was given time to freshen up and change before she would join the Vanes for dinner, and I went with her to her room. I was to be stashed in the servants' quarters. Sir Harry, Lady Frances informed Mary, had just returned from a long trip to Scotland.

In the room, I watched Mary run her hands over every piece of cloth in sight. I set to opening the trunks and pulled out three of her best gowns.

We had one of the housemaids follow us, seeing to our every need. "Will you need hot water?"

Mary turned and smiled. "Please," she answered. "I will require as much as thee can bring me."

I had all but forgotten that servants were not addressed in the familiar. In the New World some kept up the practice, but with indenture being over after a time, it had become confusing and had really fallen by the wayside in Newport. I got a kind of sinking feeling that only worsened the more I stayed in the Vanes' house. I can't say I had begun to think of myself as equal to the Dyers, but they honestly treated me as if I were, and by their example, so did others. Maybe I had grown in my own estimation. Whatever gains in stature the New World had given me, suddenly began to ebb like the tide. For the first time in years, I felt like I was nothing but an Irish servant. I did not like the feeling.

As she prepared to bathe, Mary talked of all her painstaking efforts in the flax fields, at the dye tubs, at her spinning wheel, and loom. She feared that everything she made over the last fifteen years paled in comparison with the finery in this room. Nothing she brought with her would do, she concluded. The entire contents of her trunk, too homespun and old fashioned, would make her look like a country bumpkin in this setting. I could see that she was working herself into a state over what to wear to dinner, so I hung the gowns near the bath, hoping the steam would freshen them. The dresses all had a damp sea smell, as if they had been wrapped in garlands of rotting seaweed. I shook out her best, dark blue dress, waving it over the vapor. A vigorous brushing would spruce it up, I thought. We dressed her hair in a small bun at the back of her head, with ringlets pulled forward framing her face.

We entered the drawing room that evening slowly and nervously, surprised to find them all in black. I was supposed to wait there until the butler could show me what to do. So I found an inconspicuous chair by the door. Harry glanced my way, walking in, but only nodded.

He caught the puzzled expression on Mary's face and said, "We look like Boston over here these days."

"Well, at least you have not cut your hair," answered Mary. "You look well."

"And you are as lovely as ever. That marvelous air agrees with you. You have met my Frances?"

"Yes, this afternoon. She was most kind."

"So many people want to meet you. Lady Frances has been swamped by requests. We'll have to do something."

"Not on my account, I hope."

"Yes," replied Lady Frances. "Everyone wants to hear about your adventures. You are very much in demand."

"Wait 'til they hear about the thrill of dirt floors, churning butter, and making soap."

"Are you still having to be self-sufficient?" asked Sir Harry.

"No. I jest. We have a substantial market now, by New World standards, of course. However, everything I own seems so woefully inadequate."

Turning to his wife, Harry remarked, "Mrs. Dyer's skills with the needle were legendary in Boston. So much so that the clergy were obliged to devote entire sermons solely to the sin of her good taste."

"You must take your share of the credit there, sir. I believe Reverend Wilson is still going on about your red vest," Mary replied.

"Tell me all the news as we go in," he said while taking her arm. "Thee will seat her at my right," he told the butler as they approached the table.

Through the door I could see a room lined with liveried servants waiting for any request from the Vanes. No one came for me, so I sat outside the dining room feeling like yesterday's fish, not knowing what to do with myself.

"Mr. Coddington has written me about the charter," began Harry.

"No doubt he told you he had the backing of the rest of the island when he had himself declared governor for life," said Mary, taking her seat.

"I am aware of the friction. I had no idea, as you know, that he acted alone when he had the Roger Williams charter nullified."

"Mr. Coddington's actions came as quite a shock."

"Many of my colleagues want to see Rhode Island lead the way in the fight for religious freedom," continued Harry. "Rumors of strife and disagreement are very bad for the cause."

"Yes. I realize that. Governor for life doesn't carry the ring of freedom in my ears—does it in yours?"

"Didn't I tell you, Frances? Was I right?"

Seeing them smile at each other, Mary asked, "Right about what?"

"He said that you never hesitated to let people know exactly what you think of them," answered Lady Frances. "We didn't invite guests tonight as I know you two will have a lot of catching up to do," said Lady Frances.

Mary began by asking, "What great events have you participated in while we have been held captive in the dark? What happened in Scotland?"

"Well, you know that from the moment of the king's death, Scotland declared itself for young Charles."

"Yes," said Mary. "It would seem that the Scots have the whip hand over us, for whichever side they cast in with inevitably becomes the majority."

"Quite. But one mustn't forget that they are motivated by their own interests—particularly in maintaining their own church. They could be persuaded to change sides. The Scots have proposed that if Charles were to embrace the Covenant and become champion of the Presbyterian cause, they would not only declare him their sovereign, but also would march to England, unite with the Royalists and help him restore his kingdom. He has already tried, but has been twice defeated. They invaded England on September 3. Sixteen thousand of them were trounced once again by our dear friend Oliver Cromwell. Young Charles led the troops until he had to flee. I heard that he hid in a tree at Boscobel. With a price of a thousand pounds on his head for his capture, it is remarkable that he escaped. Apparently, people whispered, 'the king, our master, your master, and the master of all good Englishmen is near you and in great distress: can you help us to a boat?' It worked and he lived."

"Did you want to see him dead?"

"Good Lord, no."

"It must be difficult for you to return after all these years and find so much changed," said Lady Frances.

"I am afraid that I may be very much at odds with you both."

"How so?" asked Sir Harry.

"To put it bluntly, I do not believe in your cause as strongly as you do."

"The king's execution was very hard on my wife," said Harry.

"Really?" asked Mary.

"Yes. I still think it was terrible, " stated Lady Frances.

"I disagreed with it myself," added Sir Harry. "Oliver Cromwell wants to rebuild the kingdom as alike to the old as possible. He was not even completely in favor of abolishing the House of Lords."

"Then why did it happen?" asked Mary.

"It was declared unnecessary, burdensome, and a danger to the liberty, safety, and public interests of the people of this nation."

"But liberty is more in danger now than it ever has been in history," Mary protested. "Merciful heavens, Harry, you must know what jeopardy we are in. You know why I have had to make this journey. Surely, you must fear for your own estate."

"When the dust settles, the country will be stronger. But I'll be honest with you. We are down to ninety members in the House. There is only one from London and three from Wales. Herefordshire and Lancashire are not represented at present."

"In time, things will be put to right," said Lady Frances. "There is much talk these days of not subjecting this fragile free state to the rude winds of popular judgment."

"Does all executive order come from the House now? You must forgive me, Lady Frances, for asking so many questions. You can't imagine how frustrating it has been having so little information coming our way."

"Not at all," said Sir Harry. "I can tell you that we have a Council of State made up of forty members who make up the main executive authority."

"And Cromwell is president, is he not?"

"Yes."

"So what about the army—these soldiers I see everywhere? How big is it now?"

"Forty-four thousand men."

"Good Lord. Why so many?"

"Don't think this tender republic is not threatened. Ireland and Scotland united against us could be our undoing. The king's death seems to have brought the unlikely coupling of Protestant Scotland and Catholic Ireland into accord. We have the native clans, the gentry of the Pale, and the Protestants of Ulster, all lined up against us."

"Does Oliver Cromwell envision Britain in three equal parts then?"

"Well, for the time being we have a subdued Ireland and Scotland, with England being the most equal part of the three. Cromwell has been given lands worth four thousand a year for his efforts. Your old friend Reverend Hugh Peters made a spectacle of himself by calling out, 'He'll be king of England yet.'"

"Sir Harry, you must forgive me for asking this, but have you taken leave of your senses completely? What is to become of us? What will happen to England? We have no king. No House of Lords. We have a shadow of Parliament and a ruthless tyrant grabbing more power for himself at every turn."

"I believe in religious freedom," shouted Harry. "I believe in the cause of a true Parliament."

His wife made clucking sounds to hush him up. "In these desperate times, Mary, we have tried to keep our focus on the issue of religious freedom."

"Would Ireland be free to remain Catholic then?" asked Mary.

I lost my composure all together and let out a war whoop from my spot behind the door.

"Cromwell feels that God does not side with the Irish," began Harry. "Therefore, since they are outside the kingdom, they must be brought in. We cannot risk having Prince Charles arrive in Ireland and raise a force against us. Desperate measures have to be taken to protect the whole country from sinking into chaos. We have to suspend mercy in times such as these, or the government will not hold," he concluded.

Mary's voice got louder. Without Mr. Dyer to send cold looks her way, there didn't seem to be any force in the room to stop her. "How can the government hold if the country is torn apart?"

"We have God on our side," Harry said.

Tempted to emit a loud "Ha!" I restrained myself.

At this point, I still did not know what Cromwell had done in Ireland yet. I still hadn't heard a word. The conversation was leading me to dark thoughts and I had a tingling feeling at the back of my neck.

Mary carried on in the same confrontational path. I was pretty sure our stay in this house would not last longer than this one night at the rate she was going. "I don't see how you can say that, Harry. How do you know which side God is on? Are the Presbyterians convinced God sides with you? Are the Catholics?"

"What we are hoping and praying for," said Lady Frances in a smooth and calming tone, "is that at the end of this whole process, England will be a better place. We hope that good people such as you can practice their religions, whatever they may be, free from persecution. Is this a concept you could find yourself in agreement with?"

"You must forgive me, Lady Frances, for my bluntness. Your husband and I go back many years and we have seen our way through trying times before. I feel I must make my convictions known if I am to remain here as your guest. Believe me, I will understand if you feel you cannot put up with my views. However, I simply must express them. I have no kind feelings towards Oliver Cromwell. None at all. I see him as a ruthless upstart who has usurped the authority of the Crown. I am in my heart and in my soul, a Royalist—a loyal subject to his Majesty, King Charles II. There is no confusion in my heart. The religious question does not take precedence over my loyalty to the king. The only part of the parcel I am not in complete accord with is a return to a National Church. I do not want to see a whole gaggle of bishops take their place in the House of Lords either, if it is ever restored, that is. I don't like the intermingling of church and government."

"Then we have our common ground," cried Harry. "Our ideal is one and the same. We both want religious freedom."

"Yes, but not at the expense of the whole foundation of the country. Not at the expense of civil liberty. Not if we have to go under military rule to get it." She sighed. Then to my surprise I heard her silvery laugh peal out and her hosts joined in. "How am I going to do this?" she asked. "How have people managed any polite discourse? Are not the battle lines blatantly obvious?"

"You'd be right at home with the gentry. They're our most vociferous and open foes. One must remember how hard hit they have been, particularly in the purse. Hand in hand with them are the disinherited Episcopal clergy," added Harry. "I am a bit of a crossover. I have betrayed my class."

"Well, I don't see how we could ever return to being an Anglican nation now," said Mary. "I think you may have accomplished your mission there."

The butler came for me, dragging me away. Housed on a tiny cot with the other servants, packed in two stuffy rooms above the kitchen, I felt pretty downcast over my surroundings. No one asked me if I had anything to eat, so I was out of luck as far as dinner was concerned. As it turned out, I didn't miss much because the Vanes were in the habit of serving the staff tasteless slop. Homesick for the delicious food of the New World, as much as for my husband, and my own home where I was queen of the castle, I wondered what misguided adventure had led me to this pass. Then I happened to notice one young girl who was with child. I introduced myself to her and learned, as soon as she opened her mouth, that she was Irish. I asked her what she had heard of Cromwell's invasion. She crossed herself, fighting back tears.

"The whole of the population has been reduced by a third," she cried.

I dropped to my knees right there.

CHAPTER EIGHTEEN
The Emerald Isle

We did not become unwelcome guests in the Vane home as I had hoped. On the contrary, both Lady Frances and Harry seemed to hang on every word Mary said. Rounds of invitations came and she delighted all with her wit and charm. As the summer grew stifling and close, the Vane household made plans to move out to their estate called Belleau. Mary decided to accept their invitation and go with them. London had become suffocating, and both of us viewed it as nothing short of a filthy breeding ground for any number of ills. Buckets of waste were dumped out windows, landing on heads and walks, everywhere. We had no word from home.

Seeing to her estate proved tricky. I began to worry that her financial affairs would not be settled by the end of summer. A sneer curled on the lips of the lawyer who told her he would handle the sale of her properties and send the money along to the New World in due course. She trusted no one. I knew she would not consider leaving until she had the coin in hand. The lawyers planned to outlast her; all they had to do was bide their time until she couldn't stand the separation from her family any longer. I fully believe they intended to send her home empty-handed, and once the ship left the Plymouth wharf, they would proceed to line their own wicked pockets. I prodded her to bring Sir Harry Vane along, hoping that the sight of him would get them quaking in their boots. This strategy failed to inspire them to get on with the job. They remained stubbornly planted. I think that as far as they were concerned, they might as well give their malicious schemes a try as they were operating in the first year of Cromwell's England. A new seal had been forged. It had a map of England and Ireland on one side, and on the other, a picture of the House of Commons with the inscription "In the first year of freedom, by God's blessing restored."

We took a dusty journey out of London. As the carriage turned the last corner of the drive and the great house came into view, Mary remarked that she felt as if the upheaval of war had fallen into the mists of time. It did not take long for her to drift, body and spirit, into the peace of the English countryside. For her, the estate existed in its own little world: lovely, soft, and romantic. Guests arrived, and leisurely pursuits followed.

As for me, shoved in the back rooms again, desperate to get home, I tried my best not to complain. Hoping the estate would provide us with greens from the garden, at least, I learned to my disappointment that the fare was just as bad as it had been in London. Tasteless boiled mutton and broth, served up in a suffocating back room behind the kitchen, day after day, nearly had me lose my appetite altogether. Harry Vane never looked at me or talked to me at all. Fine, fine, but at least provide a decent meal, I wanted to say. Plus, the girl I met on the first night at their house, the one with the swollen belly, would not say who the father was, but the talk of the kitchen was that she carried the master's child.

Mary knew of my unhappiness, and to her credit, she kept assuring me that she would make good on her promise as soon as she could swing it. Once she found herself settled for the summer, she let me know the good news that she had made all the necessary arrangements for me to make the journey back to dear, old Ireland.

I traveled by carriage to Liverpool where I boarded ship and crossed the Irish Sea. Up on deck, when I caught the first glimpse of the blessed island, I couldn't stop the tears from flowing like a river. The land itself, more emerald than I even remembered, seemed to cry out to me in pain. As soon as I set foot in my village, I learned that seven of my nine brothers were now in heaven. Wee Owen, studying to be a priest, was saved by the cloth. Jimmy, still alive, had been seriously wounded. All the rest were killed in the fighting. Mother nearly fainted when she saw me. Her mind went blank for a second and I worried that in her grief she may have forgotten me. She cried and squeezed the breath out of me. She asked about Moira. Happy to report that she arrived safe and well, led to another great hug. I asked about me Da. Looking over my shoulder her face took on a waxy expression. Saying nothing, she took me by the hand. His bent head, slumped forward in the little chair, made me rush to him and kneel at his feet.

My mother whispered in my ear. "The grief is goin' to kill him."

That night everyone crowded into our cottage. Da held court much in the same way I'm doing now. I heard all the tales. Ireland tried to side with the king. Cromwell put a stop to all our efforts. Now the English were arriving in droves with laws drawn up by their sham Parliament, to dispossess us of our lands. Settling in huge numbers, Protestant, and a breed apart, it was clear to me that they would be with us forever. They considered us a conquered people.

In September, William Dyer joined us after his ship landed in Plymouth, England. With John Clarke and Nicholas Easton, he came to labor day and night on a new and better charter. He sent for me and though I was loath to leave, I had to go. My priest assured me that I was not cursed. Granted absolution, he truly convinced me that I would be blessed. Mother said she would pray for me day and night. She bid me to watch over Moira and to see to it that she landed a good husband. My Da took me as far as he could in a borrowed cart. His hands shook and his back bent nearly double. I told him all about Newport and the riches of the land and sea. I wanted to see that dreamy look in his eye. He was always a great one for adventure. At the end, he grabbed my hand and said, "You'll go far, my girleen. Keep your wits about you. Don't forget us."

I met up with Mary and William who had been traveling around England that summer, visiting relatives. We all headed back to the Vanes. I wondered how I would be able to stand the sight of Harry. As the architect of a war that took my seven brothers, I really wanted to run him through with a carving knife. Crammed into the shameless quarters and ordered about by their cooks and butlers, I knew I would be working non-stop on Mr. Dyer to get us all back home. Being next to nothing in their eyes drove me to distraction because I longed to find a way to boast of my fine house and husband. While I desired to shout this news day and night, I knew that would only make things worse for me in the servants' quarters. A glum passenger in that coach, I said but two words on the whole journey.

William started right in with, "We need to get back before we are too deep in winter." When Mary remained silent, he added, "Perhaps we can entice the Vanes to come over for a visit next summer."

"You misunderstand me as usual," she answered.

"I beg your pardon?"

"A visit from the Vanes, which is about as likely as a visit from the pope, is not the thing that will change my mind."

"Change your mind?"

Looking him full in the face she said, "I have decided to stay."

"What?"

"I have given this a great deal of thought. Obviously, it is not an easy decision. I hope you will come to support me," she added, as she turned to look out the window again.

William glared at me, but since I knew nothing of this, I merely shrugged.

"No, I will not support you. Not financially, nor in any other way. Your place is at home with the children. How could you even consider doing anything else?"

"Nothing is settled. My whole effort will be for naught if I leave now. I do not trust those lawyers. I cannot board ship knowing I am abandoning my estate. The children need financial security."

"No. The children need you, period. I need you. You don't know for certain these men will cheat us. You fear that they will, but you do not know this absolutely. If they behave in a way that is injudicious, we will not be without recourse entirely."

"Oh yes, we will. Look around you, William. The gentry are in the process of becoming impoverished. Cromwell is taxing them to death. It won't be long before we are not allowed to take anything out. We have to get it while we can."

"What of the children?"

"Don't ask me such a question, William. Do you think this is easy?"

"No. You are skin and bone, Mary. You are worrying yourself sick. I don't think any amount of money is worth it."

"It's all I have."

"What on earth are you saying? What the devil do you mean, it's all you have?"

"When I lived with the Barretts, my estate was the only thing that kept me from being treated as less than a servant. I don't know where it came from. I only know it was meant to be mine. Don't you see? It's all I have of who I am."

William brooded silently for a time. His anger and frustration showed plainly on his face. Mary said nothing further. We jounced along in silence, the narrow coach suddenly stifling to all of us, until William said, "What makes you speak like this?"

"I guess in the spiritual sense, for the first time since we left Boston, I feel more at home."

William's eyes widened. He looked as if he were about to say something, but then changed his mind. I had not met this new fellowship she found as it all happened while I was away. I only knew that Lady Frances was involved with a group who called themselves the Seekers, but I thought they were a harmless bunch of Protestants in search of some better preaching than they were finding in church. They had questions, Mary told me, and I did not give it much thought after that because as far as I was concerned, the whole lot of them were always riddled with doubt. What took place over the summer, I did not know. Harry desired to write a book about his daft notions of a second revelation, and I had learned that he sought Mary's help. He and Lady Frances fancied themselves as leaders of this group; they both wanted to be like Anne Hutchinson, but as far as I was concerned, neither were fit to lick her boots, God rest her soul.

"How do you plan to live?" asked William.

"I have enough from the sale of the sheep, if I'm careful. When my land here sells, I'll have more."

"That money does not belong to you."

"I believe it does."

"It belongs to our family. I can insure that not one penny of it falls into your hands," he added.

"Who do you think you are?"

"Your legal husband, that's who."

Mary raised her chin and said, "There are others who will support me."

"Who?"

"Friends."

"Oh for God's sake, Mary. Grow up. Get on with your duty. We have six children to house, dress, feed, and provide with a Christian upbringing. Six children who are not, I might add, languishing in the lap of luxury at Belleau."

"How can I give the children the guidance they need if I don't have a sense of who I am?"

"You will never know any more than you do at present. Casting about with a set of idle wanderers, in search of God knows what, won't accomplish anything."

"It would help if you showed some faith in me, some backing. William Hutchinson always backed his wife."

"There is a world of difference between you and Anne, Mary."

Now we were really in for it, I thought. She fired her most lethal look and I almost believed I might see him turn into a toad right there on the spot. I knew that if she had had a stone or a rock in her hand at that moment, she would surely have pitched it at him. I wanted to hit him myself because he had all but insured that she would remain. Why did he choose that moment to cut her off at the knees? Did he entertain the notion that he could undermine her confidence, make her meek and send her seeking shelter in his loving arms? If he did, she was right about him misunderstanding her, as usual. If I could turn back the clock to one moment that would have altered the course of her life, it would have been that moment in the coach when Mr. Dyer told her she was no Anne Hutchinson. What he said to her that day hurled her in a direction that she could not stop, even if she wanted to.

She knocked on the door and asked the driver to stop. Stepping down onto the dirt road, she set off on foot. William told the driver to go on.

"Let me out. I'll walk with her."

"Drive on," he said.

I wondered if I should jump.

Turning his dark gaze on me he said, "What has been going on over here?"

"Nothing is going on. I was as surprised by her announcement as you. I want to get home just as much as you do, probably more. The Vanes have all but kidnapped her for their own purposes, so if you happen to be looking for a culprit, I'd start there. Harry is the consummate politician, and you know how much Mary attracts attention. He is using her for his own gain. I'd start with him if I were you."

We both clammed up then and we got two miles down the road before he told the driver to stop. I made a move to get out. William put a hand over the door. "If you do not move your hand, Mr. Dyer, sir, I will have no choice but to bite it. Don't think I won't because I will. The roads are full of desperate men. You should be ashamed of yourself for leaving her alone out there, unprotected."

He sighed. "Very well. Go. God help the robber who runs into you."

"Mistress, " I cried breathlessly when I found her. "Is it true? Are you not goin' back?"

"I can't. Not yet. You can go if you want. I won't stop you. I'm not leaving without my money."

When at last we caught up with the coach, which had mercifully remained where I left it, thirst, hunger, and exhaustion led her to climb on board. Mr. Dyer had just been sitting there in a right funk while we were walking along the road. We bounced along in silence for the rest of the journey.

At Belleau, William Dyer marched up to Harry Vane and demanded to speak with him alone. After being ushered into the study, William stated his case, asking his friend to do whatever he could to discourage Mary from staying. Sir Harry tried his best to placate Mr. Dyer. Yet he knew of his wife's affection for Mary; he was aware of their plans as far as the Seekers were concerned, and was not very forthcoming.

In frustration, William turned to Roger Williams and Dr. Clarke, who were also visiting Belleau at the time. He implored them to talk her out of it. They reminded her of her duties, but were met with open hostility, both by Mary, and by their hostess. William carried through with his threat to see her go without financial support. My wages were lowered because he knew I would give them to Mary. I told him how much I had been sending my parents, and begged him not to cut them off too. He asked me for their address and promised not to leave them in the lurch.

Mr. Dyer sailed home with his partners, triumphant in the charter, but without his wife. He informed me that my passage had been taken care of and that I was free to cross at any time. He reminded me of my duty to the children, saying it should take precedence over my duty to Mary. I knew what he was saying was true, but I couldn't leave Mary alone.

After William's departure, Mary's resolve faded. Lady Frances and Sir Harry, both visibly pleased with her decision, did nothing to quell my rising anger. I wanted to tell them, flat out, that they could not keep her, but of course, I couldn't. They waxed on and on about how she had done the right thing. Their efforts only made her uneasy. I noticed she slept but a few hours a night.

Returning to London with the Vane entourage did little to change Mary's heavy mood. Invitations arrived, new clothes were required, and Mary's frustration over William's actions soured her every waking minute. She had to make do with alterations made to gowns no longer worn by Lady Frances. A new fashion for ladies that year took society by storm. The top of the bodice, now cut straight across, exposed the chest and shoulders. Mary's longing for a gown in this new shape grew quickly to the level of obsession. I suggested we just take the scissors to one of the cast-offs and hope for the best. Wouldn't you know it, she figured out how to reshape it entirely?

In late October, after we had gotten as far as hemming this dark red satin dress, Lady Frances entered her room. "I came to see what magic you have worked. That color will look beautiful on you, Mary."

"Yes. It is lovely. I've taken the trim off another one and changed it a bit. I hope you don't mind."

"Heavens no. Why should I?"

"Well, I cannot forget that these are your garments. I thought perhaps you might not want them changed."

"It is I who have changed. Each child born adds another inch. I couldn't wear them again even if I wanted to. Do whatever you like. I came in here because I have something to tell you. We will be knee deep in Royalist spies and sympathizers at the navy ball tonight."

"I thought they were ordered to stay twenty miles from London."

"Naturally, the ban is proving impossible to enforce. They are determined to see the House of Lords reestablished. Inroads and converts are made everywhere."

Mary gazed at the folds in her lap, saying nothing.

Lady Frances pressed on. "Knowing how you feel about this matter made me think I should warn you. Stay on guard. These people will stop at nothing."

"You are speaking of our countrymen. They are not a breed apart," snapped Mary.

"The aristocracy has always viewed itself as a breed apart. They have remained consistently ruthless. Divest yourself of false illusions regarding these people, Mary."

"I fail to see Oliver Cromwell as a saint, Lady Frances. I don't see the soldiers stationed on every corner a Godsend either."

"I don't expect you to agree with me, or to change your opinion. I am only warning you to keep your eyes open. I would not be very happy to learn I have a Royalist spy under my roof."

"Surely you do not believe I could be capable of such a thing?"

"Not as you are now, no. However, knowing how you feel about the monarchy and seeing what this war has done to people has affected my trust."

"Would you rather I not attend this ball then?"

"No, not at all. Do not misunderstand my intent. I'll be interested to hear how much you pick up. So will Harry. We don't want you to be stolen away from us, that's all," she added.

With a rueful smile Mary said, "I am not at all diplomatic enough for intrigue. I would be a thorn in either side, I'm sure."

Later that evening, when they returned home, I could see plainly on Mary's face something had happened.

She grabbed my hand and ushered me to her room where she shut the door. "I met him. I talked to him."

"Who?"

"My father! William Seymour. I'd been keeping to my usual task of answering questions about the New World, when I spotted this handsome man with thick, iron gray hair. Drawn to him right away, I pinned Lady Frances and asked who he was. When she told me, I nearly fainted. So I said, 'Can you introduce me? I think he is a family friend.' Then Harry took me over and within seconds I found myself staring right into the face of my father."

"Are you sure, Mary?"

"Yes, there is no mistaking the resemblance."

"What did you say to him?"

"I didn't waste a second. I just put it to him immediately and asked him if he had once been married to Lady Arabella Stuart."

"You didn't!"

"I did! Who knows if I'll ever get another chance?"

"What did he do? Was he horrified?"

"His eyes turned very cold. 'Why do you ask me such a question?' he said. I swear I felt as if he were looking right through me. Never in my life have I seen such a penetrating gaze. So I asked him to forgive my boldness and then I carried on saying I was a very curious creature and that I had only wondered if he were the same William Seymour. He told me he was, very icily, I might add. I thought I wasn't going to be able to breathe. I shook like a leaf, Irene. He stared off over my shoulder, giving me every indication that he didn't want to discuss the subject. I carried on anyway, and with the nerve of a canal horse, I asked him if he didn't agree that she had been treated very unfairly. He answered saying that they were both young and foolish. He was about to turn away, so I put my hand on his sleeve to stop him and asked if they'd had a baby. 'What the devil are you asking me these questions for, woman?' he said. 'What possible business is this of yours?' I felt the inside of my mouth turn to powder. I looked at him pleadingly, begging him to recognize me. There was a half second where I thought I detected a flicker of surprise, but it was gone in a flash. So I went on to tell him that my guardian, a woman named Mary Dyer, same as myself, placed me with the Barrett family as their ward. When she died, she whispered his name, so naturally, I thought there might be some connection. My nerve started to fail me then and I could feel my lip quivering. Then he decided to put a stop to this whole business and said, 'Lady Arabella lost her wits in the tower. Rumors of a baby came as a result of her madness. She starved herself to death. Is your curiosity satisfied now?' With that he turned and walked away."

"Holy Moses. What a brave woman you are, mistress. I cannot believe the risk you took."

"I had to. Who knows if I'll ever get another chance?"

"And what do you make of his reaction?"

"I don't know. He looked at me in horror. Yet, I know what I saw. He just couldn't bring himself to go any further."

My eyes darted back and forth wondering what I should say, and what this news was going to do to her. My goal was pretty standard. If we could focus on the good and throw away the bad, I thought we might be able to stave off disaster. The path was fraught with peril. "But if there was a baby, he had to deny it," I told her. "He would have died in the Tower too, and the child would have had no chance of survival. None. He must have made up his mind to deny her, you maybe, altogether."

Mary sat cross-legged on her bed holding a looking glass to her face. Picturing her black hair gray, she sat there telling herself over and over, that he was her father, that she had not been wrong, that the resemblance was uncanny. "What of my mother? Was what he said true? Mad? Starved herself to death?"

"They always say that about women. Maybe the jailer was given orders not to tend her if she grew ill. Maybe they told him not to feed her. It wouldn't be the first time a woman received such a fate for being disobedient."

"Why is it so hard for us, Irene?"

"Because they get away with it. Even on slave plantations the white masters deny their offspring. What will you do now? Will you do anything more?"

"The best thing to do at this point," she answered, "is to leave it where it lies. I have a father, but he does not want me. Maybe he never wanted me. Maybe he arranged for me to be kept with the Barretts for that reason. You know, Irene, even if that were true, it's better than remaining forever in the dark. I feel like I have seen some kind of origin. It gives me an inkling of who I am. He is quite something, obviously. That in and of itself is better than nothing. This truth will never set me free anywhere, except deep within myself. I do have a duty to protect my estate, to pass it on to my children unharmed. That much I do know."

During the next weeks, Mary fell ill. A fever, which caught most of London in its grip, found its way into the Vane household. Their children took sick first. After days of nursing them, Mary collapsed and had to be confined to her room. During the days of tossing and turning, sleepless nights, and wild dreams, she cried for William and the children. The first day she felt well enough to get up, she confessed to Lady Frances that she felt bad about staying.

"You are run down, Mary, that's all. Once your strength returns, you can resume where you left off."

"And where was that?"

"Settling your estate."

"What success will I have? People like me will be in rags soon. I am sorry. I don't mean to insult you or your husband, but the writing is on the wall. What hope do I have?"

"You said you felt at home with us."

"This is not my home. I belong with my family, not with yours. You have been very kind— too kind. I feel as if I have overstepped the bounds."

"Because you were ill?"

"Yes, partly, but I cannot forget that I am here without my husband's blessing. I should make arrangements to return."

"You have to stay the winter. You can't sail now. You must wait till spring. Besides, I need to ask you a favor."

"What would that be then?"

"After you have fully recovered and are well enough, would you consider traveling up to Cumbria to meet George Fox?"

"Why?"

We were all walking in the upstairs hall when this came up. Too rainy and miserable to think of taking a turn outside, we had been trying to do the same indoors. I felt like sticking my foot out and tripping

Lady Frances. I think I might have, if the damage hadn't already been done. Just when we were getting somewhere, she had to come up with this plan. Where would this hairbrained expedition lead? Not to Plymouth and to a ship home.

"I heard he has taken up with Margaret Fell of Swarthmore Hall. Her husband is Judge Fell. I could arrange an introduction. I would love to go myself, but I can't. You are the only person I could trust to give me a fair accounting of the man. Would you consider doing this before you go? Strange things have happened to people around him."

"What kind of strange things?"

"The whole Fell household was turned on its ear. Fox wandered in one day when their parish priest was over visiting. The two men fell into a vehement argument. When Margaret arrived home, her daughter came running up to report that a stranger had gotten into a fight with their pastor. Margaret rushed to her clergyman's defense, but soon found herself agreeing with Mr. Fox. She invited him to church the next Sunday. He asked if the service was for hireling priests only and then proceeded to turn the place upside down. Within days, the whole household, even the servants, were converted. Judge Fell was stopped on his way home and told that his family had been bewitched. Mr. Fox has gathered a great following in the north. His sect is called Quakers now."

"Odd title."

"Children of the Light changed their name to the Religious Society of Friends. The group has grown in leaps and bounds. Quaker is a derogatory name given to them because some are so moved by their service, or this man's preaching, that they shake."

"So you are counting on my skepticism."

"Yes, that and your strength and wisdom. You are the right person to go."

"How is it that we have not heard more about him? Why hasn't he come here?"

"He spent the whole of last year in a jail in Derby."

"Why?"

"He was arrested for blasphemous opinions. Then he refused to join Cromwell's army and was jailed for another six months."

"Is he a Royalist?"

"Good heavens no. He has not made any political declarations."

"How would I get there?" asked Mary.

"By coach. You will have to ride the last part and you will have to be very careful. Go by way of Ulverston. Do not attempt the shorter route. One cannot reach Swarthmore Hall until the tide is out. The shifting sands of Morecombe Bay present a great hazard. You seem very thoughtful. No doubt you'll require some time to think this over."

"The fare would present an obstacle."

"It will be paid by the Seekers. You will report to us upon your return. You may consider yourself hired."

"Is this some special exception in my case?"

Lady Frances raised a hand to stop her. "No, no, no. We have been looking for someone to send."

"I'm not sure if I believe you. I would need to take Irene."

"Naturally. You could come back and return home in the spring if you like. It wouldn't be safe to sail in your present state, Mary. We have to fatten you up first. Any illness befalling you at sea could be fatal in your present condition. You are not strong enough yet."

"I am curious to meet this man. Perhaps I need to get out of London. I never seem to do very well here. Too many memories." With that, she excused herself and we returned to her room.

CHAPTER NINETEEN
Swarthmore Hall

The trip took five days. Leaving London by coach, we stopped at Oxford, Armscote, Warwick, Birmingham, Lichfield, Chester, Liverpool, and finally Pendle Hill. After a good night's sleep at the inn at Lancaster, we sought information from the innkeeper regarding the ride across Morecomb Bay.

"It must be done at low tide," he said, " but don't let the look of the sands deceive ye, now mind. The ground can look as firm as rock. Yet there are those that have lost their footing. Many a horse has gone down, before he knew what hit him. And if ye go around, that would be another day's journey."

"What is the best way to pull out a horse if it gets stuck?"

"Ye shall grab the reins and pull then. You have to be very stubborn about it. It may take a while, now mind. Don't give up, or let the horse rest. The only hope ye've got is to become a mule and pull that creature out. Sometimes, the sand gives way. Other times, it takes what it wants."

"How long would it take to sink?"

"Can happen quick as a wind picking up on a still day. Or can take as long as a dull sermon. There is no telling. It's uncertain stuff, that sand. Very uncertain indeed. There was a man, now mind ye, who went straight across at high tide. They say his horse flew."

"Who was that?"

"George Fox. Went to Swarthmore Hall, he did, home of Judge Fell, if ye please, and bewitched every woman under his roof."

Mary smiled, pulled on her gloves, and thanked him. We hired two horses. She mounted a lovely mare, whereas mine had the look of a dumb, thick plug. We took our time approaching the bay, eating a good meal for once in Cartmel, and then looking around the town before heading slowly out to the bay. Seeing the lay of the land, she questioned the sense of riding clear around the estuary. How maddening to go miles one way, and then back up the other side when a quick dash across could make short work of the problem. Low tide must be the answer, she concluded.

"I don't want to risk it," I declared. I had known her long enough to foresee we'd be in this pickle. When Lady Frances said, don't ride across the sands, I wished right away she would have found a better choice of words. Mary was so bold about everything, and she simply could not, would not, be told she couldn't do something. I was beginning to think that maybe she was William Seymour's daughter after all, because he was told he couldn't marry Lady Arabella and look what happened to them.

"But surely those who sunk in simply misjudged the tide. I want to get this journey over with. George Fox rode at high tide and made it. Reports of the shifting sands are most likely exaggerated," she added.

So we chanced it, in spite of my misgivings. Proceeding slowly and cautiously, without incident, Mary got three quarters of the way across, when she felt her horse crumble below her. Getting one foot down in the mushy sand, she managed to stand, grab the bridle and pull the reins over the mare's head.

"Easy, girl," she cooed, as she began to tug. "Stay back, Irene," she ordered me. "Don't come any closer."

I watched helplessly as her horse thrashed, struggled for firm footing, but then sank in deeper with every move. Then Mary felt her own feet going down. She looked the horse in the eye and said, "Come on, girl, let me pull you. I'll get you out."

"I can get up close and throw a rope, mistress."

"No," she barked. "I won't allow it."

With that she proceeded to pull and pull with all her might. As she continued to sink, she kept stepping up and forward, only to feel her feet give way. When she sank in up to her knees and the horse even deeper, I decided I had seen enough. I would not stand by and watch her die. Within seconds my calm resolve turned to near panic, as my horse faltered too. I got off and pulled him.

"I told you this would happen," she cried. "Why didn't you obey me?"

"For the same reason you didn't listen to me! I cannot sit there and watch you go under."

"Why didn't we go by way of Ulverston?" she yelled, getting right mad now and yanking on the reins. "God!" she screamed. "God help me." Not with a plaintive cry, but a desperate one, she cursed her fate, cursed the fact that we were alone in this predicament, cursed the Vanes for being so selfish as to send her off alone, knowing the risks. She cursed herself most of all for allowing them to influence her, cursed herself for not following William. It all came out in a torrent.

I tried to cheer her up by saying, "I'm sure you've forgotten someone. You left out Cromwell. If you want to curse someone, curse him. He deserves it more than Mr. Dyer does."

My attempt at jollying her along did nothing. Her eyes started casting about in true fear. "Where is God? Where is your God now, Irene?"

By this time, I was up to my knees. Indulging in some Protestant debate, as to the exact location of God, did not appeal to me in the slightest. Not seeing any way out now, I felt it was a certainty that we were both goin' to die and be buried in Morecomb Bay. Smothered with a mouth full of sand, in a matter of minutes, was what this expedition had come to. "Hail Mary, full of Grace. The Lord is with thee. Blessed art thou among women, and blessed is the fruit of they womb, Jesus. Holy Mary, Mother of God," I whimpered. "Pray for us sinners now and at the hour of our death." I cried. Then the words "Ye've got to be a mule and pull the creature out" came back to me. It was as if I heard them. "Pull yourself together," I shouted. "Pray be calm. Be a mule. Be stubborn."

Wouldn't you know it, but it turned out that we were both obstinate enough to get the job done. I concentrated all my efforts on pulling one of my legs up. I thought my boot might come off my foot, but at last I got it dislodged. Then I threw my leg forward until it landed on hard sand. I felt sure I could pull myself out, if only I could grab a hand, a limb, a branch, a rope—anything. In vain, I clutched the sand that just slipped through my fingers. My leg still stuck in the sand, now on such an angle, pulling it out could well break the ankle. So be it, I concluded. Animals chew off their paws to get out of traps. When my forearms were submerged, I gained a bit of leverage, and with every ounce of strength that I had, I managed to free my leg. Once out, I thrashed my horse and pulled the reins. I went at the poor beast as if possessed. I heard the mud give way. The horse got his front legs out, but the rest of him with that great bulk and weight remained lodged. A sound came out of me that was not even human. Every dead ancestor I ever had, and the will of my seven brothers, all seemed to find a place in my throat. I shrieked this unearthly cry, just like the banshee. The terrified horse went bounding forward, thrashing at first, but then standing free! I grabbed the reins and mounted in one motion, how, I still do not know. The horse would have run till it dropped dead, it was so afraid of me. We pranced around in a circle where the sand was firm.

"Go," yelled Mary. "Save yourself."

I got hold of a good hemp rope from the saddlebag and tossed it to her. Tying it around her waist, she gave me the signal to drive my horse forward. I could hear Mary crying in pain, but I kept digging my heels into the ribs of the poor beast until I heard the words I wanted to hear.

"I'm out," she yelled "Stop, I'm out."

There was nothing we could do for her horse, but stand there and watch the poor thing die. We shivered from the shock. Doubling up on my mount, which by now I had gained a newfound respect for, we carried on at a timid walk. I don't think either of us breathed until we got off the sinister, shivering sands.

When at last we reached the other side, we carried on to our destination slowly, keeping the horse at an unruffled pace. Off in the distance, we could see the neat town of Ulverston. After making a few inquiries, we found the road to Swarthmore Hall. As we got to the top of a hill, we found ourselves at a nice little spot with a creek running through. We came to a halt and dismounted. With our destination now in plain sight, we gave the horse the chance to slurp up large drafts of water.

Dipping a bit of linen in the creek, Mary washed her face and neck before slaking her own thirst. I did the same. "Sweet, cool and pure. Almost as good as New England, but not quite." She gazed up towards the Hall.

With its bay window climbing three stories, the handsome building gave off an air of respectability. "The occupants of such an establishment would not seem likely to fall prey to bewitchment by a clever stranger," I said.

Mary led our surviving horse up the lane. By the stone wall, we came across a man wearing a leather apron and an old hat, digging in the garden. Thinking he must be the gardener, she asked him if he would be so kind as to direct us to Judge Fell. He laughed.

"That would be me," he said. Then he explained that he had been in the process of planting a tree, to celebrate the birth of his seventh daughter.

After introducing ourselves and describing our purpose, the judge asked her casual questions about Sir Harry Vane. Then he showed us to the door and called for one of his girls to get us settled.

We met Margaret Fell by the great window, with her babe in arms. Something of an instant friendliness passed between them, as Mary raved over the view.

"Oh Good heavens, how marvelous you are to come all this way. I can't imagine how you managed alone. Did you have any trouble getting a horse? Well, of course, you're here now, aren't you? And been in the New World and back again? How is Lady Frances? You must tell me all about the Seekers. Judge Fell will want to hear about Parliament. My girls simply must hear about your adventures, and my boys want to ask you about the crossing. We've been looking forward to your visit. Wherever did you get that lovely jacket? Had to be London. We're terribly plain and countrified here."

"I must apologize for my appearance. I have been on the road for days and I lost my horse to the sands," said Mary.

"What am I doing? What am I thinking of? Where are my manners? Girls, why didn't you stop me? We have not given you any time to settle in! I do apologize, Mistress Dyer. I will see that you are shown to your room. Henry! Thee must take Mistress Dyer to her room."

"Yes, ma'am."

"Have Betsey bring her some hot water, please. I do hope you'll be comfortable here. Swarthmore is not Belleau, but it is a dear old place."

"It's lovely. This view must surely be one of the finest in England. You cannot imagine how glad we are to be here."

I nodded in agreement, thinking privately that only the heavenly hosts knew how true her words were.

Mary turned her head back to our hostess, as we got ready to leave, and said, "I'll see you at dinner then?"

"Indeed. Or come down before if you are ready. I'll be camped out here by the fire. Join me whenever you wish."

To my great surprise, and delight, I was not sent off to the servants quarters, but instead was given a small bed in Mary's room. Invited to dine with all of them, I was beginning to think that I might have been bewitched already.

At dinner that night, we heard all about George Fox from the Fell girls and from Margaret, herself. They all took after their mother, boisterous, gregarious, and generous, both with their feelings and with their praise. In spite of all the good cheer, I found my suspicions growing. The girls gushed on at great length about how he told them they could develop their gifts and talents well beyond their dreams. Judge Fell's business kept him occupied elsewhere that night, so we did not have the privilege of his opinion.

"I spent my entire life looking to the Bible and studying the Bible as if the key were in the learning," said Mistress Fell. "He told me that we couldn't find the living presence through books or learning, or history, or the clergy, or any other way, but by experience. This was a completely new way of worship for me."

Mary and I both looked at each other. This woman could have been quoting Anne Hutchinson verbatim.

So Mary asked, "Revelation does not come to everyone. What is the method?"

"Sitting quietly and going within. Maybe some of it rubs off from George Fox. Who knows? I only know that if I had not met him, I would have gone on fulfilling my duties, but remaining virtually in the dark. After meeting him, I know what he says to be true. I know it from experience."

"And your husband?"

"He is not unconvinced, no matter what he might say. He leaves his study door ajar when we have meetings here. He says he is too old to take on new habits, but I feel he is converted in his own way."

"How does George Fox support himself?" asked Mary.

"What a strange question? I have no idea."

"He does not work for his daily bread?"

"No. He spends most of his time traveling. He has never asked for any assistance, if that is what you are getting at."

"Forgive me," Mary said quickly, with a hand extending to Mistress Fell's arm. "I heard of him turning up at all these different places and I wondered how he managed the finance."

"It never occurred to me to ask," said Margaret. "I'm sure he will be happy to tell you if you want to know."

"I didn't mean to be rude. I suppose it is one of the cruder aspects of living in the New World. Lots of people cross the ocean in some sort of disguise and stay that way until they are unmasked."

"Are you saying he could be a wealthy man masquerading as a weaver's son?"

"No. I don't know what I'm saying. I will have to meet the man myself, obviously. I can see he has left a profound mark on you."

"He will on you too, Mary. He will. You may doubt me now, but mark my words, this man will change your life."

"He won't address you in the familiar," said one of the girls. "Did you tell her that, Mother? You will think he has mistaken you for a servant."

"He sees everyone as equals and addresses them as such," added Margaret.

"Then why not simply address servants in the familiar?"

"When he addresses judges and priests and magistrates in the same speech commonly reserved for servants, it has a more pronounced effect. I think that's why he does it. Of course you could ask him."

After dinner, we begged to retire early. The combination of the journey, coupled with the struggle on the sands, in short, the whole incredible day, had left us exhausted. Mary expressed doubts about our mission. She told me she feared this meeting with Fox was going to be very awkward. She declared to me that night that she simply would not be bowled over; she did not want the Fells to be disappointed, but she feared they would not be happy with her reaction. In the first place, she told me, there had been nothing said by Margaret that she hadn't first heard from Anne. She suspected Fox might be a bit of a rake, taking advantage of these good people.

"Lady Frances will be disappointed too. Everyone who wants fundamental change sees the need for someone to emerge as a leader. Surely this man is not the one. I'm going to ask the question about money. I hope it doesn't result in bad feeling all round. I like the Fells, and would like to consider them friends, but my first obligation is to the truth. I am determined to ferret it out."

"He's no goin' to convert me," I stated. "If he does try something with you, he'll not get you. Not over my dead body. I may have to drag you out of here the same way I did in Morecomb Bay."

A week went by before we had the chance to meet the famous Mr. Fox. From an upstairs window, Mary saw him come up the lane on a good horse. She called me over so we could have a good look at him. He wore his hair long and shaggy. I knew at once, by that first glance, that there was no messing with this man. I heard he had been beaten and jailed many times, but he certainly did not look any the worse for wear.

I would have bet he was about as tough as an old shoe. Going hand in hand with his strength and resolve, I noticed a warm face; I could see how he gained so much trust. You would either fear or love a man like him, but you would never change him. So I summed it all up by saying, "He doesn't look like a rake."

Mary had not put a cap on her head that morning, as we had been busy washing and starching them. When she heard Margaret's booming voice, she picked up one nearest at hand, but found it was still damp. Deciding to leave it off, she hoped it would not be noticed. We had washed her hair that morning and dressed it plainly in a bun.

We expected him to make some gallant move or statement, but he did neither. He was introduced to us, but said very little. We noticed his leather breeches. His shirt, very fine, spotlessly clean, and made from good linen, gave him the look of a man who had come from solid English stock.

Mary began by asking, "How is it that you have arrived so unscathed?"

"Did thee expect to see me in tar and feathers?"

She threw back her head and laughed. "No. I was so much more disheveled after my ride across the sands."

"My horse seems to know the way well enough."

"Come in by the fire," announced Margaret. "I will see that you get something to eat."

"No," he protested, putting up his hand. "I thank thee, but I have been well fed this morning."

"He eats like a bird," she added to Mary. "Did you know that Mary asked a very interesting question? She wants to know how you finance all your journeys."

"I am sorry, Mistress Fell has put my question to you so bluntly. I am here at the behest of the Seekers who have a great interest in your work. It behooves me to ask questions, however curt, so that I may take back an accurate picture."

He looked at her, but said nothing.

Margaret, accustomed to this behavior, simply carried on, "Mary comes from the New World. She lived in Boston. They were banished with Anne Hutchinson. She lives in Newport now. Can you believe she raised a flock of sheep? All on her own. You kept sheep too, didn't you?"

"Yes. I did tend sheep."

Mary asked, "Did you not find it peaceful?"

"Did thee?"

"Yes, actually I did," she answered. "Their gentle ways were a great comfort to me at times. I sold them off before I left. Sometimes I dream I am back in the pasture with them."

"Will thee keep a flock again?"

"I don't know. I don't know what I'll do when I get back."

"Isn't there a new daughter in this house?" he asked, turning to Margaret. "May I see her?"

"Yes, yes. I'll go and get her."

Mary tried to think of things to say, but found she was at a loss for words. She looked at me for help.

"I'm Roman Catholic," I divulged. If Mary was exasperated with me, she did not show it.

He smiled, but did not say a word. Totally comfortable in the silence, there seemed to be no such thing to Mr. Fox as an embarrassing lull in conversation. Mary and I were very grateful to Mistress Fell when she returned with the baby.

That night in our room we were both confused. Poised to defend Mary against his efforts of persuasion, I felt a bit helpless. So far, he had made no move to win her over. In fact, he didn't even seem the slightest bit interested.

The next morning, we were told that a meeting for worship would take place at Swarthmore.

"Don't expect him to preach," we heard.

I started to head upstairs. Mary grabbed my arm. We were standing in the hall. "Please come with me," she begged. "I want you to hear what he says."

Curiosity got the better of me, so I joined her. Chairs, set up in the large room off the hall, seemed harmless enough. We sat quietly waiting for him to start. When nothing happened, we peeked around the room at the faces of the servants seemingly deep in prayer. The silence continued. Some shuffling of feet and the odd cough disrupted the quiet, but no words were spoken. I got antsy and could not help but think of all the chores I had to tackle that day. I had an uncomfortable feeling in the pit of my stomach. I thought Mary might have been going through the same agitation as she folded her arms across her front and tried to shift in her chair without making any noise. Every once in a while she opened one eye slightly, and looked around. No one paid any mind.

Then George Fox stood.

Finally we are getting somewhere, I thought.

He paused before speaking. "Nothing that was ever made was not made by God."

That was it. He sat back down and the silence resumed. Mary's cheeks, however, burned bright red.

Afterward, she asked him why he chose those words, why he had said what he said. To her frustration, he did not reply.

Then she said, "I thought you were a man with answers."

He smiled. "Then thee must think of me as a man with questions."

"You have doubts?"

"Doubts, despair, troughs, dark passages, I have known these aplenty."

Looking slightly agitated, she proceeded. "Where do you find comfort when you suffer?"

"When I myself was in the deep, shut up under all, I could not believe that I should ever overcome; my troubles, my sorrows, my temptations were so great that I thought many times I should have despaired. But when Christ opened to me that he was tempted by the same devil, and overcame him and bruised his head, and that through Him and His power, light, grace, and Spirit, I should overcome also, I had confidence in Him; so He it was that opened me when I was shut up or had no faith. He gave me his spirit and grace which I found sufficient in the deeps and in the weakness."

"The Lord does not come to me!" she blurted.

They stared at one another then. She waited for him to say something, but he didn't utter a word.

"Could we talk about this some time?" she requested.

"We will go into the orchard," he said.

She motioned for me to follow. They sat on a small bench under a tree. I made myself comfortable on the grass, a few feet away. Mary told him about Anne's meeting, of the days in Boston, of the journey to Pocasset and Anne's death. She relayed her conversations with the Indian brave. Stating that she had all but given up hope of finding what she had sought for so long, she asked him if he could tell her what he had said to Margaret because Margaret had become so convinced. "What did you say to her when you first arrived? Can you remember? Can you tell me what you told her?"

"When I arrived here, I came upon Lampitt, a priest. He talked of high notions of perfection. He said he was above John; and made as though he knew all things. But that crooked and rough nature stood in him, and the mountain of sin and corruption. The way was not prepared in him for the Lord. I told him that now he could see a thief, and join hand in hand with him, but he could not preach Moses, nor the prophets, nor John, nor Christ, except he were in the same spirit that they were in."

Mary's mouth fell open. "That is exactly what Anne Hutchinson said to the ministers of Boston! She said they could preach no more than they knew. Didn't she, Irene?"

"Aye, she did indeed."

"I think we tried to do the same thing in Boston. We were met with such opposition and then of course we were driven out. After that, we went back to the old way, as you say, going to church, hearing the sermon, but feeling cut off."

"Yet the way has been prepared," he stated.

Mary smiled. "I suppose it has. In fact, perhaps a field has never been so well plowed as this one. Only these openings you speak of have not yet come to me."

"The first step to peace is to stand still in the Light and by the same Light thee might see Christ that died for thee to be thy Redeemer and Savior, and thy way to God."

"Will you pray for me?" begged Mary, almost in a whisper. "I get so tired," she added, but stopped as he immediately bowed his head. I could tell that Mary was loath to take her eyes off him, but she dropped her head in prayer instead. As she took a deep breath, I could see her body relax. She remained very still beside him.

I slipped away into the orchard.

Mary told me later that in time she grew quite sleepy; feeling as if she could slide right off the bench and onto the grass. She did not remember how long they sat together there. She sank into an underwater feeling, describing it as peaceful and calm. There was no trouble in that gentle state, she said: no worry, no doubts, no fears; it was as if she sat in a period of nothing, which did not need to be filled up; no thoughts occurred to her as to how to fill it up; the fullness was there in the blankness. That's how she explained it. There she remained, until she felt his hand on her shoulder. She opened her eyes to see him stand.

"Where are you going?"

"It has been revealed that I must walk in the fields," he answered. As she watched him walk away, she moved to the grass where she lay down on her back and gazed up at the sky. The light was soft and pale all around her. Her mind went all the way back to the moment Anne placed the newborn Samuel in her arms. The baby radiated a kind of glory he brought with him from the other world. His breath on her face felt as gentle as the mist on a New England pond. The pure hand of God was everywhere, she thought, in everything. Then the words "Nothing that was ever made was not made by God" returned to her thoughts.

That evening, in our room, Mary confessed to me that maybe George Fox could be the man to heal England's troubles after all. "What if Cromwell were to meet him?"

I spat out the window. "It wasn't anything Fox did, though, mistress," I told her. "What you are describing is what I would call an epiphany. It was you feeling the power. It wasn't him."

"No, but Margaret said that she never felt it till she met him. His method is the key here, Irene. He has a method that works."

Our room had a lovely warm glow from the oak paneling and the soft light filtering through ivy. Mary spread out across the four-poster bed. She never looked lovelier. I couldn't find any words to talk to her of this peace she had found. Bless her, I recalled thinking; bless the Fells, and bless Mr. Fox too, I thought. From my perspective, it was as if she had found a kind of absolution too.

I did nothing. I let it all happen.

I still don't know whether that was right or wrong.

We remained on at Swarthmore through the summer. Lady Frances sent word twice, but Mary made no move to leave. It was her wish to linger as long as she could in the company of the man simply known as Fox. Eden, or the Paradise we were all looking for in Boston, seemed to lie around him in a celestial cloud. He snatched heaven and brought it down with him, she told me. She insisted she could see it surrounding him and emanating from his skin, from his hair, from his eyes. When she sat with him in meeting, she told me she could feel it; she felt the warm glow, the light, the peace, and the bliss. Why would she want to veer anywhere from this joy? Swarthmore had become her hallowed home.

We took trips to the beach and to the shores of beautiful Lake Windermere. The loveliness of our surroundings gave us all comfort. I was the only one who wanted to leave.

"The rest of the country needs to know about this," she announced one day. "England first and then New England. What the Puritans sought, I've found. Anne knew they were all off course."

"What are you thinking, mistress? Your children need you. We have to get home."

"I understand," she said. "Did you know that Fox is absolutely convinced that women can throw off all yokes around their necks?"

"You can't throw off children! They are God's greatest gift, a blessing He has yet to bestow on me, I might add, and never will as long as I have an ocean between myself and my husband." She got quiet, so I started to worry. "We are goin' back in the spring, aren't we? I told Sean I'd be back in September."

"I know."

So I pushed for us to return to London at least. I reminded her that we were on this mission at the behest of the Seekers who wanted their report. We began the ride back to London with me full of high spirits and hope.

We got as far as Lancaster, where we stopped for a bite to eat. In the tavern, we heard the news of a terrible commotion in Ulverston, resulting in the arrest of George Fox. She mounted her horse at once and I followed, heading straight back to Swarthmore. Waiting for the tide at Morecomb Bay, she paced back and forth, standing on one foot, then the other. Part of her wanted to bolt, I know, but she understood that I would tie her to a tree before I'd tempt my Maker twice.

By the time we finally landed back at Swarthmore, night edged around the house. By the great window, we found a bruised and limping Fox, hobbling towards Margaret Fell. One look at his face and Mary burst into tears. "Tell me what happened," she cried, sinking down to the floor by his knee.

He began slowly. "I was moved to go to the steeple-house at Ulverston, where there were an abundance of professors, priests, and people. I went near Priest Lampitt, who was blustering on in his preaching. John Sawrey, the justice, came to me and said that if I would speak according to the Scriptures, I should speak. I told him I could speak according to the Scriptures and bring the Scriptures to prove what I had to say; for I had something to speak to Lampitt and to them."

Mary nodded, moving to hold his hands. Seeing that they were black and blue, she only stroked his leg instead.

"The people were quiet and heard me gladly, till this Justice Sawrey incensed them against me and set on them to hale, beat, and bruise me. The people, in a rage, fell on me in the steeple-house, before his face, knocked me down, kicked me and trampled me."

"Did you try to get away?"

"No. Some tumbled over their seats for fear. At last he came and took me from the people, led me out of the steeple-house, and put me into the hands of the constables, bidding them to whip me, and put me out of the town. They led me about a quarter of a mile, some taking hold by my collar, some by my arms and shoulders and they shook and dragged me along. Blood ran down from several, and Henry Fell, running after me to see what they would do with me, they threw him in a ditch of water, some of them crying 'knock the teeth out of his head.'"

"Where did they take you?"

"When they haled me to the common, with a multitude following, the constables and some other officers gave me some blows over my back with their willow rods, and thrust me among the crowd, who having furnished themselves with staves, hedge stakes, or holly bushes, fell upon me and beat me on my head, my arms, and shoulders till they had deprived me of sense, so that I fell down upon the wet common."

"They could have killed you," cried Margaret.

"When I recovered again and saw myself lying in the watery common and the people standing about me, I lay still a little while and the power of the Lord sprang through me, and the eternal refreshing revived me so that I stood up again and in the strengthening power of the eternal God and stretching out my arms to them, I said, with a loud voice, 'Strike again; here are my arms, my head, my cheeks.'"

At this Mary wept, bringing her dress to her face.

"There was in that company a professor, but a rude fellow, who with his walking rule-staff gave me a blow with all his might just over the back of my hand, as it was stretched out; with which blow my hand was so bruised, and my arm so benumbed, that I could not draw it to me again. Some of the people cried, 'He hath spoiled his hand for ever having the use of it any more.' But I looked at it in the love of God, for I was in the love of God to all who persecuted me, and after awhile the Lord's power sprang through me again and through my hand and arm, so that I recovered strength in my hand and arm in the sight of them all."

"A miracle then," said Mary. "This won't be the last time this kind of reaction is provoked."

"No," he said sadly.

Mary studied him as he sat by the fire. His face was swollen, black and blue. She knew that he suffered blows before. She wondered if it would break him eventually—if men would succeed in beating the light right out of him, turning him bitter.

She put her hand very softly on top of his. She began, "In a small way, I know what this feels like. I had a baby back in Boston, a baby who did not live. I was told she was very misshapen, although I never saw her myself. Later, the word went around that I had given birth to a monster. They dug up the grave and said my baby had horns and hooves. I remember well, the jeering looks, the mean stares, and the shouts from rude people. I lived in terror that they would kill me for bringing evil to the settlement. We were driven out, but I never felt safe. I have lived in fear till now. I know that if we try to bring this message to the people, we will be met with more of the same. How will I keep from running in cowardice? How do you go into market places and steeple houses knowing you will be met with this horror?"

"The power of the Lord is over all," he affirmed. "The power of the Lord is over all."

We woke up the next morning to the smell of fresh rain on wet grass. As the events of the night before came back, Mary sat up in bed wondering what to do next. She told me then that we would not be leaving. "Not with Fox so badly bruised," she added.

"The Vanes will send someone to fetch us if we don't return soon."

"Well, let them," she said, getting out of bed. "I'll explain it all eventually, but not now. Not when Fox is hurt. Not when the town is so riled up. Not when Lampitt has proved himself such an enemy. I cannot get over how a priest could misperceive Fox's intentions. Lampitt probably fears losing his congregation more than anything else. Fox has a way of seeing right through people. Have you noticed? This incident in Ulverston doesn't have anything to do with theology. It has more to do with the little fiefdoms of the clergy. Their congregations are their customers and they will beat, fine, and imprison anyone who threatens their turf."

"Aye. The most vicious behavior you will ever see comes from Christians trying to show how much religion matters to them. That's why you cannot mess with it. It's one thing to carry on as we do here with the silence, but it is quite another thing altogether to go storming into churches telling them all to change."

"So how are the Friends to proceed then? How will they survive in the face of all this?"

"Is this your concern?"

"I must not allow my husband, the Vanes, or Dr. Clarke, to dissuade me from my mission. Remaining in the company of Friends is of paramount importance to me. No matter how long it takes, I will not go back to Newport until I can take them with me. Otherwise, I will be in danger of losing everything."

My Irish temper started to boil over. "You're in danger of losing everything now! How long can you stand to be separated from your children? What about your husband? What about mine? How long are they expected to do without their wives?" The color rising up to my face scared her.

She fell back on the bed weeping.

I thought I'd said enough and should just wait for her to come round. I was sure she would. Up in the top room, I took up my weaving. I started to think how awful it would be for me to have to set off for Newport by myself. If we could only have gotten as far as London, I thought the Vanes would put an end to this. The loom sat in front of the window. I watched Mary go off through the orchard in search of Mistress Fell. She found her friend out in the garden. It must have been a morning for tears, because as Mary approached, Margaret wiped her face on her apron. She came towards Mary with her skirts gathering moisture from the grass. They walked together until they paused by the back door, just under my window.

Mary put her hand on her friend's shoulder. "Can I help at all?"

"I love him," said Margaret.

"Fox?" asked Mary.

Margaret nodded.

"I love him too," stated Mary.

"I know. I know. We all do. But I think in my case, it may be different. I still love my husband, but I don't dream of him at night. I don't long for him. When Fox came up the lane yesterday, looking like he did, I thought I'd die."

"I had the same reaction, Margaret. I think what you are feeling is what we all feel. Naturally, there is a tremendous amount of love amongst

us all. I can feel it at meeting. I can feel pangs going through me like
Cupid's arrows. When I was courted by my husband I felt something
similar, but even that was different. I was young. I knew nothing. What
I have encountered here is all encompassing."

"But I'm quite certain that things have gone to a different level
with me."

"Does he know?" asked Mary.

"Yes. I believe he does."

"And what does he say?"

"Pretty much what you have just said. That I'm feeling the power."

"Then why the tears?"

"I'm ashamed for my husband's sake. He has been very good to me.
He is a kind man and a tolerant one. I have no cause for complaint."

"I don't want to go back to my husband," said Mary.

I knocked over a heavy bucket. I'd been leaning over it so I could
hear. Now I'd made a racket, causing them both to look up. I ducked.

"Really?"

"I don't see how I can go back. I am not the same person anymore.
William will be the same. He will go on about the business of running
the farm and our household, but I will not be the same and he will do
everything in his power to put me back in my place. Why should I be put
back there? You know the story of Jesus and Martha? I used to think
Jesus was so unfair to tell Martha to forget about trying to feed the men
He brought with him into her house. He told her that she should listen
to what He had to say instead. Women had to serve their guests by law
in those days, and how different is it now? I used to think she must have
been furious at Jesus, this vagabond, who wandered about, never con-
cerning Himself with mundane chores, and then coming into her house
and telling her not to bother serving all the guests. But now I see He
was right. Spiritual matters come first. Take care of the spirit first.
That's what He was saying. Why should she have to worry about what
everyone was going to eat? They weren't worrying. They wanted to hear
Jesus. Just think if she had scurried about the kitchen missing her chance
to hear Christ. When Anne Hutchinson was killed, I vowed that if I ever
found another teacher, another leader even remotely like her, I would
not veer off to my own concerns again. That is how I feel about Fox. I
came to talk to you about it, actually. I do not want to leave him, or if I
do, I want to be certain, at the very least, of being with other Friends. I

don't want to return to that Vane camp alone and have them ridicule everything I have found."

"Well of course you should stay with us then, Mary," said Margaret.

"Have I been of any help?" she asked.

"At least I know I am not alone in my affections."

"He says Christ was his way to God, but I think Fox was mine. If I sit beside him, I feel it. Sometimes, when I start to settle in, I think of him, of his hair, of his eyes, of his smell, and I am flooded—right off. I know he wouldn't want me to do that, but I do it all the same. I love his face. I love the toughness and the sweetness mixed together. I love his guts. I admire him more than any other person I know."

Fox walked out the front door just then. Both women rushed to his side.

Feeling beside myself now, I did not know what to do. The dear children's faces came to me. I feared that she'd forgotten them. I knew that simply couldn't be true. Maybe she didn't want to face the sense of being at odds with the whole town. She could go home, describe this experience and they would have no clue whatsoever what she was talking about. I knew the feeling because I had lived it, having been separated from Ireland, my family, and my faith. Then it occurred to me that perhaps she had been bewitched. What was I supposed to do about that with nary a priest in sight? Being the only link to Newport in Swarthmore Hall put a huge burden on me. Should I just head home without her? If I were to go off alone, she might never get back. Wasn't it my duty to help her find her way home? Yet if I acted like Mr. Dyer, going for the firm common sense approach, I knew she would buck me and all would be lost.

So I turned to my usual sources. I prayed. I prayed and prayed to the Blessed Virgin, who had never failed me yet. Calling in reinforcements, I wrote to my priest, asking him to inform my mother and ask for her prayers too.

Chapter Twenty
Fox Meets Vane

When Mary and I finally left Swarthmore, we rode to London with an entourage of Friends, including Fox. The Vanes dispatched a messenger as promised, and the Fells sent him packing. Mary wrote a brief letter saying she had most assuredly not been bewitched, but had become a member of the Religious Society of Friends. Convinced that the Vanes would join as well, she arranged for a meeting.

The air, thick with tension as we entered the Vane establishment at Charing Cross, could have been cut with the proverbial knife. The winter of 1653 had been one of the coldest people could remember. The mood sitting over England was one of pure darkness. Parliament had been so reduced in size that it was now called the Rump. No quick solution to the war had presented itself and Sir Harry, left with a burden too large to carry, had degenerated into an ugly mood. The bad weather, interpreted by all to mean this, that, or the other thing, only added to the sense of despair. Some saw it as a sign that God did not sit favorably with Cromwell after all. The cold rain presented little hardship to Mary and me, not after our years in the New World. We arrived at Charing Cross cheerfully, but could plainly see that her former host was miffed over her deserting him.

Harry began by saying, "How did you make your way here? By coach?"

"No, we rode," she replied.

"Good horses?"

"Yes. Very good."

Turning to Fox, Harry said, "Do you work your same magic on the beasts of the field then?"

"Why does thee want to know? Is thee not happy with thy mount?"

"I assure you I am perfectly happy with my horses, sir."

Mary swept through a quick explanation of the choice of pronouns, but to no avail.

"I am curious about something, Mr. Fox," said Harry. "Perhaps you would be so kind as to enlighten me. I have been asked by Mr. Dyer to oversee Mary's stay in England. It is my duty to see that no one takes undue advantage of her situation. Her allowance has been reduced, as I'm sure you have no doubt found out. Lest you think this reduction is temporary, I assure you it is not. It will not be increased while she is here. Do you hope to benefit financially from your association with her?"

I saw the color rise to Mary's face, "Do not answer that question. There is no need for such rudeness, Sir Harry. While I can appreciate your concern, I came here to assure you that nothing untoward has happened."

"Oh I see. This man simply enjoys your company, is that it?"

"Perhaps we should leave," she said, turning to me and lifting her chin.

Fox stood his ground.

Harry walked toward her with an arm outstretched. "No. Wait. I've blundered. Forgive me, please. I do want to hear what you have to say. Lady Frances will kill me if she hears I sent you away mad. Please, do sit down."

I remained standing, but everyone else took a seat.

Mary took a slightly more congenial tone, willing, at least, to give her old friend the benefit of the doubt. "What do you want to know then?"

"I will address my question to thee, Mr. Fox," he said in the most patronizing of all possible attitudes. "Has thee known a second revelation?"

Mary sighed. She had explained Sir Harry's odd theology to Fox and warned him of it in advance.

"What did thee miss the first time?" Fox asked.

I helped matters greatly, by bursting out laughing.

Harry flew into a temper. The whole tale of the Strafford and the steward handing over the keys to the treasure room came tumbling out. According to him, the Lord Himself gave him direct order to both open the velvet casket and betray his father and the king. Fox remained still, listening without emotion, until Harry ended his speech by shouting, "And for God's sakes take your bloody hat off your bloody head when you are in my house."

Mary turned and swept out of the room.

Fox said a few words to Vane, and then joined her on the street. She apologized for her friend's behavior, but Fox only raised a hand admonishing her to cease defending him. "He is a spoiled, arrogant man," he stated.

On our way to the market the next day, Mary and I stopped over at Charing Cross to meet with Lady Frances. "I am so sorry, Mary. So very sorry I sent you up there. Harry has thrown it up to me all these months. If I could take back my words that day in London, when I asked you to go up to Swarthmore, I most assuredly would. I feel simply awful."

"Dearest heart," said Mary, "How could you spend one second in regret? I have known nothing but the greatest joy. My trip to Swarthmore became my salvation. Margaret Fell told me Fox would change my life. I didn't believe her at first. She was right though. My life has changed, irrevocably, and for the better too. I feel I owe you a tremendous debt of thanks which can only be repaid by showing you what I have learned."

At this Lady Frances stood. "Don't even try, Mary. Save yourself for that band of ruffians you call friends. Don't, for one second, think you can drag me down into that bog."

Mary sat quietly for a second. Then she said, "It is quite the opposite of what you say. It saddens me to hear you say so. But I know the root of your fear. I will be preaching next week in Gloucester. I would like you to come. If not, we can separate religion from our friendship if you like. I know you believe in religious freedom."

"What do you mean 'preach'?" asked Lady Frances, whose mouth had fallen open.

"Fox says I am ready."

"What will you say?"

"I don't know. I will, of course, wait upon the Lord."

"Oh, this is folly. Don't let this man make a fool out of you, Mary."

"It has nothing to do with him."

"You are following him like some dumb sheep. I never would have thought you'd fall so easily. What did he do to you?"

"He only helped me on my path to God."

"You are bewitched."

"Lady Frances, I am obeying the Lord, not George Fox."

"Do you love him?"

"Yes," says Mary. "I love him, as I love you."

"We begged you to come back. Do you have any idea of what Sir Harry has been through?"

"You must understand that I had my reasons for staying and they were sound."

"I see nothing sound in a woman of your class traveling around with such a tramp. No one has answered the question of his finances. Are you and Margaret Fell supporting him?"

"He has a small income left by his grandfather and some interests in shipping."

"How do you know this?"

"I know. That's all I can say. He is not what you think."

"What, pray tell, is he then?"

"He is simply a man with a good method. He is the founder of the Religious Society of Friends, which will make its mark on this country and the New World as well. He is no different than Martin Luther, or John Calvin, or any other Protestant leader. He simply has a different way that is more Puritan than the Puritans."

"He is a dissident for the sake of being a dissident and nothing else. You have let him mislead you into thinking he is more than he is."

"This is very rich coming from you, Lady Frances. Oliver Cromwell is not a dissident? Murdering the king was not an act of dissent?"

"How dare you! You have become a bloody, stupid fool, Mary. You will leave this house at once."

Outside, I spat on the ground. "Well, " I said, "You killed two birds with one stone there."

"Be still and cool in the light," she answered. "That's what Fox told me to do. It works for him. It worked for Christ. It had better work for me too, or I'll make myself a laughing stock, just as Lady Frances predicted."

CHAPTER TWENTY-ONE
The Preacher

The rain beat against the wall of the little inn in Gloucester, the night before Mary was about to preach. Puddles of muddy water oozed under the heavy door. Guests lingered by the fire, deep in their cups, singing. Mary and I heard them from our room upstairs. We planned to retire early, but as the night progressed we found ourselves tossing and turning. Even after the revelry stopped and the singers had all departed we still could not settle. We decided to sneak downstairs in the dark and head outside for a bit of air. Below, all had grown quiet. Flagons smelling of ale remained on the tables, the only reminder of the crowd who had filled the place earlier.

We found a small flax wheel by the hearth. It had been so long since our hands touched a spinning wheel. In the basket nearby, Mary fingered a pile of fibers. I remembered all those nights in Boston and Newport when Mary spun her worries into thread. So I said, "Why don't you spin for awhile? I'm goin' to find something to drink."

"Who do you suppose is spinning at the hearth in Newport now?"

"It isn't me and it isn't you." I located some brandy. "Do you want some?"

She shook her head. I poured myself a hefty glass. I had nothing to feel guilty about.

"Do you think it could be my little Mary? Samuel probably brought in the flax last summer. Do you think Will helped him? The younger children would have done the scutching and swingling, the soaking and bleaching. You know what always amazes me about growing flax? There is so little to be had from all that peeling."

With flask in hand, I said, "There is a husk over everything." I thought I was getting right smart from the brandy.

"The layers of learning and Bible study and church have to be peeled off; because they are the outside layers. Underneath is the truth of going inward; that's where the precious threads are to be found."

She got up then and opened the front door. I followed her outside. The rain knifed our faces. "Do you remember," I asked, "how the snow creaks under foot when it is really cold?"

"And the water freezes in the washbowl overnight."

"And the children slide on the frozen ponds?"

"Wet feet, and icy skirts, and biting wind. I remember. Eighteen winters I spent in New England."

"But you survived," I told her.

"Six living children. One dead, one stillborn, one miscarriage."

"One stillborn, three miscarriages," I contributed. She put her arm around me. "The crowd is goin' to be here in a few hours, mistress."

"What can I say that they have not heard before?"

"They haven't heard about you. They haven't heard about the New World. They know nothing of the natives. Remember when Anne said, 'Ask the beasts of the field and they shall teach thee?' We know more about life than men do. We know about the stuff of life."

Back up the stairs, she crept into bed, just as the sun was about to rise. She drifted into a dream where she clearly found herself reunited with Anne. She saw her standing on a hill. Mary felt herself reaching for her, heart glad to see her. Running toward her with her arms outstretched, Anne waved her on. Then she woke in our small room under the sloping ceiling. "It all has a purpose," she said. "Everything leading up to this moment has had a purpose."

In this frame of mind, she descended the stairs.

When the time came, Mary knew she was ready. I couldn't get over it. People were spellbound and many became convinced Friends right then and there. Later, they held a great meeting. We traveled on towards Wales the next day. As we gathered up our things and closed our satchels, she looked around our room at the inn.

She turned to me and spoke. "I'm not the same woman who came in the day before. My mouth has been opened."

On April 20, 1653, at the request of Lady Vane, Mary stepped over to Charing Cross for dinner. She dressed quite plainly that evening, prepared to do battle.

Later, when she returned to the inn where we were all crammed into a loft, she looked so upset, I knew something had happened.

"Irene, it's gotten so much worse. Cromwell has really done it now. Don't spit 'til I finish. I may even join you."

"What has he done?" I asked.

"Well, when I arrived, a footman ushered me to the library. I saw at once that both Lady Frances and Sir Harry had been crying. I paused at the door, uncertain as to whether I should intrude, but Lady Frances rushed over to me with open arms. I sat down and waited for him to speak. Then he recounted the whole sad story. It is worse than we imagined, Irene. Well, maybe it is not worse than you imagined, but I never thought England would sink this low. Cromwell has been speaking of declaring himself king! He said, 'unless there be some authority and power so full and high as to restrain things in better order, it will be impossible in human reason to prevent our ruin. What if a man should take it upon him to be king?' He appeared in Parliament not even dressed for the occasion, wearing an old black coat and gray stockings. He brought a party of musketeers from his own regiment. Cromwell stood and said, 'This time I must do it.' Then he proceeded to ramble on in a vicious tirade about injustices, greed, uncleanness, embezzlement, petty jealousies, sins, drunkenness and then he said to the House, 'It is not fit that you should sit as a Parliament any longer. I will put an end to your prating. You are no Parliament. I say you are no Parliament. I will put an end to your sitting.' Then he turned to a guard and said, 'Call them in! Call them in!' Harry jumped up saying it was not honest, whereupon Cromwell shouted, 'O Sir Harry Vane! Sir Harry Vane! The Lord deliver me from Sir Harry Vane.' They were all herded out like a flock of sheep, with Cromwell calling out names saying one was a drunkard, another a whoremaster; Wentworth he called an adulterer; he called an alderman a thief, and Harry, a juggler, without common honesty, as well as to blame, entirely, for the whole business. So that's it then. England is in shambles. First the monarchy, then the Lords, and now the house have been demolished. Without the House of Commons, the people have no power. You can spit now."

"What happened next?"

"Harry cried over his political career and all his broken dreams. I tried to comfort him by suggesting an arranged meeting between Cromwell and Fox."

"Boy, wouldn't you love to be a fly on the wall for that? Will Harry be able to pull it off?"

"He wasn't very keen on the idea. He got very sarcastic suggesting a fat lot of good it would do the country, to have Fox march into Whitehall with his hat on his head, addressing Cromwell as a servant. Lady Frances reminded him that I was a guest, so he stopped abusing Fox, in favor of a new tactic. He asked me about my numbers."

"Your what?"

"My numbers. He wanted to know how many members we had in our society. I told him to forget trying to use us as a political faction. He accused me of being unpatriotic, so I left."

"He is really twisted up about the hat issue, isn't he?"

"Well, Fox is right about him being arrogant. I hate to see him out of politics though. And I cannot believe Cromwell wants to declare himself king."

"Parliament has been dissolved before," I told her. "Then they need money and some sort of government gets put back together."

"The old guard is completely gone, though, Irene. Whatever comes back will be handpicked by Cromwell. He is destroying what took centuries to build."

"Aye. It's all going to play itself out now, without any influence from our old former mayor of Boston, Sir Harry Vane. What is done here is done. Hope lies in the New World. England may as well consider her best days behind her. She is played out. We have to forget all this nonsense and go back to building our own future."

"Soon," she said. "Soon."

I started to get my hopes up. She really looked to me like she meant it this time. If things had been different, we probably would have hopped a ship shortly after that. Fate, Cupid, or bad luck, intervened though, and the greatest diversion of all crossed our path shortly after that. How was I to know she'd fall in love?

It took some time for the enormity of Cromwell's actions to filter down to the common man. Many felt the affairs of Parliament had little to do with their lives in the first place. As from time immemorial, the fields were plowed, cultivated, and planted. Pastoral life continued, as it always had, both in times of war and peace. Yet a cloud of uncertainty hung over everything and the simple joys of festivals and plays disappeared from village life. When England turned Puritan, they took all the fun out of everything, as usual. The Old Globe Theater closed down and traveling troupes of actors were no longer allowed to perform. Friends continued to speak on market days and crowds carried on, showing up to hear them. We often arrived at these affairs, wet from the rain, and bedraggled from sleeping wherever we could find shelter. If we were lucky, homes were sometimes graciously thrown open. If not, inns or stables, or often open fields, had to suffice. Whether she was with Fox, or with other Friends, Mary continued to preach. They held meetings for worship in obliging fields, barns, and homes. The smell of wet clothes, mixed with horses and hay, lingers in my memories of those times. Country sounds and the love I could feel drifting and mingling with the aromas of newly turned earth and bodies warm with exertion. If all went smoothly, the peace of meeting would only be broken by the songs of birds chirping, or children playing outside, or a Friend, moved to speak, breaking the silence. I continued to slip off to Mass wherever possible. No one ever said anything about it, or tried to steer me away from the one true faith.

On one such market day, in the town of Cheltenham, a well-dressed gentleman rode up to hear Mary. She had been inviting interested parties to attend a Meeting, which was to take place in a few short hours. From the crowd a farmer called out, "Do you call yourself a priest then?"

She belted out the answer. "We are all preachers."

"Then who interprets the gospels?"

"Anyone who can read."

"It is not a woman's place," shouted another.

"There is a part of God in each and every living soul. None have need of an official interpreter. I lived for years as an Anglican, and then as a Puritan. During the whole time, I dutifully went to church, but I felt very cut off from the Lord. I studied the gospels, but to no avail. It was not the way to the living Christ. When He came to me and filled me with his light, my life was changed forever and I had no further need of church."

"You are a blasphemer," cried the man who first spoke out. Others joined in shouting, "Whore! Instrument of the devil!" A man picked up a rock and hurled it at her. As it pealed past her shoulder, she turned to avoid the blow. More objects suddenly came flying in her direction. A large cabbage hit her on the head.

The well-dressed gentleman dismounted and rushed to her side. "Stop it, all of you. What kind of hospitality is this? Is your own faith so weak that you throw rotting vegetables at this woman? She has come to invite you to worship with her and this is how you behave? If you have no desire to attend, then be off and leave her in peace. I for one plan to join her, and I invite her Friends and any other interested parties who have peace in their hearts, to travel with me to my father's house."

While he spoke, Mary looked up at the concerned face on this impressive young man. When he finished, he offered her his hand.

"Christopher," she cried.

I knew right away he was the one. The great love of her life. She introduced me and thanked him.

"I heard you lived in the New World. Am I right?"

"Yes."

"And do you plan to return?"

"With all my heart," she said. "I have six children and a husband on the other side of the ocean."

"And you are here because of the Society?"

"As soon as I can get an interested group of Friends to go, we will set sail for Newport."

"And where is this place? Is it in Virginia?"

"No. To the north. On the Island of Aquidneck."

"Come," said Christopher. "Come to my house. Bring as many as you like. We'll put you up tonight."

The Meeting took place in the great hall of the Holder estate. Christopher became a believer that very day. The bulk of us were fed with the servants. Mary was invited to dine with the elder Holders. When she told me of the invitation, she rifled through her things looking at me in desperation. We had pared down her wardrobe to almost nothing. In her role as a preacher, she dressed very simply. I had a feeling that her lack of adornment may not last forever and I had prepared for an event like this. From the bottom of my satchel, I produced the red satin dress that had once belonged to Lady Frances. You should have seen her face! Housed in a handsome guest suite, we had time to bathe, refresh the gown and dress her hair. When she descended the stairs, Christopher stood waiting for her at the bottom. The sight of her put him over the moon.

I learned from Mary that his wife and baby had died in childbirth. Too grief stricken to remarry, he said he had made inquiries about her whereabouts. So happy to see him again, she bore him no ill will for not marrying her when he had the chance. The two of them seemed to get on like a house on fire.

Before bed, as I brushed her hair, I said, "Women are being hung all over England for adultery."

She turned to me and grabbed the brush out of my hand. "How dare you!"

"What? It does happen."

"Not to me, Irene."

"But you said you loved him once."

"Yes, when I was a girl. I was not married then, I was not a mother."

"Fine. I did not mean any harm, mistress. I know he has feelings for you."

"Friendship. That is the extent of it. We grew up together. That's the end of it."

She went off to bed in a huff. I left her then, not sorry for what I had said.

When the band of Friends packed up to move on to London, he asked if he could come along.

Looking into his bright blue eyes, Mary smiled and said, "I have a very good feeling about this. You are most welcome."

I could have added that I had a very bad feeling, but said nothing. I liked the man well enough. In fact, I was pretty dazzled by him too, but I never lost sight of my duty to Mr. Dyer. This new twist was going to delay things further. Then in my scheming mind, I hatched a plan. If I could convince Christopher to cross over, if I could light a fire in him for the adventure of New England, I knew she would go with him. So from that point on I made friends with him, seeing him as my ticket home.

CHAPTER TWENTY-TWO
The Secret Revealed

On July 4, the empty House filled up again with a selection of Puritan Nobles. It was called the Little Parliament, or the Barebones Parliament, named after one of its members, Praise God Barebones. Harry, not invited to join, found himself left out of the fray for the first time since all this business began.

Cromwell called them "a people chosen by God to do His work and to show forth his praise." It did not take long for word to filter back to the streets of London that the Saints, as they were called, were proving to be a disappointment. In the end, he managed to convince some of the moderate members to vote for dissolution before the others were even awake. A few of the more stubborn members rushed down to remain in their seats, and declared that they had been sent there to do God's work. One of the officers, forced to give them the boot, heard this plea and stated, "God has not been present here these past twelve years."

Mary and I were in London with Christopher Holder on the night of February 8, 1654. The night Oliver Cromwell, who on December 16 had taken the oath as Lord Protector in Westminster Hall, was to be banqueted and driven through the streets to Whitehall. The whole of London was practically berserk. The sight of him parading in his musk-colored suit, heavily embroidered in gold, with his colonels around him, and lines of soldiers carrying torches, sent me round the bend. I never expected to see him in person, and when it happened I screamed and shook my fist. "Shame on you, shame on you, you murderous, cursed louse." The tower guns' saluting drowned out my wailing. I glanced over at Mary and saw that she had fallen to passionate weeping.

Christopher took hold of her arm and led her away, suggesting we walk to a quieter spot.

"I hate him," she cried.

Responding to her distress, Christopher said, "You are not alone in that sentiment."

She looked up to see if he mocked her, but saw only his kind and calm expression. Christopher, being well educated and worldly, had an ease and charm that we both found comforting. As we made our way along the crowded streets, drunken citizens were shouting comments, and Mary wondered if London itself had gone mad.

"Have they forgotten everything?"

We rounded a corner and she suggested we get something to eat.

As we warmed our hands around a flagon of hot water, Christopher told us the Protectorate wouldn't last.

"Why?"

"The English people still judge events by portents," he answered, as he tore a hunk of bread in two and dipped it in his stew. "Look what happened with the river ebbing and flowing in an uncharacteristic fashion; a comet has been seen; part of Saint Paul's fell down; I have even heard rumors of the ghost of King Charles walking in Whitehall." He stopped.

Mary looked at him with her eyes filling up with tears. "If only it were true. If only his ghost could appear and turn Cromwell around."

"Like Hamlet? End the Protectorate by indecision? You really are quite the Royalist."

"It's in my blood," she answered. "Yours too."

I shook my head vigorously. I knew where she was headed and I tried to stop her.

But Mary only gazed into his eyes. Then, in spite of my efforts, she said, "The murdered king was my uncle."

The stew no longer commanded Christopher's attention. His spoon dropped to his plate as he sat there, spellbound. "How?"

"No living soul in England, except Irene, knows this story, Christopher. You must never tell anyone. I believe I am the daughter of Lady Arabella Stuart who died in the Tower. She married William Seymour in secret. There were rumors of a baby. I am that baby."

Christopher lost himself in her gaze, speaking in a manner common to Friends, which was in silence. I did not see how it was possible for her to look across the table, into the eyes of Christopher, and resist falling in love all over again. I spotted another group of fellow travelers and went off with them. The sounds around us became louder, more drunken, bawdier, and more debauched, as the night wore on.

All I could get out of Mary the next day was that she had done the right thing in telling him, even though she was not quite sure why.

"We have become a part of something larger than ourselves," she mused. "Each of us will be called upon to play a part, and when the time comes to be tested, we will draw strength from one another and be happy in that knowledge."

Joy written all over her face made it plain to me that she was very happy. I wondered how she would ever see herself going back to William now. She told me that as Christopher had reached across the table and as he took a hold of her hand, he said, "I will not forget this night."

We remained in England through yet another fall and winter. I told her flat out that I couldn't stand it any longer. I had to go home. "You have to go home too," I added.

"We will," she answered. "We will."

At this time, word spread through England that Fox, who had been jailed, was about to be hanged. Friends who came to visit were beaten with a great cudgel—as was Fox almost daily. Since Cromwell had been declared Lord Protector, a rumor of a plot against him, with George Fox and the Quakers scheming to bring in King Charles II, eddied around London.

Housed at the Mermaid Inn, at Charing Cross, Fox was to be kept there until word came from Cromwell.

Some days later, early on the morning of March 9, Captain Drury came to the Mermaid Inn to escort Fox to Whitehall. Mary had high hopes for the meeting. Her excitement scared me. The fire in her had grown to such a boiling point; I feared it would consume her, if she were not careful.

The appointment went surprisingly well. We heard that when Fox had made a move to leave, Cromwell turned, grabbed his hand and said with tears in his eyes, "Come again to my house: for if thou and I were but an hour of a day together, we should be nearer to the other." The Lord Protector said he wished Fox no more ill than he did to his own soul.

After that, Fox was free to go.

Friends set to work. Immediately upon hearing of Fox's release, they wanted to get as many people into London as possible. Several great and powerful meetings were held in and around the city. The crowds grew so dense, the throngs of people so thick, they could barely get Fox

in and out of the buildings. His popularity grew to Christ-like propor-
tions. Things really took off from that point. A joy in this momentum
that went beyond words, beyond all feeling, filled up Mary's heart every
day with gladness. She ate, slept, and breathed the movement. Doors
opened, fellow Friends offered their homes, class barriers and social
distinctions melted before our very eyes. I was never introduced as Mary's
servant. Friends roamed as a pack, picking up steam every day, convinced that they had a solution to offer the English people and from
there, the world.

In August, a ship brought mail from home. The tears jumped to our
eyes when we read that Samuel had married Edward Hutchinson's
daughter Anne. Little Charles, three now, had learned how to fish.
William's letter, full of concern and worry, begged her to come home.
Despondent for days afterward, she wrote back saying we would be in
Newport soon. Her estate, still not settled, made that statement seem
very untrue to me. She did not write that since the day she met George
Fox she had seldom veered more than a few days' journey from him. She
did not tell them that Christopher Holder had not left her side since the
moment they were reunited. She left out the fact that she had another
family now, one bound by spirit, not bound by blood. All she could say
was soon, soon, but the months turned into years and the gap became
harder and harder to bridge.

As the numbers of Friends in England multiplied, so did the ar-
rests. Friends jailed all up and down the kingdom were hard-pressed to
remain free for long. Once authorities heard they would not swear an
oath, they were hauled into court, pressed into swearing an oath, then
jailed for refusing to do so. For declining to doff their hats to a judge,
they were likewise thrown in the clink. However, they were not the only
people in England finding themselves on the wrong side of the law. England, divided into eleven areas, had each one headed up by a major
general. Local militia, supplemented by troops on horseback, enforced
their edicts. All this was funded outside the regular military budget, by
yet another tax on the beleaguered Royalist gentry. The country, for all
intents and purposes, turned itself into a police state, and England could
no longer be described, in any way shape or form, as merry. Much as the
general court in Massachusetts tried to legislate all the fun out of everything, these major generals were held to no laws, but those of their
own choosing. Hapless citizens were brought before them for sins of

swearing, drinking, gambling, dress, and all kinds of licentious behavior. Maypoles fell to the ax; feast days were replaced with fast days— even to the extent that soldiers were sent around on Christmas day with permission to enter any house where they smelled a roast cooking. Can you imagine?

Thurloe, who headed up Cromwell's spreading intelligence service, had people from impoverished Lords to scullery maids working for him everywhere. As hatred for Cromwell increased, so did plots of attacks on his life, and with each one uncovered, Thurloe's power doubled.

Cromwell managed to form a new Parliament by handing out certificates of admission; no one got in without one. He beseeched them in the name of God to devote themselves to the work.

Fox went to Wales in 1655 with two other Friends, in order to continue spreading the word. Near Launceston, they were taken prisoner while traveling. They met up with the major general of the region, protested their illegal arrest, but were told that the major general could not stay and talk with him because he was afraid his horse would get cold. This is what English justice had been reduced to. He said the guard must take them on to the castle at Launceston. Nine weeks passed before they were brought before a judge. During that time, folks from the countryside nearby gravitated towards the three Friends. Once again rumors spread of an impending hanging.

Word of this reached London. I thought I was making some progress on the issue of getting home till this happened, but that is how things went in those years. Some suddenly would find themselves in desperate trouble, needing us to concentrate all our efforts on getting them out of their various predicaments. This case in Launceston was no exception. We mounted our horses and along with Christopher Holder, and our new friend William Robinson, we rode down there to bear witness.

When the judge arrived, a large crowd had gathered to hear the trial. The prisoners were guarded through the streets, with the doors and windows crammed with people. They were brought in before Judge Glynn, then chief justice of England. We managed to get seats in the courtroom.

The judge began by asking, "What be these you have brought to court?"

The guard answered, "Prisoners, my Lord."

The judge started right in with, "Why do you not put off your hats?"

They did not answer.

"Put off your hats," yelled the judge. "The court commands you to put off your hats."

Fox was obviously ready for this. "Where did ever any magistrate, king, or judge, from Moses to Daniel, command any to put off their hats when they came before him in his court, either among the Jews, the people of God, or amongst the heathen? And if the law of England does command any such thing, show me that law either written or printed."

"I do not carry my law books on my back."

"Tell me where it is printed in any statute book, that I may read it."

"Take him away, " snapped Judge Glynn.

Brought back some time later, a new question faced them.

The judge looked pretty smug in my estimation. His eyes seemed full of sparkle. "Where had they hats, from Moses to Daniel? Come, answer me. I have you fast now."

I looked at Mary. "English justice at its finest," I whispered.

"Thou may read in the third of Daniel," replied Fox confidently, "that the three children were cast into the fiery furnace by Nebuchadnezzar's command, with their coats, their hose, and their hats on."

"Take them away, jailer!"

Later, they came back in again. This time the judge had the guards forcibly remove their hats. The Friends received the hats and quietly put them back on their heads. Then Fox asked the judge for what reason had they lain in prison for the past nine weeks, since he had raised no other subject with them but hats.

The judge had the jailers take their hats off again, and they once again ended straight back on the heads of the Friends.

By this time I was really trying hard not to laugh.

The judge asked Fox to explain his position regarding hats.

Fox replied that it was an honor of men, an honor they seek from one another. Then he quoted Christ who said, "How can ye believe, who receive honor of one another, and seek not an honor which comes from God only? I receive not honor from men."

The judge then brought in an indictment.

Peter Ceely, the man who had arrested them, came forward. "May it please you my Lord, this man went aside with me, and told me how serviceable I might be for his design; that he could raise forty thousand men at an hour's warning, involve the nation in blood, and so bring in King Charles. If it please you, my Lord, I have a witness to swear it."

Fox stated that if he had done anything worthy of death, or of bonds, then the judge should let the entire county know it.

The judge then said again, "Jailer, take him away. I'll see whether he or I shall be master."

Feeling they were not likely to be released for some time, they stopped paying the seven shillings a week for food, and seven a week for their horses. For this, they found themselves dumped down in a place called Doomsdale. A hole where murderers were kept after they were condemned; a pit where years of human filth have never been removed. It was said that those sent to that dungeon were never in good health again.

The first night, a few kind folk gave them a bit of straw to burn. It covered a smattering of the stink, but unfortunately, the jailer, whose room was over theirs, smelled the smoke. Enraged, he poured buckets of excrement and urine from a hole in his floor, down on top of their heads. Standing up to their calves in dung, and now saturated and besmeared, they nearly smothered from the stench.

When Christopher and William Robinson returned from the jail to the inn where we were housed, they looked as white as ghosts.

"How bad is it?" asked Mary.

"Worse than anything we have seen yet," replied Christopher, who could not even look at Mary.

"I am going in," she announced

"No. No," I said. "You can't."

"That would be the wrong course," added Christopher.

"You mustn't," said Robinson. "He wants us to make an appeal."

"What is happening? Is he being beaten?"

When Christopher described the conditions, a fury rose in Mary that got her to her feet. "What if he falls ill? What will happen to us if we lose him?"

"They won't succeed, Mary," stated Christopher "I have never seen anyone as tough as he is. Even in that place of filth and darkness, he can find his way. You must write to Sir Harry Vane. No one in good conscience can justify such treatment."

"Chief Justice Glynn can have Fox put to death, at any moment, just for refusing to remove his hat. What recourse do we have? We have none. We have no real Parliament, nor a House of Lords, nor any other governing body to whom we can appeal. No one represents us. We have no king. We have only Cromwell. How can we get through to him?"

"Numbers," said Christopher. "Remember when Sir Harry asked of our numbers? If a large enough crowd arrives here to witness this trial, it will give them pause in Whitehall. When word gets out as to how Fox has been treated, Friends will come. Cromwell will fear the numbers. Do you think he feels safe in his bed? He is no safer than Fox is. Don't forget, there are no civil liberties protecting him either. That is why he has Thurloe and his henchmen. He knows he can be overthrown at any moment. These rumors of Quakers joining forces with Royalists are born in that fear. We need to send word to Friends the length and breadth of England to get down here any way they can. It is the only chance we have of saving Fox."

So we got busy. Sure enough, good people flocked in from the country and more groups of Friends headed south from London. Eventually, word filtered down from the top. The door would be opened and the prisoners would be let out on the Castle Green for the Sabbath. The tide swelled in their favor as Meetings, held week after week, saw each one nearly doubling in size.

Spring drifted into summer and once again our chances to catch a ship slipped away. Why didn't I just leave? I made up my mind to, but somehow I couldn't bring myself to do it. Deep down inside I had faith that her maternal instincts would bring her home.

I knew Mary wouldn't leave as long as Fox remained in such a terrible place. Much to the dismay of the local priests, the crowds kept swarming on Launceston until they became a multitude. Help finally arrived from the most unlikely source. Reverend Hugh Peters, so concerned by the throngs flocking to those meetings, told Cromwell he could do no greater service to George Fox than to keep him imprisoned in Doomsdale. So, on July 13, 1655, the three prisoners were suddenly released, with all conditions the judge sought not accepted. He wanted Fox to promise not to hold any more meetings. This Fox could not do; he wanted him to cease to travel in Wales. Fox said no. So in the end his sheer stubbornness carried the day. It wouldn't be the first time.

CHAPTER TWENTY-THREE
Heading Home

As Christopher and Mary rode side by side on their many travels, she entertained him with stories of her life in Newport. He asked her countless questions related to hunting, and fishing. He was particularly intrigued with the concept of canoe travel and wanted to hear all about the adventures of Roger Williams. Never would the New World have greater ambassadors than the pair of us. In this mission we were united. She recounted all she knew about native worship, their hunting and fishing methods, their forms of shelter both when traveling and in camp, their methods of preparing food, their system of bartering, and even their language. She taught Christopher how to converse freely with the Narragansetts! I did my bit describing the lobsters up to two feet long, the wild turkeys we cooked with oyster stuffing, the clam chowders, and all the seafood we gathered right outside our door in Newport. The harbor teeming with ducks, the shores littered with nuts and berries, and the woods so full of game that feeding a family was simply a matter of heading into the forest with a musket in hand; I spared him nothing as I told him how the shores and the woods of New England provided for the natives for centuries, while in England, citizens were facing arrest for cooking a goose on Christmas day. As we described the life I was so desperate to get back to, he shifted in his saddle and said, "I'm going there one day."

"What day?" I asked.

"Soon," he answered.

"Sooner, rather than later," I added. "William Robinson wants to come too."

Mary envisioned a settlement of Friends in Newport. Once her estate was settled, she planned to give them land to build their houses and help them get started.

Privately, I implored Christopher to ask his father to lean on the lawyers and get the matter finished. "We can go in the spring," I told him. "She has some of the choicest land in Newport, and you know there is none better in all the world. Don't miss this opportunity. People are leaving England in droves. We need to act now before it's too late."

I knew Christopher to be ambitious and he clearly was up for the adventure. He never mentioned pulling any strings, but before long, the words I had waited for years to hear, finally arrived as music to my ears. Her estate settled, and her English property sold.

The Friends coming over with her were to form the nucleus in New England. From there, the movement would spread. That's what she hoped for. She had already written to Mr. Dyer regarding the land. The shoreline between the wharf and their farm, if developed, would spread the town out towards us. Young Charles, five now, knew only Moira and young Mary as his mothers.

We were standing on the shore of the west coast of England on a windy day in March. We had been traveling and preaching with a big entourage. This time, we even had Fox in our midst. Spring was fast approaching, yet she had not booked our passage. Looking out to sea, I could tell by her face that she was longing for home.

"Your mission has been accomplished, Mary. You have your money. That was the obstacle, so you said. I there something else keeping you now?"

Her face crumpled up in tears. "I don't know."

"Is it Christopher?"

"It's everyone. Everything."

"Well, I can not do this anymore. I have to go home."

She threw her arms around my neck and cried, "Please stay. Please don't leave me."

"I can't stay any longer. I just can't. I haven't started my family yet. I don't even know if I still have a husband."

Fox came upon us then. I blurted out our conversation along with my frustration in the matter. He placed his hand on Mary's shoulder, and to my great relief, urged her to return.

We got all set to go. I could hardly keep from jumping up and down with excitement. Any time during this period that Mary received a letter, or someone approached with news, I held my breath. Wouldn't you know that it would be Harry Vane who would bollocks up everything.

Word came that he had been ordered to appear before the Council of State on July 29. It was thought, by some, that his writing was seditious. He had to post a bond of five thousand pounds before being taken by ship to the Isle of Wight and imprisoned in Carisbrooke Castle. Mary fussed about this, saying she owed them a visit before leaving. I lost my temper and informed her that I would not see another summer go by.

"We could go and see them and sail in September," she suggested. "I've got to try and convince them to come to Newport. Their estate has been taxed to the gills for years. Now it is being subjected to the skill of lawyers. They will be ruined, Irene. He has to jump ship."

"We have to board the ship. I don't want to go back there and be shoved in the servants' quarters and treated like dirt. I don't want to sit and look at the man who lost me my brothers. I don't care if he is ruined. The fault lies with him. I am getting on that ship and I'm going."

Her tone grew very chilly. "I never made you stay, Irene. You have been free to leave at any time."

"I didn't want to leave you. I don't want to now, any more than I have all along, but I have run out of choices. I have to go. Sean told Moira that if I don't get back soon, I could forget coming back to him."

"You can sail with me after I see the Vanes and still make it back in time."

"That was our plan the first summer, remember? I told Sean then I would be back in September. That was six years ago! We have to get home. If you weren't so selfish, you'd come with me."

"So, that is what you think of me?"

"No. Well, yes. You're neglecting your children."

"I think you should go then. Your passage has been booked. I will see you are escorted to Plymouth."

"Mistress, don't let the Vanes suck you down with them. Come in September."

"That is my intention."

"Give me your word. Let me go home and tell Mr. Dyer that you gave me your word."

"Fine. I will be home in September."

With that we parted ways for the first time since I was sixteen.

On my trip home, I felt so alone I could hardly stand it, but my hardships fell behind me when I finally set foot in Newport. My Sean forgave me. He felt so strong and powerful that when I hugged him, I went weak in the knees. Moira had everything in hand, just as I knew she would. The two of us talked for two weeks straight.

Mary did not arrive home that September, or October, or November. The fall, brighter and prettier than I had remembered, came and went without her. I cursed Harry Vane, day and night. Mr. Dyer seemed so angry; I truly think he had begun to see himself as a widower. I heard that Mary journeyed to Raby Castle, ancestral seat and home of Harry's parents. They were holed up their with Lady Vane, Harry's ancient, bejeweled mother, who by all reports was encrusted with bitterness and blamed him for everything. We had no further word after that. I thought she must be locked up with the last vestiges of the aristocracy, not to have returned.

The first really cold night in December, I had a terrible dream. Mary called to me, asking me not to leave her. I told Mr. Dyer about it the next day, but he paid me no mind. About a week later, I dreamt that I walked out with her to Roxbury Neck to visit Anne. The pair of us talked to Mistress Hutchinson through a wall. It was cold in my dream and I felt terrible that Anne was even colder. Weeks passed. We headed into January. I stayed close to the fire, telling everyone that I'd forgotten what these winters were like. The wind seemed to go through my bones. One day, as I sat at my spinning wheel, I thought I heard Mary's voice. Then one night I dreamt of Boston again. I saw the town, and then the jail. The sight of Mary curled up in a little ball near frozen, all hunched up in the corner, scared the daylights out of me. Everything seemed so real; I could even smell the place. Waking with a start, I was too disturbed to go back to sleep.

I went straight to Mr. Dyer in the morning and told him, flat out, that something was wrong. "Mary must be in jail," I added. Then I told him of the two women we had heard about when we were back in England, two Quaker women who landed themselves in a Boston jail the previous year.

He laughed at me and said, "What for?"

I tried to explain how it was in England, how Quakers were slapped into detention right and left, but he had no sense of it, because he hadn't seen it yet. He never saw it; Puritans were not treated that badly back in the days when he and Mary lived in London. The bishops didn't like them, but that is a far cry from lock-ups. Stands were being taken in the

New World now too, I told him. We knew that the *Speedwell* carrying Christopher Holder and a few other Friends had been turned back and forced to sail home as soon as they arrived in the Port of Boston. I did not hesitate to add that Mary Fisher and Ann Austin, the two women who traveled the year before, were stripped and whipped, before finding themselves in clink. "They were also searched for witch marks by Reverend Wilson and Thomas Weld." He seemed to think that they had provoked the magistrates. "These are people that believe, totally, in the equality of the sexes," I continued, trying everything in my power to persuade him. "They will not doff their hats, not even to the chief justice of England, and they say thee and thou to everyone, refusing to accept any class distinctions. They travel about like this in bands, where all of society's laws are thrown to the wind and church is gone for good. People go crazy sometimes when they see this, sir. I've seen whole towns come out with stones and pitchforks. We know how Boston will respond. Governor Endicott is ten times worse than Winthrop."

"Mary couldn't possibly have sailed to Boston," he insisted, becoming angry with me. "She wrote a year ago saying she intended to go from Plymouth, to Barbados, to Newport. Even if she'd gotten this far, I would have been contacted. I know how these operations work, Irene. If they can send someone on their way, they will. Governor Endicott could not put my wife in jail and not contact me. There are no laws on the books at present against Quakers. These dreams you are having are just your caring nature. You are not used to being separated from Mary, and so naturally you worry. I'm sure Sean says the same thing, does he not?"

I had to say yes, because it is exactly what he said, but I knew for certain that something wasn't right. You can't convince a person who doesn't have the sight what it's like to have it. So I went back home, discouraged, and was going on and on about my feelings to Moira, who reminded me that our cousin Bridgett had been in Boston a few months.

"Why not write her and see if she can find out anything," she suggested. "She could go down to the jail at night and do a bit of snooping."

I wasted no time at all in writing a letter to my cousin in Boston. Then I had to sit back and wait for an answer which I knew would take a few weeks, provided Bridgett could find some kind soul to write it for her. While I waited for the reply, another dream woke me with a start. This time Mary screamed my name. Screaming with all her might, she told me she'd die if I failed to hear her. I flew over to the Dyers in the

morning and beseeched Mr. Dyer to listen to me. He didn't dare smile
this time, but his attitude remained maddeningly unchanged. He only
jabbed at the fire and stated cynically that Mary remained in England,
suiting her own purposes.

"We have no choice but to wait and see," he said.

It was a full two weeks later before I found out what had really
happened.

Chapter Twenty-Four
Jail

Mary rode her horse down to Plymouth and boarded her on the small ship that would become her home for the next two months. She didn't get to leave till November, as the Vanes were in a sorry state, tending Harry's old mother, burning furniture for fuel, and scrounging the grounds for food. Mary thought they would have starved without her, just because they were so plain useless. Harry's mother castigated Harry, daily, over betraying his father, and ruining their fortune. Mary's efforts at getting them to Newport failed because Harry still clung to his futile cause. "England is a ship without a rudder," he said and "I cannot abandon her in this state."

Early winter storms tossed the ship across the Atlantic to a fare thee well. There were times when the women on board went white with fear and the men became truly grim. Two horses in the hold, including Mary's beloved Bay mare, died from injuries brought on by rough seas. The wretched slop bucket, the close air, and the horror of being shut in when the seas were too rough to open the hatch, made the discomfort all encompassing.

After a brief, lovely stay in Barbados, she sailed north in late December, arriving in January 1657. She met a widow named Ann Burden who needed to go to Boston to settle her husband's estate. Desperate to get home, she thought she could board a ship to Newport as soon as she landed. They had no plans as far as the Society was concerned, so she thought she could do it unnoticed. The pleasure of sailing into the Boston harbor, seeing the windswept pines and the growth of the town, quickly faded when it became clear that their ship was to be boarded. The two women stood together as the officials rifled through their belongings.

The officer pawed through Mary's trunk. When he found her books and pamphlets, his face took on the look of one who had caught a thief red handed. "Quakers!" he boomed.

Before Mary could get help of any kind, she was thrown in jail.

After suffering a strip search and a whipping, they were locked in a cell, without heat or light. The first night, they lay together face to face as their backs were still raw and bleeding. The January winds blew mercilessly through the cracks in the wall. Inwardly, Mary fought to control her anger, while outwardly, she kept whispering to Ann that the power of the Lord would see them through. Yet, she knew that her survival depended solely on the jailer, William Salter. If she could not reach his Christian heart, in one way or another, they would end up carted away on the back of a bitterly cold night. So when he came with their food, she talked to him as a fellow Bostonian, describing where her house had been so many years ago. The next day, she told him of her children. She asked if he had a family. Ann asked for hot water so they could clean their wounds. On the third day, he complied. By the end of the week, he gave them a bit of straw, which they packed next to their skin.

Through long, empty hours Mary sent messages in her mind to William. She knew that if she could contact him somehow, he could get her out. Yet she was given no means of communication, and even at the time of her arrest when she had begged the officials to send word, she was denied.

During the day, Mary kept her ear next to the wall facing the street. Once she called out when she heard someone talking close enough to hear, but that brought the jailer who told her that if she continued, he would be forced to take action. She resumed listening obsessively, desperate to hear a familiar voice.

Then to Mary's dismay, Ann fell ill. A hacking cough and fever threatened to rip her only source of warmth and comfort from her arms. Without her cellmate, she would not be able to stay warm enough to live. As she tended her, trying to bring down the fever by sponging her with cold water, she remembered the night that she and I fought together for little Maher's precious life. Then it came to her. Knowing that I was blessed with the sight, she tried to communicate with me by going within. In her mind, Mary screamed to me. "Save me," she cried over and over. "I will freeze to death if you don't hear me. Save me, Irene. I'm locked up in the cold." She kept this up all through Ann's illness, all through her slow recovery, and all through the rest of January and February. Then one day, as she kept her vigil by the wall, she heard a voice that brought tears to her eyes. It was a thick Irish brogue.

"Who is there? Who is it in the jail? Tell me your names. I am here to help."

It was not my voice Mary heard, but one she knew in her heart she could trust.

"Come tonight," Mary shouted just as Ann burst into song. The jailer opened the door and told them to be quiet. That evening Mary dared to hope. When she heard a faint knock on the wall, she was ready.

"William Dyer of Newport. Can you get word to William Dyer that his wife is in jail?"

"Aye," came the reply. "My cousin works for his family. I must away."

Mary, who had been crouching by the wall, fell on her knees. "The power of the Lord is over everything," she said to Ann. "It is over everything."

I got word when the ship came in. I took off for Mr. Dyer, running like the wind. "My dream," I gasped. "It's true. She's in jail. She's in Boston."

"Boston? What is she doing there?"

"Freezing to death. My cousin spoke to her through the wall. She said to get word to you. You must go to her at once, sir. She is in danger, just like I told you. Mortal danger. Jesus, God, why did you not believe me?"

"What is the charge?"

"My cousin said they have passed a law against Quakers."

"She sailed into Boston and declared herself a Quaker?"

"No, they came on board the ship and went through her things. She's been there almost two months. You know how cold this winter has been. Please get her, sir, I beg you."

"Don't cry, Irene. I'll do what I can. I can not understand why she went there."

"Maybe it was the only place she could land. My cousin told me they arrested them right there in the harbor. You've got to get her to Newport. She was stripped and whipped."

"Did a boat come in from Boston today?"

"Yes. My cousin Bridgett was on it. It leaves in the morning."

"Go back and tell the captain I plan to sail then. Express our gratitude to your cousin and tell her I will see to her expenses. Where are the children?"

"They're at the beach. What shall I tell them?"

"Nothing yet. Tell them I have to go to Boston and ask Samuel and Anne to keep an eye on things."

"Aye. I don't know whether to laugh or cry. Think of it, sir. She could be home soon."

"Charlie won't even know her."

"It will work out, if we can just get her here. Bridgett said they are shut up in a dark cell without any heat at all. It's a miracle they've lived this long. I'm going to pack a hamper of food. She's probably near starved. I'll send along some warm clothes."

"Right. Thank you."

William headed straight to the home of Governor Endicott once he landed in Boston. Surprised to hear that the Mary Dyer housed in his jail was the wife of this respected citizen of Newport, the governor held him to a heavy bond and ordered her release. William did not hesitate to pay. Mary was to be released into his custody and kept from any communication with others in towns between Boston and Newport. Endicott insisted that she must never, under any circumstances, return. Once William Dyer agreed to these terms, the governor said she was free to go. William was shown to the door and escorted to the jail. The wind was blowing hard that day and as the door to the jail opened, he saw the two women crouched together in the corner of their cell.

He fell to his knees before her. "Mary."

"I knew you would come," she said. "I knew it. Meet my friend Ann Burden. We did not know of the laws passed against Quakers, William. We had no idea."

"I have posted bond for you. We can leave at once. There is a ship in the harbor. Irene sent along clothes and food. Come."

"What of Ann?" asked Mary. "I can't leave her here."

"You must," said William. "We will work to secure your release, Mistress Burden. I promise you, we will do everything in our power to get you out."

"Give Ann the clothes and the food then. I will help you, dear heart. I promise."

After a tearful parting, William and Mary walked down to the docks. "Irene told me you were in jail," he admitted. "She said she kept dreaming about Boston. She even dreamt one night that she went out to visit Anne on Roxbury Neck and talked to her through a wall. She described the cell exactly. I didn't believe her. I thought you would sail into Newport and I would have the chance to tease her about her Irish superstitions. I doubt I'll ever tease her again."

"The Lord opened her," said Mary, "and revealed our state."

William drew his wife to him and whispered, "I want to get you home."

When the ship came into sight of Newport, throngs of people ran down to greet them. Mary inhaled the sight of her children. Wee Charlie jumped up and down on the shore—a strong husky boy of seven. Young Mary had grown into a beauty. William, a strapping young man with the same cheery smile, could not suppress a wide grin. Samuel stood with his arm around his wife. Maher and Henry ran around leaping in the air with excitement.

Mary came toward me with her arms outstretched. Wouldn't you know it, but we both burst into tears.

"I owe you everything. My life, my children, everything."

"I'm so glad to see you, mistress. Look at you. Skin and bones. Oh wait till you get this good food and air into you. I haven't stopped eating since I came home."

"Sean is well, I gather?"

"In fine form entirely."

Back at the house, Mary took her chair by the hearth, sipping ale as the family bustled around telling stories and preparing a feast to celebrate her return.

"I started a lobster stew this morning, Mother," said young Mary. "Irene came in and said, 'Chowder, forty people.' That was it! I knew better than to question her, so I simply started cooking."

"How did you know it was the one thing I craved more than anything in the world? I cannot find the words to tell you how proud I am, Mary."

"I have not minded the work, Mother. I have missed you though."

"You're supposed to say 'thee'," said Henry.

"Father doesn't," answered Charlie. "He says he's not goin' to turn Quaker and I'm not either."

"Hush!" cried young Mary.

"There is no cause for scolding. Those who allow the Light to fill them will be refreshed."

"That's it?" asked Samuel.

Mary smiled "It's that simple."

"You know what?" said Will. "I think your form of worship will suit life over here."

"Why?"

"I think it is tailor-made for the New World. The older religions are all about duty and structure— about society and our place in society. We are not bound to the same rules here. Look at Irene. She started as our servant and now she is our friend. It's what you are saying, isn't it, Mother? Its what you mean with the 'thee' and 'thou' business, isn't it? That we are all equal."

"Precisely. I have chosen to address servants in the familiar. George Fox takes a different route, but the end result is the same: we are all equal and should address each other as such."

"It won't be that easy in Virginia," stated Maher.

"Why so?" asked Mary.

"Because of slavery. What do Quakers say of slavery?"

"The same seed of God is present in everyone. Slave owners have managed to convince themselves that their captives are not the same animal that we are. No one will convince George Fox of this because it isn't the truth."

"What about the Dutch? What will they think?" asked Maher.

"That remains to be seen."

"Will saved us from being attacked by the Dutch," boasted Charlie.

"How?"

"Father and I went out in the shallop in the early morning when their ships were in the harbor getting ready to attack. I jumped in the water, swam under the boats and tied up their rudders. It is not quite as effective as guns, but it did the trick."

"I can swim," said Charlie. "Will taught me. Can I show you? I can swim to Goats Island."

"You'll have to wait till summer, my love."

"When will we have a meeting?" asked Henry. "Do we wait till Sunday?"

"Tonight, after dinner, when our friends are here."

William, who had been silent up until this point, feigned a slight cough. Mary looked at him, but said nothing. The children's eyes went from one parent to another until Samuel changed the subject.

Through the course of the evening, Mary answered question after question about England. Wishing she could give better news, she saw nothing but sad looks on the faces at her table as she described Thurloe's spies everywhere. When the subject turned to the Society of Friends, expressions brightened. As the last pie was finished, we moved upstairs where benches had been set up to face each other. Mary spoke briefly and then asked all to sit in silence.

As spring breezed into Newport, Mary's strength returned. Attempts at getting Ann Burden released were successful. Meetings were held in the Dyer home to begin with, and then moved on to other homes as the numbers grew. William did not join her in this work, but he did not openly oppose her either. The family settled into a happy and productive time. Letters were sent to England and Barbados, but it was not until May that she heard any word from her fellow ministers.

Samuel came into the kitchen one day while we were in the process of shucking oysters. He said, "A group of Quakers just landed in Providence."

A queer feeling came over me that I immediately shoved aside. Saying nothing to Mary, who was clearly energized and excited, I wished they hadn't landed at all. Maybe I wanted life to stay the way it was for a time, with all of us living peacefully together in dear, tolerant Newport. Everything had been going so well, and now things would change. We cannot stop life from happening though, no more than we can stem the tide, or interfere with the hand of fate.

The next day after traveling to Providence, Mary and I knocked on the door of Catherine Scott, only to have it opened by Christopher Holder.

"Christopher! My goodness. What are you doing here?"

"I should have known you would find me. Come in. Catherine is at the market."

"Tell me everything," she said.

"I heard about Boston. I sent word to Barbados, but it did not reach you in time."

"I assumed you had been sent back to England."

"I was, but I returned on the *Woodhouse*. Have you heard of our miraculous voyage?"

"No. I have heard nothing."

"Come in. I will get you some ale. I don't even know where to begin. You know that the *Speedwell* was sent back. A nice circuitous route I took the first time. You can imagine my frustration, finally getting here, then jailed, then sent back to England. I guess you were already at sea by then. Well, we knew we would have the problem of finding a captain to take us with these new fines in place, so we waited until we had our own ship. The *Woodhouse* is a small vessel, so small that we had trouble locating a crew brave enough to work her. Once we set off, the captain said that the Lord led her across the ocean as a man leads a horse by the head. What a voyage. I cannot tell you of the power of our small band. Everyone from the first expedition decided to return. Not a one chose to remain in England; they braved the uncertain seas, they came knowing that they may be jailed on landing, yet none were deterred. We had meetings every day. William Robinson came with me and Humphrey Norton too."

"Wasn't Humphrey Norton the Friend who offered to take the place of George Fox in Launceston?"

"One and the same. He did great service in Ireland. It was revealed to him early on that we must take direction from the Lord. 'Cut through and steer your straightest course and mind nothing but me,' we were told. We heeded His voice and were saved on more than one occasion."

"How did the captain receive this?"

"He may have doubted us at first. But one day Humphrey Norton became convinced we were about to be pursued by an attacker. The Lord revealed that we would be carried away as in a mist. Later that day, we saw a great ship heading right for us. But a fog rolled in and we knew, to our utter relief, we would be saved. From then on, we heeded nothing of longitude or latitude, but kept to our guiding Light. We were given the direction to head southward until the evening before we were to hit land. We met in the evening and saw the shore at the time it had been prophesied. Then, under the power, the word came to us that the seed in the New World would be as great as the sand of the sea. We all heard it in union and burst into tears of joy."

"Christopher. What you have described is wondrous."

"We are going to take hold here, Mary. Don't you see? Nothing can deter us. Nothing. We know that we'll prevail. How has it been since you have been home? How is the family?"

"Wonderful. My children have grown into good people. I am at last complete, no longer tormented by the separation. Like you I am happy."

"Catherine's children have all become Friends. In knowing her, I feel I see something of Anne Hutchinson. Mary Scott is probably one of the finest young women I have ever met."

I saw Mary swallow. A mere pause in conversation ended quickly, as she rushed in to cover up her feelings. What else could she do? And what could he have done either, knowing he would soon be seeing her with Mr. Dyer and all her children. We knew it was just as well that he turn his affection elsewhere. Only I knew what it cost her.

Standing and walking over to the fire, so he would not see her face, she asked, "Is everyone from the *Woodhouse* still here then?"

"We put off five Friends on shore at New Amsterdam. William Brend plans to go to New Haven, John Copeland and myself are going to return to Boston. We have not worked out a method as yet."

"You will be treated worse than before," I told him. "I hate to be the spoiler, but Mary nearly died in prison."

"We are willing to take such punishments as are meted out. They will not have jurisdiction in the end. I am certain."

Mary turned, looking a bit anxious. "But you will stay awhile in Newport and enjoy our beautiful summer, I hope."

"Surely you are chomping at the bit for some of my lobster stew," I added. "You're no goin' to deprive me of keeping my promise. Why don't you just stay put in Newport."

"Have no fear. I have missed your cooking as much as I have missed you, Irene."

"Oh, what could I do with those tasteless, worn-out fixings I had to prepare in England? Wait till we get some of this fare into you, then you can be a proper judge of my cookin'."

"Sometimes I think you did not do this place justice. We are in paradise here—back in the Garden of Eden. Only it is a new Eden, an American Eden."

Mary looked at me and smiled ruefully. "That's what they used to say in Boston."

"We must be a part of the new seeding."

"I have missed your enthusiasm, Christopher, just as I have missed you."

"You led me here, my friend. I have you to thank."

CHAPTER TWENTY-FIVE
The Fate of Friends

The first group of Friends in Newport, springing as they did from the old followers of Anne Hutchinson from Boston, began as a close-knit group. When the *Woodhouse* passengers arrived, more meetings were held, and the group started, much to Mary's delight, to grow and flourish.

Having these Friends from England here in Newport worshipping on her beach, was a blessing that she could scarce contemplate without crying. Two parts of her had come together; those that knew Fox joined forces with that original group, the antinomians, as the clergy used to call them; she was the bridge between the two. It gave her a heady feeling. She told me that she vowed to help those *Woodhouse* passengers and friends in any way she could. Since I didn't know then what was down the road, to my eternal shame, I told her that sounded like a good idea.

As the first chill set into the August nights, our friends made plans to travel in order to spread the word. Meetings would continue in Newport, in their absence. Their presence had been such a source of joy that we were all loath to see them go. I knew that if they remained in Newport, they would be safe. I tried to talk up all the simple joys of life: building houses, raising families, worshipping freely, and setting on down the road to prosperity. To travel outside Newport, with the intention of converting settlers to their beliefs, was a path fraught with peril, and I told them this plainly. Yet I could not deter them. They were still fighting a war. Mary wouldn't dream of dissuading them; she and I both knew that they would not be hindered anyway.

The plan was to begin in Plymouth Colony, with Christopher Holder and John Copeland entering the settlement. In the event that Friends would be driven out, more would move in to take their place. So they left, with many well-wishers in Newport seeing them off.

They had great success in Sandwich, a town of Plymouth Colony where, as Humphrey Norton later stated, a great fire was kindled and the hearts of many did burn within them.

In the town of Plymouth, they did not fare as well and were met with opposition. Holder and Copeland were immediately escorted out of town by a constable. Norton arrived next and found himself led directly to the authorities. They questioned his belief in the Light as a means for salvation.

He answered, saying, "The grace of God that brings salvation has appeared unto all men." For his statement, he was conveyed fifty miles in the direction of Newport. Then William Brend, Sarah Gibbons, and John Copeland came along next. In the town of Scituate they made converts because the citizens witnessed their cries to forgive the magistrates who whipped them. Mr. Brend, an elderly gentleman, won the hearts and minds of many, who could not believe they would take the lash to such a gentle soul.

Then word came back to Newport that Humphrey Norton had been imprisoned in New Haven, and very badly treated. Mary made plans right away with William Brend and Mary Wetherhead to travel to New Haven in order to raise objections.

The day before she was to leave, Mr. Dyer entered the kitchen, just before the noon meal with a dark look on his face. "I gave my word to Governor Endicott that you would do no such thing. Have you forgotten that John Winthrop Jr. is the governor of New Haven? How well do you think he will receive you? What if his mother is there with him?"

Mary, leaning over the fire stirring a stew, stood up straight to face him. "Your word does not rule me, William. I'm sorry that you were put in such a position, but I have no choice in the matter. I am called to do this work and I must heed."

His answer came swiftly. "This is your own voice you are listening to and your own puffed up image of yourself. It has nothing to do with God."

Chopping onions, sitting by the table, I held my hand to my forehead. He had been so good up until now. I honestly thought it would all work out, that she would carry on with her ministry and he would accept it. Now I realized I had been living in a fool's paradise. This was the very reason, I thought, that I had such a time convincing her to leave England. This was what she dreaded. On the other hand, I felt the same way Mr. Dyer did. I couldn't bear the thought of her flying off, getting in the thick of all this trouble either. I was just starting to see her shape return to normal. She had been so happy too. This was not the road to contentment. Mr. Dyer was right about the promise he made. She could be slapped into jail anywhere just for violating the command issued by Governor Endicott. I had lived in New England long enough to know that all these little towns feared this kind of thing more than native uprisings, or forest fires. They had to establish order, and they hated strangers wandering in to their settlements causing problems. She was about to barge into John Winthrop Jr.'s jurisdiction. I just sat there, knife in hand, eyes tearing up from the onions, lost in my own confusion.

Then Mr. Dyer spoke again. "You were released into my custody. In effect, I am your jailer now. I forbid you to go."

Mary's mouth fell open. She threw the spoon on the table and took off to the beach. I ran after her.

"Throw off all the yokes," she told me. "That is Fox's position; it is my position; it is the position of all the Friends I know, male and female, but it is not my husband's position."

"Nor is it the law," I said.

"Then how do I do this, Irene? William simply wants me for himself."

"As do all husbands."

"But he doesn't care a fig for my abilities."

"Maybe you can wait a couple of days and see if he softens. You always throw everything at him too quickly. Men are slow compared to us. You have to treat them like a loaf of bread. It has to be kneaded, then left to rise, then kneaded again. You know what happens if you rush the bread."

She accepted this strategy. We were okay for a few more days, but that was not to last. Just like it had been in England, news would filter in and then everyone would jump on their horses and go flying off, just to get thrown in jail. We heard that dear Humphrey Norton, a man special to me on account of his clear gift of the sight, suffered being branded on the forehead with an "H" for heretic.

We had to leave then. Sean had a fit and I had to placate him. He tore into me about my condition, but I told him I knew beyond a shadow of a doubt that the baby I carried was goin' to make it. He accused me of having no way of knowing. Can you imagine? I could not let Mary go off without me, so I ignored his wishes and joined her.

Once landed on the Connecticut shore, we sought the company of our friend, but were prevented in having any discourse with him by John Winthrop Jr. He sneered at us, looking us up and down as if we were diseased. At the sight of him, bitterness rose in Mary's throat like poison. The governor, being the spitting image of his father, right down to the same long nose and pointy beard, did not help. Memories of the defiled grave of her baby came flooding back. He took great pleasure in telling us to leave; we were led from the town, put on horseback, and driven off. When the constable slapped the back of Mary's horse, she lost her temper and yelled to all in sundry that they would suffer for Humphrey Norton's sake.

Arriving back in Newport, Mary returned to an angry husband. Convinced that she had done nothing to further her cause, he told her she probably made things worse.

"Humphrey has been released. He's going to Plymouth. He is not deterred as easily as you, William."

"You could stay home and help the people you've encouraged to settle here, Mary. John Rouse and William Leddra came from Barbados while you were gone. They were very disappointed not to see you."

"Do not think that by making me feel guilty, William, you will succeed in keeping me here." With that she went off in search of the new arrivals.

John Copeland and Christopher Holder set out on their mission with the intention of returning to Boston. Knowing they could not arrive by sea, they found passage to Martha's Vineyard, some fifty miles to the east. They found no welcome at all there and were shortly ordered to leave. After hiding for a few days, they met up with Indians. Because Christopher knew enough to communicate, they made instant friends. The natives took them by canoe to Massachusetts.

After landing at Cape Cod, they crossed the cape and found a town which was at that time without a minister. They held a meeting in a clearing by a stream, newly named Christopher's Hollow. By the time they were ready to leave, they had a group of convinced Friends. Buoyed up with their success, they went on from town to town, toward Boston.

By the time they arrived in Salem, word had reached Governor Endicott. He made sure they were ready. After the Sunday service in the

Salem Congregational Church, Christopher stood to speak. No sooner had the first words left his mouth, than he found himself grabbed by the hair. A handkerchief and then a glove were shoved right down his throat till he choked. Not just gagged, mind you, but choked until he nearly lost his life! He fell to the ground writhing and turning blue. Had it not been for Samuel Shattuk, a church member, who managed to pull away the hand of the town commissioner, Christopher would not have lived through the service that Sunday.

By Monday, Copeland and Holder were safely housed in a bare cell in Boston. Thirty-three stripes with the lash was their official welcome. Shattuck, for his kindness to them, was banished.

Now, in late September, the nights started getting colder. By order of the deputy governor, the prisoners received the horrific news that they were to be whipped twice a week. The first whipping would be fifteen lashes, with each successive scourging increased by three lashes. The prisoners resolved to continue to pray for forgiveness for their attackers. Each time the whip was raised and their backs burned and stung, they repeated their prayers. Back in the cell, they did what they could to clean the wounds, but with the flesh having no chance to heal between lashes, more and more of it fell off their backs in great chunks. Infection, of course, sat in wait for them like the demon in Reverend Wilson's sermons.

In October of 1657, while Holder and Copeland were still in jail, and we were able to do nothing for them, new laws were passed against Quakers. A fine of one hundred pounds would to be inflicted on anyone bringing a Quaker into the colony, forty shillings for every hour that one should entertain or hide a Quaker. Any Quaker caught returning after having once suffered, if a man, was to have an ear cropped, for a second offense another ear, and for a third, have his tongue bored with a hot iron. If the offender was a woman, she was to be severely whipped and on the third offense have her tongue bored.

After two and a half months in a cold bare cell, with backs so subjected to the whip they never stopped throbbing, with every movement putting them near tears, the men were finally released. They set sail for Barbados, and there they spent the winter.

On a cold wet day in the winter of 1658, Mary and I headed over to Dorothy Brenton's house, across and beyond Newport to Brenton's Point. With too much ice on the path for horses, we opted in favor of setting out on foot. We did not get past our own gate before our feet got soaked through. Dorothy, inching her way slowly towards joining the Society, ever since Mary's return, dropped hints earlier that week that her position of hold out was about to come to an end. This mission of convincing Dorothy kept Mary trudging along through the cold. Confined to her hearth through the whole of January, as Newport had been hit by one wicked storm after another, we needed any kind of diversion. Past the town, we viewed the long, lonely stretch of land we had to cross before Brenton's Point. The wind whipped through layers of shawls and cloaks; our feet hurt from the cold, and ice clung to the hem of our skirts. As flurries of snow swirled around us, we had trouble making our way along the path. Mary bid me to hold on to her waist as she fretted on my account, just as I worried about her. We could hardly hear each other over the wind. She remarked that expedition was about as wise as our trip across Morecombe Bay. Somehow this struck me as a portent and I began to wonder if we hadn't done something really foolish. When we heard the sounds of horses snorting in the cold, we shouted for help. A young man in a cart fitted with runners came to the rescue. We were safely delivered to the Brentons, frozen right through.

By nightfall, I heard Mary talking more quickly than usual. I saw her drop her shawl as if she wanted to throw it off her. As I leaned down to pick it up I noticed how red her face looked. We were in front of the Brentons great fire, enjoying a flagon of ale, and I could have put it down to that, but some instinct made me reach out with my hand and feel her forehead. Mary had been struck with a terrible fever. We ganged up on her and got her into bed. Dorothy sent word to Mr. Dyer that Mary would remain with them until she could be moved. To appease her, and because her mind was probably made up already, Dorothy made an announcement. She declared that she would follow Mary with every bit of dedication she had displayed in her days as a devotee of Anne Hutchinson.

Mary shook her head vehemently at these words, saying it was not about her, but Dorothy said, "You know what I mean, and I mean it. My hesitation had nothing to do with the Society. It just took me awhile to come off Anne and on to something else."

Mary closed her eyes then and we saw two fat tears run down her cheeks. I wiped her face as I sponged her. She grabbed my hand and squeezed. Pneumonia set in where it held her in its grip for the rest of the winter.

Word reached us that two Friends, William Brend and William Leddra, had been captured in the woods outside of Salem. They were taken to Boston, and Mary could do nothing to help them except to send letters to Edward Hutchinson. We lived for the mail that winter, sending the younger boys down to the wharf daily in search of ships and news.

We heard that the Friends held in the Boston jail had not fared well at all. Under the jurisdiction of a cruel jailer who desired to profit from their labor, they were forced to go five days without food and were given twenty lashes apiece with a three-corded whip. Poor old William Brend, the sweetest man you'd ever want to meet, had his head shoved down to his ankles with irons snapped shut, holding his neck and ankles locked together. After being kept like this for sixteen long hours, he was taken to the mill the next day and put to work. When he refused again, the jailer flew into a mad rage and went after Brend with a rope. After twenty blows, the rope unraveled, which only made the jailer more maniacal. He came back like a crazed lunatic with a thicker, stronger rope, this time dipped in tar. In his frenzy, the jailer's mouth foamed up. In a deranged rage, he struck William Brend until he reached the unheard of number of one hundred and seventeen blows.

When the town heard of this savagery they appealed to the governor. Endicott sent in his surgeon who came back saying that the flesh hung in bags under Brend's arms, and would rot off his body before anything could be done to repair him. From sneaking outside the jail at night, Bridgett learned from other prisoners that Brend had turned cold and that he could neither hear nor see. When talk came of having the jailer appear before the next general court, the clergy defended the jailer's cruelty by saying, "William Brend endeavored to beat our gospel ordinances black and blue, if he then be beaten black and blue, it is but just upon him."

I barely finished describing this tale before Mary began crying. She sobbed from a place deep and low in her chest. Still clogged up with phlegmatic coughing, the crying caused much laboring and gasping for breath. Her head sunk down to the table. I could think of no words of comfort, so I stroked her hair. William, fearing something had happened to one of the children, rushed to her side. She spilled out the news between gulps.

He said, "You people have to forget about Boston. You have to admit that it won't do anyone any good to beat your heads against the authorities in Massachusetts."

"You are wrong!" she croaked. "We will not stop until we have our legitimate right to practice our religion as we see fit."

"You will not succeed in stripping the Boston clergy of their power! You will not succeed in changing the minds of the magistrates, any more than Anne did."

"Anne is respected for her efforts."

"Anne is dead, Mary! We founded Newport so that we could establish religious freedom. We got a charter. We can welcome as many Friends here as you like. Don't go trying to inflict your will in places you cannot change."

"We have to do something about these unfair laws against Quakers! I don't know how long it will take, or what we will have to suffer in order to meet our mission, but those laws will be changed. When I leave this world, I want to know that my children, and the children of my friends, will not be beaten to death for their beliefs."

"I have given my word that you will stay here. Does my word mean nothing to you? Does dishonoring your husband mean nothing?"

"No. I would not have asked you to make that promise—even if it meant that I must remain in jail. I cannot promise that I will not return to Boston. I cannot make that promise to you, or to any other living creature."

"Why?"

"It may be revealed that I must journey to Boston for the purposes of my ministry. I have to obey the word of God."

"God does not ask such things of people!"

"He does! The *Woodhouse* sailed here without a compass. God led those good people here for a reason. He spoke to the prophets and he has spoken to us. Does it stand to reason that he would speak once and then never again in all of history? We have to make the way clear. One day, our numbers will be as great as the sands of the sea."

"Are you saying that you fully intend to martyr yourself?"

"I am saying I will do what is asked of me."

"This is inconsiderate madness." He grabbed his hat and stormed out of the house.

Mary kept on weeping. I rubbed her back and said nothing. The last thing I wanted to do was encourage her. I remember feeling deeply frightened by what I heard. So what did I say? "Things will be better in the summer. Christopher will be coming back."

Chapter Twenty-Six
The Ear Cropping

By spring, the joy of all joys came to me at last. Mary placed a healthy newborn son in my arms. Happy at last, I felt the curse had been lifted for good.

The beleaguered sufferers returned from Boston in time to let the summer sun and native salves heal their torn backs. Christopher Holder sailed to Newport by way of Bermuda, announcing that he felt ripe to return to Boston. He hooked up with his old companion John Copeland. They were both arrested right away, that August, in Dedham, Massachusetts.

Governor Endicott said, "You can be sure that you will have your ears cut off."

A few days later, Christopher found a cellmate in the form of John Rouse, who felt moved to ally himself with them. He received the same sentence. All three, subjected to twice weekly beatings, were put constantly to work. Word spread throughout New England, and Friends streamed into Boston from Newport, Providence, Sandwich, Salem, New Haven, and Plymouth.

Mary and I walked to Boston by way of the old trail. I had my wee Sean in an Indian papoose Mary got for me. Catherine Scott, along with her daughters Mary and Patience, joined us from Providence. I went along to keep Mary from being noticed. Mr. Dyer was dead set against her going.

On September 17, 1658, they found themselves face to face with the magistrates. Endicott pronounced, "You are greater enemies to us than those who come openly; since under pretense of peace, you come to poison the people."

Then they were asked for proof that the Lord had sent them.

John Rouse answered, "If we were evildoers, the judgments of God would be heavier upon us than those we suffer by you."

Taking offense to this, the governor said, "Quakers have nothing to prove their commission by, but the spirit within them, and that is the devil."

Copeland answered, "We have seen some of your laws that have many Scriptures in the margin; but what example have you in the Scripture for cutting off ears?"

After calling each of them by name, Endicott said angrily, "It is the sentence of the court, that you three have each of you his right ear cut off by the hangman."

They were taken back to the prison. On September 16, the marshal's deputy read the order. "To the marshal-general or to his deputy: You are to take with you the executioner, and to repair to the house of correction, and there to see him cut off the right ears of John Copeland, Christopher Holder and John Rouse, Quakers; in execution of the sentence of the court of assistants, for the breach of the law, entitled Quakers."

When the prisoners were brought into another room, John Rouse said, "We have appealed to the chief magistrate of England."

Holder added, "Such execution of this should be done publicly, and not in private; this is contrary to the law of England."

The marshal answered, "We do it in private to keep you from tattling."

The executioner took hold of Holder first. He brushed aside his black hair, and the marshal, seeing this, turned his back.

Rouse says, "Turn about and see it."

The marshal, full of dread, weakly said, "Yes, yes, let us look on it."

The two others stoically submitted to the knife. When the deed was done, they said, "Those that do it ignorantly, we desire from our hearts the Lord forgive them; but for them that do it maliciously, let our blood be upon their heads; and such shall know in the day of account, that every drop of our blood shall be as heavy upon them as a millstone."

As if they had not been punished enough for one day, after the ear cropping, they were whipped again.

Outside the jail, a large crowd gathered. We had entered the town very carefully. I thought that if I could restrain Mary from making a public spectacle, we could get in and out before anyone figured out she was even there. She dressed plainly in gray and wore a cap with a large fold in front that covered most of her face. Catherine convinced her on the trail that it would do no good to anyone to have her identity discovered. We all agreed that Catherine would be the public voice.

We were surprised by how much Boston looked the same. A pretty time of year, the light filtered through the trees giving a golden hue. We went first to the spring to get refreshed—just as we had all those years ago. The town had grown in size of course, but the central core of the settlement we once called home, remained as prim and ordered as ever.

We met up with the big crowd down by the jail. In a clear, loud voice, Catherine expressed her objection to the ear cropping. Before we even had a sense of what was happening, Catherine, for her words of criticism against the ear cropping, found herself sentenced to a public whipping! They came right up, and dragged her to the post. Mary and I clutched each other as we heard the fabric of her dress tear. Rough hands pulled and ripped. She writhed, but without the use of her hands, could not cover herself. Her daughters on either side of us, whimpered. Our dear friend, a beloved mother, respected citizen of Providence, sister of Anne Hutchinson and leader to whom we all turned in our times of troubles, faced her former neighbors, stripped bare to the waist. Oh, but she put us in mind of her sister. Tied to the whipping post, the only part of her she could move was her head, and that she held high. All the women standing near her called out to her.

I screamed at the top of my lungs. "God save you, Catherine Scott. God love Anne Hutchinson!"

She carried the day, I tell you. In my heart, I know that no matter what I could ever do or say would hold a candle to how magnificently Catherine carried herself that day. My God, she was splendid. Each stroke of the lash brought more of New England over to the Quaker side.

Her attacker ended with, "If you come hither again, there is likely to be a law to hang you."

In a voice loud and strong enough for the crowd to hear she declared, "If God calls us, woe to us if we come not. I have no question that He whom we love will not make us count our lives dear unto ourselves for His name's sake."

Endicott boomed out his answer. "We shall be as ready to take away your lives as you are to lay them down."

The long walk back home grew soggy with tears. I didn't know what I could do for Mary. The brutality stirred something up deep inside her. Maiming Christopher was not what she intended, she told me, when she encouraged him to come to the New World. She felt guilty for bringing her friends over.

Just as the first snows started to fall, we heard of the death of Cromwell. "Good riddance," I said after I spit into the slop bucket. If I could have walked to his grave, I would have, just to have the privilege of spitting on that too. Mr. Dyer, reading from a pamphlet, told us that after accepting the name, style, title and dignity of king, his health proceeded to fail him. The death of Lady Claypole, his favorite daughter, who starved herself and broke down her own health entirely, took the wind out of his sails. Apparently, he went downhill after that.

He died on what he called his lucky day, September 3, the anniversaries of the battles of Dunbar and Worcester. Only eight months earlier, he had been vested in a robe of purple velvet, lined with ermine. He sat on a raised chair of state, holding a scepter of gold, with people all around him shouting, "God Save the Lord Protector." Yet as he lay dying, Cromwell asked his chaplain a question: "Is it possible to fall from grace?" After being assured by his minister that it was not possible, Cromwell said, "Then I am saved, for I know that I was once in grace."

The arrogance of this killer, this blackguard, this usurper, this treasonous pile of pus, never failed to amaze me. He named his cursed, hopeless excuse for a son as his successor.

"Richard will follow in his father's footsteps, it seems," said Mr. Dyer as he put down the pamphlet.

Mary stood with her hands on her hips. "No, he won't."

"He will sit on the raised chair of state in Whitehall with all honors and duties given to the king."

"Not for long."

"How can you be certain?"

"We will see the restoration of the rightful king."

"Are you privy to some information of which I have been left ignorantly in the dark?"

"No. I see it as a natural course."

"How dear do you think King Charles will hold your cause?"

"Friends in England have expressed high hopes, William. The current thinking is that King Charles may harbor a place in his heart for those who have been persecuted. He will believe in justice, and he will be sworn to uphold the laws of England. Once the Great Seal is broken, the power of the army will be subdued, and the power of Parliament will return. Richard Cromwell is not the man his father was. England is sick to death of this whole mess. Thurloe won't be able to maintain his hold. Richard is not anywhere near shrewd enough to hang on—not in the face of the present mood of the people. Tumbledown Dick is what he is called in London."

"Would it give you more peace to see the king restored?"

"Yes. Of course," she added, looking at him as if what he just said was rather puzzling.

"Then I shall pray for such an outcome."

On the nineteenth of October, in the flaming fire of fall, the General Court of Massachusetts met again for their regular session. Pastor Norton petitioned the court to write a law that would see Quakers banished upon pain of death. It passed by a feeble majority of one. A man named Wozel, who had been absent due to illness, was so taken aback by the decision, he immediately made his distress known. Weeping with grief, he said that if he had only known he would have crept on his knees to register his vote. It was recorded into law on the twentieth of October 1658. According to the new law, anyone from the cursed sect called Quakers could be apprehended without warrant, and driven from town to town until they faced trial. If proven that they belonged to the pernicious sect, they would be sentenced to banishment on pain of death.

CHAPTER TWENTY-SEVEN
On Pain of Death

Mary's patterns of eating and sleeping went all out of kilter. Thoughts of how to reach those in opposition plagued her night and day.

"Christians hanging Christians. Who would have thought we'd come to this, Irene? Remember what we envisioned when we sailed to the New World in 1635? Remember Winthrop's talk of the city on a hill? We were supposed to be the ones who would shed light for other nations to take example by. Will the citizens of Boston have to face the sight of us hanging from a halter before they get it? This is nothing more than a government promoting its own ideology at the cost of Christian lives. How can the Boston magistrates be made to listen? Do they really want the deaths of Friends on their consciences? Will they go so far as to hang a woman—only for her religious beliefs?"

"What woman are you speaking of?"

"It could be any one of us, or our daughters, or our daughters' husbands. We have to think of some way to get this law changed."

"It will have to come from England then, don't you think?"

"Once England is put to rights, maybe that will happen. How many will die in the meantime?"

"No one has to die, mistress, unless they do it willingly. Shouldn't we all just stay out of there until the law is changed?"

"But then it won't be changed."

On winter nights while the rest of the family slept, Mary crept downstairs to her wheel by the fire. She spun, she wove, she fashioned lace and embroidered a wedding dress for her daughter. Some nights I'd be up with the baby, and if I saw candles burning, I would pop over and keep her company.

One night William, stumbling down the stairs, asked her why she did not sleep.

"I have to do something for Mary. I want to give her something."

"But why the secrecy? Why not do this in the daylight? Why not work with her?"

"It has to be a surprise."

"Why? She is not planning to marry soon. She won't give the Brenton boy the time of day."

"I don't know what will happen this spring and summer, William. If I am called away, I want to go, knowing that I did something for my daughter."

"Called away? How can you be called away?"

"Have you understood nothing?"

"I understand that you are needed here, my love. You are needed more than you know. Do not tell me you are thinking of Boston."

"I do not know how much will be asked of me."

"By whom?"

"By God."

"Mary. God does not ask such things of anyone. He does not ask people to submit themselves to cruel jailers and ignorant magistrates. He asks only that you care for those whom He has given into your care."

"Precisely. Those whom He has entrusted to me will be suffering under cruel and unfair laws. I have a responsibility to see those laws changed."

"Have they not made themselves plain enough? They do not want you there."

"They have shown themselves to be plainly wrong."

"It seems you do not hold us very dear."

"My love has grown since I joined the Society. But just as my love has grown, so too has my family."

"Your children will hear that their mother was mad."

"I don't want my children and grandchildren to go through life subjected to mean stares and whippings. I don't want them to be hated for their beliefs. I don't want them to have to suffer the same pain and grief I have had to suffer. When I see those looks of hatred directed at me, sometimes I have no further wish to live."

"You get no hateful stares here. No whippings. To contemplate any move from this loving shelter is wrong. Leave off the Society of Friends outside Newport. Live your life here. That is not too much to ask."

Mary held out her hand to him. She could see that his eyes were filled with tears because for the first time, he had a sense that she might do some crazy thing and he knew now that he would not be able to stop her. "I know. If circumstances were different, I would take my place here and fulfill all my duties as wife and mother joyfully, but how can you ask me to sit docilely by while Friends are put to death?"

"These men are in a hanging mood, Mary. There is no way to stop them."

"They will be stopped."

"How?"

"The power of the Lord is over all."

"God wants you to be a wife and mother. God never asked anyone to stretch from a halter. It is contrary to every teaching."

"He does not want His people hanged either. Don't you see that?"

"I only see that you must stay out of Boston."

"I may not be able to, William. If I am called, I must go."

"Do you think that by climbing the ladder to the gallows tree, you will show the world the depth and breadth of your faith? You will only succeed in making them wonder if your faith is real."

"There will be those who will die for religious freedom."

"Promise me you won't be one of them."

"I cannot make that promise, William."

"Do you not care for me at all? Do you not care for our children?"

"Think back to our days in London, William, when I was pregnant with Samuel. I thought that in making the crossing and coming to the New World I could die. So did our friends there. So did the ship's captain. When Puritans were being persecuted, you thought the risk was worth it. I want our children to be free to come to the truth."

"They can do that here."

"I want them to be able to do that anywhere, either in England, or any town in New England. I am devoted to this principle, William. Devoted."

"I remember a time when you were devoted to us."

"But don't you remember how I searched, how dark the world was at times?"

"It seems to me that it is darker now. I don't think you've seen any light but what shines from the halo you've put over your own head."

"Whether you understand my beliefs, or refuse to understand my beliefs, William, I am unmoved."

He stared at her in silence. He looked at me for help. For once, words failed me. My mouth turned to powder. I was about as useful as a dumb sheep. Then, with his back bent in resignation, with his head bowed, he turned and put one weary foot in front of the other and climbed the stairs to bed.

In the spring of 1659, word came from Harry Vane that he was back in Parliament, at last. The army, increasingly ill at ease with both the new Protector and his handpicked Parliament, demanded a recall of the old Rump. After four months in office, Tumbledown Dick Cromwell's relationship with the army had dissolved to the extent that he did not even have a personal guard.

Wouldn't you know it, but the first problem before the new House was to raise the money needed to cover the cost of the funeral of that pompous piece of work, Oliver Cromwell.

Sir Harry wrote that England went plain nuts over the whole affair: Cromwell's corpse was embalmed in sheet lead and wrapped in an earthen shroud. He was not interred until November 3. Crowds of mourners passed through three rooms in Whitehall that were draped in black and decorated with escutcheons. They then arrived before Cromwell's wax effigy, standing draped in ermine and velvet with the gilt sword of power at its side, and in its hands were the scepter and orb. When his body was taken to Westminster Abbey, it was escorted through jammed streets by lines of infantry in new red and black coats—still unpaid for.

After the funeral, army pay, also in arrears, brought another pressing problem to the new House. They resented being commanded by a mere civilian and had plans of wresting control of the army from young Dick. As soon as these sentiments were voiced, Vane spoke to his old cause. All the power, he said, should rest with a true Parliament, representing the people. Harry wrote that he was not without hope. He felt that he must explain the old cause to the new members, describe what the civil war had brought, and make them understand that England had covered itself in blood for a reason. Revolution, Vane thought, was not so much of a memory to be defended; it was a dream they had not yet seen to fruition. In conclusion, he added to Mary that her Royalist dreams had not gone up in the smoke of civil war, but were very much still present in England.

Mary, who was sitting sewing, got to her feet. "He says nothing of the Massachusetts law."

"He must not have heard," I answered. "He spoke mainly of himself, as usual."

By summer, Mary finished her work on the wedding dress. Wrapping it carefully in linen before packing it away in her great chest, she placed it tenderly on top of the old ball gown and sprinkled dried valerian leaves to protect it from moths.

She took to rising early and spending hours on the shore watching the early morning light slip across the ocean. Every bird crying overhead, every duck diving for fish, every clamshell lying open on the beach, and every tree bending in the wind, reminded her that there was nothing ever made that was not made by God. God is in everything and God is everywhere, she repeated to me. I started to believe that she'd be all right, as long as we could keep any news from reaching her. How was that possible? As if Newport wasn't cut off enough from the world, I wanted to put it in a barrel, and seal it up, so we could keep our Mary safe.

In September, our friend and neighbor, William Robinson, rode from Newport with Christopher Holder to a new Friend's house. On this ride, he said he clearly and distinctly heard the word of the Lord. It became very clear to him that he was being asked to go to Boston and lay down his life in service. Christopher vowed to go with him. Marmaduke Stephenson, a new arrival from Barbados, told them that he sailed to Newport under a direct order from God.

I didn't know what to make of these movings of the spirit and hearings of the word. I knew saints had these kinds of episodes. But I also knew what this would do to Mary, so I resented them and told all in sundry that they were just plain daft. I joined forces with William, saying that God doesn't ask us to be martyrs, even though I knew in my Catholic heart that it does happen from time to time, but not to one of my own. Besides, I reasoned that since they were all Protestants, they had to be wrong anyway. Much as I liked the Friends and had a soft spot in my heart for all of them, especially for being so good to me, I would have done all I could to help them except affirm their callings to die.

Patience Scott, a little girl of Catherine's brood, told her mother that she heard a definite moving of the Lord to go to Boston and bear testimony against the persecuting spirit. Catherine, who was unable to travel, sent for Mary. They decided that a group of her friends would go. Mary, in her capacity as minister, would be their guide. My Sean told me he would lock me up if I set off again, but I knew he didna' mean it. Young Mary wanted to join us, but Mr. Dyer wouldn't let her go.

We set out from Providence on a warm, sunny day. Mary wondered if she too would hear something by direct voice. She made herself ready to hear, but no revelation came, thank the Lord. I suppose it didn't help, with me praying one way and her, the other.

Eventually, she decided that it did not matter whose ears had been opened, only that His will be obeyed. "It is fitting that He spoke to a nine-year-old girl. Do you know why, Irene? Because no one doubts her."

"Aye."

"The enemy must be looked at in love. That's the hardest part. I fear neither the whip, nor the gallows, as much as I shudder at my own fury. We have to remain in an attitude of patient forbearance; we have to have hope for forgiveness; it is very important that we don't lose sight of this; we must hold our persecutors in the light. You know my natural inclination was to hate these men passionately and to fight them to the death."

"Mine too."

"I can't forget that these are the same men who defiled the grave of my baby and who branded me as the devil's whore."

"I can't forget it either. Nor can I forget that they locked up a mother of twelve children, kept her in the freezing cold, and drove us out of Massachusetts with a pregnant Anne trying to keep a brave face."

"I have to remind myself all the time to stay in obedience to His will."

"It's hard to be sure which is which," I added. "Mostly, I'm pretty sure He just wants me to keep going."

We kept a watchful eye on Patience as we traipsed along. Her expression never wavered from one of grim determination. Mary Scott's forehead remained knit with worry for Christopher. It was no secret that she loved him deeply and hoped to marry him. I noticed Mary always grew quiet when the subject came up.

Once in Boston, everyone was arrested. I got off on grounds of being Catholic and refusing to own up to being a Quaker. I ran to the docks and found a ship sailing for Newport. Sending word to Mr. Dyer, he wrote back right away to Governor Endicott saying that he was aware of promising to keep his wife from returning. He added that although he was sorry she had chosen to reenter Boston, he felt it behooved him to ask what law of England the magistrates were acting upon. He argued that they had become far worse than the Anglican bishops they sought to escape, and he begged for mercy, describing his wife as a tender soul.

Banished on pain of death was the sentence meted out by the General Court of Massachusetts. I could hardly believe my ears. I guess I thought they'd never do it, or they'd make exceptions for the women, but they surprised me once again. The ends they needed to go to in order to display their misbegotten Christianity stupefied me.

We hit the trail back home, once again, in a now very familiar state of rejection. The path now had a familiarity to it that struck me as ironic. We were always heading to Aquidneck, putting one humiliated foot in front of the other. How many times were we going to get exiled from Paradise?

Christopher continued on his travels. Robinson and Stephenson hiked northward through the woods to Salem. The circle of Friends worshiped in secret, but it didn't take long before they were discovered. Robinson and Stephenson found themselves captured and marched back to jail in Boston.

In the pale light of late August, as Mary ambled along the shore in Newport, the sound of sobbing broke her meditation. Coming around the point, she found William Robinson's ten-year-old son lying on the wet rocks, crying his eyes out. After offering what little comfort she could, Mary spent the day searching for solutions as we worked in her kitchen garden. For the first time I could remember, she wouldn't share her thoughts with me. I feared the worst

Late that night, Mary tiptoed into the rooms where her children slept and kissed them, one by one. She put a few things in a satchel and slipped out the door. The sky, bright with stars, threw down enough light to guide her. Just past her front gate, Mary spotted me coming toward her.

"Where are you goin'?"

"I might have known," she sighed. "What are you doing out of bed?"

"I could ask you the same question, but I think we both know the answer. Were you not even goin' to say goodbye?"

"I couldn't. I didn't want William to know."

"He'll know soon enough."

"I have to go to Boston, Irene. I can't leave my friends in jail without giving them support. They need to see a familiar face."

"Do they need to see that face with a noose about the neck? Some-one else can go. I'll go."

"It doesn't mean the same thing if you go."

"I'll send Bridgett then. It doesn't have to be you."

"Yes, it does. I'm ready."

"What good does it do anyone to get yourself killed? What good did it do my brothers? Ireland was still conquered."

"It will be free again."

I grabbed Mary by the shoulders. "I have seen this look before. I know it for what it is. I put Samuel in your arms that day. Do you re-member? The Almighty asks more of the living than he does of the dead. It's no great trick to martyr yourself. What are you trying to prove?"

"That this place is worthy of more. Don't you remember what it looked like when we first saw it? I could scarcely even breathe. It was beyond heaven. These magistrates are wrecking all our chances. We have to make them change. It will be worth it in the end. The rest of the world will look on this place and envy us our freedom. I brought these people here, Irene! I aim to see they are not disappointed." Then she lowered her voice again, glancing nervously toward the house. "I am as responsible for them as you are for your son. I told them to follow the light, only to see them beaten to jelly. I have felt every lash as if it were on my own back. I cannot sit here in the comfort of my hearth and see my friends put to death."

My eyes filled with tears. "We have come so far together, you and I. I do not want to live here without you."

"The best thing I ever did in my whole life was to pick you out of that crowd in London."

I started to cry. "God love you, Mary." Then it hit me. "I'm coming with you then."

"No. I have to do this alone."

"No, you don't." My mind raced around thinking of something to say. I came up with a terrible lie. "I have been moved of the spirit to go. I have had a definite leading."

"That is your own will."

"Then how did I know to be out here then? How come I have my things packed? How come I have the food ready? Do you even have any food?"

She sighed, "No."

"Do you have winding sheets?"

"No."

"Do you have a rosary?"

She smiled. "No."

"All right then, we'll be off."

"But you won't tell? You won't try to stop me."

"Much as I'd like to, I see that I can't. I do want to be with you, though, for however long I can. Chances are, Endicott will not have the stomach to hang anyone. Let me go get wee Sean over to Moira." I dashed back into my house and was able to scribble a hasty note for Mr. Dyer.

As we started out, she said, "That's what I'm hoping for, you know. If Governor Endicott won't hang me, maybe he won't hang them."

"May the curse of Cromwell be on him."

Off we stole into the night. Scurrying away as fast as we could, Mary darted under the cover of trees whenever she heard a strange sound, or detected footsteps approaching. She seemed as jumpy as a young deer. A few bands of natives passed us, that was all.

We got about twelve miles a day. By night, after a simple meal, we rolled our blankets and covered ourselves with our cloaks. Sleep did not edge in like a welcome friend. My thoughts darted around. I told Maher and young Will, the day before we left, that I thought she might try something like this. I told them that if we seemed to be missing, to act quickly, and have their father write the governor. I kept wracking my brains trying to think of something else.

CHAPTER TWENTY-EIGHT
The First Execution

Entering Boston undetected, in the early morning light, we turned the corner at School Street and headed up to the spring. After refreshing ourselves, we talked about how many times we used to do this in the early morning, how we'd be doing it still if Harry Vane hadn't lost the election. We passed Anne's old house and the Winthrop's. Half the leaves on the huge maple tree in the Hutchinson yard had begun their red march. A beech, down the street, showed its first tints of bright yellow. What was not evergreen in Boston, had turned the autumnal corner and now veered toward glory. With Anne gone, and the Winthrops dead, I wondered what they would have thought of this crazy turn of events. John Winthrop Jr. came out against the law banishing Quakers on pain of death. So if he opposed it, I hoped there must be some way to break through. We strolled over to the churchyard linking arms, and dropping down to our knees at the baby's grave. Then we headed over to her old house. Every speck of the dirt in that yard looked familiar. William's well-built house stood as solidly as ever, sheltering another family now. Standing by the gate, Mary's eyes filled with tears.

"Look at my roses."

When the front door opened, we hurried away. She wanted to go to the jail next. I found a thousand reasons why we should do that later, but she didn't listen to any of them.

As we approached, she grabbed my arm and said, "Isn't that Christopher?"

Thinking that the lack of food and sleep had caused her eyes to play tricks on her, and sure she must be mistaken, I could have fallen over when he turned and greeted us.

"Mary! Irene. What are you doing here?"

"The same thing you are, I imagine. I came to visit the prisoners."

"I'm on my way to England," he announced, drawing us aside. "I'm going back to get the advice of George Fox. We have to do something about this law."

"Then go, Christopher. Go now. I will go into the prison. Don't get yourself arrested. They'll hang you."

"No, Mary, it is you who must go. Does your husband know you're here?"

"Get yourself on a ship, Christopher. You must listen to me now. Mary Scott loves you with her whole heart. You should be marrying and building a family. I have had six children. You have none. Get on a ship and away with you. You'll do Friends more good in England than you will here. Get a hold of Sir Harry. He's back in Parliament now. You could get this law repealed before anyone is sent to the gallows."

We heard the door of the jail open. I stopped breathing. The marshal came out and to my horror recognized them both.

"This man is on his way to England," said Mary. "Put him on a ship, sir. He comes from a very highborn family who will threaten your charter if you hang him. Take him down to the wharf and send him on his way. The governor will thank you. He said himself he doesn't want to hang him."

The constable looked at both of them. "Is your passage booked, sir?"

"Yes," he said, looking reluctantly to Mary. "But let my friend here go and take me in her stead."

"You people are always trying to exchange yourselves one for another. Yet you all show no regard for our laws."

Deliberately, I think, Mary lost her temper. "We came to look your bloody laws in the face!"

At that her hands were tied behind her back and they carted her off into custody. I screamed my head off, until they threatened me with prison. Knowing I would not do her any good in there, I clammed up. Quakers talked a lot of being full of the power. I do not know what was inside me at that moment, but I turned and hit Christopher. If I'd shot him with a musket, he could not have looked more crestfallen. "Save her," I shrieked, as he was led off down to the docks.

I learned that, once in prison, she would remain there until the general court met on the nineteenth of October. I stayed on in Boston with Bridgett. The two of us snuck out at night. I talked to her while Bridgett kept guard.

Mary was chained to the wall this time; she was utterly alone and unable to contact her friends. The first night she thought she heard William Robinson shouting, but he was stopped before she could answer. She slept in intervals. At one point she dreamt she would be executed when she woke. For the first second, when she opened her eyes, she felt relief. Then she remembered. Ice ran through her veins, as she broke out in a damp sweat. Be still and cool in the light, she told herself over and over. As she was fed nothing, Bridgett and I tried to get food to her and blankets, but we were turned away. So we snuck by, in the wee hours of the morning, and talked to her through the wall. The nights grew colder one by one. Harvest time came and went without her.

She told us about the two men who intruded one evening; one wore the garb of a minister. I didn't know who it was, but later learned that they ordered her to disrobe, and then peered at her body, holding a candle close enough to burn her with hot wax. Mary said she kept her eyes fixed on the jailer the whole time. He stood by the door of her cell.

The men pinched and prodded.

The minister asked, "You're the mother of a monster, aren't you?"

"Nothing that was ever made, was not made by God."

"You are the devil's whore! You took him in your bed!"

"He must have left a mark," said the other. "Look at her again. Lie down," he shouted as he yanked her legs apart. "Some say the devil goes in the back door. Bend her over."

"Do you see anything?"

"Its too dark to see anything. Bring the candle closer."

Mary kept her face steady.

"You sirs best finish up here," reminded the jailer. "I have other duties."

The minister asked, "Will you repent?"

"I ask the same question of you, sir."

"Redemption is possible even to the worst sinner."

"I shall pray for you then."

"You shut your filthy mouth, whore." He shoved the candle in her. "We will rid this town of vermin like you. It will give me no pain to see you die for your sins."

"Christ died for yours."

"See that she is whipped," said the minister to the jailer, and with that they left.

The jailer came back in with food and drink. The sight of his offering, and the look of compassion on his face, unleashed the tears. He unlocked her from the chain and told her that he had the watch that night.

"There are two men here who have been asking to see you," he told her. "I shall bring them by later."

After eating the food, she crept to the corner of her cell, tried to take care of her burns and then hugged her knees to her chest.

"Were you called?" was the first question William Robinson asked of her when the jailer let them in.

"No. I did not hear by direct revelation. God put a messenger in my path. I found your son grieving on the beach. I thought that in coming to Boston, I might be able to prevent your deaths. After today, I fear I have only made things worse."

"It does not matter," they both declared at once. "We are willing."

"Then I must make myself willing too," she said. " But I have been tempted in here. I seem to cling more stubbornly to life than the pair of you."

"Perhaps they will stop short of hanging a woman."

"I was searched for witch marks this afternoon. They will have no scruples against hanging me."

The jailer told them they would have five more minutes.

"We will spend it in prayer," stated William Robinson. He stood facing Mary, with Stephenson close beside her. Her communion with them left her comforted.

When the jailer pulled them away, she dropped back down to the dirt floor. The jailer took up her wrist and as she heard the irons snap shut, she felt more peaceful. The door of her cell slammed shut.

Just as she nearly drifted off to sleep, she heard the word. It did not come from somewhere in the room. The sound came from inside her head.

"I am with you, Mary."

She stopped breathing while her heart pounded. No pain, no discomfort, troubled her any further. She felt elevated to the most unbridled joy imaginable.

The law had no dominion over her after that, no jurisdiction at all. With the Supreme Being with her, she knew with rapturous certainty, that she would soon be with Him forever.

This is all we need, I thought, when she told me the whole story later that night. I could not say I didn't believe her. I just knew that there was no stopping her now.

On October 20, they were brought before Governor Endicott and the other magistrates. As she entered the courtroom, I saw a lovely soft look on her face. She seemed so happy that I felt puzzled. Her hand traveled up to her ear. It was a gesture sent to remind me that she had heard the word.

Nothing had come in the way of intervention from Mr. Dyer. At least, I had heard nothing and did not know why. I thought he might be operating behind the scenes or something. But as I had expected to see him in the courtroom, and did not, I feared he was too angry with her to defend her any more.

The first order was directed at the keeper, as he was asked to pull off the prisoners' hats. Endicott began by telling the prisoners that he had no wish to hang them. But imprisonment, whippings, cutting off ears, and banishment on pain of death had not stopped them from coming.

Seeing that Endicott was about to pronounce their sentence, William Robinson asked that he be allowed to read a paper he prepared in prison. He thought that if the magistrates knew the true meaning of their actions, they might be forced, by conscience, to reconsider. Endicott denied his request, saying, "You shall not read it nor will the court hear it read."

Robinson then placed the paper on the table. Endicott picked it up and read silently to himself.

When the governor appeared to have finished and looked up, Robinson asked again if the court could hear it read.

Endicott once more denied his request. Then he cleared his throat and in a grave tone, he said: "William Robinson, hearken to your sentence of death; you shall be had back to the place whence you came, and thence to the place of execution, to be hanged on the gallows till you are dead."

I thought I might meet my maker then and there. Bridgett clutched my hand. My breath came in little, panting gasps. I prayed that Governor Endicott would stop short of hanging a woman. If he chose that course though, he might order her to have her tongue bored instead.

Stephenson was called. Endicott said, "If you have anything to say, you may now speak."

The prisoner remained silent, even though he too had prepared a paper, which he submitted.

"Mr. Stephenson," announced Endicott, "you shall be had to the place whence you came and thence to the gallows and there be hanged until you are dead."

Then it was Mary's turn. As she stood before Endicott, she looked him squarely in the eye. She thought only of the Lord Jesus Christ who she knew beyond a shadow of a doubt stood beside her at this moment.

"Mary Dyer. You shall go to the place whence you came, and thence to the place of execution, and be hanged there until you are dead."

"The will of the Lord be done."

"Take her away, marshal."

"Yea. Joyfully, I go."

A wail pealed out of me, so I had to be dragged away. Bridgett walked me up and down the town. My mind went on fire. I sent word to William, but I knew he wouldn't be able to get to Boston in time. I thought if I could talk to Endicott, I might get somewhere, but I knew that he wouldn't, in a million years, grant me an audience. So I slept that night in the grass, across from his front door. I thought that if I could catch his attention in one sentence, I might be able to get in a few words.

When he came out of the house the next morning, I was ready for him. "Governor Endicott, sir, do you remember Sir Harry Vane?"

He stopped. "Yes."

"Did you know he's back in Parliament?"

"Yes, I heard the Rump was recalled."

"Did you know that he keeps trying to get the Quakers to join with his Parliamentary cause? Do you know that he fears their fellowship with the Royalists because their numbers are so great that they will be able to bring back King Charles?"

"That is absurd," he announced, planning to dismiss me altogether.

"I stayed with them in England, sir. So did Mary Dyer. We lived with them for months. You would do well to listen to me, sir. Quakers are up and down the length of England, Scotland, Wales, and in Ireland now too. The Society keeps on growing. When you make martyrs of them, the numbers multiply. I saw it happen over there. If you hang a woman as well known as Mary, you will not be able to stem this tide. She traveled all over England at the right hand of George Fox. If you don't believe me, write to Hugh Peters of Salem. He'll tell you."

"You best be on your way, mistress," he said. "Or I'll have the marshal escort you."

I could only hope that he would think over what I told him and that my words would give him pause to consider his own neck. There was nothing else I could do. Still no word came from Mr. Dyer.

On October 27, the fateful day, Marshal Michaelson and Captain James Oliver brought them out of jail. Cries of protest erupted. I ran to get some word to her, but as the prisoners were immediately surrounded by a band of two hundred armed men, my efforts failed. With a crack, the drums began to pound. Troops on horseback led them through the streets of Boston. The shouts of friends and foes alike were drowned out by the relentless, ferocious beating. Drums roared through the streets of Boston, as the law of banishment on pain of death was about to be enforced. The drums, meant to drive fear into the hearts of the prisoners, to drown out any words spoken to the crowd, to express the power of the government, scored on all three counts. Yet all three prisoners strolled hand in hand, smiling. The trees along the way howled their chaos of color. Friends who had poured in from near and far shouted greetings, but the thundering drums usurped their efforts. The firm grip of the law, both visible and audible, asserted its presence.

The marshal turned to Mary and shouted in order to make himself heard. "Are you not ashamed to walk hand in hand between two young men?"

"No. This is to me an hour of the greatest joy I could have in this world. No eye can see, no ear can hear, no tongue can utter, and no heart can understand the sweet incomes or influences and the refreshings of the spirit of the Lord which now I feel."

We marched to the gallows tree by the Frog Pond, in the Common. Old Gooseberry himself, Reverend John Wilson, stood by the ladder. His face, now a thousand lines of craggy bitterness, sneered at her in abject disgust. Flanking him was Pastor Norton, the minister who burned her with his candle. Together they made up the two worst Protestant offerings the church had ever spit out.

His first remark was addressed to William Robinson. "Shall such jacks as you come before us now with your hats on?"

"Mind you, mind you, it is not for the not putting off the hat we are put to death!" he answered. Robinson, the first to go up the ladder, ascended with a deliberate step. The rope, dangling from the thick branch of the tree, went around his neck. On the platform, the executioner bound his hands and legs and then tied his neck cloth around his face.

Robinson told the spectators to mind the light that is in them, which is the light of Christ of which he testified and was prepared to seal with his blood.

Incensed by this remark Wilson yelled, "Hold your tongue. Be silent. Would you die with a lie in your mouth?"

Robinson answered, "I suffer for Christ in whom I live and for whom I die." The pace of the drumming reached a feverish pitch. Shoved off, Robinson's body dropped. As he hung there swinging, I could not keep from crying. Bridgett had hold of me 'round my waist. I thought back to the moment we met him in London. He was a prosperous young merchant then: curious, sophisticated, comely, and kind—desperate to hear of our adventures in the New World.

Now it was Mamaduke Stephenson's turn. My eyes raked the crowd for any sign of William, or anything that could save Mary. As he reached the top of the ladder he cried, "Be it known unto all this day that we suffer not as evil doers, but for conscience's sake. This day we shall be at rest with the Lord." His head stretched upward before he was turned off.

Mary moved somewhere between waking and sleeping. I saw her eyes go from tree to tree. Obscene, macabre—the Common lay before her as if it had drenched itself in blood. Then she delivered the full force of her look, the look her husband said would kill someone some day, at Wilson, her first pastor in New England. She stepped up to the base of the ladder. Then her expression changed and she managed, for a second, to gaze on him benevolently, as if she pitied him. I thought she really had become a saint then. His face remained like a piece of granite, as usual. Yet she could look on him piteously, even at the moment of her death, because she knew that his wrath was his failing.

For the first time in my life, I felt like I was the Holy Mother witnessing the crucifixion. Seeing Mary go up that ladder had to be one of the worst moments of my life.

The executioner had nothing to wrap around her face.

Wilson stepped forward and said, "Take my handkerchief." He reached up to the heavens waving the white cloth, the universal symbol of surrender. The hangman had to descend a few rungs in order to grab it. Mary's eyes found mine.

At the top of my lungs, I screamed, "Blessed is the fruit of thy womb!"

After he tied the handkerchief over her face, the noose slipped around her neck. There was a commotion behind me. I heard Will's voice.

"Stop! Stop! She is reprieved."

On a horse that looked lathered near to death, he waved a piece of paper. I raised my arms to him, but he flew straight to the marshal. Mary did not move. Pulled off the platform now and falling, but falling slowly, it was into soldiers' arms that she landed. The handkerchief was removed and her coats were loosened. She looked for her son, but did not see him. The crowd jeered

"Let me die as my friends have died," she cried to the marshal. "I am ready. Let me go."

"Governor Endicott has ordered you released into the custody of your husband." He grabbed her arm and pulled.

Mary tried to scramble back up the ladder.

"No!"

The bodies of Robinson and Stephenson lay at her feet. She looked at them in horror, her eyes wild with panic. Constables ripped the clothes off them, leaving them stark naked before the crowd. It took three men to hold her. In her furious twisting and writhing, she screamed at Wilson.

"You want to hang Quakers. Hang me!"

The bodies of her friends were tossed into a waiting cart.

When she was led back to her cell, alone, like a horse wearing a halter, I could not get to her. That night in prison she wrote a statement, to be submitted to the court, where she said that her life was not accepted, nor availed, in comparison with the lives and liberty of the truth.

The next day, put on horseback and escorted by four men to a point fifteen miles outside of Boston, she was given a horse and a man to accompany her, which she dismissed, preferring to walk back home.

I caught up with her then. She trembled in my arms.

"How could William do this to me?"

"He wanted to save you."

"I am not saved. I was so close, Irene. There are no words to tell you how awful I feel. I can't get the image of the bodies, hanging, and then stripped and heaved into a cart, out of my mind. When I close my eyes, I see them."

"God rest their sweet souls."

Through every step we took, through the riot of red and yellow leaves, Mary ranted and raved. Her rage would not be contained. For her husband, she felt nothing but the deepest wrath. She thought it was his fault. Not only had he interfered with her mission, he impeded her obligation and obedience to God's will. He sent her son to do the deed. What would she say to him? What would she say to her friends, or her children? What would she say to the Robinsons?

"Now, it would not be fair at all to take this out on young Will. You should have seen his face. He would have taken your place to save you and there is no finer lad in all the world."

"I refuse to go back as William's prisoner. I simply can't do that, Irene."

"Well, it's a bit of an imaginary imprisonment, don't you think? It won't amount to anything once we're back in Newport."

"I won't live in the same house with him. I mean it, Irene. I have to figure out how to escape. Maybe I'll go to Barbados, or Bermuda. I have to go somewhere, away from William. If he is going to hinder my ministry, I will have to leave him. I will not consider living in my husband's house as his prisoner."

In Providence, we stopped at Catherine Scott's. Mary suggested they hold a meeting for worship as quickly as possible.

The next morning, Mary took Catherine aside and told her what she told me.

"Will was desperate to save you. I hope you don't hold this against him. That would be most unfair."

Mary's eyes filled with tears. "I was almost there, Catherine."

"If you don't go home, Mary, your children will be confused for the rest of their lives. They will think you are punishing them; that you don't love them. I hope you will restore your household to peace before you think of going anywhere." Catherine's mouth took on a line that we had seen in Anne's face with every baby she delivered.

"I only want to get back to where I was. I was at the top rung of Jacob's ladder. I want so desperately to get back," she said.

"If you got there once, you can get there again. Surely, we don't need to be at death's door to know peace."

"I wanted to be with Anne."

"Aye," said Catherine. "I suspect that when my time comes I will feel the same. This was not your time. We must not question the ways of the Almighty. If you had been meant to die that day, no one would have been able to intervene. For some reason you were chosen for this fate, and the Lord must have other plans for you. Trust in that, Mary."

Thank God for Catherine. What she said made sense. Young Will was saved from his mother's wrath. Sadly, his father did not fare as well.

CHAPTER TWENTY-NINE
Shelter Island

Back at home, as soon as the children were in bed and asleep, and I was raking the coals of the fire, Mary confronted her husband.

"You tell me," said William, "if the situation were reversed and the children had come to you crying, what you would have done? You tell me."

"I would have told them exactly what you should have told them, which was that I had been moved of the Lord to action and must, in obedience, give my life in His name."

"You say that now. Do you not think that if you had been looking into Will's face, or Mary's, or Maher's, or Henry's, or Charlie's, or even Samuel's, that you would have been able to give them the same answer?"

"If you had all been with me, I would have said my good-byes and still climbed that ladder. You must not ask a mother to choose between her duty to her family and her duty to God."

"A mother who turns her back on her family is not obeying God!"

"You never wanted me to have this faith, did you?"

William grabbed the poker, jabbing the logs in the fireplace till they sparked and crackled. Then he heaved a huge log on top the heap.

"You throw that log the same way they threw William Robinson's body onto the cart."

At this, William turned to her slowly and sighed. He studied her face carefully. Then he said, "What is the matter with you?"

"Nothing."

"The hangman disposed of Robinson's body according to the duties of his job."

"You will never understand. I know that now. I came to this conclusion some time back, actually. I am not staying here this winter."

"Where do you think you're going?"

"I can sail with the Coddingtons to Shelter Island. There is a new family there and they are the only people on the island except for the natives, but more Friends will arrive in the spring. They will welcome company and I can translate for them."

William looked at the floor. He slid one boot forward and then said, "Perhaps you will be safer there."

"From what?"

"From this inconsiderate madness."

"I'll go first thing in the morning." She ran up the stairs; he sank into a chair by the fire. The poker, still in his hand, dropped to the floor as his hands came up to his face to cover the tears.

I slipped out the door.

The Coddingtons welcomed Mary and brought her in with open arms. Anne Coddington joined the Society of Friends in England. William Coddington became a Quaker largely to please his new young wife. Initially, we went over to take a look at Shelter Island. Mary wanted me to stay with her for the winter, but I refused to leave my family. By this time, I was expecting my second child. My allegiance had to shift. Mary understood. Yet, I felt I had to know what her circumstances would be on that island. I didn't know the Sylvesters, and I knew they lived there alone. I had to make sure they would be good to her. I also thought that I could be on hand to convince her to return home, if she decided the isolation would be too much.

As we sailed with the Coddingtons on their shallop, the Sylvesters' beautiful island came into view. It sat nestled between the two northernmost tips of Long Island. Nathaniel Sylvester grew up on a plantation on Barbados. He purchased the Shelter Island in a trade for six hundred and fifty pounds of sugar. He planned to grow tobacco, which everyone in sundry told him would be too hard, but he was not deterred. He brought slaves with him, and hired Indians to work alongside them. When we saw the enormous pines, we could not fathom how his plan would work.

Mary moved into a little log cabin built by John Rouse the previous summer. It sat in a lovely birch glade, and was only steps from a long, utterly deserted beach. For the first time since the hanging, I saw Mary's face brighten. For some reason which I failed to understand, she adored this tiny home.

"It's beyond me, mistress, what you see in this speck of an establishment, when you have one of the finest houses in Newport."

"This is mine, Irene. That's the difference. Nathaniel said I could buy it."

"Why on earth? He'll let you have the use of it."

"I want a place of my own."

"It's so lonely here."

"Precisely," she said. "No magistrates, no ministers, no town, no hard faces."

It broke my heart to hear these words. I knew how deeply she had been affected. In her near-death experience, she had looked out over a crowd who couldn't have cared less whether she lived or died.

"It had to be a strange kind of madness to kill a Christian woman over her Christian beliefs."

"Exactly. What will make them change this stand they have taken against Quakers? We have to get religious matters out of the hands of the government. Church and state have to be two separate bodies, like they are in Newport. The question plagues me night and day, Irene. If they truly believe they are doing God's work, what will make them stop?"

For some reason, I thought of Cromwell. He was always saying he was doing God's work. "When did Jesus ever talk of work?" I asked. "I don't think God works at all. Why should He? Why should the Holy Mother? Isn't it how we envision Paradise? A place with no work?"

She laughed then. "You see things so clearly, Irene. How do you do it?"

"I haven't had to spend my life in a Protestant muddle," I told her. "Begging your pardon, of course. I know every church has gotten mixed up in the affairs of men, and every time they do, they sully themselves."

"They feel justified in cutting Christopher's ear off, beating William Brend to a pulp, and killing William Robinson. How can we convince them to be more fair?"

"If they had listened to Anne and brought her ideas of grace into their hearts, everything would have been different. Do you ever think of that? What if they had opted for grace over works, like she wanted? There would have been none of this sorry business. She would be governor of Boston by now. When they drove her out, they drove out goodness and mercy. Since then, they've had to keep going to greater lengths to justify themselves."

"How can they possibly justify what they did to Robinson and Stephenson? How?"

"I don't know. They'll think of something. Some kind of pamphlet will come out before too long. Mark my words."

If I had known they'd use her, I think I would have stayed on the island with her and brought my family over somehow. But we can't always save the ones we love. They get away from us in spite of our best efforts. There is a lesson to be learned there too. I never did manage to figure out what it was, though.

CHAPTER THIRTY
The Second Execution

As fall smashed into winter, Mary made no plans to return to Newport. Her snug cabin, warmed by the fire, kept the Atlantic winds at bay. A wheel, brought in from the main house, allowed her to keep up with her spinning. She became a great source of support for the Sylvesters. In no time flat, they became totally devoted to her. Giselle, being a new transplant from England with no contacts to draw on, save her sister Anne Coddington, would surely have perished from loneliness without Mary. Mr. Dyer made no effort to bring her back to Newport. Mary soaked up the isolation. The sense of being alone in a wild place, free from scrutiny, cut off from the trails and river routes of the mainland, offered her time to get over the horror of Boston. Shelter Island wrapped her in the peaceful silence of the woods, and when winter pounded the shore with storms, she felt perfectly snug in the comfort of her cabin. Some nights she saw herself living alone like this until she grew into old age.

The cramped little cabins of the slaves who lived alongside the natives became Mary's village. When a small group of braves approached Mary asking if she would hold a Meeting for them, a crack opened up around her heart, and a great shaft of light broke through. A powerful Meeting took shape in the woods. Joined by slaves before long, it grew into a service unique to the New World. Watching the snow falling softly on the blankets of her flock, Mary saw the hand of God in this, in everything that led up to this meeting, and her anger ebbed, usurped by love.

I managed to get over for a visit in mid-winter. I arrived frozen solid. I had a small trunk with me, packed full of her possessions. In her hasty retreat, she had not taken much. We laughed as we lugged the chest to her cabin. As I opened it for her, my eyes fell on a winding sheet. Some impulse had me throw it in at the last minute. She remarked that

I made sure she was ready for anything. I told her I had heard of her work with the slaves and would send more things over if she felt they were needed. She warmed me up by her fire, talking the whole time about the meetings. The next morning, bundled in a bear coat of Nathaniel's, I witnessed the most profound event. While I could barely understand the slaves, I saw them writhe and shake, dance and shout, cry and wail. The natives danced, said their traditional prayers, and made sounds that I can only liken to Irish keening. Mary spoke of the Holy Spirit, with her face all lit up with sweetness. I wept with gratitude through the whole thing. Now, after all these years, it's how I like to remember her best.

I took back a letter with me for William.

"My Beloved Husband," she wrote, "I am writing you today to beg your forgiveness for my anger when last we spent the night together under the same roof. My time on Shelter Island has given me a deeper understanding of God and God's will and how that applies to me. I believe I was led here for a purpose, for a very high quest. The part you played in saving me from the same fate that befell William Robinson and Mr. Stephenson, was not to be my fate after all. I now see that you did not intervene in God's purpose for me. I was wrong not to see how you are led and guided and that you so often have my care and safety in the forefront of all your thoughts. Therefore with tenderness and love for you, my dearest husband, I do humbly beg your forgiveness."

I cannot report on what Mr. Dyer thought of the letter because he never made a comment on it of any kind. I think that he and I both, along with all our other friends, just hoped for the best and believed that at some point in the near future, life would return to normal.

My wishes were shattered as soon as I heard the next batch of news. I heard before Mary did. If my hair hadn't been red, it would have turned, right there on the spot. Sean asked me to calm down because the look on my face scared him. I ran up and down the length of Newport, to every Friend's house and begged them not to tell her. Everyone said she'd hear anyway, but I held them all to a promise, nevertheless. Did I think of requiring the same oath from John Winthrop Jr.? No, I did not.

Nathaniel had to go over to New Haven to do a bit of business. He took Giselle along, but Mary stayed behind.

The young Winthrop met up with them and said, "I would have walked on my knees from New Haven to Boston if it would have stopped the law banishing Quakers on Pain of Death."

Nathaniel answered by saying that they were all looking to England for help now.

"Have you not heard of the document the Boston magistrates sent to England?"

"No."

"To prove to the world that they were not cruel, or overly harsh, to prove that they had no malice in their hearts, to justify their actions, they had outlined their reprieve of Mary Dyer. They said that she willingly accepted their action and had gratefully quitted their jurisdiction, promising never to return. I'm glad she's finally coming to her senses."

Giselle, incensed for her friend's sake, gave a full accounting of this to Mary as soon as she and Nathaniel returned to Shelter Island.

The minute Mary heard, her life was over. Guilt washed over her like a wave crashing upon a rock. What would Christopher Holder, George Fox, and Margaret Fell think of her now? All the brave actions taken by Quakers the world over were cheapened by an act of cowardice. Friends everywhere would think she let them down, let the cause down. She simply couldn't live with the shame. If one Quaker gave in anywhere, it would allow the justices and magistrates everywhere to have the idea that Friends would capitulate. She feared she would be remembered as a woman who cowered at the sight of the gallows; a woman whose faith did not sustain her; a woman who did not have the courage to go through with her mission; a woman who acquiesced, thanking the authorities for releasing her into the custody of her husband; a woman who didn't have the guts to die beside her fallen comrades. There would be the stories of Robinson and Stephenson and then the meek little Mary Dyer thanking Governor Endicott for letting her go. How would they get the law repealed now? This lie discredited the whole Society.

She saw only one way to undo it. One way. No other way. Marching straight back into her cabin to pack her things, determined to die for her cause, she vowed to make them face the truth of their actions. She would put their ideals to the test. What would the city on the hill make of her this time?

Packing only a few provisions and a blanket, she left on horseback without telling anyone. On her way out the door, she thought to include a shroud. She hoped some kind soul would give the winding sheet to the executioner and prevail upon his decency. The memory of Robinson's and Stephenson's naked bodies haunted her still. She did not care for the thought of all of Boston gawking at her bare corpse.

An Indian horse ferry, on the other side of the island, took her over to Long Island. From there she would figure out how to proceed. Feeling certain that her connection with the Manhansetts would see her through, she set off, determined to find her way to Boston.

April winds and storms felt good against her face. After she crossed Long Island, she found another horse ferry to Aquidneck and then set off on the old Pequot trail. Through the hours following the twisting and turning path, serenaded by the optimistic chirping of mourning doves, she watched wildflowers pop up on the forest floor, buds open out on the trees, and the great migration whir overhead.

Word reached the Dyers through the Coddingtons. Mr. Dyer wrote a letter to Governor Endicott and sent it with an Indian runner. Mary was already in Boston by the time William's letter came across Endicott's desk. Though William explained that he had not been with her and did not sanction her decision, he begged the governor for her life.

"If her zeal be so great as to adventure, oh let your favor and pity surmount it and save her life," William wrote. "Let not your forward compassion be conquered by her inconsiderate madness. I only say that yourselves have been and are, or maybe, husbands to wives, so am I: yea to one most dearly beloved: oh do not you deprive me of her, but I pray give her me once again and I shall be much obliged forever, that I shall endeavor continually to utter my thanks and render love and honor most renowned. Pity me. I beg it with tears."

Endicott threw the letter down. He had no care for William Dyer and his troubles with his wife. He turned and gave the order to have her found and brought before the General Court on May 31.

The air was hot and heavy with scent the day Mary came once more before the court. Governor Endicott addressed her. "Are you the same Mary Dyer that was here before?"

She replied, "I am the same Mary Dyer that was here at the last General Court."

"You will own yourself a Quaker, will you not?" he asked.

"I own myself to be reproachfully called so."

"You must return to the prison and there remain until tomorrow at nine o'clock; then, hence you must go to the gallows and there be hanged till you are dead."

She looked him in the eye. "This is no more than what you said before."

"But now it is to be executed. Therefore prepare yourself tomorrow at nine o'clock."

"I came in obedience to the will of God, the last General Court, desiring you to repeal your unrighteous laws of banishment on pain of death, and that same is my work now and earnest request. I told you if you refused to repeal them, the Lord would send other of his servants to witness against them."

"Are you a prophetess?"

"I speak the words the Lord speaks in me. Now what I spoke of has come to pass."

"Away with her, away with her."

When Marshal Michaelson came for her in the morning, she greeted him with calm resolve. As she stepped outside, she nodded to Friends who gathered outside the jail. Looking into the quiet face of Mary Scott, she smiled. Bridgett and Moira screamed, "God love you, Mistress Dyer!"

The drums began to pound again and the soldiers kept their pace. The sky, dark and heavy, threatened rain at any minute. A wind blew in from the south, a certain sign that a storm was pending. Up King Street to Corn Hill Road, and then across the fields of the Common to Rope Walk, she struggled for breath in the oppressive air. As she got to the great tree, the memory of the last episode came flooding back. Reverend Wilson, keeping with his habit of fulfilling the work, held his place again. Someone called out to her to return from where she came and save her life.

"No, I cannot, for in obedience to the will of the Lord I came, and in his will I will be faithful to the death," she answered.

Captain John Webb said, "She has been here before. She has had the sentence of banishment on pain of death and has broken the law in returning. Therefore, she is guilty of her own blood."

"I came to keep blood guiltiness from you, desiring you to repeal your unrighteous and unjust law of banishment on pain of death, made against the innocent servants of the Lord. Therefore, my blood will be required at your hands who willfully do it. For those that do it in the simplicity of their hearts, I do desire the Lord to forgive them. I came to do the will of my Father, and in obedience to his will I stand even to death."

Then Wilson, who could not contain his irritation any longer, decided to show her the path of the righteous, "Mary Dyer. O repent. Repent and be not so deluded and carried away by the deceit of the devil."

Mary turned her eyes to him and said, "I am not now to repent."

Pastor Norton asked if she would have an elder pray for her.

She told him, "I never knew an elder here."

Asked if she would have the people pray for her, she answered that she desired prayers from all the people of God.

A scoffing voice from the crowd cried, "It may be she thinks there are none here."

She regarded the crowd of somber faces. They were huddled together on this gray morning, dull and cheerless in their sad colors. "I know but few here," she answered. Asked again if one of the elders could pray for her. "No. Bring me a babe, then a child, then a young man, then a strong man, before you bring me an elder in Christ Jesus."

From the crowd she heard another question. "Did you say you had been in Paradise?"

"I have been in Paradise all this time," she said, "and now I am about to enter eternal happiness."

Captain Webb gave the signal. Up the ladder she climbed. Once again, Wilson offered his handkerchief and the hangman brought it with him. He tied her ankles, just above the top of her boots. With trembling hands she moved her skirt out of his way. Then he bound her hands behind her back.

As he covered her face, she whispered to him. "Walk in the light."

The drummers accelerated their nimble hammering until the executioner shoved her forward. Mary dropped with a crash.

The crowd stood by very silently, watching her body swing. All drumming, all noise, all talk ceased, while the crowd witnessed the death of a woman executed for her religious beliefs, the first woman to worship with slaves and Indians together. A gust of wind blew across Boston, catching Mary's skirt, puffing it full with a snap. Her dress billowed, as a sail does when suddenly grabbed by the wind.

General Atherton observed, "She hangs there like a flag."

Then a chorus repeated his words until a deep voice boomed, "She hangs there like a flag for others to take example from."

They cut her down and ripped her dress and skirts from her, tossing them aside. Mary Scott handed the winding sheet to the hangman.

He made no move to accept it until she said, "Please man, in the name of God."

He put the sheet on the ground and rolled her up in it, moving her body with his foot. The fibers, spun by Mary's own hand, the flax grown by her husband and sons; the scutching and swingling applied by her children; all the hands in her family worked together to make that shroud. The ponderous flax brake, the motion yielding the twice broken bark, wielded by her husband, rendered the precious fibers. Strands often likened to the fibers of the soul had been combed by her own fingers. All the nights when she couldn't sleep, she sat by the great fire and turned her wheel. She wove the cloth in her back room in Newport; it had a window facing up the hill to the cemetery. Now this piece of cloth, fashioned by the hands of her family, was the only covering, the only clothing, the only shelter, between her body and the earth. The hangman threw her onto the waiting cart.

The people of Boston simply turned and headed back to their homes. There was work to be done. Time had been lost. Wilson hobbled along home, very slowly. His gout bothered him that day. I heard that past the frog pond he sneezed twice, instinctively reached for his handkerchief, and then remembered that it had gone. After wiping his nose on his sleeve, he probably started to think about his sermon. I expect he would direct his remarks to the men in his congregation; he would remind them to keep a close watch on their wives. He would tell them about William Dyer, how he allowed his wife to dress in showy ways, and in doing so, let the devil right in his front door. The comely ones are the ones to watch, he would insist. He would say that it all started with Eve. He planned to call the devil's whore by name, Mary Dyer. Hangs like a flag indeed.

Everyone tried to keep the news from me. I felt it all along. I saw it in William's face. I knew she had gone. At the time of her death, I went into labor. My first daughter, Mary Anne O'Neil, came into the world, and made me smile through my tears. I was born under a lucky star, my children. Sent out into the world alone, with nothing but a rosary in my hand, I could have lived my life in the back rooms of an English estate, or I could have died on the streets. Fate intervened, and I found a friend, in the truest sense of the word.

 EPILOGUE

William Leddra, the Friend who sailed to Newport from Barbados with John Rouse, became the fourth Quaker to hang in Boston. After being imprisoned in December of 1660 he was chained to a log of wood and kept in an unheated cell for the length of the winter. He was charged with refusing to remove his hat. He was also accused of being in sympathy to those who had been executed. He made an appeal as an English subject to be tried under the laws of England, but it was to no avail. When he was cut down and stripped, the hangman said, "He was a comely man. But then Mary Dyer was a comely woman."

Friends in England knew something had happened in Boston long before the first ships arrived with the news. George Fox, who was imprisoned in Lancaster, recorded the following entry in his journal: "I had a perfect sense of their sufferings as though it had been myself, and as though the halter had been put about my own neck though we had not at the time heard of it."

On May 25, 1660, General Monk rode to Blackheath with the regiments of the old Ironside army, decked out in full array, to welcome back King Charles II. London went mad with joy. When the celebrations died down, Thomas Brinley, now accountant to the king and father of Anne Brinley Coddington and Gissell Brinley Sylvester, told King Charles of the letters he had received from Newport and Shelter Island describing the execution of his daughter's friend, Mary Dyer. A first edition of George Bishop's book called *New England Judged* was given to the king. Samuel Shattuck, the man who removed the glove from Christopher Holder's throat in the Salem Church, Nicholas Phelps and Josiah Southwick, all Salem Quakers now banished on pain of death, sailed to England with a petition. It read:

1. Two honest and innocent women stripped stark naked and searched in an inhuman manner.
2. Twelve strangers in that country, but freeborn of this nation, received twenty-three whippings, most of them with a whip of three cords with knots at the ends.
3. Eighteen inhabitants of the country, being freeborn English, received twenty-three whippings.
4. Sixty-four imprisonments of the Lord's people amounting to five hundred and nineteen weeks.
5. Two beaten with pitched ropes, the blows amounting to one hundred and thirty-nine.
6. An innocent old man banished from his wife and children and for returning, put in prison for above a year.
7. Twenty-five banished upon penalties of being whipped or having their ears cut, or hand branded.
8. Fines, amounting to one thousand pounds, laid upon the inhabitants for meeting together.
9. Five kept fifteen days without food.
10. One laid neck and heels in irons for sixteen hours.
11. One very deeply burnt in the right hand with an H after he had been beaten with thirty stripes.
12. One chained to a log for the most part of twenty days in winter time.
13. Five appeals to England denied.
14. Three had their right ears cropped off.
15. One inhabitant of Salem, since banished on pain of death, had one half of his house and land seized.
16. Two ordered sold as bond servants.
17. Eighteen people of God banished on pain of death.
18. Three servants of God put to death.
19. Since the executions four more banished on pain of death and twenty-four heavily fined for meeting to worship God.

In addition to this list, Friends in England arranged to lay their sufferings before the Privy Council. Edward Burroughs, right before his appearance in front of the king, had just heard of the death of William Leddra. He said, "There is a vein of innocent blood opened up in thy dominions which will run over all if not stopped."

The king replied, "I will stop that vein."

"Then stop it speedily, for we know not how many are soon to be put to death."

"Call the secretary and I will do it presently."

Burroughs then asked him to send it immediately, but the king said he had no occasion to send a ship. He added that Burroughs may send it if he wished.

Christopher Holder went at once to inquire when the next ship would sail. When they learned that none were scheduled to leave for months, he persuaded a captain to let him pay to send a ship without freight. Then Burroughs returned to the king and asked if Samuel Shattuck could take the message. The king, thinking this an excellent idea, gave his approval.

When Samuel Shattuck sailed into the port of Boston, the authorities tried to have him arrested. He insisted on appearing before the governor. Endicott ordered him to remove his hat. When he did not move, Endicott angrily ordered it thrown to the ground. Then Shattuck gave his credentials as the king's messenger and presented the mandamus. Staring at him in utter disbelief, Governor Endicott reluctantly, but obediently, picked up the document. It read:

"Charles R.

Trusty and well beloved we greet you well. Having been informed that several of our subjects here among you, called Quakers, have been and are imprisoned by you, whereof some have been executed and others are in danger to undergo the like; we have thought fit to signify our pleasure that in behalf for the future and hereby require you are to forbear to proceed any further therein; but that you forthwith send the said persons to their own kingdom of England..."

Endicott's face paled. In a quiet voice he said, "We shall obey his Majesty's commands."

In the long, bloody history of Europe no ruler, nor any nation, had ever written a law against the persecution of people for their religious beliefs. What he held in his hands was the first document of its kind. He issued an order. "To William Salter, keeper of the prison at Boston, you are requested by authority and order of the General Court, to release and discharge the Quakers who at present are in your custody. See that you do not neglect this. By order of the court."

As Samuel Shattuck left the governor's office, the servant who had returned his hat, stopped him in the street.

"Why did the king throw in with your lot?"

"He did not like seeing his laws broken and his subjects put to death."

"But who were they to him—a few fanatics and one mad Quaker woman?"

Samuel leaned forward and whispered in his ear. "Not a mad woman, but his first cousin."

Fearing more repercussions, the magistrates of Boston decided to send their pastor and Simon Bradstreet over to England in an attempt to justify their actions. When they had completed their crossing, and sailed into port, they saw a man standing on shore wearing leather breeches and a broad-brimmed hat.

"Who is that?" Bradstreet asked the captain.

He glanced ashore and said, "You're in for it now. That is none other than George Fox himself."

When they disembarked, Fox said, "Did thee put four people to death for no other reason than being Quakers?"

Bradstreet responded in the affirmative.

Fox said, "Then thee killed them out of thine own wills and not according to any law of England." He then introduced the distinguished gentleman standing beside him. "This is William Robinson's father. He is in the process of mounting an investigation into the death of his son." Two more men rode up. When they removed their hats, the two men from Boston thought that they were being shown some respect at last. But as the men dismounted, they turned their heads, brushed back the hair and revealed the handiwork of the Boston jailers. Fox said, "Perhaps thee will remember Christopher Holder and John Copeland."

No justification was ever presented to Parliament. The two men boarded the ship and sailed home.

On Saturday June 14, 1662, Sir Harry Vane lost his head on the scaffold. For his part in delivering the casket letters leading to the executions of both Strafford and King Charles I, he was executed. He died bravely, wearing a scarlet vest and reminding the crowd of his quest for a true Parliament.

Before Vane's trial a rumor went about London that while he had been in New England, he had debauched both Anne Hutchinson and Mary Dyer, and both of them had given birth to monsters as a result.

Hugh Peters, who could not live down the rumor that he had been the actual executioner, also lost his life.

In 1680, William Penn asked King Charles II if a debt of eighty thousand pounds, owed to his father, could be paid with wilderness land in America. On March 4, 1681, a charter was granted deeding him the territory west of the Delaware River, between New York and Maryland. Quaker immigrants, following William Penn to Pennsylvania, became as great in numbers as the sands of the sea.

Ratified on December 15, 1791, the Bill of Rights pronounced that Congress could make no law restricting the free exercise of religion. The four Quakers who gave their lives in Boston, for the cause of freedom, did not die in vain. By their deaths, they set in motion the law of the land, which created, forever, the separation of church and state. Herein lies the beacon of light.